Tell us!
Talk about this book on
Twitter using the tag
#debris

JO ANDERTON

Debris

BOOK ONE OF THE
VEILED WORLDS TRILOGY

ANGRY
ROBOT

ANGRY ROBOT
A member of the Osprey Group

Midland House, West Way
Botley, Oxford
OX2 0PH
UK

www.angryrobotbooks.com
An appetite for Art

Originally published in the UK by Angry Robot 2010
First American paperback printing 2011

ISBN 978-0-85766-154-8
eBook ISBN 978-0-85766-155-5

Printed in the United States of America

9 8 7 6 5 4 3 2 1

DEBRIS

1.

The great silver bones of *Grandeur*'s hand reflected the morning light and it looked, for an instant, like the giant statue was holding the sun itself. I couldn't have arranged a more perfect moment to lead three veche inspectors into my construction site. We paused, blinking away the after-image of the statue's skeletal palm.

"As you can see," I said, "her construction is right on schedule. If I may, my lords, I still do not understand the need for this impromptu inspection."

"You and your statue represent a significant investment to the veche, Lady Tanyana," the oldest of the three said. "Considering the amount of kopacks we are paying, surely you do not begrudge us the opportunity to oversee that investment."

I met his bland expression with a false smile. There was something jarring about this man. So ancient he walked with the support of a cane – in an era where such ineffi-cient aids were unnecessary – but still managed to do so with an undeniable aura of authority. The large silver bear's head, inlaid with opals and flecks of gold, hanging by a thick chain around his neck marked him as a member of an old family.

"Of course not, my lord," I answered. "What I do not understand is the need to do this today, without notice, and outside of the prearranged inspection dates." And why him? Why would the veche send one of their most senior members to inspect the construction of a statue, no matter how grand she was?

The other two inspectors, younger men, were already peering at the bindings in *Grandeur*'s feet. The insignia on their garish, bright yellow woollen jackets marked them as sitting members on the Construction for the Furtherment of Varsnia. More the calibre of people I'd expect on an inspection. If I'd expected one at all.

"You're worried there has been a complaint?" The old man wandered, slowly, peering about, tapping at the ground. "Hmm. Good, strong pion-bonds. Clean systems. I don't see why anyone would complain about this construction site."

I gritted my teeth. "Neither do I, my lord. But what other reason would there be?"

"Indeed."

That was not an answer, not an Other-cursed answer at all.

"My lady?"

I glanced over my shoulder. Volski was the first of my circle to arrive. He usually was. His gaze flickered to the inspectors, and his mouth pinched into a small, concerned frown. "What are they doing here?"

I lifted a hand, gestured to quiet him. "We are being inspected," I whispered.

His eyes widened. "But why, my lady? Has there been a complaint about our binding?"

I shook my head, and wished I had an answer. "I don't know. Other's hell, Vol, I've got no idea what's going on." I drew a deep breath, calmed myself. "Just warn the others as they arrive, won't you?"

Volski nodded and stepped back to wait outside the gate to the construction site. I hurried to the inspector's side. He was smiling as I approached. A cheeky, impish kind of smile that made me shudder.

"Your circle is loyal to you, aren't they?" He continued to tap the ground with his cane.

"Yes, my lord."

My critical circle made me – nine skilled binders who worked below me, in harmony with me, to manipulate pions and alter the very structure of the world. Everything was made up of pions, from the steel in *Grandeur*'s finger bones to the sun-spotted skin that stretched across the back of my hand. I saw them as lights, a myriad of tiny fireflies. Some were brighter than others: those on the surface layer of reality were easy to see, eager to please, but weak. I could manipulate them with little more than a coaxing whisper, but any structure I built with them would not last the first brush of wind.

It was the stronger pions, the dim lights that kept themselves hidden, that my critical circle and I could manipulate. It took all ten of us to pry the pions free, to entice their cooperation and set them to work. But once we did, oh, the wonders we could create.

I glanced up at *Grandeur* with a smile, breath deepening, my palms itching just to start. There was so much work left to do on her, and how the pions were calling me. From all across the construction site they flickered a coordinated phosphorescent dance – in time to the twitch

9

of my fingers, the beat of my heart – to work with me, to bond with me, to build *Grandeur*'s wonder high into the sky. I was used to the enthusiasm of my pions, but this seemed stronger than usual: their caress like a tug, their call a demand.

Perhaps they were feeding on my frustration. There were pions in all of us, in everything, and we were all connected by their light. I could ride that, I could control that, if only the veche inspectors would let me get on with my job.

It took a moment to collect myself, to draw my focus back on my body and the elderly inspector in front of me. The pions dimmed. They never truly left, of course, but only the shallow ones still shone if I wasn't concentrating on them. If I wasn't letting myself get carried away by them.

The inspector's smile deepened. "Impatient, are you?" he said, with a chuckle. "Don't fear, my lady, we will not keep you long."

The rest of my circle arrived as I answered a pointless set of rudimentary questions. Yes, I had two healers on site as the edict required. Yes, my raw materials were sourced from veche-accredited mining operations and handled by an experienced circle of lifters. I'd worked with them before. Six point circle, a high number for something as straightforward as carrying heavy rocks, but all in the name of safety.

Hardly seemed worth dragging an old family veche member all this way just to ask questions like this. Why were they really here?

From the corner of my eye I watched Volski organise the site. He spoke to each member of my circle, sent the healers to their usual corner to set up, and admitted a ragtag band of debris collectors. It was unusual for collectors to arrive so early. Debris was the waste created by all our pion manipulation. Our work on *Grandeur* would certainly produce a lot of it, but we hadn't even started binding so there was nothing for them to collect yet.

Finally, when the first slabs of raw stone started to arrive, I could make my excuses. I had a statue to build, after all.

"Yes, of course." The elderly inspector and his fellows withdrew to the fenced-in edges of the site, near the healers' small white tent. "We won't hold you up." But they didn't actually leave.

"You're staying?" I asked, before I could stop myself.

"Of course." Another of those Other-cursed smiles. "To watch you work. Wouldn't be much of an inspection if we didn't, now – would it?"

"I suppose not, my lord." I gave him a small bow, as his status in the veche deserved. "If you will excuse me."

Just what I needed.

I hurried over to my circle, where they stood in a tight knot in the centre of the site, and held up a hand to silence any questions before they could be asked.

"Veche inspection," I said. "Don't let it worry you." I clapped my hands together, forced a hopefully bright smile. "Let's get started."

The members of my circle spread out to surrounded the statue, evenly spaced, and began gathering pions. Across the site the tiny particles of light flared up again, fast and eager, in response.

I turned to *Grandeur*, and found myself grinning. Such enthusiasm was infectious. All around me it was building: bright lights and raw energy, swirling, coalescing in

11

vast daisy chains around my circle, around me. Flashing, brilliant particles brushed against my skin, stirring the bonds inside my very body, linking us all together: the statue, the circle, the world. Me. I pushed down a sudden and unseemly need to laugh as the thrill of it tickled through me. Better than any food, better than passion, better – dare I say it? – than the syrupy black coffee with a dot of caramel cream Thada at *Keeper's Kaffine* poured for me every morning.

This was me, the truest me. Tanyana Vladha. Pion-binder, architect, centre of a circle of nine and good – Other-damned good – at all of it.

"Help me up there," I whispered to the pions. They hardly needed convincing.

We fashioned stairs out of the very air. Tied thousands of tiny drops of water with miniscule fragments of sand, and ash, and whatever trace metals the pions could find, and froze them, then burned them, crushing them together until something like glass appeared. And we did this with every step I took, binding and rebinding, until I stood on the bones of *Grandeur*'s incomplete palm, eight hundred feet high.

The tension of a site full of riled-up pions travelled through her steel beams and hardened glass tiles in a constant tremor. Nothing she couldn't handle, I was sure. I had designed and built her to be strong.

"Are you ready to begin, my lady?" Volski's pions carried his words to me, up a current of wispy blue lights that smelled of dust. Each member of my circle was different. Llada bullied hers along on a solid track of authoritarian purple. Tsana's touch was green, sharp as the eyes of a child.

"I am." The tiny bright particles couldn't speak, of course. Rather, they replicated the vibrations of my words, carrying and depositing them where instructed. I could ask them to shout across the whole of the site, if I wanted, but these words I kept for Volski alone, "Are the inspectors watching us, Vol?"

A pause. Either Volski was collecting his thoughts or – and, I thought, more likely – his pion stream was struggling to push its way through to me. The construction site was so full of light, countless different streams and loose particles attracted to us but not yet incorporated; a single thread could get tangled on its journey.

"Of course they are," he answered, finally. "You really don't know why they're here, my lady?"

"Vol." It took several attempts to get down to him. "Don't let it upset you." I opened up my pion thread and sent my words to everyone in my nine point circle. "Let's use this opportunity to show these so-called inspectors, and the veche, just how good we are."

The pions, at least, surged with agreement, even if I couldn't quite make out all of my circle's reply.

"If you say so, my lady," Volski said. Then, after another pause, "The first block is on its way to you now."

I stepped to the very edge of *Grandeur*'s palm, lifted my arms, spread my hands wide and urged the circle on. They gave everything I could have asked for. Colours surged as the pions they had gathered travelled up their threads toward me, like blood through veins. From nine points spread out across the site below me, my pion-binders coaxed power from the world around them and sent it all up to me.

"The block is nearly there!" Tsana's words came across clipped, and I hoped she wasn't tiring already. *Grandeur* was, well, a grand lady. She would take many more sixnights to complete, and for the two hundred thousand kopacks the veche was paying, I'd make sure we built her well. For moons we had crafted her, from sturdy, sand-filled legs to the crystalline squares of her glass-sewn gown. Hands, face and neck were all that remained to be done. But a face takes longer to sew than a dress, expression needs time and care. A light touch, the delicate detail.

The rock the lifters hauled past the hem of *Grandeur*'s sparkling, crystalline sleeve was enormous. To my architect's eyes it was a tangle of bindings, of tightly knotted energy giving it structure and form. Dense with material, shining with ore and sand and potential. I would build a hand from that rock.

"Have you got it yet?"

I took a small step from the edge, feet steady, steel the only thing between me and the ground. The obliging pions in the girder shone a bright path to follow. The boulder wobbled as it rose, jerking in the sky. The lifters were having trouble.

"Hurry, my lady," Volski murmured by my ear.

I shook out my fingers. "Ready now?" I whispered to the lights buzzing around my head like fireflies. I must have looked like flame from the ground, a tiny lit wick in an enormous candle. The toes of my boots hung out over space and a humid updraft.

It seemed we had, in fact, already loosened a lot of debris. Debris was always followed by heat.

I cupped my hands, repeating the gesture, and imagined holding the boulder there in my palms. The pions caught on quickly. They had trailed over my fingers like streamers woven from flowers. Now, they wrapped around the rock, cupping it in a tight, bright mesh. "Good little girls and boys," I whispered again. Then I sent down to my circle, "Patience, Tsana, Vol. Art and beauty, these things should not be rushed."

Laughter does not carry up the circle. But I imagined a smile brightening Volski's ever-serious eyes. "Lifters are getting weary. The site is thick, so don't work them too hard."

It was a lot of stone to lift so high and hold for so long, even without a throng of pions clogging the sky.

I brought my cupped hands together, with more care than I had placed my feet. Falling didn't worry me; if I couldn't create myself something safe to land on, then I had nine people below me who could. But the pions guided by my hands, with their jostling, in their zest, they needed a focused mind and a firm grip.

A gust of wind, warmth-tipped, billowed my jacket. The high collar of densely woven wool tugged at my throat. I locked fingertips and sent the pion horde drilling. They rushed to their duty, pushing inside the rock, sticking to its bindings, prying at its knots. Undoing its old form, and preparing it for a new existence in *Grandeur*.

Once I could feel every grain as though they were pressed against my fingers – from smooth iron-ore to fine sand – I instructed Volski to give the lifters some rest.

The rock was a sudden weight, and I braced my feet on the steel beam, leaning into the wind to compensate and regain my balance. I was not alone. The circle throbbed below me, around me, and even as I fed pions into the rock, even as they set about their dismantling and reconstruction, the circle found me more.

Sweat on my neck, clammy wool. All part of the thrill, wasn't it?

First, cement separated in a flurry of mud. I padded the hand bones with it, filled out the palm, was careful to lift my toes as it solidified at my feet. Next, more steel.

15

Another gust of wind, and I staggered a half step onto thankfully dry cement. My interlocked fingers jerked in reflex. Particles tugged in an attempt to escape, but I had knotted them so tightly they could not slip out of place. Somewhere below me, the structure rattled. Just wind, surely, trying to knock *Grandeur* around like it was doing me.

"Are you all right?" Tsana asked. "The wind's come up."

"I noticed," I snapped off the words. "Be quiet and keep working. We're being watched, remember."

Tsana was silent. The pions didn't carry sulking, either.

Fingers are hard to fashion. I guided pions to the square-end edges of the metacarpals and set them to building knuckles out of steel. *Grandeur* was a statue, so she was hardly going to flex her hands or pick anything up, but I needed sufficient mass there and a strong enough supporting structure to keep the fingers stable. *Grandeur* had her arm outstretched, hand cupping. When I'd vied for the contract to build her I'd described this as a poignant way to show that Varsnia, even as wealthy and advanced as we are, was not beyond lending a helping hand to lesser nations, not beyond carrying an extra weight. Didn't mean I believed it, of course, but it had certainly convinced the veche.

Another shudder ran through *Grandeur*'s frame. Fine dust from her shoulder trickled in a soft waterfall behind me.

"Did you feel that?" Tsana put aside her hurt ego.

"Of course." I was standing on it.

With a frown, I peered over the edge. The distant ground was hard to see with heat waves adding their haze, and a sky thick with lights. My circle was still complete and distinct, linked by varied colour and dotted with light like dew on a spider's web.

Movoc-under-Keeper stretched out beyond the construction site, a sprawling city of dark stone and bright lights. Threads of thin, sharp pions surged between buildings, carrying light, carrying heat. Down along the Tear River, further south of the Keeper Mountain, factories burned. Thick patterns of orange rose above a rubbish disposal. Twisting, complex green over carpenters working. And on top of it all, the mess of the everyday. Lives made up of pions shifted, prodded, caressed and coaxed into action. It would be easy to say Movoc wasn't built of bricks, of cement and steel. It was erected on a frame of pions, it lived through them, and was lit by them. A true city of the revolution.

All this was normal. Nothing amiss. Just a few more pions than usual, overexcited for reasons I did not understand. And the wind, battering *Grandeur*'s glass dress. Swallowing vertigo, I returned to the steadily solidifying knuckles.

"Tanyana?" Tsana's pions sped by so fast they took most of her voice with them. "I think something's wrong."

I completed the knuckles, each a hub of steel with half a dozen smaller pins extended, ready to brace fingers. Only an eighth or so of the boulder's total mass had been used. I drilled for more ore, removed it, and started construction of five thick beams.

"I need details, Tsana. Anything you say is useless to me without details."

The wind hit again, harder still. And below, my circle flickered. No, not just my circle – all the pions in the construction site. Gone was their light, their colour. All I saw, for a slow and breathless moment, was Movoc as it would look without the pions that gave it life. The city was grey, wet, and darkness haunted its corners.

They returned in a flurry, somehow faster, somehow thicker, and wilder than before.

"There's too much interference, I can't keep the pions focused." Tsana's words spilled around me. "I don't understand why–"

Llada burst in. "Systems are failing all over the site! The lifters are down: two of their stones have dissolved, they're trying to contain the third but, my lady, they can't even maintain a circle. The bonds in *Grandeur*'s feet are loosening. Her hem. Her ankles. Other, we're losing pions and I can't stop–" Her thread of purple lights whipped free of the circle, thrashing unrestrained against the sky, and her voice disappeared. It only took her a moment to rejoin us but it was far too long for someone with her pion-binding skill.

Other, what was happening?

I took a deep breath, and put all thoughts of the inspectors out of my mind. I didn't need this now, not now while they were watching and reporting on me, but worrying about them would only weaken my focus. The safety of my circle, indeed my entire construction site, was my main priority. I would deal with the effect on my career later. "Everyone, come in close," I said. "Tighten the circle and you should be able to bring–"

"They won't listen to me!" Tsana's jarring, sporadic voice peppered me as her pion thread tore violently through my fingers. "Too many–"

"Can you hear me, my lady?" Volski, at least, remained calm. "You need to get this place back under your control."

"I know. Shorten your threads–"

"My lady? Can you hear me?"

Other damn us, we couldn't even get through to each other. The site was just too bloated, overrun by wild, fierce lights. Any pions I sent down to my circle were surrounded, torn from their threads, and riled into abandon until they joined the powerful and unruly throng. And I didn't understand why. The pions were my friends, and had always been. When I called them from their home, deep in the layers of reality, they responded with enthusiasm, with joy. Not this.

This felt like madness, and the very idea sent a chill over my skin.

When we controlled them, pions could change the very structure of the world. But mad, like this, and out of our control, what would they do now?

"No," I whispered to myself. "No, I won't let–"

A great screeching sliced through my words. The finger bones, being carefully constructed only a moment before, writhed in the sky like pockets of termite-infested timber. I focused all my attention on them. I let go the circle below me, I ignored the chaos infesting the rest of the site and the inspectors, observing it all, scribbling away only the Other knew what in their reports. All I saw, all I knew, was those finger bones, and the tiny particles of energy bright within them.

"Enough of this," I told the pions. My pions. Stern, but kind, I was a mother, a teacher, a firm hand. "We have a job to do. Enough."

But they couldn't hear me, or wouldn't. So I approached them, balancing on hot steel beams wet with condensation. I reached up to the closest finger bone, placed my hand against its stretching, writhing not-quite-metal-anymore form so the pions in me and the pions in it could touch, could mingle.

"Listen—"

But then, only then, so connected to the finger bone, so focused, did I see them.

Pions, yes, but not like any pions I had never known. Red, painfully red, and buried so deep inside reality that even the collective skill in the building site below hadn't seen them. When I tried to communicate with them they burned like tiny suns and heat washed over me, and anger, such a terrible tearing anger I could feel from my head to my chest and deep, deep inside me. In my own pion systems.

Gasping, I stumbled back. They bled out from the finger bone, infecting the particles around it, undoing all the bonds I had made. I spun, and they were everywhere. It wasn't the wind battering *Grandeur* around like she was little bigger than me. The crimson pions whirred around us like a nest of furious wasps. Bereft of any guiding structure they crashed indiscriminately against my statue, against my circle, the earth, the street. They infected every pion they touched and tore apart every system in their way.

Desperately, I stumbled back to the edge of *Grandeur*'s palm. My circle was holding on by only a few stubborn threads. Volski. Tsana. Llada.

I drew all the clean pions I could gather into a single, solid thread and thrust it back down toward my circle. "Can you hear me?" I had to penetrate that mess, I had to warn them. "It's not the wind, do you understand? Let everything else go, look to the sky, the edges of *Grandeur* and you might see them. There are pions!"

I was answered only by screaming below. Not passing my ears, not touching my senses with a brush of colour and scent. Below.

The finger bones fell. Two crashed onto *Grandeur*'s palm, only feet away, and there they lay, writhing. One dripped, hot like melted cheese, over the side. The other curled over itself in a snake-sex frenzy.

Where had the others gone?

More screaming and great thuds. I swallowed, clammy in my jacket, too hot.

I had to take control. I was the only one who could. Not even my circle, skilled though they were, could see pions this sharp, this deep into the world.

I ran hands through my hair. My short fringe stuck up hard, styling cream rearranged by sweat.

Take control, but from whom? Who had coaxed these crimson pions from the deep places they must have slept in? Who had disturbed their dormancy? Pions could not be created, just as they could not be destroyed. So this anger, this burning rage, must have always existed, somewhere deep inside all things.

Why had it been set free?

Legs folded beneath me as I shook tension from my wrists, and reached out with open, cupping hands.

The fiery particles slipped through my fingers. Not around them, like water, but through them. Like reflections on a wall, like shadows. Like my fingers weren't even there.

"No!" Focus. Touch them, command them. Pions had listened to me since I was a child, been keen to please me, never hating me, never too wild to be caught, too angry to be soothed. "Don't let this happen!" My voice broke, I took shuddering breaths to try and control myself. How could I hope to control pions if I couldn't even do that? "I don't know who's doing this, but you don't have to listen to them. I'm here. You know me. Trust me, and come back. Come back to us."

I could have been talking to empty air. Nothing changed, the chaos, if anything, grew fiercer. And while my fingers passed through them like I wasn't solid, those particles hooked themselves into the pion-bonds in my coat, my hair, the outer layers of my skin and dragged me forward. *Grandeur* shook. I could feel her swaying, as her systems were ruthlessly undone. Creaking eased around me, below me. Somewhere glass shattered. The threads of *Grandeur*'s dress, pulling away?

No. I wouldn't let this happen. Not to me, and not to all the people below who trusted me, who relied on my strength and my skill not only to work such wonders, but to keep them safe while we did so. I would not let them down.

So I stood, braced, haloed by blazing fire. I called out to the pions again and opened my arms wide. They rushed over to me from all across the site, and further out too, from the rest of the city, as far as my call could reach. I gathered every clean pion I could summon, anything that wasn't crimson and furious and blind, and wound them into tight, complex threads. Unstable without my circle's strength to support me, surrounded by the chaos of the construction site, still I tied my threads into all the weakening pion-bonds below me. I stitched up *Grandeur*'s feet and legs where she had been rapidly dissolving; I injected solidity into the decaying finger bones; I recombined the lifters' stones and helped them reform their tattered circle; I caught the edges of my own, frayed circle, and bundled them together.

"It's Tanyana! She's taking control–"

"–restoring integrity! That's amazing, my lady, amazing–"

"–can you come down? The bindings in her arm are still loose and we need–"

Voices flashed at me, snippets of sound. The circle flashed with them, lightning strikes of panic.

I strained to hold them all, to control so many pions and keep their threads safe, solid. And it looked, for a moment, like I was winning. I, and my binding, was stronger than the furious crimson pions trying to undo us. *Grandeur* strengthened, the circles below hardened into solid colour and began channelling fresh pions of their own. More binders were joining us, emergency and relief crews, and I even allowed myself to smile, and whisper to my pions, "There, do you see? We can do it. Together we are strong."

Until all the bright and furious lights slowed in their whirling chaos, then stopped, hanging like too-close stars in the air around me. They flashed, coordinated, and my stomach clenched as they gathered into a wide and terrible thread of red light. And attacked.

They did not attack *Grandeur* again. Not the circles below, not anything else in the construction site. This time crimson pions attacked me, and only me. They crashed into me, through me. And all my threads were torn from my control, and all the systems inside my body cried out and jumbled up, and I stumbled forward, toes on the edge of *Grandeur*'s palm. I burned, and the sky burned with me, for an instant of tortured brilliance before they all disappeared. The bloat of crimson, the normal few, every last pion that lit Movoc-under-Keeper was gone.

And in their place, darkness. A sea of the wiggling-worm stuff.

Tanyana, is it? Welcome. And a single voice, a whisper more imagined than real.

Metal screeched and shuddered at my feet. Strangely numb, I turned to see *Grandeur* crack below her elbow. For a moment we hovered, her arm and I, in a strange hand-shake eight hundred feet in the air. She took her time deciding which way to fall. Then the sky tipped, pions pushed, my soft-soled feet slipped forward, and I was free.

Silver knuckles shone, bright in the sunlight of a clear day, and even as I fell I squinted back to watch them arch toward me, filling the blue sky. She was *Grandeur* to the end. Not content to throw me to the earth and away from the safety of my nine point circle, she had to slap me on the way down.

2.

When I opened my eyes again the world was empty.

I lay, propped up on hard pillows in a bed that creaked beneath me with each breath. The room was not my own. A white-painted ceiling; beige walls dotted with washed-out pictures; a chair in each corner; a small table. A lifeless room, certainly not home. But that was not what made it empty. The pions were gone. The walls were colourless and hollow without them, the tiled floor dull and flat. No bright connections between particles, no flickering eagerness, no foundations of light.

Empty.

A man sat beside the bed. His skin was pallid, surprisingly free of freckles or sunspots, his hair so blonde it was almost white. His eyes were a faint, dirty kind of green.

His jacket was dull. His striped shirt, his woollen pants: there were no pions in them either.

"Where are the pions?" I tried to turn my head and ask. But pain surged up like a tide at the movement, and my mouth felt full of cloth and too weak to form proper words. I wavered, and from the corner of my eye caught sight of what had once been my left hand. Wrapped in thin linen I could see through it to something dark that wound its way over my fingers. Fingers too misshapen, twisted, and thick to be mine.

Those former fingers cleared my head. Those former fingers were terrible enough that I could turn my neck and speak.

"Where am I?" My voice was raw and dry. "Who are you?"

Face like a statue, the man watched me. Not impatient, not bored or even caring. Nothing. "I am glad to see you awake, Miss Vladha." His voice reminded me of ice over a lake. Cold. Smooth. Dangerous. With a strangely halting hand he drew an insignia from his jacket and showed it to me, a roaring bear's head ringed by nine concentric circles. "I represent the national veche. I am here about the incident."

Grandeur. Oh, Other.

I gathered what authority I could. What had happened at the construction site – those crimson pions and the chaos they had wreaked – that was not my fault. "Do you know who summoned them?" I asked. Something tugged at my face with the croaking words. Dimly, I was aware of the thin, almost paper-like gown I wore. It crinkled softly beneath the weight of blankets. It was mostly transparent, and I knew I should have been embarrassed beneath the man's constant appraisal. I wasn't. Because there were bandages between gown and skin. A dark shape beneath sheer green.

He blinked. A long and precise movement. "I beg your pardon?"

"The crimson pions." I swallowed hard. Other, I could have killed for water. "They disrupted our systems, they undid my bindings. They pushed me. Do you know who unleashed them?"

26

"The only person responsible for your statue, Miss Vladha, was yourself."

He had misunderstood me. "No, no. I was attacked. Pions too deep for the others to see, but I saw them. They broke *Grandeur*, they pushed me off the edge. You need to find out who did this!"

The veche man shook his head. Sharply to the left, then to the right. "Listen to yourself. You know how impossible this sounds."

"But there were–"

"Pions the members of your own nine point circle couldn't see, let alone three qualified veche inspectors?" He lifted the corner of his mouth in a precise sneer, before dropping it back to the expressionless thin line. "The incident has been before a veche tribunal. The inspectors reported none of this. Neither did your circle, or the lifters, or the healers. No one. *Grandeur* was your contract, Miss Vladha, and you must take responsibility for it."

A veche tribunal?

Unsettled, I glanced around the room. How long had I been sleeping here? Why would the veche hold a tribunal about *Grandeur* before I could attend? Panic rose like the returning of blood to a limb. This couldn't be right.

"No." I seized the edge of the bed. "The veche can just open a new tribunal. If you're not going to listen to me, then they will. You just sit there and I will–" I tried to swing my legs over the side of the bed. Pain flared along my left side and instead of storming out to find justice, and answers, I fell back against the pillows.

The veche man watched, and offered no help. "As you can see–" his voice maintained that emotionless monotone "–you are in no position to do anything. The tribunal is closed. The veche, whom I am here to represent, will not open a new one. People with injuries like yours often find themselves confused. I suggest you put these supposed memories behind you. I suggest you concentrate on the future."

Injuries. "What happened to me?" I swallowed. "What have the healers done to me?"

"The healers did the best they could. Your wounds were more extensive than you realise. Trauma to the brain has rendered you unable to see or manipulate pions. The veche extends its well wishes in this difficult time."

What was he saying, in that uncaring monotone? The brain? Pions?

I touched my head with gingerly soft fingers. No padding there, no pain.

Had I dreamt up that wild, crimson force that had thrown me from *Grandeur*? But it was all so vivid, and I would not have fallen, could not have fallen, unless I had been pushed. But he didn't believe me. "What does this mean?"

"You have cost the veche significantly, and we will give you the opportunity to pay us back. Once you can get out of bed." He didn't even offer his hand as he stood, but I found myself looking up to watch him go.

The door to my room opened up to a white-tiled corridor. After the veche man had left a gradual stream of men passed by. Most wore long white coats over their clothes and talked in hushed tones. What was this place, some kind of hospital? Strange pictures on the walls caught my eye. Faint sepia ghosts of arms, legs, and what had to be someone's waist, although I couldn't understand why anyone would hang an image of a waist on a wall. In each of those glimpses I thought I saw jewellery. Bracelets, necklaces.

That was odd, surely. For a hospital.

Odder still, because these images hadn't been created using pions. What were they, drawn by hand? With ink – actual, physical ink? Or were they photographs? It was hard to imagine anyone still did any of that. And yet, if they had been rendered, I wouldn't have even known they were there.

Rendering was reasonably common nowadays. It involved the manipulation of tiny particles – water droplets, all kinds of dust, even hapless insects in the wrong place at the wrong time – and arranging them in just the right way to catch and reflect carefully directed light so an image resolved itself, apparently out of thin air. A truly skilled nine point rendering circle could create a life-size duplicate, detailed right down to the pores on their subject's skin, of shimmering light and colour that could stand like a statue or attach itself to a wall like a painting.

The left side of my body felt heavy, weighed down by dread, by the wrongness of it all. I lifted my left hand, placed it in my lap, but couldn't bring myself to peel back those bandages, to look at those fingers.

"You have to come back," I said to the particles of light that had always been my friends and would not, could not have abandoned me now. "Do you hear me?"

I wrapped my right hand around the ruin of my left and slowly, slowly began to squeeze. Pain like fire, like the burning of hot lights, sparked deep beneath my skin. Still, I squeezed, as though I could just force the pions back out from wherever they were hiding. Maybe, if they saw how much I needed them, they would return.

Pions had always come when I called.

I remembered running through the tight corridors of the textile factory my mother had worked in, prying loose the pion streams of their small and ungainly circles with nothing more than a whispered word. My mother was not a skilled binder, but she did what she could to provide, widowed and burdened with a precocious little brat like me. It was so easy, it had always been. A hook of my finger, a smile and a call and the factory workers' thin aubergine pions lightened to sharp pink, flocking around me. The other members of the factory circles must have hated me, but I never even noticed. Not with so much light all gathered in my hands.

I squeezed, gasping in difficult, hitching breaths. Push past the pain. Pions were there, somewhere, deep in a world that had always opened up for me, that had never felt as solid and impenetrable as this.

My first year studying at Proud Sunlight was when I really started to realise that I was different. I didn't come from a wealthy family with a strong pion-binding ancestry; in fact, I could only afford to attend at all because of the scholarship my skills had bought me. And I was young, compared to the rest of the students, a sixteen year-old girl surrounded by men and women at least four years older and all vastly more experienced.

They were surprised, so surprised, that I could keep up with my lessons. Keep up, and exceed them. Three moons into my first year and an experimental circle in the military sublevel collapsed in on itself, threatening to drag most of the riverside wing with it. I still remembered that feeling, standing in the middle of the churning, tattered remains of their six point circle, fearless, at peace, because the power and the energy rolling around me was my friend. The only friend I had in such a strange place.

I'd opened my arms to it. I'd let those pions play across my skin, touch my own systems, grow to know me, to trust me. As they always did. And I'd whispered calming words, like a mother to her child. And I'd stroked their tense formations, like soothing a wild beast. Working together, the pions and I unravelled the circle that had so entangled and enraged them, and then put right the building they had almost destroyed.

And I'd realised, in the aftermath, that I might be different and I might be poor, but with pions beside me none of that mattered. With my skill, with their help, I'd form myself a new identity.

So this wasn't possible, couldn't be possible. They had to come back, they couldn't leave me. We were all connected: the pions gave me strength and I gave them purpose.

I squeezed harder. Something tore beneath the bandage and I gasped at the sudden rush of pain. But no lights came with it. It was like the pions just couldn't hear me any more, as I couldn't see them. The world had become a barrier between us.

And I was alone. And everything I had worked for was gone.

"What are you doing?"

I flinched, and released my left hand as I looked back to the doorway. An entirely different man stood there. Worry wrinkled the edge of his green eyes – nothing like mould, closer to the Deep Salt Sea – and he brushed a fringe of rich dark hair across his forehead.

"I'd leave those bandages alone, if I were you. They're there for a reason, you know."

I frowned at him, and croaked, "Just leave me alone." Alone. Could I really be more alone than this?

He shook his head. "He didn't even offer you any water, did he?" He produced a large, full glass with a flourish. "Those men, the veche ones I mean, they never change. Don't even think to offer a thirsty lady some water." And he smiled at me, all white teeth and shining eyes. What, exactly, did he think I had to smile about?

"Devich," he introduced himself as he swept into the room, white coat billowing. He helped me hold the glass to my lips, tip it and ease the precious fluid into my dry and aching throat. Despite everything I sighed when it was gone, rested my head back, and realised how much I had needed it.

He watched me, expectant, like a loyal dog.

"Tanyana," I finally said.

He poured more water into the glass and placed it on the table beside the bed, just within reach. "I know who you are." And his eyes were so heavy with concern, with worry and even fear, that his look caught a lump in my throat. I swallowed on it, hard. "And I'm so sorry for you, my lady. So sorry." He knew about *Grandeur*, then. And the pions. "But I'm here now and, oh, Tanyana, I will try and help you. I will."

Could he bring my pions back? Because that was the only way to help me now.

He began dragging something large and covered with a white sheet through the doorway. Almost too large. It ground horribly against the wooden frame, the sheet caught twice in the wheels and almost tipped the whole trolley over. I caught glimpses of metal, but couldn't begin to guess what it actually was. Devich, red-faced, yanked and dragged until the contraption came through. It left two large dark marks either side of the door frame, and with a nervous laugh and ruffle of his hair, he glanced down the corridor and quickly shut the door.

"What is that?"

He laughed again, self-deprecating. "Ah, in good time. This is first." He rummaged beneath the sheet. "Here." He produced a clear glass tube, apparently empty. "This will help with the pain. I feel almost as bad as those veche men saying this, but you're going to need to be able to concentrate. And pain is never helpful, is it?"

"Concentrate? On what?"

Another nervous laugh, and he didn't answer. "Let me show you how to apply it." Devich walked around to the left side of the bed. He began untucking the blankets that covered me and instantly I tensed. His face fell. "I'm sorry, my lady. I'm sorry to have to do this to you so soon. And I... I don't even want to test you. But they are waiting. And I know it's not fair, and I don't want to push you..." He seemed to flounder, eyes on the floor, tube in his hand.

With a groan, I reached for the water. Again, I filled my mouth, my throat. It washed through me, so fresh and clean. Everything I did not feel. I watched him from the corner of my eye and wondered if I could trust him. I almost wanted to. Because of the smile, perhaps. Definitely because of the water. But perhaps it was the sorrow in his eyes and the hitch of his voice, so real compared to the veche man's statue face and false sympathy.

"What test?" I placed the glass back on the table carefully. My right hand shook. My left side ached.

Eyes to the floor still, Devich mumbled like a shameful child, "For debris."

"Debris?" Something quivered in my stomach and had nothing to do with my injuries. The same terror I felt confronted by a world without its pions.

"The veche need to know if you can see debris, they need to know if you will be a collector. A debris collector.

33

As quickly as possible. You see, the longer we wait the harder it is for the networks to–"

He'd stopped making sense by that point. I could see Devich's mouth moving, but no words came out. All I could hear was *Grandeur*, as she fell. All I could think of was emptiness. A debris collector? That was impossible. I was an architect, a highly skilled pion-binder. Nothing less.

"That's not possible," I breathed out the words. "I'm not a debris collector."

Devich looked up, he clasped the tube at his chest. "I hope so, my lady. I truly do." Then he tried for a smile, it shook slightly. "Now, let me help you." He unscrewed the tube. "This is for the pain, and to help you heal."

"What is?" The tube still looked empty to me.

"The–" He paused. "Oh. Of course. You can't–" He floundered again.

"I can't see them." I had no way of knowing what the pions in that tube were doing, and what they would do to me.

I allowed him to lift back the covers and expose my left side. The strange gown was tied at the seams, and he undid them with fumbling fingers. His touch was very warm. A layer of cloth bandaged me down the entire left side of my body. Carefully, tip of his tongue caught between his teeth, he lifted my leg, my arm, and undid them.

Someone had embroidered on my skin. Thick, ugly dark lines woven from face to thigh. My left hand seemed to be held together by the stitching alone.

Devich sucked in a sharp breath. "Oh, you poor thing."

I rather agreed. Instead, I asked, "Who did this? Do you know?"

He just shook his head. "They didn't tell me. The veche brought you here, to me, as you are now."

Devich squinted at the glass tube and held it above my left hand. I breathed in sharply as one rounded end rippled, like the glass had just turned to water, and pulled back to create an opening. He lowered it, then, so the newly formed edges rested softly on my stitches. He held it there, for a moment, then repeated the action, moving along the left side of my body. Face, arm, chest, leg. His touch was sure, gentle. He glanced up at my face and whispered apologies, even as he cradled my hand in his.

Whatever those invisible particles of once-were-light did seemed to work. Wherever he touched me a cool, numb sensation slid over my injuries, easing the roaring ache. When he finally finished he bandaged me again and did up my gown. "Here." He discarded the tube, and handed me more water.

"Thank you." I drained the glass again. "Well, are you going to tell me if I'm a collector?"

With a sad nod, Devich pulled the sheet away. It revealed a bizarre-looking station of buttons, flashing lights, flickering dials and quiet screens, all topped with a large dome, something like a birdcage in clear polymer. Its wheels squeaked as Devich pushed it closer to the bed.

Crammed into that ungainly chamber, I saw the truth. Truth twitched and floated aimlessly, truth vibrated and wiggled. I saw debris.

Debris was the waste created by pion manipulation, and Other did it look like it. It looked like little clumps of squirming dirt, the dark and dim-minded younger sibling to the pions' lightness, their energy and colour.

It could not be controlled, it did not have the ability to unbind and rearrange the very structures of the world.

In fact, all debris could do was interfere with existing pion systems. Too much debris left uncollected could slow down the working of a system, weaken and ultimately undo its bindings. It was dangerous, if left unchecked.

And I realised I had seen it before, in the moment before *Grandeur* hit me. Squirming darkness turning my construction site into a dumping ground. But I hadn't known what it was as I fell toward it. I had not understood the implications.

I sat straight, raised a hand. Devich grunted, pushed the station closer. I leaned over the edge of the bed, ignoring the pull of stitches and smothered pain, and brushed warm polymer with my fingers. Inside, the debris scurried haphazardly; it didn't react to my touch. The debris had none of the semi-sentience, the playfulness, that allowed binders to persuade, to coax, or control pions.

"Ah well, that answers the first question. Looks like you can see it."

I glanced up to meet Devich's flushed face, and took my hand away. "You can see it too?" Maybe there was hope for me, if Devich could see debris, and he could still bind pions, then–

But he shook his head. "No. Would make it easier, but then who'd operate this?" He pressed his hands to a clear glass panel and all the lights that ringed the polymer cage started flickering. "Collectors fill the chamber for us." Something beeped beneath his fingers. "They check it from time to time, so we know it's still full." Odd-looking dials moved and the filament inside half a dozen or so valves began to glow. "Not easy working with something you can't see."

Wasn't that my whole life, now? Living in a world created and run by things I could no longer see.

What was going on inside this bizarre machine? The dials and the valves were a throwback to old, pre-revolutionary technology, before critical circles were discovered. So what was powering this thing? Fire? Steam, gas, water? If so, then there'd be exhaust, surely. And noise. I'd almost believe a pair of poor abused rats turning a wheel. But what was Devich doing, then? Hands on a glass panel, eyes slightly unfocused, whispering under his breath. That was pion manipulation if I'd ever seen it in action.

"Now we need to measure how well you can see it." He cast me what I'm sure he wanted to be a reassuring smile. How could I be reassured with debris floating around like that?

Devich's fingers twitched and I stared at them, hard, trying to read what he was doing with the pions from his movements alone. Something in the debris chamber shifted, and I looked up quickly to catch the end of a strange haziness on the other side of the poly.

"Tell me," he said. "What do you see now?"

The debris was clearer now, clumped together in distinct groups. It looked like the deposits of several dogs on someone's unfortunate courtyard. "I see debris."

Devich was a statue of patience. "Yes, but what does it look like this time? Describe it for me."

I did, analogy and all.

"Very nice." He chuckled, twitched, muttered. "Count them, will you?"

"Why? You said you couldn't see them. How will you know if I get it right?"

"This isn't an eye exam, Tanyana. I need to know if you can tell the debris apart, or if it's all one hazy mass."

Eye exam? Arrogant statue of patience that he was. "And that will make a difference?"

"A big one."

I counted six deposits.

"Very nice, very nice indeed." More of that same strange fuzzing in the chamber. "You need a challenge, my lady."

"I'm nobody's lady." Not any more. I was not longer the centre of a nine point critical circle. And I did not need reminders of it.

"Will you look again and tell me what you see?"

The debris had changed. No longer distinct clumps it had become something flat, dark. Like the shadow of a featureless building. The poly cage began to mist up, and Devich removed one hand from the glass panel. He opened a door in the side of the machine and turned a small crank. A fan whirred, and the condensation faded.

I leaned over the edge of the bed again, and wished I could stand. Wished I could face Devich on my own two feet. "It's hard, this time." I squinted in a vain attempt to work out what the debris was doing.

"To see it?" Devich's voice was carefully controlled.

"No." Oh no, I could see it. But I couldn't understand it. It had become squares, rectangles, shapes with too many sides to name, of thin black or grey. They stretched across the cage like the webs of a tribe of particularly disorganised spiders. Were they holes? Gaps in the air, or little solid sheets of paper? "I don't know how to describe it."

"Can you try?"

I gave him my jumbled description, and his fingers flew.

I touched the poly, lightly. It felt warm, the whir of the fan a slight vibration. The debris flickered and its webs redrew themselves, crowding around my fingertips. The poly grew warmer. With a small shudder, I sat back. "So what does it mean?"

"It means you are as highly skilled with debris as you were with pions. Few collectors see more than a haze, or a shadow of the stuff. Not like you."

"I am a collector, then?"

With a sigh, Devich lifted his hands from the glass panel, and the whole machine turned off. He replaced the sheet in silence.

"Yes. And you need a suit."

"Suit?" Why did such a small word seem to echo so, in this unhomely room?

"All debris collectors wear them." His green gaze held mine. He hesitated. "Tanyana, I can't do this to you, not if you don't want it. I mean–" he fidgeted, fingers plucking at each other with startling violence "–that's not what they would want me to say, but after everything that's already happened to you. I could pretend. If you wanted. To spare–"

The door slammed open, and Devich jumped. Pale, he turned, his hands still plucking their guilty twitch. Two veche men this time, impossible to tell apart. They stood, shoulder to shoulder, filling the doorway.

"You have tested her?" one said.

"Can she see it?" the second continued.

Their voices were the same, their unmoving hands, their stiff, expressionless faces.

The edges of Devich's mouth pinched. "I–"

"Answer us."

Devich swallowed, throat bobbing visibly. "Yes, I think so, but I might need to do further tests."

"No, that will be enough."

"But it was difficult to–" Devich tried to speak, but the veche men cut him off.

"Step aside."

"She will come with us."

Devich, too pale, almost green, cast me a silent, fearful glance. Then the veche men entered the room, bringing their chill with them. Devich gripped his testing machine and forced it out into the corridor. It screeched against the wood again and left a deeper gouge.

In its place, the veche men brought a bed. It floated above the ground, obviously on pions I could not see, and was made of a kind of silver poly mesh.

"What are you doing?" I straightened.

"You will come with us." The men stood at either end of my bed and gripped the blankets. "You will be suited."

"I don't know what that means? Wait! Stop!"

Holding the blankets above and beneath me, the veche men lifted. Together, they carried me as though I was no heavier than a child, and deposited me on the bed. The jarring set off pain in my hip and behind my knee. I held my left hand with my right and pressed it tightly to my chest.

"You will be suited."

I looked up to the veche man closer to my head, about to argue, but stopped. A line ran along his chin, impossibly fine. It curled up to meet his mouth. Dark. Thin. Like a seam.

The bed moved. They floated me out of the room, down a long, tiled corridor that echoed the tread of their shoes. We passed few people, and they all looked the other way as I tried to meet their eyes. They all glanced fearfully at the veche men, nodded, twitched fake smiles. Still, we kept moving.

Down a ramp, along another corridor, down a second ramp. Down and down until I thought we had to be far underground, because even *Grandeur*, surely, could not have been this high.

Finally, two large doors swung open and we came to a stop in a wide, circular room. It was filled with more strange machinery, and as I levered myself to my elbows I noticed a table, smooth and chrome, awkwardly star-shaped. Lamps surrounded it, and burned it into brilliance. "What is that?" I asked.

"You will be suited here, miss." In the sharp glare of lights reflected on metal, I caught those lines on his face again. More of them. They ringed his eyes like spectacles, they dipped down from his nose like a puppet.

That's what it was. These veche men, they looked like puppets.

"But what is that?"

Then Devich appeared. "Tanyana." He held my hand, his palm cool and dry. "I'm sorry." His hand squeezed mine. "Please trust me. I'll be here."

Someone stepped out of the bright-lights-on-silver glare. A faceless shadow, a brush of displaced air and then something sharp pierced my upper arm.

I tried to jerk away. "What–?"

Numbness seeped through me like bleach through cotton. Hands from the bright lights took my blankets away. They undid my gown, they peeled off bandages.

I turned my head toward Devich, on a neck gone to damp and dissolving sponge. My mouth wouldn't form his name, no matter how hard I pursed it, or how I lolled my tongue around like so much flopping fish.

"I'm sorry," he repeated, and leaned close. His breath reminded me of maple cakes, the kind Thada brought in

41

from the western colonies and kept aside for me. I was suddenly hungry, then nauseous, in alarmingly quick succession. "I'll be here, I'll look after you." Devich's enormous eyes swam close to me, rich with concern, before floating away.

The shadow hands lifted, and laid me gently on the silver table. My skin was too bright, naked under the lights, my stitches too dark in comparison. I couldn't feel temperature anymore, not hot nor cold.

Shadows hovered at the edge of my vision. When one leaned in, close to my face, I could only make out pale blue eyes, distant with concentration. The rest was hidden in a tight mask of shiny silver fabric. Only when I tried to touch it did I notice my hands were clamped to the table, encased in a large-fitting glove of the same chrome metal. A lift of my sluggish head, and my feet were the same.

My tongue slipped in and out of control. "What...?" Had I dribbled? I couldn't feel wetness, but something in my slurring mouth convinced me that I had. "What... doing?"

The blue eyes sharpened, stared at me, and skin bunched around them. A frown.

"She's too awake." There was a woman behind the silver mask. It moved as she spoke, rippling into mesmerizing waves.

"Give her another shot." I knew the monotone of the puppet men.

"No," Devich said, from somewhere that made his voice sound like he was wedged inside a can. Tinny and muffled. "Too much and we will dampen the nerve-networks. She's strong. That's all."

The blue-eyed woman watched me for a moment more, indecisive, before retreating from view. Then a

42

whirl beside me, mechanical parts and crackling pion-power. A hooked finger of thick metal, of pumping fluids and sizzling energy, rose from beneath the table to arch over me. The tip came to rest against my wrist. It was heavy and solid; I could feel its pressure.

"Don't let it frighten you, Tanyana," Devich murmured. "It's strange, I know. But this will give you your suit. You won't feel it."

Maybe I should have closed my eyes? But within the finger hidden parts whirled, lights flashed, then tubes opened to merge fluids into startlingly beautiful pinks and blues, and I couldn't look away.

I felt it when it entered my skin. Not with pain, not the sharp of cutting or the excruciation of foreign bodies, but dull pressure and unemotional awareness. Needles plunged from the fingertip into my wrist, injecting things that wriggled up my arm like parasitic worms.

Blood slicked from my skin to darken the chrome table. It flowed slowly, like mud.

Then my shoulder twitched. I saw it from the corner of my eye. Steady, in rhythmic succession the muscles spasmed, starting behind my shoulder blade to end near the base of my neck. Then the top of my arm did the same thing, then near my elbow, and finally down, partially obscured by the finger, close to my wrist.

"That is good," a puppet said, without emotion.

"But we've only just planted the network." Devich sounded concerned.

"Continue."

"Not if it is too strong. I will suit her, but I won't hurt her!"

"Continue."

Over and over my arm twitched, as the wriggling

43

below my skin intensified. Then, suddenly, the finger clicked loud and echoing, and everything stopped.

I blinked down at my wrist as the finger lifted. All I got for my trouble was a hazy image of blood and wire.

The finger withdrew. Another rose in its place. Wide, with a thick hinge at each knuckle, and brazenly golden amidst so much chrome and white light. This one also hovered above the mess of my wrist and I winced as it lowered, though I felt nothing, and loosened more saliva.

"Shhh," Devich murmured. "Don't be afraid."

The fingertip opened like an insect's jaws and clamped over my wrist.

"Be a good girl, keep still. Just a moment."

The pressure on my wrist – all around it – grew until I was certain it had to break. Then the finger clicked like its thinner brother had done, folded in on itself, and withdrew.

There was something on my wrist when I lifted an uneasy head to peer at it. Something that glowed. Not with the lamplight, but with its own power. Colder, artificial. If I could have shuddered, I would have. A good, long one that touched every hair, that eased out every creep.

Not only did the thing on my wrist glow, but it moved too, spinning in a slow, encircling rotation.

"This is your suit," Devich explained.

Suit? It was some strange bracelet, more like jewellery than a suit. Then I remembered the photographs on the walls, the adorned wrists, the ankles. The waist.

The waist? What about the neck, what I had assumed was a necklace? Would they stick needles into my throat, pierce my blood and breath and plant something that wriggled, that crawled, that glowed and spun?

44

My body remained numb, heavy and limp, and I couldn't struggle.

The first finger whirred into existence again, this time down at my right foot. I couldn't see it properly, but I knew it would be hovering, pumping its fluids and charging its pion-power. Anticipation of its weight, its pressure, its penetration ran unfelt tremors through me.

If my legs twitched the same as my shoulder, I didn't see it. The fingers repeated their ministrations on both of my ankles, then over on my left wrist. Strangely, it felt no different on the stitched-up skin there. I almost threw up when two fingers, larger than the ones that had destroyed my wrists and ankles, latched onto my waist and pushed down hard.

I stayed awake until three new fingers rose around my head, thin and tentacle-like. They arched above me, and clamped themselves over my throat so hard darkness spotted my vision. Then there were needles. And crawling things. And pumping fluids. I felt it all in that numb way, the way that assures you there will be pain, oh, there will be pain, but not now. Not just now.

Devich whispered from his distant can as two of the fingers withdrew, and ejected the empty glass tubes that had held their colourful fluids. "Let it go. You've done so well, Other knows, better than I thought you could. So let it go, let them finish, and sleep. Can you sleep for me, my girl?"

As I closed my eyes I saw Devich's face, the cheekiness in his slightly upturned mouth. Not, Other help me, the metallic arch of the fingers. Not the new canisters that slid in to replace the empty ones they had ejected. Not the things that filled them, fibrous, soft and wiggling in the glass, as they lowered themselves past my face and into my throat.

• • • •

I was still on the table when I woke, but I was covered by a grey blanket of roughly woven wool, and the lamps were dimmed.

Devich stood beside me, holding my hand in his.

"Why did you do that to me?" Something pressed against my throat as I whispered. Small twinges of pain told me the numbness was wearing off. "I'm sick of this. People keep doing things."

"Oh, Tanyana." He pressed his forehead to the back of my hand. I could only see him from the corner of my eye; my neck was stiff with a strange combination of deadness and blossoming ache. "You have been suited, my girl."

Your girl? I wanted to explain in no uncertain terms why, exactly, I was nobody's girl, and certainly not his, but heavy eyelids and the threat of more drool stopped me.

"Hurts," I managed instead. "Pions hurt, now this hurts. Had enough. No more."

"The pions?" Devich's head jerked up, expression alarmed.

"Pushed me. No one will listen. But they did."

"Pushed you?" He hesitated, as though searching for the right words. "I– The suit, it will hurt for a while. So will the stitches. Until the networks stabilize. Until your skin heals."

Stitches and scars and suit, what did they look like? Was I still me?

"Can you forgive me?"

I couldn't quite move my mouth to answer him.

Devich sighed and stood slowly, joints creaking and back stooped, tired like an old man. "They will take you home now." He squeezed my hand. "You need to rest and to heal and then, then, I would like to see you again." He leaned close. "If you'll forgive me."

As he called to the puppets, as he held onto my hand, I knew I already had. If not for his self-deprecating laugh, if not for his soft touch, then at least for the water he had given me, when no one else would.

3.

I learned to cover the suit if I wanted to sleep.

Any resemblance to jewellery ended with the silver. The fixtures were large and ungainly, as wide as the length of my middle finger. They were thick too, half an inch at least, so I couldn't pull sleeves down to cover them if the jacket was too tight, and most of the boots I owned were now unwearable.

Worst of all was the way the silver bands moved. At the centre of each was another ring, a thinner version of the whole apparatus that spun slowly, constantly. I hadn't gathered enough courage to touch it. This extra ring seemed to float on something liquid, it moved so smoothly. Around the floating ring were symbols, signs and letters of scrolling silver, and these were the bastards that glowed. As they moved – not with the floating ring, not with any apparent symmetry or reason – they flickered. Some dipped into dull nothingness while others rose from the silver shining, beaming their arcane meaning proudly.

I couldn't decide what Devich and the puppet men had fitted me with. Six bands of silver drilled into my skin were hardly what I could call a suit. If it was liquid, then why didn't it spill when I moved my hand? If it was solid, then how in all the Other's worst dreams did it move? And I wondered, dimly like a dull headache, what the pions were doing. Surely they were there, spinning the silver, shining the ciphers.

The veche returned me to my apartment after the suiting, and left me there. I lost track of days. No one visited. Not the puppet men, not Devich. No member of my circle. I couldn't do much other than throb with my collective pain and hope I was healing.

I went through the days like I was a puppet myself, someone else pulling the strings. Slowly my hand knitted together, fingers started to look like fingers again. Twisted. Stunted. But fingers. A few days, and I could bend my left knee. I slid from my bed each morning and struggled the length of the apartment, moving, walking as much as I could. Gradually, my strength grew. I cleaned my wounds, washing the bandages in my bathroom sink. I stared at myself in the mirror each morning, wondering what kind of scars would they leave.

Then I sat in the study, shutters drawn and only one lamp burning low. I had to turn the lamp on manually: remove the small latch on the side of its base – the Other-damned thing was stuck, and I snared a fingernail in the process – stick my finger in and twist and curse until the valve opened enough to allow the pions to flow. For countless days I did nothing but peer at its light and wonder why I could see it, but not the pions that drove it. I supposed that was the point. In a factory somewhere on the outskirts of the city pions were being asked to create this light. Then, when they knew what was expected of them and were ready to perform it, they were rushed down one of the many great systems that spread across the city, just so they could arrive here, in this lamp, to bind this light for me. I didn't really know what they were doing to create the light. I was an architect, not a lamplighter. The pions had to be generating some kind of reaction, inside that ornate glass tube on its sculptured brass fittings, but I didn't know what it was. I'd never bothered to learn.

I thought about the pion-binder, sitting in a lamp-light factory with hundreds of others all bound in complex critical circles, coaxing an enormous number of pions across Movoc-under-Keeper to give me this small amount of light. A man, I decided, after much staring and thinking, there in the semi-dark, balding and fat. With poor hygiene. The members of his circle can't stand the way he stinks. And he sits there, in seven-bell shifts, after which he is even more pungent, and earns maybe two hundred kopacks a day with the rest of them.

I sat for days alone in the study, at least a sixnight and one, probably more. Days covering my wrists, ankles, waist and neck with blankets.

What was I doing?

Giving up? That didn't take long, did it, Tanyana? A little push, a few cuts, some creepy statue-men and a bit of new jewellery and already you're sitting in the dark nursing your misery. That's the Tanyana who worked her way to the centre of a nine point circle, is it? Did you win the contract to build *Grandeur* by sitting around? Do you remember how you did all that? Hard work, skill, determination. Hardly the traits of a debris collector.

I stood, left the room, and opened the valves for every light in the apartment.

I shouldn't be a debris collector. And I wouldn't be, if someone hadn't pushed me. If the veche knew I was telling the truth.

I rinsed my face and hair in the bathroom basin, and rubbed as much of myself as I could with a wet towel. I worked honey-scented nut oil into my skin, and dabbed vanilla onto my neck and wrists. My stomach gurgled with awakening hunger at the smell, and I allowed myself a chuckle as I pulled open the lacquered closet. Bears growled down at me from its corners, their eyes inlaid with beechwood, their teeth glinting mother-of-pearl. My hands shook slightly as I pushed aside the high-necked navy jackets I had worn on construction sites. Instead, I pulled on thick pants and a pale angora sweater. I had lost weight, and even these small, shapeless clothes were baggy on me. I rubbed gel over my hands and ran them through my short blonde hair so it stuck out around my face, not that different from the sleep-messed look, to be honest. I owned little in the way of cosmetics and jewellery. Nothing dusky to compliment my pale, almost grey eyes. Nothing to cover the freckles and sunspots endemic of a fair complexion subjected to too many days working in the sun. The only adornment I had to add was a watch that would remain hidden in my jacket.

The watch was a gift from Jernea, the old architect who had mentored me through university, given on the day I earned my own critical circle. It opened with a small catch: inside concentric circles rotated slowly, tracking and chiming with the bells. No pions had crafted it, and none worked the gears that moved it now, all it took was the turning of a tiny wind-up key. Old-world technology and craftsmanship, and that meant it was at least two centuries old. For that, it was precious. For the skills that were lost, far more so than its polished brass and coloured glass inlay.

At the door I squashed my feet into heavy black boots. I pulled on a dark coat. It was cut for a man, but far more comfortable than any ridiculously-long-sleeved-draped-across-the-shoulders-and-narrow-at-the-waist woman's wear would be. Outside I pressed fingertips to the pion-powered lock. It had a flat, crystalline panel designed to read my touch alone. Normally, I would have watched pions buzz about my fingers, glancing against those busy within my own body and checking I was, in fact, the person who lived beyond the door they guarded. Now, I only felt a tickling over my skin and had to take the security they provided on faith.

Outside, a crisp Movoc morning breeze carried the tolls of thirdbell up from the city centre and set the skin on my face tightening. It irritated my stitches. I turned into it, discomfort or no, and started to walk. Slowly, shuffling, limping slightly. But at least I was walking. The centre of Movoc-under-Keeper was more than bridges, grand old houses, and romantic spots where pions danced. I could find veche chambers there. The project halls. The tribunal.

The veche couldn't silence me. I would give them no choice but to listen.

Where pions should have stretched from rooftop to rooftop in light-beaded banners there was only empty, cloud-grey sky. Movoc was a strange, dim place without the busy lights and complex systems that gave it life. It felt haunted. Not only because of the countless unseen presences I just knew were there, hidden beneath it all. But things just seemed to move, to work, all on their

52

own. Metallic doors opened or closed themselves, so did the windows. I had to cross the street to avoid a fountain I had once thought of as beautiful. It was built with gaps in the stonework, so the complex bindings could be better appreciated and the very colour of its pions added to its form. Now it just looked like a lot of blocks of carefully shaped stone suspended in thin air, dribbling water that came from nowhere. Unsettling. Unnatural.

I passed beneath a walkway between two tall buildings of silver and glass. It floated, unattached to anything, roaming left and right, up and down, to collect and ferry passengers between the towers. And I flinched, every time its dark shadow passed over me, because to my limited senses, the damned thing should have fallen. It didn't, and it wouldn't, while its bindings and systems still supported it. But I couldn't see any of them. I couldn't even tell whether the circle that set it up in the first place had done a good job, and were up to date with their maintenance.

I was watched the whole way. A lone, scarred, bandaged and slightly glowing woman was not a usual sight for the centre of Movoc-under-Keeper. I kept my head down, my slow progress steady. But I could feel them, and catch them in the corner of my eye. A gaggle of young, rich girls flocked around a table at the open window of a coffee house. I turned, slightly, at the sound of their surprised, screeching cackle and realised they were pointing at me while they did it. What must I have looked like to them, compared to their beautiful hair, artfully painted skin and layers of lace-tipped silk? Frightful enough for a young boy in a miniature enforcer's uniform to take one look at me and run, bawling, to wrap his arms around his mother's knees.

With each look, each expression of shock, of disgust, of fear, I lifted my head that little bit higher. But I was grateful that the walk was only short, all the same. One of the advantages of being a pion-binder paid two hundred thousand kopacks by the veche was the closeness of my apartment to the city centre and the Keeper's Tear Bridge.

As I neared Tear River, Movoc changed. Newer, pion-built complexes withdrew, to be replaced by older, smaller buildings with leadlight windows. Small garden plots, bumpy stone roads, narrow streets. I realised, as I walked, how lovely these buildings were without pions to distract me. Bears carved out of stone roared from cornices. Welcoming faces made from small pieces of multicoloured glass smiled above doors. And images of the river was everywhere, etched into the sandstone to flow, one building to the other, wrapping Movoc in the Keeper's Tear.

I had missed all that beauty, looking only for the lights within the stone.

Like most veche buildings the tribunal hall was close to the Keeper's Tear Bridge. As I neared it, I started to wonder if this was, in fact, the only reason I was here.

Beside the bridge, on the eastern bank, stood a building of bluestone and quartz. My design. I had surrounded it with gardens, with pine trees cut to catch the snow and create smaller, pale mirrors of the building's domes. It climbed in ice cream scoops, rich like a dessert. Sun caught in the crystal, water from melted ice or summer rain kept the stone streaked and mottled with rich blue. When the gardens bloomed the clover was a mix of white and indigo, of snow and moist bluestone. A structure of beauty, a place of warmth. An art gallery, where people met to sip wine beneath paintings and sculpture, renderings and light shows. My first commission from the veche as the leader of a nine point circle.

I stalled in front of it, toes between pathway and springy grass.

"My lady?"

I didn't turn. Couldn't have been for me.

"My– My lady?" Closer, more insistent. And a voice I knew – Other, I knew.

"Volski?"

"It is you! My lady!"

"Don't call me–" but my words were whisked away as Volski wrapped me in his arms.

My stitches roared their protest up through my throat. "Put me down!" I screamed, and he dropped me. I caught the fuzzy edge of his shocked expression as I sank to the path and plunged my left hand in lovely, cool grass, stitches screaming all over my body and the suit burning like fire.

"What's wrong?" He dropped to his knees beside me.

I could see feet gathering on the path. "Nothing," I gasped at him, struggled to stand, and finally took his offered hand. "Please, I'm fine." Sure enough, a small group had gathered on the pathway to watch me struggle. Older men, suits grey. An aging woman with silver peeking through the dye in her hair pressed her hand to her lips, partially obscuring an exaggerated "O".

Volski understood. He always had. He scowled at the crowd, held my elbow to help me balance, and maintained an affronted silence. His calm air dispersed them. It took away the drama, and made me thankful I hadn't run into someone like Tsana. When the path was clear again he led me to a bench opposite the gallery, and murmured in my ear, "You don't look fine." His face battled between concern and a fatherly frown. It was easy to think of Volski in a fatherly way. A good ten years older than me, with a solid, square jaw and serious dark eyes he was honesty and responsibility in human skin. We had worked together when I was merely the centre of a three point circle, and I had taken him with me every time I rose. He had been an anchor, reliable and constant. "I was worried about you, my lady."

And he had left me scarred and alone.

I lifted my chin, and held back a wince as the stitching in my neck pulled. "You certainly found a fine way to show it."

"I would have liked to show it. I would have liked that very much. But I didn't know what happened to you, I didn't know where you were. They only told us you had survived a sixweek and one after the fall, and that was because Llada and I went to–" he broke off. "What is it?"

I must have looked as cynical as I felt. "I don't need your excuses."

He swallowed hard. "We are cowards. I know that. We were afraid, we felt guilty. But after what Tsana did to you, can you blame us?"

Blood drained from my face, left me icy and light-headed. "Tsana?"

He frowned at me. "You don't know?"

"That's why I'm here." I pointed to the veche chambers hulking on the other side of the gallery garden like an ugly older brother. "To get some answers. And make them listen to me." Volski started to follow my finger but his gaze became stuck on my suit where it spun slowly, bright against inflamed skin.

"Other," he whispered. "What is that?"

"Oh, this? This is my new suit." I let out a long breath. "They tell me I'm a collector now. A debris collector."

Volski's face fell the way it would if I had told him someone we both knew had just died. "No. Not you."

"Sadly yes."

"Is that because of–?" He swallowed, neck bobbing visibly. "Of what happened."

"Yes. Whatever that was."

"There was a tribunal, my lady. It wasn't her fault."

"No, apparently it was mine."

"You weren't at the tribunal. We could only go by the evidence."

"Don't you think that's a little strange, Volski? To hold a tribunal while I was in a bed – or missing, or dead, for all you seemed to know – and had no chance to defend myself?"

Emotions fought over his face. Uncertainty, grief, guilt. Not the righteous anger I would have preferred. "What else could you have added?"

"That it wasn't my fault, that it wasn't an accident!" I gripped Volski's arm, drew him closer. "I tried to tell you then, I tried to warn you, but the circle was failing, I don't even know if you heard me." A new emotion now. Fear. Was I that terrifying, with my new lights and bandages over my face? "Someone must have summoned them, set them loose on the construction site. It was their fault, not mine!" I broke off, panting. Weakness shook over aching skin. This might not have been the best idea. Not yet, anyway.

"Them?" Volski whispered. His eyes darted over the seat, the street, the gallery. Anywhere but me.

"Pions." I tried gripping him with both hands, but the fingers of my left had started to swell, and they wouldn't

57

respond. "They broke our circle. They pushed me off *Grandeur*'s palm."

"Other, Tanyana, your hand doesn't look good," Volski said.

I glanced down. Sure enough, the bandage had lifted. Dark stitches crawled out of red, puckering holes.

He stared at the wounds in horror. "Maybe you should calm down. Maybe you should go home."

Calm did settle on me, but not the kind he wanted. A hollow, hopeless cold. "You used to trust me, with your pions, your work, your life. Why don't you believe me now?"

"Tan– my lady." Volski patted my right hand like I was a pet. "I want to believe you, of course, but I didn't see anything. We didn't see anything. There were no pions pushing you. It was an accident. That's all."

That's all? "If I fell, Volski, just fell, then please explain this to me." I held up my mangled, swollen left hand. "Please tell me–" my tongue was a lump in my mouth at the words "–please tell me what Tsana did."

Confusion. Pain. Grief. Volski grieved for me though I was not dead. "It was an accident."

"Tell me."

He swallowed hard again, and took his patting hand away. He looked to the gallery, its permanence and beauty. I couldn't bring myself to do the same. I would find no comfort there. Instead, I watched the emotions on his face. Wondered if he wished he had not noticed me at all. "She panicked, when *Grandeur* started to come down. You wouldn't have believed it, Tanyana. On the ground, with all that glass and metal and stone falling on us, it was all we could do to keep ourselves alive!"

"Yes, it must have been terrible." And yet the very

image of peace and quiet from my position, eight hundred feet up and falling fast.

"Nosrod caught you first, he made a webbing, soft, strong. Ingenious. But it disintegrated. Must have been the panic, we all felt it. Nothing we created would hold."

That, or the furious crimson pions none of them believed existed.

"Llada did... something like cushions. Worked well. For a moment. And then–"

"And then?" I felt very quiet and still. In my mind I could see myself falling, the scrambling attempts of my circle to save me, and the pions destroying everything they tried. I could see it as clearly as if I had been awake still. As if *Grandeur* hadn't knocked me out from the start.

"And then Tsana, she panicked, and she constructed glass."

"Glass," I whispered.

"It was an accident, the tribunal said–"

"Fell through it, did I?"

"Y-yes."

"Lots of blood, I imagine."

He nodded, looking ill. "It was terrible. Just horrible."

I stood too quickly, swayed, and grasped the back of the seat.

"Where are you going?" Volski leapt to his feet, hands out to hold me, but I leaned back and steadied myself. "Can I help you home?"

"I'm going to the tribunal chamber. They need to know–" I blinked dizziness away "–I need to tell them!"

"Let me help you!"

But I didn't need Volski, not any more. He buzzed around me like a fly as I crossed the gardens, climbed the steps, and entered the tribunal chamber.

Tribunals were held in a grand old hall built of smooth marble. Carvings glared down from a high and imposing ceiling. I glanced up at them as Volski and I walked the long path to the single desk barring the way to the tribunal chambers. The Other, his face twisted and monstrous, seemed to follow us. Why had they carved so many of him? His distorted form, his red eyes, his long and leering tongue. A horde of Others surrounded the Keeper Mountain, where a single large light fitting had been installed. I supposed it was symbolic, the way *Grandeur* was supposed to be symbolic. The Keeper was more than just a mountain; in the old world myths he was a guardian too, a barrier between us and the terror of the Other. He was a light holding back the darkness.

Volski, I could tell, was more concerned with the people around us than the Other on the ceiling. The hallway was crowded, hushed words rose to the ceiling like humming smoke. Eyes watched us, whispering mouths turned our way.

The desk was a wide slab of roughly cut stone with a polished surface. A bored-looking woman sat behind it, a lamp in the design of a lily lighting her face.

I stormed the desk in my tired, shaking style. She looked up, eyelids heavy, her own pink handprint on her cheek. "Documentation?" she droned, before I had opened my mouth.

It wasn't what I had expected, and I realised I didn't really know what to say. "I– er– I need to speak to someone." Who? "Someone who presided over a particular tribunal." How were tribunals identified? Dates? Numbers? I turned to Volski. "Do you remember the date it was held? Do you have anything to prove–?"

"Don't bother." The woman behind the desk

straightened. No sleepiness remained in her face. Her hazel eyes were sharp, her face suddenly angular and hard. "No documented slide, no tribunal. No point."

"No." It wasn't that simple. "I need to speak to someone about a tribunal that was held without me. I need them to set up another one, or reopen it, or whatever it is they do. What's the word? An appeal! I need an appeal. To tell the truth!"

She lifted an unimpressed eyebrow. "Listen. You can't walk in here and demand to talk to a veche representative. They're not dogs to bark at your command."

"But—"

"I said no! The veche calls you to a tribunal, not the other way around. Who do you think you are that you expect the veche to jump when you shout?"

I realised the whispering had gone quiet.

"What about me?" Volski, until this point hanging back uncomfortably, leaned on the desk beside me. The silver veche bears on his strapping navy coat shone in the lily-light. "Can you help me?"

The woman let out a rather overstated groan. "And what do you want?"

"He's just going to ask you the same thing!" I jumped in. "But you'll listen to him, won't you, because of those damned pins on his coat."

She gave me a firm, level look. "We are all equal before the veche. No matter how... dirty."

"Other's shit."

"One more word like that and I'm throwing you out." She lifted a hand. Enforcers I hadn't realised were there materialised from the crowd. Their bears were roaring, furious and large, and they shone from belt buckles, hats and shoulders.

61

"You can't just—"

"Tanyana!" Volski slapped a heavy hand on my shoulder and I gasped into silence. Bastard had hit my left side. "I assume you cannot direct me to a veche member who oversaw a particular tribunal?" he asked the woman behind the desk, and positively reeked urbane diplomacy. "Even though I was there?"

"That kind of information is sealed." She glared at me. "For what must seem at the moment to be obvious reasons."

I glared right back.

"What kind of information can you give me?" Volski pressed on.

"Transcript slides are available to the public. All sensitive information removed, of course."

"May I have one, then?"

So, as it turned out, I needed Volski after all. The woman grudgingly gave up the records: two small glass sides, each about the length of my finger and as thin as a fallen leaf. Every word crowded inside them was written in pions. They held answers more securely than any lock could have. At least from me.

"I haven't given up," I told the woman behind the desk, even as Volski started to walk away. "I won't let this stop me."

"How exciting for you."

I followed Volski to one of the few empty stone benches that lined the hallway. The enforcers watched us, the crowd watched us, even the woman behind her desk. My bandages were hot. My stitches ached.

"What more can I tell you?" Volski asked. "I told you about Tsana, I explained—"

"I don't think this will help." I pressed the bandage down on my hand, looked up and held the shocked gaze of a wealthy woman in satin and pearls. Wasn't the bell a little early for pearls? What did she have to look so scandalised about? "I need to tell people what really happened. I need to make them understand that I shouldn't be, well, like this." I scowled as the unruly bandage started to curl. "How will reading those lies help me do that?"

Volski was silent for a heavy moment. "Tanyana. It's all we've got."

We? This was hardly his fight; my circle had made that very clear. He would leave, as soon as I let him, as soon as his failing sense of duty and guilt abandoned him. But when would I have this opportunity again? "Fine. The stitches then, tell me about the stitches."

Volski held the slide out at arm's length, and lifted it so he could peer through it. A gentle flick of his fingers and the pions inside leapt out of the glass, shining their words in a bright golden light that I could only imagine. All I saw was a faint mist that gathered in the space between Volski and the slide. He scanned, mouth moving, fingers occasionally twitching. And frowned. "Are you sure you want—"

"Tell me."

Even so, he hesitated. "Your injuries were horrible."

I laughed, a little too loud. It echoed from marble floor and walls. An enforcer twitched my way before realising my bitterness wasn't actually a threat. "I know that already."

"The glass—" he hesitated, coughed "—you fell through the glass on your left side. But, you see, falling steel beams had already hit you, on the head, so the healers had to choose." Volski lowered the slide, dismissing its invisible information. As the mist dispersed I saw three tiny dark specks form. I looked away, horrified. Debris. "They saved your life, did things in your head you do not want me to read out. But it meant you weren't strong enough for them to heal the glass cuts. So they had to resort to stitches."

"I see." Did that help, knowing where the Other-cursed patterns in dark fibre came from? Didn't make them any less sore. Wouldn't make them heal faster. But, at least, I knew.

"And what does it say about pions in there?" I bit off each word. "Does it detail the chaos? The crimson pions that tore up everything you tried to do to help me?"

"You know it doesn't. I was there, I didn't see them, none of us saw anything like that." Volski hesitated again. "It does include the inspectors' reports, though. They determined that you tried to do too much, because you felt like you were under pressure, and pushed yourself too far. You created so much debris that it destabilised the systems, but you didn't realise that was happening." He swallowed. "It was a mistake to do an inspection without more warning." He coughed. "The veche has even set down a new edict: three days' notice, in all cases, from now on."

Those Other-damned inspectors. I stood. This time, Volski didn't follow. "Thank you, Volski. I'll leave you alone now."

He still didn't stand. "Can I see you again? Is there anything more I can do to help?"

I snorted. "Do you really want to?"

"Of course!"

"My door is open to you. Always open."

"But where–?"

I started walking away. I didn't need to watch Volski pretend to care about the crazy, damaged woman he once respected. A few steps, however, and I stopped. Looked over my shoulder. "Who did they replace me with?"

"Who? Oh." Volski fidgeted and looked uncomfortable. "They made Llada the centre. Brought in someone new to fill her spot. Not the same, though. Not without you."

That was nice to say, at least. "Llada?" I could imagine her bullying the circle the way she did her pions. Didn't think it would last. "Not who I would have chosen."

I left Volski sitting in the veche chamber, the tribunal slides between his fingers.

As I limped my way home, I came to realise just how much of a fool I had been. I should not have left Volski so abruptly while he was offering help. I should have taken what favours I could get. But he wasn't the only avenue still open to me. If I couldn't reopen the tribunal just by asking nicely, or rudely, then maybe I wasn't asking the right people. I had been an architect for the veche. Surely someone in Construction for the Furtherment of Varsnia knew someone who could ask nicely and not be ignored.

When I made it home, the courtyard was not empty. Devich stood there, pressing the lock, bending over, frowning at it. How long had he been standing there, doing that?

I said, "I should have known you'd come the one day I step outside this place."

He spun, smiled at me, blinked confusion. "Good to see you walking."

I pushed past him, touched the pion lock, opened the door and let him stand there as I leant on the door frame.

"Tanyana." His gorgeous green eyes swam with emotion. It took me a moment to realise that was because the suit on my wrist was shining in his face. "Will you let me in?"

I lowered my hand. "Are you going to give me a good reason to?"

"Hmm." He lifted a finger to his lips, tapped with exaggeration. "So I can admire your beautiful home?" And he winked. With his smooth cheeks and the boyishness in his smile I couldn't imagine anyone as different from Volski.

"Not quite good enough."

Devich dropped his finger, and his act. "I have this, to ease the pain." He took another glass tube from his pocket. "And I'd like to come inside to make sure you are healing."

A sneer twitched on the edge of my lips, but I stepped back to let him inside. I crossed my arms as much as I could without hurting my wrists. "I'm sure you say that to all the girls you trick, tie down and mutilate."

The glance over his shoulder was guilt-ridden and puppy-eyed. Dangerous combination. "Only the interesting ones." His voice was thick.

Scowling, I closed the door. "What do you want? What more could you possibly do to me?"

"Tanyana, please." He took a half step closer, before simply twitching his hand. A hopeless gesture. "Forgive me. I didn't want to. I'm so sorry I hurt you."

"Hmph." I approached him, setting the buckles on his pale jacket sparkling.

It was strange, I suddenly felt powerful. In my hurt, my ugliness, I was stronger than him in his tailored shirt and polished boots.

I held out my hands. "What is this?"

"Your suit, my– Tanyana."

"Try again."

He smiled, sad and slow. "I will explain. I'm here to help you." He flicked a glance back at the door. "Now that you're well enough, they let me come and see you."

I lowered my hands, still scowling. My wrists had started to ache again, right up into the elbow joint.

"Please." He said that an awful lot. "Sit down. Do you have tea? Can I make you some tea?"

I gave in to him, and pointed him to the kitchen. As I settled into my reading chair I could hear him rattling around. The clang of cutlery, the hollow knock of cups, and finally the hiss of heated water. It was rather pleasant, to have Devich in my small kitchen.

Too pleasant. I reminded myself to scowl as he entered the study, cups fitted with knitted warmers balanced in his hands. My stitches pulled.

"Here." He handed me a cup, and I wrapped my hands around the warmth. The light from my wrists created sparkling patterns on the dark liquid, the crests of a false ocean.

He sat on the footrest, knees close to my own. I didn't shift away.

"Explain."

He took a sip of his own first. This seemed to involve sniffing the tea, blowing away steam, and gradually touching the rim of the cup to his lips. "To be a debris collector, you need a suit. See, you can't go around picking the debris up, not with your bare hands. No one can do that. So we need to make suits. Special suits. And that's what you're now wearing."

"But these don't look like any suit I've seen." I flicked my wrist, wincing slightly at the stiffness there.

67

"True. Your suit is dormant now."

"Dormant?" Suits weren't dormant. Suits were wool and buttons and dye.

Another sip. "It'll be difficult while you're healing, particularly if you're going to insist on running around upsetting your stitches." His eyes slid to the red, angry skin of my left hand. I had to fight not to slip it from the cup and hide it between my knees. "When we can be sure everything has stabilised then I'll show you." The edges of his cheeky smile peeked above the rim of the cup. "It's not something I can really explain."

I gulped my hot tea down, enjoying the warmth it left in my throat and stomach. "Why are you here then, if you refuse to explain anything?"

"Told you." He placed his still-full cup on the floor and shuffled forward. His hands rested lightly on my knees and his raised eyebrows challenged me to pull away.

I sat very still. The heat of his palms travelled through my pants to leave a tingling.

"I'm here to help." He leaned in closer. "You're tired, Tanyana."

I didn't pull away, but I did make a face. "You should try sleeping with these sometime."

"It's the small things that are hard to get used to at first. Here." He kept one hand on my knee as he slid open the buttons on his jacket and pulled dark cloth from a pocket. "You might need to wait a few more days for your skin to heal, there's nothing I can do about that. But these are for you."

There were five of them, tight circles of a dark cloth that stretched in my hands. "What are they?"

"To cover you. So you can sleep." He took one from me and ran his fingers along it, demonstrating the elasticity. "These will hide the light." He placed the fabric back with its fellows. "Helps you sleep." And the cloth would hide the horrible metal bands from the rest of the world. He didn't say it, but I could read it in his face.

I had never hidden before. Would I do so now?

Devich collected his cup from the rug.

I lifted an eyebrow at him as he sipped, carefully. "Is that all?"

Crestfallen, he replaced the cup on the floor. "Well, I still need to help you with the pain. Show me your wrists."

Wary, I did so, shoulders tense, ready to snatch them away.

"How are your wounds?" He inspected the suit and lifted bandages along my arm.

"Healing slowly."

"Do they hurt?"

I described the pain, the changes and the rises and the rare, rare dips. He listened, expression hidden.

"I will show you some exercises. Keep the muscles working, and they will heal faster. Pay special attention to your neck. You need to keep the blood vessels and nerves there healthy."

I lost track of the bells as Devich tortured me some more. He bent my wrists, he rolled my ankles and bowed me from the waist. He massaged the tender muscles around my shoulders. Hurt like the Other's own claws, left me feeling twitchy and sore and irritable. The monster even waited for his tea to cool to room temperature before drinking. What kind of Other-spawn would do that?

Finally, he loosened more pions across my skin, to ease the damage he had done. "It hurts now, I know."

"Oh, do you?" I wrapped myself in my arms as he took

the cups away, determined to stay in the chair for at least another sixnight, and possibly never move again.

"It won't hurt as much tomorrow. Trust me."

"Why would I ever trust you?"

Devich smiled, and drew his jacket from the corner of my desk where he had tossed it. His sleeve disturbed two old-fashioned graphite pencils I had bought for the novelty, never imagining I might actually need to use them. I watch him rearrange them. His hand was shaking.

Was I really that horrible? To look at, to touch, to force himself to speak to?

"Because I know a lot more about debris than you do, Tanyana." He kept his back to me as he shrugged on his coat. "You might be able to see it, but I've spent my life studying it. I worked with suits more primitive and painful than yours will ever be. I coached dozens of collectors, helped them through the beginning, when everything is nasty, painful and new. You're not the first collector I've visited to teach them how to sleep, whose knotted shoulders I have eased, who's resisted the exercises I designed for their own good. You're not the first, and you will not be the last." Smiling, open and easy, he flicked buttons into holes. "You're not the first, Tanyana, but by Other, you're the strongest."

Curled into a chair, sulking, I snorted a laugh. "What could possibly make you think that?"

"You can't know how quickly you tied to the network. Some collectors take weeks to heal as much as you have in the past, what is it now, sixnight? Yes, it's only been a sixnight. And your suit is generating, it started generating the moment it touched your skin. You are strong, Tanyana. Please, in the coming moons, with the coming changes, remember that. You are strong."

I had no idea what to say, so I didn't reply.

"And do your exercises." Grinning, Devich left me. I heard the door close, the sizzling click of the pion lock, and silence. Lovely silence.

The skin around my suit stung when I pulled the dark covers on. My left hand screamed protests. But it was worth the discomfort to sit in darkness – actual darkness – and silence. Didn't have time to move from my chair before I fell asleep.

4.

"As you appear well enough to make a scene in the tribunal chambers–" a puppet man, standing in my doorway, passed me a small white card "–you are doubtless well enough to begin collecting. Leave now."

I stared at the side of his neck, at his jaw, his eyes. Nothing. No seams, no wooden hinges. But I had seen them. I knew it. "How do you know that?" Two days since Devich had been here, two days since I had met Volski in the city. Had Devich told them? But I hadn't told Devich about the tribunal records. "What are you doing? Following me?" But how could these wooden puppet creatures have followed me without being terribly obvious?

"We know that you are ready to begin collecting, Miss Vladha."

I met his dirty-wall eyes and wondered what was going on behind them. "And what will you do if I don't?"

His expression didn't change.

"I am not a debris collector," I hissed at him. "I don't belong with those people. I was pushed, do you hear me! This isn't right, it isn't fair!"

The puppet expelled a long sigh, the most human thing I had seen any of them do. And in that movement I caught a glimpse, tiny and almost hidden by pale hairs, of a line etched down his neck to disappear beneath the collar of his shirt. Fine, thin, dark. But there. Definitely there. "You tried to reopen a tribunal, did you not?"

"Other's hell, how do you know that?"

"Let me assure you, Miss Vladha, that if you do not follow our instructions, if you do not meet up with your collecting team by breakbell this morning, you will be brought before a tribunal of your own. You will repay the veche for the damage you caused, and for the skills you have lost, one way or the other. If not through the collection of debris, then through a sentence of manual labour in the colonies. Abandon your duty, and the veche would have no choice but to strongly condemn such a blatant waste of your newly acquired talents. And as you might imagine, miss, there are few positions for a woman with no pion-binding skill at the edges of civilisation."

Something inside me quailed. I tried not to show it. "You wouldn't really want that. Set up a tribunal and all I'll do is tell the truth. That's the last thing you want." But my voice shook, however much I wanted it to hold steady.

"You refuse to understand, miss. The truth has already been told. Backed up with testimony by senior veche inspectors, no less. The matter is ended." No change of expression. No bluff to call, no threat to challenge.

I looked down at the card in my hand.

Sublevel, 384 Darkwater
8th Keepersrill, Section 10

"Eighth Keepersrill? Are you mad?" Dawnbell had just

sounded. How did he think I could travel so far before the next bell?

But when I looked up the puppet man had gone. Too silently, too quickly.

I rubbed my face as I closed the door, and resisted the need to return to bed, pull blankets over my head and pretend none of this had ever happened. Instead, I wrapped my piecemeal suit in the black bands Devich had given me. They were easier to fit now, the skin around the silver mostly healed. I had discovered in my first, nervous proddings of this newly touchable skin that the suit went further into me than it appeared. When I tried to squeeze my finger under the edges I couldn't find a gap between skin and silver. It was a part of me now, deeply.

I had discarded most of my boots – left them on the street for beggars with small feet – so the shoes I pulled on were not as high as I would have liked, not as tight to my calves or made of the kind of hard leather that could keep out cold slush and street-funnelled wind. I made up for it with heavy woollen pants and stockings underneath them. The shirt I picked was the same snow-mush grey as my pants, with sleeves long enough to cover my wrists. Then I wrapped myself in my comfortable jacket, tucked my watch into a pocket and again, I stepped out into the city.

The early morning was icy cold. A faint pink smudge lit the clear sky, edging the Keeper Mountain in rose-gold. I did up both layers of buttons on my jacket, wrapping it tight around my chest. Still, the wind pried at it, insistent.

I strode out into the near-empty street. Ice clung to the edges of lamps and crowded the rims of windows.

The dawn gave Movoc back some of her colour. Dour buildings of pale stone glowed. Dull iron gates, window bars and lamps burnished to faint gold. The ice that coated the streets glistened like mother-of-pearl. And it made my heart ache, to remember the colour I knew hid below this borrowed, reflected light.

I wasn't entirely sure where the eighth Keepersrill was. Further away from the city centre, for a start. From the street outside my apartment I could see the faint tips of the Keeper's Tear Bridge, the bear flags sagging beneath the weight of icy-heavy dew. I turned my back to it. If I followed the Tear down, away from the city centre, eventually I would come to the eighth rill. But this was the second, and I didn't know how many effluent inlets washed their filth into the Tear between here and the eighth. I had less than a bell till breakbell. Walking would take too long, and I wasn't willing to risk that. I needed to find transport, and that meant I would have to pay for it.

I fingered the rublic in my pocket. The disk fitted comfortably in my palm and gave off a slight heat. Sadly, that was all it was good for now. I could no longer read the pions that would have told me how many kopacks I owned.

Time seemed to rush ahead of me, leaving crunching noises in the ice. I dug a hat from my pocket – a leather cap that fit snugly on my head and was inlaid with tightly knitted wool – pulled it down over my ears and jammed my hands into my pockets. Then I headed for the Tear.

Movoc-under-Keeper had started its life – back in the dark days before Novski developed his theory on critical circles – huddled around the Keeper's Tear River. The Tear had always been the life of this city. Its waters rushed, clean and clear, even in the middle of the coldest winter night. It provided Weeping carp to hungry primitives, and introduced them to the great bears that hunted the large, dark-scaled fish. Hundreds of years and a pion revolution later, Movoc-under-Keeper still huddled around the Tear. All levels of veche built their buildings as close to the bridge as possible, anyone with kopacks to spare bought apartments with views of the water. Other's teeth, even *Grandeur* would have faced the river, if she'd lived long enough to gain a face.

When Novski's critical circle revolution changed the city, two large roads were built on either side of the river. Movoc's arteries. I headed for Easttear.

The traffic began to pick up as I neared the river. Men mostly, rugged up with jackets and leather caps like mine, heads down and shoulders hunched, hurried against the sharp wind that rose from the water. Few women. Bracing the cold, wrapping oneself up in clothes that hid shape, hair and feminine beauty, was hardly very ladylike. There were those who had no choice: the cleaners, spinners, and governesses. This close to the centre of the city, however, most women could afford to behave like ladies. Even the women of my circle, when I had one, only grudgingly resigned themselves to jackets and caps on a construction site.

The driver of the first landau that slid past glanced my way, but didn't stop, even as I waved as frantically as my stitches would allow. Either his coach was full, or he had just ignored me. I frowned, and tugged my cap down where it had started to ride up and expose the bandages over my left ear.

The landau looked bizarre without pions. It glided several feet above the ice, silent and smooth, all polished ebony with sparkling silver fittings. Its driver sat at the front, exposed to the morning chill while his passengers rode in insulated comfort, hidden behind darkened glass. The driver held his hands out, fingers loose over invisible reins, mouth working as he coaxed and guided a complex tangle of invisible lights.

I knew what I should be seeing. A landau was usually festooned with bright streamers, and carried on long legs of pion threads. They looped around the base, threading through the nooks and the hooks where wheels and springs would have been, back when horses used to draw them. There were usually six long spider-like legs of many bright and diverse colours. So what looked like gliding to me now was actually crawling. Crawling on light.

The second coach ignored me too.

I had known my life would be different now. But I hadn't imagined that something as simple as signalling a landau to take me down the Tear River would become this much harder, this quickly. My high-necked, tailored jackets had given me status. Their quality said I was a skilled binder, one who earned enough kopacks from her craft to have clothes like that made to measure. Their silver bear-heads shining from the shoulders told how many times I had been employed by the veche, and how many successful commissions I had filled. The insignia stitched into the neck, difficult to see unless one stood close, demonstrated which university I had graduated from, and with how much honour.

Wearing those jackets, I did not have to stand in the slush of melting ice at the edge of the street and wave at coaches as they glided past. Coaches came to me; they sought me out like loyal puppies hoping for scraps. Without them, I was just another person in this too-full city.

77

A coach finally did pick me up. A much cheaper-looking affair than the silent and dark landaus I had watched gliding past. It had wheels, for one thing. Not all binders were strong enough to create large insect-legs of pure energy, and had to rely on pion systems working in a gearbox and driveshaft to help propel and steer the carriage. This one was painted in a pale lacquer, peeling in places, and one of its steel-mesh stairs was loose.

"Where you headed?" The driver squinted down he slowed the coach beside me. He didn't stop it, so I was forced into a fast walk to answer him. As fast as I could manage, at least.

"Eighth Keepersrill," I shouted over the rattle of wheels and icy stone.

His eyes widened as he realised I was a woman. But then, I didn't look that much like a woman, dressed the way I was. Surprised most people the first time, which had always been the point. I didn't appreciate the assumptions that came with wearing skirts, long hair and glittery pieces of jewellery. As the fatherless daughter of a textile factory worker, I'd spent most of my life fighting against just those same kind of assumptions. But I was not a weak pion-binder, and I was perfectly capable of doing great things, powerful things, and living my own life my way.

At least, I had been.

"What Section?" He slowed the coach further.

Swallowing my pride, I tried to sound grateful. "Tenth." And I smiled. I actually smiled at him.

He nodded. "Get on."

I didn't give him the opportunity to bring the Other-damned coach to a stop. Ignoring the pain in my stitches, I grabbed one of the rails, pulled myself up and yanked a door open with the other hand.

Three men were already crammed into the interior. One read from a small slide, one seemed half asleep. The third was industriously picking at the seat's worn cushions, undoing the cheap fabric with his fingers, and then repairing it with a whisper to whatever pions would listen to him. Better than boredom, I supposed. As I swung myself in they squeezed closer together, making a space for me. I wedged myself between the door and the man with the slide. He wore a bulky coat that made loud crinkling noises as I pressed against it.

I was suddenly hot, and sore. I flipped the edge of my cap up to reveal my ears, and hunkered away from enquiring eyes. The stitches on my face and the bandages on my neck stood out like a snow-rabbit in spring. My cheeks reddened beneath them, a warmth that sent every thread, every puncture itching.

What I would have given for the comfortable interior of an expensive landau. Temperature-controlled, silk on the seats and a selection of slides to choose and read from. Daily missives from the veche, mostly, but better than staring mindlessly out the window. Which was all I could do now.

We rattled and bumped our way further from Movoc's centre, and out into the poorer areas of the city. With each stop a passenger left, and was almost immediately replaced by a new one. I tried not to let my mind wander over the buildings and what I would do to fix them up. Re-stone the plain wall there with a criss-cross of brick and ornamental shale. Refashion the entire roof on a particular hovel, where it sagged precariously in the middle. I'd fix the roads too, not something an architect would usually stoop to do. Even the most beautiful of buildings can be ruined by uncared-for streets.

Twice, when the coach slowed to ease the passing of men and women on foot, I saw stiffly walking figures, too pale to be real. One stood beneath a lamp. The other walked alongside the coach, close to the window, and met my eyes through the glass. The puppet men. They probably wanted me to see them, to know they were ever watching. I sank down further in my uncomfortable seat.

Finally, the coach came to a squeaking halt and none of the other passengers made to leave. I opened the door, gasping as icy air hit me.

"Eighth Keepersrill, Section ten," the driver called. I tugged my cap down and, gripping the handrails, swung myself around to face him. There were a few shallow in-dents leading up to his seat and I climbed closer.

The driver whistled lowly. "Agile, aren't ya?"

He couldn't feel the strain in my muscles or the sting-ing of my scars.

"How much?" I asked.

He drew a rublie from his pocket. It was battered, the small lights that ran the edge flickered unsteadily. I was surprised it still worked. "Eight hundred."

"I beg your pardon?"

He blinked, a small frown creasing greying eyebrows. "Eighth Keepersrill ain't 'round the corner, you know."

I knew. How much time did I have before breakbell?

"I shared a small cabin. It was cramped and uncom-fortable. As far as I could tell, you drove us in circles to get as many people crammed in there as possible. If you expect me to pay eight hundred kopacks for that kind of service, your brain has either frozen, or you think I'm some kind of idiot. Do you think I'm an idiot?"

The driver's eyes bulged. "Miss, that's the fare—"

"I will pay you two hundred."

He choked on something, and spluttered, "Two hund–"

"A quarter of the fare for a quarter of the space. That's fair."

"That's robbery!"

I flicked open my lapel and drew out my watch. As I opened it, scowling at the circles, at how Other-damned close they were spinning to breakbell, I'm sure he got a good look at the bear inscribed on the polished brass, its glass eyes deeply blue and teeth opaque white.

I snapped the watch shut. "I'm sorry, I didn't hear you."

The driver paled, like a man who just realised he'd made a nasty mistake and tried to swindle someone far above his social standing. Or thought he had, at least.

"Nothing."

"Good. Two hundred?"

"Yes, miss. Of course."

I handed him my rublie and watched intently as he touched it to his. The lights flashed as the two connected, then flickered green to indicate a successful transaction. I took the rublie with a nod, glad he had no idea that I couldn't see how many kopacks were registered to me, let alone how many he had taken.

"Thank you." I leapt from the side of the coach. Only when I landed in an inch of sludge and sent sharp pains into my ankles and left leg at the impact, did I realise it probably wasn't the best idea. Despite that, I straightened under the driver's appraising gaze.

He lifted gloved fingers to his hat. "Miss."

I turned as if to go, then stopped. "Oh, one other thing."

"Miss?"

How much pride did I have to swallow in one day? What would it take to make me sick? "How much was on there?"

"Uh...?"

I shook my head, tried to pretend exasperation. "On my rublie. How much was on there?"

"On yours? Ten thousand, miss. You must have seen–" He started to pale again. It made the whole thing easier, to know his day was turning out just as well as mine.

"Thank you." I spun, before he got any grand ideas about getting his hands on my rublie, and hurried away.

Ten thousand. Ten thousand! I'd expected the veche to take my payment for *Grandeur* away, but ten thousand? Had I paid for my time in the hospital, for Devich and the veche men to suit me? Ten thousand wasn't enough to keep my home next moon, ten thousand wasn't enough for the new clothes I needed to fit over the Other-buggered suit. Ten thousand would keep me eating for a while longer, but only if I was lucky, only if I stuck to flatbread and cheese that would have been more appropriate to grout tiles with. I could stretch it out, but not forever.

How much did a debris collector earn?

I peered up at the first intersection. Where in all the Other-cursed hells was Darkwater?

Was it really worth it? If I didn't turn up in, oh, I probably only had a few turns of the third wheel left – then what was the worst that could happen? Tribunal, colonies, some nonsense about civilisation? They meant nothing. I had no life left to take away, no purpose, no health. And soon enough, no home.

What more could they possibly do to me?

I stared at the street signs. One had fallen off long ago, all that remained of its metal fixture was rust and ice. The other had been scrawled on, all semblance of a name scribbled out with thick black paint.

"Are street signs too much to ask?" And now I was talking to myself. "Other's hells! That's it. I give up. I'll take whatever you veche bastards think you can dish out!" I yelled at the sign, and the whole run-down, garbage-riddled eighth Keepersrill, Section ten. "And you can shove your collecting team up the Other's hairy—"

A hand gripped my shoulder. I spun, ready to shout the rest of all the expletives I had ever learned into the face of whoever had been stupid enough to interrupt me.

But the dark eyes I met were calm. I could see my stupidity in their depths, my useless railing. "You must be Tanyana."

I gaped at the man. He was tall, wrapped in a long brown coat that almost touched the sludge on the street. Pale blond curls escaped a tattered hat.

"How do you know my name?" I choked over the words, struggling to get myself back under control.

He glanced at my coat, at the smooth leather of my cap and the shoes, still gleaming beneath the beginnings of a coating of sludge. "You wouldn't come here if you hadn't fallen." His clothes were heavily patched, the hems of his jacket and pants uneven. "And only the recently fallen would still be so angry about it."

"Fallen?" I whispered. Did he know then? About *Grandeur*.

He raised his eyebrows. "I'm Kichlan." He didn't offer me a hand to shake, in fact, he barely met my eyes, choosing to look over the top of my head instead. "I'll show you where we are."

With that, he hunched his shoulders against the wind and headed down the street that had lost its name. After a moment, I followed.

Tenth Section hadn't seen a repair team or a clean-up crew in a very long time. Bags of garbage clogged the corners where one ugly, hulking grey building met its twin. The stonework on the street and on the side of most of the buildings was beyond repair, and well into the replacement stage of life. Potholes dotted the road, great cracks ran down walls and all of it was crumbling in the face of the wind and the cold.

I already felt out of place, trailing behind Kichlan, suddenly aware of the quality of my own clothes. Hand in my pocket, I ran my fingertips over the rublie's bumps and grooves. Ten thousand could be a lot of money for people living in a place like this.

"Here." Kichlan stopped at a nondescript door once painted in a dark poly-mix, now peeling like snow-burned skin.

I glanced around the door, the wall beside it, even the street, but found no number. Helpful, considering the missing street name.

Kichlan turned an old-fashioned iron key in the door's old-fashioned iron lock.

A tight, claustrophobic staircase led below the frozen ground. Dim lights wavered, and I realised with a shock they weren't pion-powered.

"It's gas." I stopped by one of the lights. A small flame flickered behind heat-smudged glass.

Kichlan, several steps below me, glanced over his shoulder. His thin mouth was made firmer and more disapproving by lines drawn with heavy shadow. "Of course."

I stroked fingers along the wall below the light. A faint bump betrayed the presence of a gas pipe behind thin cement and flaking paint. "I didn't think the gas lines still worked." How long had Movoc-under-Keeper employed its factories of pion-binders to keep the lights on? A hundred years, possibly more? And who would use a potentially dangerous, unreliable substitute instead?

"Not many do. Debris collectors are the only ones who use them." Kichlan resumed his descent.

"Why?" I hurried to close the gap between us, my feet slipping on the steps' wet edges.

He snorted. "What do you mean 'why'? You can't expect us to rely on pions instead." The stairs ended at another dark door. Kichlan wrapped his gloved hand around a handle of twisted metal. "Would you trust something you can't control? Something you've never seen and can't even smell, or taste?"

I held back "I would if it's safer than gas" on the tip of my tongue.

Light spilled into the stairwell as Kichlan opened the door. I followed him inside.

My eyesight adjusted to a wide room, sparsely furnished. A low table was pressed into one corner and surrounded by ratty couches and sagging armchairs. Desks lined the wall beside the door, and cabinets crowded another, their doors closed and locked. There wasn't much else. A few empty wooden cartons that didn't seem to serve much purpose. The ceiling was high, with the bottoms of windows letting in light from the street and the occasional glimpse of booted feet hurrying by.

Five curious faces peered at me from the couches and chairs. I clenched my hidden hands in my pockets.

"Found her." Kichlan tugged off his gloves and threw them on a desk that sagged beneath the paper piled on top of it. Paper: another relic from an age before the revolution.

I started to notice the warmth in the room too, and reluctantly withdrew my hands and slipped the cap from my head. "Hello," I said, as I fussed with my hair. The problem with wearing a hat and styling cream at the same time.

"Cutting it close, aren't you?" said a pale young man lounged across one of the couches.

I said, "Streets with no names, doors with no numbers, I have trouble with them. Call it a fault of mine."

He lifted his head to smirk at me. His eyes were sharply blue, his skin heavily freckled.

"We're hard to find, Mizra." Kichlan unbuttoned his coat. "We all have trouble the first time." He hung his coat on the wall and waved his hand loosely at the free hooks.

I undid my coat. They were all watching as I hung up my jacket. I tugged at my shirt collar, feeling intensely self-conscious.

A sharp-eyed woman standing behind one of the chairs stared at my wrists. "How long?" Brown hair framed her face and bobbed as she nodded toward my suit, wrapped and dimmed by dark cloth.

My throat went dry. "Sixnight and one. I think. And maybe another day or so." It all jumbled together, the falling and the healing.

"Other." When she brushed a strand from her face her suit flashed brightly silver in the morning glare. "Doesn't it hurt, the cloth?"

I raised my wrist. "No. Not any more, at least."

Her face crinkled into a disgusted expression. "Other."

"Is that unusual?" My eyebrows lifted, tugged stitches, and I eased them down.

She snorted a soft laugh. "Unusual? You could say that."

The pale young man, Mizra, chuckled. "We thought you might be fun."

They thought?

"Natasha, Mizra, enough." Kichlan frowned at both of them. "Tanyana, welcome to your debris collection team." His voice drawled the words out a little, making them bitter, tinged with sarcasm. Hardly reassuring.

I swallowed hard in the silence. "Thank you."

"You have met Mizra."

The young man waved his hand in the air, suit glinting on a soft wrist.

"His brother Uzdal."

A nearly identical man sat in an adjacent armchair and regarded me gravely. Twins, they had to be. It was rare to see twins in Movoc-under-Keeper; it was rare to see them in the whole of Varsnia. Few lived beyond infancy.

"You now know Natasha." Brown hair, sharp green eyes. Right.

Would I remember any of this?

"This is Sofia. If you need anything, she's the best place to start."

A small, solid woman glanced up from the wad of paper she was reading. She chewed the end of a graphite pencil. Thin hair, a featureless brown, was pinned in a knot at the base of her head. She wore a shapeless dress in layers of grey.

"And this, finally, is Lad."

I wouldn't have believed it if I hadn't seen it for myself. But when Kichlan turned to Lad his voice softened, and he smiled. I'd been starting to wonder if he was capable of it.

Lad was even larger than Kichlan. Poorly cut blond hair stuck out around his head, and his cheeks had a glow to them, strangely childish beneath a fine layer of stubble. He had been sitting on the edge of an armchair and leapt to his feet at the sound of his name. He grinned at me, so widely it seemed to split his face, and shuffled forward.

"He told me about you." Lad grabbed my hands, squeezed them in his own, and shook vigorously. I hissed as he tugged at sensitive skin around my suit, and the wounds beneath my left glove. "Knew you were coming."

"Be careful, Lad." Kichlan touched the larger man's shoulder. "Be nice to the new lady."

"I am." He squeezed harder and leaned in close to me. His breath smelled sweet, like sugar drops. "He's glad you're here. Waiting a long time."

I tried to pry my hands from Lad's grip. "Thank you."

Beaming like a newly risen sun, Lad gave me one final, extra-enthusiastic shake, and released me. I staggered a few steps and grabbed at the wall for balance.

Kichlan frowned at Lad, but even so his face held none of the disregard he had shown me. "What did we talk about?"

Lad fidgeted with the hem of his shirt and shuffled foot to foot. "Be nice," he said, voice muffled, head low. "When the new lady comes, got to be nice."

It was hard to imagine a man of his size, his strength, talking like such a child. I rubbed at the throb he had set off in my hand. How could I relate to a new circle like this? No, not a circle. Not any more. They were a collecting team. I had to get used to that. Resentment from Natasha, flippancy from Mizra and nothing from his twin, disdain from Kichlan and the small one, now spiced in the middle with Lad's excessive enthusiasm. A bizarre lot.

"And how do we be nice to her?" Kichlan continued to lecture the large man.

Lad lowered his head closer to his chest and mumbled. "Don't touch. Keep back."

"That's right. Are we going to be careful, now?"

Lad nodded. In places, his hair was long and frizzy, and it jiggled wildly. "Yes."

"All right. But I'll be watching you. So you be careful."

When Kichlan returned his regard to me, his face closed up again. It was like a door, a glance of a bright room and suddenly I wasn't allowed to see any further, any deeper. "My brother is enthusiastic. He likes to meet new people."

At least one of them did. "Your brother."

"That's right." Sofia dropped her wad of paper on the table with a bang. "Lad is our special boy, aren't you?" She stood, and patted Lad's hand. He grinned down at her. "Not another collector like him, nowhere in this world."

"He's the best there is." Mizra, still prone, tipped his head over the arm of the couch and peered upside down at me.

"None better." Uzdal's voice was so quiet I barely heard it.

Did they expect me to add to this peculiar chorus of compliments? I kept my silence.

"You're lucky to be on this team." Sofia stepped between Lad and me, hands on hips, and flickered her gaze from my feet to my head. I started to suspect I wasn't entirely welcome. "And I don't care where you've come from, what you did before the accident that brought you here. A good pion-binder is not necessarily a good collector."

"Right." Accident? Did they know? Other, how could they know?

"Hmph." Her lip twitched. "Take those dark bands off, and let's have a look at you."

I ran a finger beneath the cloth hiding the suit on my right wrist from view.

"You won't need to cover them here," Kichlan said, softly, and I had the strangest feeling he understood my need to keep the suit hidden. Why all the changes in my life hurt less if I didn't have to look at the Other-damned shackles of silver and light.

I peeled each of the black strips away and undid my shirt collar so my neck was visible. My neck, and the bandages that crawled up from my left side. They felt heavy on me, even heavier than the suit, and I realised they were what I didn't want to expose to the world. Just like the suit, I didn't want my scars to be real either.

Mizra sat up to watch me, with his brother leaning behind him to get a view too. Why were there so many brothers in this team?

"Stomach too," Sofia said, arms crossed.

I blinked at her. "You want to look at my stomach?"

Mizra chuckled. "Better get used to it. No privacy around here."

My cheeks flushed as I untucked my shirt, lifted it, and tied the ends to expose the rim of silver around my waist and the white edges of padded bandages. The suit cast its own light into the room. It spun lazily, and I realised, as I clasped my hands near my waist, that each piece moved in time with the others.

Mizra whistled, the sound sharp against the room's smooth walls. "Sixnight, you say?"

"And one," Natasha whispered. "Maybe more."

Hadn't they noticed the bandages? Didn't they have questions? "Are you repeating yourselves for any particular reason?" The heat in my cheeks had turned to anger. Easier to deal with than embarrassment.

Kichlan came to my aid again. "A sixnight–"

"–and one, maybe more," Natasha added.

Kichlan didn't miss a beat "–is a very short time to adapt so well to a new suit. Particularly at your age."

I ignored that comment. "Is it?" I remembered what Devich had said to me, about being strong. Maybe this was what he meant. "What do you mean, adapt?"

"Just look at them." Mizra dropped off the couch and approached me. He was tall, I realised, and very thin. He walked, slow and laconic, like someone strolling through water. "They're glowing steadily, and the spinning is synchronised. It usually takes moons to get to that stage, filled with hard work and a lot of practice."

Had the bands ever been out of sync? I'd not noticed.

Sofia began to undress. "Right, let's get you into your uniform. We have a lot to do today and don't need you to slow us down."

My eyes widened. "What, exactly, does this involve?"

She gave me a withering look, even as I realised she was wearing something else beneath her shapeless dress. The top was like a corset, boned around her chest, but not tight enough to inhibit her breathing. Dark material, lined with more stiff bones beneath the fabric, stretched over her shoulders and down her arms, ending a few inches short of her wrists. Of course, the strange outfit left a gap at her stomach, enough for the band of silver metal and an inch or so of skin. She wore pants in the same dark fabric, finishing above her ankles. The boning continued through the whole thing and softened with the contours of her body, with her own bending, the movement of her joints and muscles.

I had never seen anything so form-fitting, so revealing, even though it covered her completely, and couldn't decide if it was ridiculous or hugely inappropriate.

A horrible thought dawned on me. "What is that?" I choked over the words.

Sofia gave me a cruel smile. "Your new uniform. Like it?"

"Other's balls."

Mizra chuckled as Lad pressed his hands to his lips, snorting giggles behind his palms.

"Now, now." Kichlan fetched a packet wrapped in clear poly from the desk and passed it to me. "You'll get used to it."

"The uniform is strong, it is warm, and it does not impede the use of your suit," Sofia said as she planted herself in front of me. "Swallow your pride, and just put it on."

She was a rather ineffectual shield, but Natasha didn't offer to help and no one seemed inclined to ask her. So the smallest woman present was the only thing between the men and me as I pulled off my clothes, and tried to squeeze into the strange black top and pants. They smelled strongly of their poly wrap. The material was a lot like the dark strips Devich had given me, too stretchy to be normal, thin to the touch, but strong when pulled.

I untied my shirt first, counting my blessings that I'd chosen a long one, and replaced my loose, comfortable woollen pants with the decidedly uncomfortable new pair.

My new team were not modest about their staring. I told myself not to care, not to feel self-conscious, and focus more on easing the material around my ankles and over stitches.

They kept quiet until I had pulled off my shirt and was trying to work out if I could keep my camisole on underneath the tight black uniform.

"You're hurt," Lad murmured.

I glanced up to see his expression shocked, eyes tear-rimmed. And I swallowed hard.

"Yes." I gave up the fight for a moment and straightened, so they could all see the bruises, the bandages, the scarring and the stitches. How strange that my new team had noticed the suit first, but maybe that was the kind of scarring they understood. And standing beneath the scrutiny of people I would have to work with, I realised the suit and the stitches were one and the same to me. Cause and effect. All a part of my fall. However much I wanted to keep them hidden, to deny their existence, it couldn't be sustained.

"So," Uzdal said, tone flat. "You're the architect."

Had I really expected to maintain my anonymity? *Grandeur* was a big statue, her fall must have been spectacular. In a terrible way.

"I told you she would be," Kichlan said, and I wondered at his wooden expression. "Powerful binder makes a big mistake, we get a new collector. Doesn't take much to work that one out."

Makes a big mistake? I bristled. "I didn't make any–"

"Why didn't they heal you?" Kichlan somehow twisted the question into an accusation. "Why give you stitches? They will leave scars. I thought healers would do anything for their fellow pion-binders, even ones who throw themselves from great heights and drag buildings down with them."

"The healers did the best they could for me." Why did this make him so angry? Had the veche dragged him from this dank sublevel to clean up all the debris I had left behind? Oh, the terrible injustice of it all.

"Is that what they told you?"

What could I say to that? I had no idea what he meant, and was at a point where I really didn't care. Instead, I sent Sofia a silent glance as I wrapped fingers around the hem of my camisole. She nodded, barely perceptible, and mouthed, "Leave it on," her voice little more than a breath.

The black top squeezed on, tight boning pressing against my chest, my shoulders and arms. I waited for pain, but if anything, the firm but yielding pressure seemed to calm my stitches. Dressed, I flexed my hands, extended my arms and turned the inside of my elbows up. The material curved with me, not prodding, not constricting. It felt like a second skin, a tough one, strong when I rapped it with my knuckles. And a little too warm.

"You don't go outside like this, do you?" Warmth in an underground room was one thing. Warmth in the middle of a Movoc winter demanded many, many more layers. And the whole uniform wasn't proper. Too much skin, too much shape.

Sofia clicked her tongue. "Of course not. It's easy enough to cover, just wear what you would normally, bar any underclothes. You won't need them."

"What's the point if we wear clothes on top of it?"

Kichlan passed Sofia's discarded garments back to her, and said, "With the uniform on we only need one layer. One loose layer. And trust me, when we start collecting you'll understand. The last thing you want is clothes getting in the way."

Sofia lifted an eyebrow. "You might have to wear skirts next time though."

94

"I have pants loose enough to go on top of this."

"Not a good idea for a debris collector to stand out." She gave me a stern look. "We need to walk around unhindered, unmolested. If you start trying to be different, trying to get attention, you'll make life harder for all of us."

Attention? That wasn't why I cut my hair short, and wore men's clothing. "I have some very loose pants."

Kichlan sighed. "As I was saying, wear the uniform beneath your clothes. Get used to it. You can be called on at any time, and must be ready to respond immediately."

"Immediately?"

He nodded. "When accidents happen – like architects who lose control of their buildings, say – we have to be prepared. Any time. All the time."

I refused to rise to the barb. "Given the effect debris can have on a pion system, I understand why."

Enough debris could slow a whole system down, leaving pions unresponsive and ultimately useless. Any system, no matter how large. And what was Movoc-under-Keeper but an enormous pion system, a system of systems, built from pions, with pions, entirely dependent on their smooth working. From fountains to landaus, nothing operated without them. Imagine running a hospital without working pions, or the heating system, or the lights. A whole city in chaos, utter darkness and cold.

"You were a skilled architect, weren't you? A strong binder." Kichlan's voice was soft again, like he couldn't decide if my past made him angry or sad. What did it matter, how skilled I was when I was a pion-binder? All that was gone now. "Before you fell."

My throat felt dry. The uniform was too hot. "Yes. Before I fell."

I held Kichlan's gaze, tried to decide if I could read sympathy in his eyes, or a bitter kind of confusion.

Then Lad broke into the silence. "He likes it." He grinned. "Thinks you look good in it. A lot."

Mizra burst out laughing as Kichlan gaped at his brother. Sofia glared at me from beneath thick eyelashes. The anger there, the resentment, was far deeper than anything she had shown me yet. The whole new-team arrangement wasn't really going very well.

"Let's go," Sofia growled the words, pulled her clothes back on and stalked to the stairs. I collected my own clothes, tugged them on, and followed.

Lad was bouncing on the balls of his feet as I stepped back into the glare of Movoc-under-Keeper. I shielded my eyes and squinted into the hard blue sky. Clouds hugged the edge of the horizon, probably flocking to Keeper's Peak and the lesser range of mountains in her shadow. I hoped they would spill over as the day wore on, keeping some warmth in the city, dulling the worst of the sharp sunlight.

"Lovely day to be collecting." Mirza hunched himself into a jacket patched together from scraps of leather and wool, and wrapped a widely knitted scarf around his neck. Guilt nudged at me. I was acutely aware of the lamb's wool cushioning my ears, of my smooth leather shoes and the heavy, wind-blocking lining of my coat.

"Aren't they all?" Natasha mumbled into the high collar of a jacket that swallowed most of her head.

Their attitude didn't dampen Lad's excitement. He giggled and repeated, "Lovely day!" over and over. He sang it, like a child with a newly learned expression, loudly, softly, without apparent tune. And he continued to bounce as Kichlan fought to secure Lad's loose scarf.

"It's going to take all day to calm him down now." Kichlan gave up on Lad's scarf altogether and muttered as he stalked past me.

Was that my fault?

As the others started down the street, Kichlan gestured for me to follow him. "I guess the most important thing I can tell you is to fill the quota."

I blinked at him. "Quota?"

He gave a little sigh and nodded. "Every sixnight and one the debris we have collected is taken away by the veche." He rustled around in a brown leather bag he had swung over his shoulder and drew out a strange container. It looked like a jam jar with a lid that sealed tightly, but was made of a dull metal instead of glass. It didn't, I rather quickly assumed, hold jam. "We put the debris in these, and they'll count the number we send back full. After a decent sixnight we'll fill seventy-two. Any less than that is a problem. Although, they'll be after–" he flicked his fingers, counted under his breath "–eighty-four now you're here."

"Wonderful," Sofia muttered, just loud enough for me to hear.

"And if we don't meet this quota?" Why didn't I shut my mouth when it wanted to ask questions like that?

"Inspection." Kichlan's face took on a thundercloud aspect, dark, foreboding. *Inspection* hung in the cold air like it was written in ice. The rest of the team held their breath. "And we don't want that."

Well, I could understand not wanting to endure a veche inspection, particularly considering their presence at *Grandeur*'s construction site when it all fell apart. But the tension I could suddenly feel felt a little extreme. What could be so bad about an inspection? A lecture, a rap on the knuckles? But those hanging-ice words told me there had to be more to it than that.

"To avoid such an event we have devised half a dozen set loops," Kichlan continued, expression still dark. "You will learn them over the next sixnight or two. They take us past places where debris congregates. Faulty lamps, old sewers. Pion systems that aren't functioning properly. It has worked, so far, to fill our quota and keep from attracting unwanted veche attention."

"Kich's idea," Lad told me, tone light compared to Kichlan's face and everyone else's heavy silence. "He decided the ways we should go and we always find some."

"Oh, Lad." A smile swept Kichlan's thunderclouds away. "You're being hard on yourself. We also have a secret weapon–" he nodded to his younger brother "–thanks to Lad, we always find the debris we're looking for, even if it's off the loop. Other teams aren't so lucky."

Lad, still bouncing and drawing further ahead, grinned proudly.

I gave a sharp, quiet sigh. "Aren't we lucky."

"You'll see," Sofia said, expression smug.

"Just remember one thing." Mizra wrapped an arm around half of Lad's wide back. "When it comes to debris, always follow Lad's instincts."

"Always," Kichlan echoed him.

Once we left Darkwater we headed from side street to side street, poking into every shadow, scrutinising every corner. I found myself immersed in a uniformity of poor brickwork, unwashed streets and cracked windows. I had no idea how I was supposed to remember the whole twisting route, let alone half a dozen different ones.

In these poorer areas kopacks weren't spent on frivolous fountains or expensive walkways that required intensive pion systems to run. Even if I still retained my pion sight, the buildings in these sections would have looked dull to me. Almost lightless. That wasn't to say they were like the ancient buildings at the city centre, built by hand in a time before critical circles. Rather, they were constructed cheaply and quickly, by smaller circles and with weaker, shallow pions. The buildings stood, barely, and did not weather the passing of time particularly well.

"Pay particular attention to shadows," Kichlan lectured me. The others were a good five strides ahead, talking among themselves. Mizra gestured wildly and Lad nearly fell to the icy flagstones in a paroxysm of laughter. "Dark in colour, debris is easy to miss in the shadows. We do not collect at night for this reason. Unless, of course, in an emergency."

"Of course."

Mizra waved his hands in the air, and now Uzdal was laughing too. Even Natasha let out a soft chuckle. Lad whooped, the sound echoing. A face peered down from a slit of a window, high up in the flat, unpainted cement wall. I glanced up to see an old man, hair thinning and face heavily lined, scowling as we trooped past.

"Mizra," Kichlan called. When the young man turned around Kichlan made gestures over his mouth, then pointed at Lad. Mizra shrugged, only to be rewarded with a clenched fist. Finally, Mizra nodded, and the laughter ceased.

Seemed a pity to me.

"Where was I?" Kichlan clasped his hands behind his back, and lifted his head. He could have passed easily for a university lecturer striding along like that. All he needed was a black cape and a bear's claw pinned to his breast.

"You were telling me about emergencies," I said, At least emergencies sounded interesting.

"Remember to wear your uniform all the time."

"So you said."

"Even at night."

I balked. "At night?"

"I told you to wear it all the time, Tanyana. And I mean it. If you are called to an incident at silentbell what will you do? Trust me, you won't be given time to dress." And then, Other's beard, the bastard sneered at me. "When the call comes—"

All the time? That was ridiculous. "How will I know if there's an incident when I'm snug in my own bed and sound asleep?" And how did he expect me to reach that state of sound asleepness wrapped in a hot, hard, second skin?

"I was trying to tell you." He tapped at his wrist. "You'll know."

The suit then. I couldn't get away from it, could I? Not at home, not in my sleep, not anywhere or any time. "Fine."

"Good." Kichlan was silent for a moment. "Should be easy for a skilled ex-binder like you to work out."

"Great." My left knee was starting to hurt.

We trekked further. More small windows opened, letting in the crisp morning air. Wet clothes and bedding were hung on wire strung between them. People stepped out into the streets. Men dressed in dark suits with small-brimmed hats tucked tightly over their ears. Women in wide skirts, heavily layered, rustled against the flagstones in rose pinks, wildflower cream and bright sky blue. Their hands were wrapped in muffs of fur dyed to match the colour of lace hemming or glimpsed underskirt.

Some wore thick hats, wide enough to keep the sun from delicate skin but low enough to protect their ears, but most donned more elaborate versions of my own: tight around the head, topped with soft moleskin and rimmed with fur.

I tugged at the lapel of my unfitted, tailored-for-a-man jacket. I played with the ends of my short-cropped hair.

"Now do you see what I mean?" Sofia hung back from the others to grace me with a self-righteous smile. "You really don't fit in, do you?"

I supposed that was a bad thing. "I don't see you dressed up like some oversexed flower waiting for the bee."

Ahead of us, Mizra let out a raucous laugh that had Lad quickly following suit. Sofia scowled. "I look like a woman of my station. You should try it sometimes." She hurried forward to smack Mizra on the back of the head.

I decided it was easier to hold my tongue than argue the point.

We didn't get much further from the Keeper that day. We wound our way through small alleys and side streets, squeezing through gaps in wooden fences, climbing a few stunted iron railings and opening rusty gates with hinges that screamed to wake the Other. I supposed it was intentional, this keeping out of the way. Away from people, away from the thoroughfares, away from space and sunlight and open sky. Because debris kept to the corners, Kichlan said, because the passage of coaches, of people, could sweep it away like dust. I didn't believe him. I was convinced, as I strained to squeeze through a cracked iron gate that refused to open any further, that the collectors were not following debris. They were avoiding people.

Then Lad, out in front and pushing along nicely despite his size, stopped. Mizra ran into his back – the experience a lot like I imagined walking into a wall would look like – and hurried to step away, expression apprehensive.

The team wrapped themselves in tense silence, all at once. I glanced from face to face, but all attention was reserved for Lad. The big man cupped his hand to his ear. Listening. He nodded, to no one in particular, and started abruptly down a different alleyway.

"Quickly." Kichlan grabbed my elbow and dragged me with him. "Once he's found it there's no slowing him, no stopping him."

I tripped on what was left of the gate and allowed myself to be half-carried, half-dragged into the alley. The stench of cat piss made me gag, while Kichlan's grip jarred into my shoulder. I struggled upright, and started running, finally able to shake him off. "Found what?" I panted behind him.

He spared me a glance, disbelieving. "Debris, of course."

I couldn't see anything, not even the Other-forsaken sludge I was stepping in. Even if the whole alleyway was teeming with dark, wiggly worms of debris I wasn't sure I would see it.

Lad turned a corner, Mizra and Uzdal close behind. Sofia, with a kerchief pressed against her nose, and Natasha, expression ugly with disgust, were a step behind them. Kichlan, probably impatient with my slow, limping run, nearly missed the bend.

"How does he know where it is?" I asked, trying to breathe through my mouth and talk at the same time. Anything to lessen the smell.

Kichlan grabbed my arm again and forced me to match his pace. His face was lit bright with flashes of sunlight and a wild smile. Somewhat mad, somewhat alarming, but alive. And proud. "He's Lad." The grin caught me and dragged out a smile of my own. "That's enough, isn't it? He's Lad. He knows."

We halted at a dead end. Roughly fired clay bricks – ugly and dark and made, I guessed, of ungainly or reluctant pions – stretched upward in a wall so high it blocked the Keeper from view. I peered at the soles of my shoes as the others shuffled aimlessly, moving boxes of rotting wood aside, lifting the worn-away edge of what was once a drainpipe and flinching back from whatever hid there. I touched an adjacent wall, just as ugly, for balance as I tipped my foot up. I had definitely stepped in something far below savoury.

Lad stood at the dead end, shoes swimming in scummy liquid. His face was hard to see in the dim alley, but what muted and grey light did penetrate it showed his lips moving slowly, his voice so quiet it was lost in a distant and incessant drip. Almost, I thought to myself, like he was talking to pions. What a strange and ridiculous thought.

Kichlan said nothing, only watched his brother. I put my foot down and leaned against the wall, just as Lad spun toward me.

"Look out!" he cried, and lunged forward as the wall gave way. His large hands fumbled with mine; I grabbed air and slippery palms but could hold onto neither. I fell backwards, into a putrid puddle of water, as a heavy shower of bricks rained down on me.

I scrambled desperately, hands beating at the falling bricks, feet slipping and kicking for purchase. And just as suddenly as the wall had collapsed, the stones stopped falling on my head. I opened my eyes to a semicircular dome of silver that wrapped around me, that shielded me from the rest of the wall.

What, by the Other's own hells, was that?

"Tanyana!" Kichlan yelled, voice muted through the silver ceiling and the Other only knew how much rock. After a breathless moment I heard scraping and the clattering of stones, then tapping.

I coughed until I could spit up the brick dust clogging my throat. "Kichlan? What is this?"

"How did it do that?" Someone – Sofia – was talking on the other side of the silver. Not, I noticed, trying to get me out from under it. "It's dormant, Kichlan. Dormant! We haven't even shown her how–"

"Give her help!" Lad shouted. "He says to be quiet and help her!" I agreed with him.

"Tanyana," Kichlan yelled again through the metal. "Don't let this frighten you. This is your suit, just your suit doing what it should do. You need to calm down and get it under control."

Calm down? I thought I sounded like the calmest person here. "How do I do that?"

A moment of half-heard muttering. "Your suit is more than bands of silver."

"I have come to realise this," I mumbled to myself. My voice echoed strangely in the tight space.

"Your suit is all this silver stuff too," he continued, oblivious. "It's in your arms and legs. It's so deep inside you wouldn't know it's there, until it does something like this."

I remembered being strapped to the veche's table. The muscle spasms from wrist to shoulder. The ache, the pressure, further down than any surface scratch could have been. Fluids pumped into me. Fibrous, wiggling things trapped in glass tubes. I had seen it happen, I had known the suit was moving deeper.

"I see."

He hesitated again. "The suit is part of you. Your legs, your arms. You know how to move your arms, don't you? Your feet? The muscles around your stomach, your neck?"

"Of course."

"Then you can move the suit."

I looked up to my wrist. Dimly, I could see a connection, where the silver on my wrist had grown, spread, flattened into the ceiling that now shielded me. The silver was part of those spinning, glowing bands. They were a part of me. And as I thought about lowering my arms that very symbol-scrawled silver bubbled back down into the bands on my wrists.

I blinked against sudden sunlight before large hands scooped me out of fetid sewage. "Tan!" Lad crushed me against his chest. "Too slow, too slow!" he cried.

It took a bit of coaxing for Kichlan to convince his younger brother to put me down. I was so grateful I even accepted Kichlan's shoulder to lean on, deciding walls weren't to be trusted. "Are you all right?" He studied my face, my head, my arms and my shoulder.

"Other of a first day." Mizra would have sounded more sympathetic if he hadn't been grinning evilly.

I fingered the top of my head and ignored him. Some of the bricks had scraped away skin, leaving dots of blood on my fingertips. And even though my uniform and suit had saved me from the worst of it, I suddenly felt sore all over. Exhausted and sore. Because from Movoc's greatest statue to one of its most decrepit walls, the city was trying to kill me. And maybe it was the dust clogging my throat, or the blood on my fingers, or the ache in my bones, but I was starting to wish it would just get it over with.

"How did you do that?" Sofia glared at me. "I thought your suit was dormant. How did you know what to do?"

"I didn't do anything." My head rang with the words. I knew I should have felt more shaken. Frightened by the wall coming down on me, confused by this suit that apparently should not have just saved me the way it had. Maybe it was the blow to the head. I just wanted to close my eyes.

"That's not possible."

"Sofia," Kichlan said in a warning tone that sent vibrations through me from his shoulder.

"Look what you found," Uzdal called from the hole I had made in the wall.

I pushed away from Kichlan's nice, stable shoulder and stumbled around loose bricks to stand beside him. On the other side of the wall was what could only have been an old city sewer. Walls chiselled into stone, not a dollop of cement anywhere, had eroded beneath a trickle of thick slop and made the foundations of at least three buildings now grown on top of it dangerously unstable. But, strangely enough, that barely caught my attention. It was the cluster of debris, squirming in the near-darkness like fat, baby snakes that held my eye.

"It was hard." Lad stood between us, stooping to get low enough to look in. "Should have known but didn't understand so you broke it. Sorry you got hurt, Tan. Sorry."

"Next time, try not to crush anyone." Mizra patted Lad's shoulder, but the large man jerked away from the touch and stomped off to huddle in a corner.

Kichlan watched his brother and sighed, before pointing a finger at Mizra and running it across his neck like a knife. Mizra frowned, but I couldn't help noticing how pale his cheeks were. "That's a great find, Lad," Kichlan said, loudly. His brother showed no signs he had heard. "Let's get it collected," Kichlan told the others in a softer voice.

He unhooked the bag he had over his shoulder and drew more metallic jars from its well-worn brown leather. He passed them out to the rest of the group. "Everyone set?"

I sat on a pile of rubble and watched as the others crowded around the hole in the wall.

"Here," Kichlan said, holding up his wrist and drawing my attention. "This is the way they're supposed to be used."

His suit flickered, more of the symbols rose to the top of the liquid and the spinning inside band stilled. The symbols pressed their sides against each other, swelled, and rose from his wrist before splitting into two solid, silver prongs. They grew, extended into the hole in the wall, pinched a small, wiggling piece of debris and drew it out.

"Debris cannot be touched." Kichlan held the debris over an open jar. "Not by hand, not by instrument, not by anything." He lowered the debris, opened his tweezers. "Except the suit." He sealed the lid. "And the jar."

I stared at the jar. Why? What was the suit made of, and was the jar the same thing? Why had mine protected me, moved without command? And could I ever get it to do something that precise, that controlled?

Kichlan gave me a sympathetic smile. "Sorry, it's been all too much for one day. And we don't usually drop things on new team members when we're trying to teach them either." He winced, and sent a guilty glance at his brother. "Just rest while we clean this up. You can try collecting some tomorrow."

Tomorrow? Another day with these people, this dirty stuff, these horrible silver appendages. What an entertaining prospect.

I leaned against chunks of ancient brickwork and let myself feel the aches. The throb in my head, matched by a larger, broader pain in my shoulder where I had fallen. Sharp twinges from stitches pulled and jolted. Had any dust found its way into my bandages? I would have to strip them all when I got home and clean everything carefully.

Sunlight lanced down from the small gap between leaning buildings. I tipped my head to feel it on my cheeks, and squinted against the pale gold. Were those clouds, edging their way over the blue sky, or my poor eyes made hazy by a throbbing head?

Dimly, I became aware of Lad whispering, "Didn't mean to, didn't know, should have told me." How could I hear him? It sounded like he was right beside me. My head was too heavy to lift, my eyes held closed by the sky's light. "Can't hurt her. Not again. If I hurt her, I can't go out any more."

He's sorry, you know. A voice from the rubble, from the sagging building. *Don't blame him. It isn't his fault.*

"I know," I whispered.

"Tanyana?" Kichlan's worried face blocked the sunlight. "Are you all right?"

I struggled to sit up, finally levering my body straight with my elbows. My mouth tasted dry, caked with the same dust that weighed down my face. I ran a tongue like paper across my teeth.

"Were you talking to anyone in particular?" Mizra crouched beside Kichlan.

I blinked, spurring tears, and my head rolled on a stiff

108

neck. "Dreaming," I croaked. I must have fallen asleep with the sun on my face.

Kichlan's smile didn't quite ease the worry in his eyes. "Well, it's been a hard day. But no time for that now." He glanced up. "We'd better get moving before it hits."

It? I squinted up, only to find low and rolling snow clouds, the sun a dull disk in their midst.

"Come on." Sofia sounded agitated. "We've got it all. Time to get back."

When I stood, head thumping to the beat of my heart, I realised they were all waiting for me. Even Lad, who no longer cowered in the corner and whispered for forgiveness, was holding two jars of debris and looking very pleased with himself. I wanted to ask how long I had lain on the rubble and slept, but my mouth was full of dust, and it took everything I had to focus on placing one foot in front of the other.

5.

Snow began to fall before we reached Darkwater. A final flurry of winter, like a childish swipe at the approaching spring. I tilted my head to catch the light, icy flakes in my mouth, and let them melt away some of the dust and the thickness of sleep. I kicked into the thin drifts that draped across flagstones, leaving dirty footprints, and feeling that bit cleaner. Its soft touch on my head soothed the throbbing, but stung in the freshly made cuts.

"That's the end of that day, then," Uzdal murmured as Kichlan worked the old-fashioned lock and let us into the sublevel. I wasn't sure what bell it was, anymore. Pale white clogged the bottom of the windows, and didn't give much of an indication of the time.

Kichlan brushed away flakes from his eyebrows and hat. "Jars in the corner, please. Tanyana." He waited for my attention to continue. "Do you see what they're doing? Full jars go on the shelves until the veche come for a collection. Empty jars only on the table. Do you understand?"

I nodded, still feeling heavy and dull, not much better than I had in the sunlight and on the rubble. He frowned at me.

"Everyone hurry home," he said, and took Sofia's remaining jars. "Don't want anyone getting caught when this gets worse." As it was bound to do. Movoc-under-Keeper loved her snowstorms.

I watched as Kichlan filled the shelves with jars, and the rest of the team left the sublevel. I counted them. Ten jars. Was that enough? Would we meet quota? I didn't want to be responsible for an inspection, not when Kichlan's thundercloud face hovered hazy but dark in my memories.

Pincers. Tweezers. How had they done that?

I clenched my fist. Silver oozed from my wrist to coat my hand and ballooned into something round and twice its size. That was a fist then.

"Tanyana?" Kichlan's voice sounded dim, like my ears were stuffed with wool. "What are you still doing here?"

Gently, I opened my hand again. Whether I moved my hand at all I couldn't tell, all I could see was the silver bulb flatten, and that was all I could feel. I cupped it carefully and slow. A flat palm. Like a spade.

"It's time to go home." Kichlan was closer. Was that Lad I could hear, murmuring and worrying in the background? "You can practice tomorrow, don't worry about it now."

I twitched the corner of my mouth. It was all the same, all part of me. The bulb was my fist, the spade was my palm. And I knew how to extend my arms, I knew how to grasp something with my thumb and forefinger. So I reached, as though there was debris in front of me. Slowly at first, my second arm, that dull silver almost-liquid grew. Then faster. I opened my thumb and forefinger and the silver split.

111

"Watch out!" Kichlan cried.

Silver crashed into the ceiling. Cement spilled in a waterfall onto my aching head. I jerked my hand back and the silver rushed into my wrist, pushing me to the ground, sending spasms to my shoulder. I could feel it, I was certain. That almost-solid, almost-liquid, strong silver in my skin, my bones, and all the spaces in between.

Kichlan dropped to his knees beside me. "Tanyana," he sighed. "Didn't I tell you? Go home. Don't, for the love of Keeper, try that again. Not until you've had some sleep at least."

I glanced up. A large hole, a good two feet wide, was cracked into the cement. At least, from this vantage point, it appeared to be only a few inches deep. "I'm sorry."

"You will be, when Sofia sees this." He gripped my hands and helped me stand. "Just go home, Tanyana."

I nodded, still numb, and climbed the stairs.

But I could go no further than the eaves of 384 Darkwater. Snow built on the toes of my boots, and I wondered how I would get home. I stank, my body hurt and my head swirled like the snow drifts growing in the street. No coach would pick me up in this state. There was a ferry on the Tear. I could try that. Did it run in a snowstorm? What bell was it anyway?

I dug my watch from its niche between my coat and the uniform skin. It rattled alarmingly. Pieces of glass fell to the snow when I drew it out. My hand shook. It had borne the brunt of the stones and rested shattered, broken, in my palm. The bear's head was unrecognisable. Glass had come loose from its inlay. When I pressed the latch the cover fell off, and the circles and bells tumbled with soft chimes to the ground.

All I could do was stare at it. My watch – my life before any of this had happened – shattered in my hand. I couldn't move.

"You need to be careful, Lad. Don't you remember what happened last time?" That was Kichlan, emerging from the sublevel.

"Course I do. But wasn't my fault, Kich. I was just following," Lad said, tone teasing between sullen sulking and genuine apology.

"Tanyana got hurt."

"Tan." Lad hesitated. "She okay, brother?"

"This time. But that's what I mean, you need to be careful."

"I will tell him." Lad's voice hitched. "Tell him to be careful."

"I know you will, Lad. I know you will."

Dimly, I wondered when I had become Tan.

"Just next time, don't listen to him so much–" Kichlan stepped onto the street and saw me. He stopped, startled, and raised an arm to hold back his brother. Or perhaps shield him.

"He knows better than me, brother." Lad, oblivious to my presence, pulled the door closed. It locked with a heavy clang that echoed from the stairwell behind it. He made a great show of pushing against it, checking, it seemed, that the lock would hold. "Can't ignore him–"

"Lad, hush."

Lad finally noticed me, hands still on the door handle, eyes wide. Perhaps I wasn't supposed to have overheard that particular conversation.

"Tanyana?" Kichlan approached me slowly, one hand half-extended. I felt like a stray cat in the snow.

"Tan!" Lad bustled up close. I thought I should probably flinch, or step back, or do something. But as it was I
stood there, hems soaking up the snow. The cold sent
chills through my legs, and I shivered.

Lad smiled at me, but this faded as I didn't respond.
He glanced over his shoulder at his hesitating brother.
"Kich?" He waved his hands, a gesture of uselessness. He
reminded me of a fat honeybee, with his hands flapping
out from his sides like that. I wanted to laugh, but only
shivered instead.

As Kichlan approached, Lad leaned over him and
cupped his hands around his mouth. "She's cold," he
whispered. Hardly conspiratorial, I would have had a
harder time hearing him if he'd spoken plainly. "Why
isn't she moving?"

Why indeed? I frowned to myself, skin on my forehead numb. Home was so far away, and there was all
that snow in the way. It was too hard, I realised. I was
standing still in the cold, in the snow, because it was all
too hard.

And my watch was broken.

Kichlan pressed his finger to his lips and Lad shuffled
over to give his brother room. "Tanyana, shouldn't you
go home?" Kichlan asked.

I stared down Darkwater. The useless signpost was lost
in thick haze, as were most of the buildings beyond it.
The roads were not left to the snow this way in the second Keepersrill. Already the snow-shifters would have
swept the powder away. I didn't expect to see them here,
their great shapes hulking dark against the white, their
wide metallic wings brushing the snow away with stiff
feathers. Their drivers knew the streets to keep to, knew
where they would be tipped for keeping a lady's skirts

114

dry and preserving the integrity of a man's shoes. There were no spare kopacks to pay them with as far out as the eighth Keepersrill.

"Tanyana?" Kichlan placed a hand on my arm and tugged gently.

What had he been talking about? Ah. Home. "It's so very far away," I murmured, and looked down to the useless silver in my hand. "It broke."

Lad made a strange hiccupping sound, like a distressed animal.

"What's far away?" Kichlan leaned closer, gaze darting over my face. His once-smooth cheeks were rough now with stubble. Heavy for less than a day's growth. Kichlan made to take my outstretched hand and I snatched it away. The rest of my watch fell, silent into the white. A breath of air, and it was gone.

He took my elbow as I wobbled.

"Home." I tried to pull away but his grip tightened, and I realised he was not so much holding me back, as holding me up. I recalled leaning on his shoulder, head throbbing and bleeding. "It's eight hundred kopacks away. That's what the bastard coach driver wanted to charge me, can you believe it?" The words rolled out of me, drawn by some invisible thread. "And my watch is gone. And it is snowing. And my head hurts." I tapped the sore spot beneath my hat for emphasis, and winced.

"That must be a long way," Lad said, very serious.

"It is indeed." Kichlan studied me.

"We got to, brother. He says we should."

Kichlan brushed snow from my shoulder in a gentle, distracted way. "Does he now? What did I say about following him blindly?"

"He's right though."

"I suppose he is."

"Who is?" I didn't like their riddles.

Kichlan didn't answer. Instead, he slipped his hand to my upper arm, like I was an old woman and he a tired but conscientious son. "You should come home with us. Just this time." He exerted gradual pressure and took slow steps, moving me forward before I realised it was happening. "Come home with us. Until you feel more yourself."

More myself? Did I even know who that was any more?

"No, really..." I tried to rouse the part of me that screeched protests. That told me it wasn't proper to go home unaccompanied with two brothers I had just met. The part that clamoured for my home, my bed, my hot water. The part that longed for the comforts of an earlier life not buried in snow, soaked in sewage, and heavy with the dust of ancient stonemasonry. But that part of me was muffled, buried underneath the rubble of the day. And Kichlan was guiding me gently, and Lad was on the other side, grinning like a child with candy in his pocket. "Is it far to go?"

"Home should never be far," Lad declared.

"No, it is not," Kichlan said, making far more sense than his brother.

So I let them guide me. I watched my feet most of the way to Kichlan's house, and kept feeling for the watch that should have rested close to my heart.

The brothers lived in the attic of a squat house dwarfed by taller buildings, solid slabs that were nightmares of poor construction and ugly design. Their house was old enough to escape such a horrible fate, but that was the only good thing about it. Its stonework looked suspiciously similar to the wall that had fallen on me, and I wondered how much of it had been built by hand rather than pions. A heavy wooden door creaked as Lad pushed it open, and ushered us into a dim room heavy with smoke and shadows. I blinked against the slants of orange fire-glow, coughed in the smoke, and couldn't see very much at all.

"We're back!" Lad called, so loudly and suddenly that I jumped a little with surprise.

"Lad?" A voice warbled from an adjacent room. "Is that you, boy?"

"He owns this house," Kichlan whispered as Lad bounded into the room. "He's a good man. He won't mind if you stay, as long as it's only one night."

So this wasn't Kichlan's house after all. He was simply, what, boarding here? Somehow, I found it difficult to reconcile. Kichlan, who organised his collection team with such authority, didn't even own his home?

"What's got you so excited then?" The voice came nearer, accompanied by the shuffling of feet. "Oh." A short, ancient man turned into the hallway. He was wrapped in layers of clothes made from what looked like mainly quilts, all patches and mismatched colours. Faint wisps of pale hair, lit a coppery gold from what must have been a fireplace behind him, escaped a tea-cosy hat to float with the smoke around his head. He carried a large pipe in one hand, and gripped the door frame with the other.

Tiny embers dropped from the pipe as we stared at each other, to touch bright on the wooden floor before winking out.

"Kichlan." The old man collected himself, tapped his pipe against his cheek, and drew a small breath of smoke into his mouth. It curled up to his nose. "You aren't going to introduce us?"

117

"This is Tan!" Lad filled the quiet to overflowing. "She had to go a long way and it's snowing and bricks fell on her, so Kich and I thought she could stay here." He paused only to breathe. "Is that all right?"

I couldn't see Kichlan's face. He stood behind me, holding me upright. But whatever the old man saw there must have convinced him. I doubted it was Lad's rambling that did it.

"Of course. You're welcome, dear Tan. I'm Eugeny, and my home is yours." He made a strange bow, touching the mouthpiece of his pipe to his hat.

"It's Tanyana." My voice sounded soft and breathless, and I tried to push more force into it. "And thank you."

He nodded. Lad whooped and clapped his hands above his head.

"Now," Eugeny wrinkled his nose, "something tells me the lady would care for water to bathe in?"

How he could smell anything through the smoke escaped me.

"She has had a difficult day," Kichlan said. I wanted to argue, to tell him I didn't need anyone to excuse or explain for me, but he was already leading me down the hallway to a set of stairs leading up to a second floor.

"I can hardly imagine." Eugeny waited until we had passed before commanding Lad to collect a couple of buckets, which he took outside. I decided they couldn't have running water, which was something of a shock. I thought every building in Movoc-under-Keeper was supplied with running water. It operated on the same, essential system as the light and the heat, with factories across the city, where pion-binders sat in large, compounded circles, gathering pions and convincing them to push clean river water through a complex series of underground pipes. Each tap was just another valve, keeping the water out until it was needed. Some of the pions were also asked to heat the water as they ferried it along, although I believed that required a slightly higher level of skill than simple plumbing.

I supposed this also explained the fireplace and the darkness. Was anything in this house powered by pions?

They might not have had running water, but Kichlan and Lad certainly had a bath. The attic room was a wide one, with a high peaked ceiling and a few elongated windows near the floor. Rugs carpeted the sound of their feet and hugged the warmth wafting up from Eugeny's house below. There were beds in two opposite corners, each with a rickety stand and water jug of its own.

The bathtub was old, solid metal with bear-claw feet and pale, chipped enamel. Lad filled it steadily, with water that looked clean enough. He heated the full buckets in Eugeny's fireplace before pouring the warm water into the bathtub and hurrying away for more. While he did this Kichlan found a thin bar of soap and a towel big enough to be a blanket.

As the bath water grew Kichlan began to fidget and look decidedly uncomfortable. There was no screen in the room, nothing to separate the tub from the rest of the attic. And as the steam rose, inviting with its promise of warmth, of being clean, I was already weighing up a little more immodesty for a nice hot soak.

"Eugeny will be cooking," Kichlan said as Lad brought the final bucket of water up the stairs, puffing from his exertions, and poured it proudly into the tub. I eyed the water and wondered how long it was going to stay so nice and warm.

Kichlan grasped his brother's hand, earning a startled expression, and Lad dropped the pail. "Clean yourself up before it cools down." He flushed redder than the warm room could account for. "We'll be downstairs until you're ready." He had to drag his younger brother toward the stairs. "Come on, Lad!"

"Downstairs?" Lad's deep voice echoed up from below. "But what about her back, Kich? Who's going to scrub her back?"

Kichlan's splutters echoed also.

I shrugged off my jacket. It dropped with a squelch to the floor. I pulled the hat from my head and the gloves from my hands and kicked the lot as far from the bath and its promise of cleanliness as I could. My pants were sodden; the only clothes to have escaped the sewage appeared to be my shirt, kept safe by the coat, and the uniform itself. Would such strange material even stain? If it was designed for daily use, perhaps it was beyond such needs as washing.

The uniform peeled off like a layer of stiff skin, and hurt like it too, where it tugged on stitches and poked at bruises.

Voices made their way up from the ground floor.

"They got to her too, eh?" Eugeny's rattling baritone was clear despite the floor between us. "Be careful around her. You know they won't be far behind."

Kichlan was too tactful to be overheard, and I couldn't make out his answer.

"I know. But your kindness mustn't put the boy in danger."

I leaned into the water and watched coils of dirt and oil spread over its taut surface.

Just who were they?

The soap was plain and made a kind of half-lather, more like a film of white than any real suds. It smelled like faux flowers, sweet and manufactured, but at least it wasn't sewage. I rubbed the flakes into my hair and wherever my skin was free from bandages before ducking beneath the water, eyes squeezed tightly shut, and rubbing again to get it out.

When I sat up and slicked hair from my brow, I realised I looked worse clean. The bandages along my neck and left shoulder had been jarred out of place, the normally thin lines of pink scarring beneath them red and puckered. I could still see some of the grit stuck around a dark stitching cord.

"Other's hairy arse," I growled. Dirty, wet, and no clean bandages. "Damn it!"

"Ah, Tanyana?" The top of Kichlan's head bobbed in and out of view at the top of the stairs. "Are you all right?"

I allowed myself a rueful chuckle. I dipped myself lower in the tub. "No, Kichlan. Not really."

A moment of uncomfortable silence. "Can I help?"

"Why not?" What was one more indignity on top of a day full of them? "Do you remember the bandages...?" I let my voice trail away. "You might as well come and see for yourself."

I hadn't realised how uncomfortable silence could get, and resisted an urge to push it, to see what I would need to say to make Kichlan's discomfort worse. More references to the Other's backside would probably not help.

"If... if you think... I will..."

Grinning at Kichlan's stumbling, his overflowing discomfort, I shifted myself around in the tub so I sat with my back to the stairs. It was big enough to allow me to pull my knees close to my chest. "This is as decent as I'm going to get, I'm afraid. I'm part of your team now. Supposed to look after us or something, aren't you?"

"Yes." The word came out as a tangled cough.

"Kich?" Lad's voice was loud, boisterous and distinctly comfortable. "See, told you! Everyone needs help with their back."

"Lad! No!"

The scrapes and bangs of a struggle reached me from the stairs. I rested my head against my knees, thankful for the warmth that added flexibility to my strained and bruised neck, and grinned against wet skin.

"No, Lad. Eugeny! Eugeny, a hand?"

More struggling.

"But, Kich, what about her back?"

"Your brother can handle it, Lad, my boy." I could hear laughter in the old man's voice. "Why don't you help me with supper? We can make something especially for your friend. You'd like that, wouldn't you?"

"Oh, yes. I guess." Lad hesitated, torn. "Are you sure you can handle, Kich?"

"Yes," Kichlan answered in a squeak.

A moment more, then footsteps descended.

"What can we make, Geny?" Lad asked as his voice faded.

"I'm coming up," Kichlan called ahead. A warning of sorts, I supposed.

I waited until he was closer before turning my head.

"What's the matter?" His thin lips and serious expression were out of place on his blushing, flame-red face. "Is it your head?"

Looking over my shoulder was not helping my aches and pains. I turned around. "No, the stitches. From the glass, when I fell. Well–" I gestured to my left shoulder with a flick of my head "–you can see for yourself."

I leaned on my knees as Kichlan touched my shoulder and back. His soft fingers were cold compared to my water-warmed skin, and they shook, but he didn't knock the bandages or brush the sensitive stitching. "The dust, from the wall," he whispered.

"And the Other knows what else," I muttered.

"The old man is good with these things." Kichlan stood. I heard footsteps retreating. "Doing things without pions, that is. Wait a minute."

Left alone in the attic I righted myself, and stretched gingerly. The water was beginning to cool.

There wasn't much in Kichlan and Lad's shared room besides their beds and bath. A hamper of old wicker slouched beside a small chest of drawers. Two pairs of boots, cleaned well but betrayed by faded and cracked leather, leaned against the hamper. Could they only have enough clothes, enough possessions, to fill a basket and three drawers? I searched the room, to the bare wooden walls, rug and freshly swept floorboards. Simple, empty.

And, as I lay in a warm bath while an old man made evenbell supper in the house below, unavoidably comfortable.

Second glance at the dresser, and I frowned. There was something on top of it, something dull, metallic and ugly in such a bare-wooden room.

I frowned at it. What was it? It almost looked like a hand. A metal hand.

"I'm coming up, miss!" Eugeny called from the stairs.

I turned my back to the old man entering the room.

Eugeny whistled lowly, a soft rush of air under his breath. "Nasty." But he didn't ask what had happened, or comment further. "Can you remove the bandages? Got the boys tearing up an old towel to fix them."

Gingerly, I unwound the tucked-in knot and began unwrapping my shoulder. "I–" I swallowed on a sudden lump. "I'm sorry to make you do that."

"No fuss, miss." Eugeny took the wet, dirty bandages as I pulled them away. "Old anyway, just sitting in my cupboard tempting the moths."

I nodded, but wasn't entirely convinced. "Well, thank you."

"Not me you should thank."

I had to rearrange myself to undo the bandages around my hips and upper thigh. Eugeny had foreseen this, and was already facing the stairs. He clasped his hands behind his back. His fingernails were short and clean.

"It's your house, though." I shifted again. "You can turn around now."

He took the remaining bandages. "That's true. But the boys wanted to help you, and they're good boys, both of them. Help an old man out. So I do the same. Now, I'm going to leave this for you." Something tapped on the bath beside my shoulder. I glanced down. Eugeny was holding a wide glass jar, filled with a yellow paste. I took it from him.

"What is it?"

"Golden roots of the waxseal plant," he said, as though that explained anything to someone who'd never heard of a waxseal plant. "When you're dry, put it on the wounds, and then replace your bandages. Ah, here we go."

I glanced over my shoulder to see Eugeny shuffle to the stairs and take a bundle of pale material from a curious-faced Lad.

"They're on the boy's bed, with your towel. When you're ready."

I realised, in the tone of that "when you're ready", that I had spent too long getting clean.

"Lad's helped me finish the apple pie." The old man shepherded Lad before him, and left me alone.

With little choice, I stood and stepped carefully from the water. As I wrapped a large, pine-smelling towel around me, something gurgled in my gut. I was ravenous.

I did as the old man had instructed. I smeared the gunk – I couldn't bring myself to think of it as golden – on my stitches. Kichlan and Lad had no mirror, so I couldn't be entirely sure I had got all of them, but I had cleaned the wounds enough times to do it mostly from memory. It stung at first, before easing the aching skin into a warm kind of numbness. Despite myself, I couldn't help a surge of affection for the old man as I tied the fresh bandages. For bits of an old towel they worked surprisingly well.

For a moment I considered leaving my uniform in its heap on the floor. Then I imagined Kichlan's reaction. I collected the dark cloth from the floorboards. It was dry. I lifted it close to my face and sniffed. Again it surprised me, giving off not so much of a hint of the sewer. I dragged it on.

The silver hand on the dresser caught my eye. I picked it up. It was heavy, and clinked on the inside as I weighed it in my palm. Where the wrist should be was a jagged hole, metal ending in burns and rust. I peered inside. Dimly, I could see thick wires coiled in on each other. They reminded me too keenly of the fibres in their metal tube, those that had become my suit. What was this hand, that it resembled the suit so closely? And why was it on Kichlan's dresser? Something told me it did not belong to Lad.

"Tanyana?" Kichlan called from the floor below. "Are you coming?"

I dropped the hand. It fell with a crash that sounded louder to my ears than it should have. I stood, stone still, waiting for Kichlan to run up the stairs. No one came. Heart knocking against my chest I collected the hand, placed it back on the dresser. It hadn't bent, or scratched, although it seemed to rattle more than before. I gave it a last pat, and hoped Kichlan didn't move it often.

Kichlan had left me a long woollen shirt and a pair of pants that were so baggy I had to tuck them into my uniform to keep them up. But I enjoyed the looseness of the material, and its warmth, and it had a fresh, woodsy smell that made me think they probably came from the same cupboard as the towel.

As dressed as I could be, I ran my fingers through my hair. It had grown longer than I usually allowed it, so it puffed out around my ears and curled lightly near the top of my neck. I replaced the lid on the jar, and descended.

I found Kichlan, Lad and Eugeny waiting by a crackling fire in a room I realised was the kitchen. It had a low fireplace built of dark stone, above which were suspended great metal plates. A round, flat tin container sat on one of them, and I guessed that was where a rich cinnamon smell was wafting from. My stomach growled again.

"Tanyana?" Kichlan spoke as I entered the room. I think he must have heard my stomach before my feet.

I found it strangely easy to smile as I met his concerned brown eyes. "I didn't know what you do with the water."

"Lad will fix it later," Kichlan said. His face was guarded, not entirely reassured. "How are you feeling?"

I nodded, and noticed I could no longer feel stiffness or pain in my neck. "Better. Thanks, I'm sure, to you all." I handed Eugeny his yellow gunk. "Thank you."

126

The old man nodded; Kichlan shrugged as though it didn't matter and turned his face away. Lad, however, beamed. "I helped Geny with his pie," he said, reaching for the tin above the fireplace. "From apples Geny got from the old woman who has a cellar and keeps them in there even when they're not the best." He barely breathed. "Geny says it doesn't help, keeping them cold like that, they still go brown but she won't listen to him, she won't." He tried to lift the metal lid, fingers dancing around the hot handle. His silver suit, where it wrapped around his wrist, reflected warm embers from the fire below. "So Geny made them into a pie, and I helped him finish it. You can eat them like that. Can we have some?"

Kichlan, exasperated, gripped his brother's hand before he could make another try for the handle. "It's hot, Lad. And no, supper comes first, pie comes last."

"Oh." Lad's face fell, but only stayed down a moment. "I can help, Geny. We need plates." He shook his brother off and buzzed to the sagging wooden cabinets in one corner of the room.

"You rile him up," Kichlan snapped at me.

The calm of a bath cracked at his tone. I bristled. "This was your idea."

"Not one of my best."

"And I'm not doing anything, he didn't give me the chance to say anything either. How could I possibly rile him up?"

"Your presence alone, *Tan*."

I clipped any possible retort when Lad, arms laden with plates, hurried between us. "You gotta sit down to eat," he told me, as he passed.

The dining table filled the second half of the kitchen. It was strange to eat in the same room as the cooking fire

127

and cutlery cupboards, and it reminded me of home. The home of my childhood, the one I had shared with my mother before my binding skill earned me enough kopacks to afford a apartment close to the city centre. I sat on a wooden chair with a faded patchwork cushion. Kichlan set two thick candles in the centre of the table and lit them with a flame borrowed from the fire. The warmth and light made the pale beech table seem deeper. I knew that colour, remembered the scent of smoke and food. I had worked so hard to leave that life behind, a world of few pions, fewer kopacks, of hungry nights and my mother's aged, worn face. Why, when Eugeny's home reminded me of it so clearly, did I actually like the feeling? I had never reminisced about the past before, I knew I had moved on to better things. Why start now?

Then Eugeny placed a thick-edged saucepan in the middle of the table, filled with a bubbling concoction of vegetables and meat. He spooned the thick stew onto rough clay plates with a wide silver spoon that had tarnished with age. The dancing bear designs on the handle gave it an heirloom air, and I wondered if anything else in his house was as precious as this piece of silverware undoubtedly once was.

Neither Kichlan nor Lad waited on any ceremony, but began eating as soon as Eugeny had served them. I hesitated. What had my mother done, before each meal? Said thanks to the Keeper, or something similar...

"Eat," Eugeny said. He gave me a sad little smile. "You'll be hungry."

I took his advice, and the moment the food touched my tongue I was lost in hunger and wrapped in thick gravy. The meat might have been beef, or something more common, even deer. I didn't care. It was tender, it was tangy. Potatoes dissolved in my mouth; turnips were rich with flavour and still a little crunchy. I had no idea what Eugeny could have done to make something so very basic taste so amazing. A hint of spice also, what was that? Not heat like Hon Ji noodles, not quite. It was like he had waved the chilli over it instead, only touched the stew with flavour.

The plate was empty before I knew it, and I was acutely aware that there was no more in the pot. Had I eaten into their meal and forced Lad, or Kichlan perhaps, to settle with that bit less?

Kichlan and Eugeny ate at a far more sedate, polite pace.

Eugeny took his time spooning the contents from his plate into his mouth, and chewed each bite extensively. Did he have all his teeth left, and were they whole? Could they be, without a well-paid healer to keep the bone sure? "Finished already?" he asked me between chews.

"It was lovely."

He concentrated on his spoon.

Lad, who seemed to be shovelling as hard as I had but obviously had more on his plate, grinned widely. Gravy dribbled down his chin. "You were hungry," he observed.

Kichlan leaned over and wiped his brother's face with a small, pale blue towel he had folded and placed beside his plate. Perhaps put there in anticipation of this very need.

"Tan was hungry, wasn't she?" Lad said as his brother cleaned him, reminding me yet again of an overlarge child.

Kichlan flicked me another *see how you rile him up* look before answering. A whole day on his collecting team and I already had a look. "Yes, very." He refolded the towel and arranged it beside his plate. "Now, finish your food or it will be too late for apple pie."

I wouldn't have believed Lad could eat any faster than he was, but he did. Kichlan, on the other hand, had left a third of his food untouched. When Lad, still chewing his final mouthful, peered hopefully into the empty pot, Kichlan scraped the rest of his meal onto Lad's clean plate. I caught a look of tenderness on Kichlan's face as his brother happily kept eating.

Nothing like the look he gave me, that one.

"Good boy, Lad." Eugeny cleared the table. I started to stand, but the old man touched a thin hand to my shoulder, and I stayed seated. "Help us with the pie, there's a boy?"

I felt uncomfortable and acutely useless as the men left me at their table and fussed with the food. It wasn't the same as being waited on by the servants of friends or associates.

The pie was good, the apples soft, the pastry cinnamon-spiced and sugary. And I told them so, Lad especially, and found myself thanking them over and over for their time, for their effort, for their food and water and soap. Finally, when the food was all cleared and I was no longer bound to sit and be waited on, Kichlan's look had become something quite different. I saw confusion there and even, if he turned his head to a certain angle, pity.

Pity was new. I was still getting used to it.

"Well, the bell is late," Eugeny said as I hovered in the kitchen door, unsure what I was expected to do next.

"Is it?" I couldn't hear the bell peals this far from the Tear River. And my watch was gone.

"You and the boys will be leaving early, I expect."

Lad was already sleepy, full and warm, wearing a heavy-lidded expression. He yawned. "Always."

I thought of my long coach ride. "Indeed."

"Bed then, I would say." Eugeny rubbed his hands together; they sounded like fragile pieces of paper.

Kichlan jerked his head toward me. "You can have my–"

"Nonsense," Eugeny cut across him, voice quiet but firm. "We will make a pallet for her before the fire. Cushions and blankets." He glanced at me. "You do not mind, do you?"

After the bath and the bandages and the food, I could hardly gripe about sleeping arrangements. "Of course not."

"Settled then." Eugeny shuffled through the corridor and into the second downstairs room. "You two go and get to sleep," he called.

For a moment Lad looked at me, Kichlan looked at Lad, and I glanced between them. Then Lad jumped up, wrapped his arms around my shoulders and squeezed. "'Night, 'Tan!" He placed a wet kiss on my ear, before letting me go and heading up two stairs at a time.

"See what I mean." But as Kichlan followed his brother he wasn't giving me the look. If anything, he seemed relieved. Maybe a little pleased.

"In here, miss," Eugeny called from the base of the stairs, where I stood listening to the brothers' footsteps over my head. What would happen to the water?

Another fire was lit in the second room, but this time nothing cooked above it. Clothes had been strung up between the rafters of the squat ceiling and the room smelled like damp cloth. Eugeny was putting the final touches on a very basic bed on the floor: draping a woollen blanket over three large cushions. The clear stems of goose feathers peeked out of a corner seam of the most worn of the three.

I'd seen more comfortable places to sleep in my time. But it was warm, and dry, and my stomach was full.

"Here." Eugeny passed me a thick quilt. "Don't mind the firelight, do you?"

I was used to sleeping in darkness, used to an apartment warmed by busy pions that had travelled across the city skyline just for me. I shrugged. "I can face the other way if it's a problem." Silently, I wasn't sure I wanted my back to the flames. What if a log fell and sent embers into my highly flammable bedding?

"Good." Eugeny fussed with the improvised bed for a moment. From the frown on his face I guessed he was worrying about more than stray goose feathers. Possibly flying embers in the middle of the night?

"They're good boys," he said again. My possible death by inflammable bedding was not on his mind, then.

"Yes." So he'd said.

"Likes you, Lad does." Eugeny glanced at me, and gave up all pretence of bed-making. "Be careful with him, girl. He's likable now, in a good mood and has his brother with him. But Lad, he's not all there. If the mood takes him..." He hesitated. "Well, you be careful."

A chill settled over me that had nothing to do with the corridor at my back, or the damp clothes surrounding me. "Tell me what you mean." And perhaps some part of my old identity as the centre of a nine point circle reasserted itself, then. I think he heard it in my voice.

"Kichlan can keep him calm, can keep him settled," Eugeny whispered to the flames. "You would not know Lad if you saw him in a dark mood. Not his fault, mind you. Just sometimes his thoughts won't go in order, his hands and feet and words won't do what he wants them to do. That's what he told me, anyway."

Eugeny approached me. He clutched at my hands, forcing the blanket from my fingers. In his intense gaze, watery eyes pale and worried, I thought I caught a glimpse of my own face rimmed by dark shadows. One hand held my wrist, vice-like, while the other pulled up the sleeve of his patched shirt.

A jagged scar tore through his upper arm and disappeared toward his shoulder. I shuddered at it, at the premonition of what my own skin would look like. My face and neck and shoulder and side.

"They stitched me up too." He confirmed my fears. "Couldn't afford the healers. Nice old woman who worked in the hospital, just emptying food trays and chamber pots is all she did, she told me about the golden root. Would have been much worse if she hadn't. Sure of that."

I was paralysed by his scar – a mirror of mine. "Why–?"

"Lad did this to me."

I balked, tried to pull away. After a moment's tugging the old man gave in.

"You find it hard to believe. Trust me, there's more than one Lad in there, more faces than you've seen. And when Kichlan isn't beside him, he can be dangerous." Eugeny pulled his sleeve down and smoothed the cloth. "But don't blame him, girl. Not Lad's fault he is the way he is. Just thank Kichlan for being there, always with him."

Still feeling numb, I nodded.

"And be careful." Eugeny pushed past drying clothes, draped in his way like enormous leaves in a musty forest. "He hurt a girl once, Kichlan told me. Veche would have imprisoned him if Kichlan hadn't been there. If he hadn't promised them he'd stay with Lad for the rest of

133

his days. He protects Lad, and he protects others from Lad. The boy likes you. So be careful."

Eugeny left me to my fireside bed. It took me longer than it should have to fall asleep on it, and that wasn't all due to the feathers sticking into me through the blanket.

6.

I woke with faint sunlight flitting over my eyelids in a drying-clothes-in-the-breeze dance, and a goosefeather poking the soft skin between my underarm and right breast. Wincing, I sat up. I couldn't remember a less comfortable night's sleep.

"Awake, are you?" Eugeny appeared, sweeping a shirt aside.

I nodded, mouth padded with dry yarn.

"Better than the boys, you are. I'll get you water, and a good meal to start the day."

Eugeny bustled from the room, feeling clothes as he went. Something caught in my throat and I coughed noisily, before wiping flecks of ash from the edges of my eyes. A pleasant start to the morning.

When Eugeny returned with a large bowl of warm water and a towel I realised there would be no bath today. My clothes had been washed and hung in the room with me. Eugeny passed me everything but the jacket with a rueful shrug of one shoulder. "Couldn't get the coat completely dry, I'm afraid."

When I left my improvised bedroom, Kichlan and Lad

were descending. Kichlan was dressed and ready, his damp hair flat and more organised than I had ever seen it. I wondered how long that would last as it dried. Lad rubbed his eyes, and from the look of his wide, oversized shirt and uneven-length pants, he was not exactly ready to face the day.

"Took hours to get him to sleep," Kichlan muttered as he caught me looking at his brother. "Can't imagine why that would be."

It was too early to be lumped as the cause of all of Kichlan's ills, so I ignored him.

Lad was snappish as Eugeny served us dawnbell supper: bread that was so over-toasted I guessed it was stale beneath the charring; eggs greasy from the lard they were fried in; honey still in its comb. Eugeny's tea was strong enough to clean streets with, and bitter. I finished the meal with a queasy lump low in my stomach.

Finally, as the sun strengthened and sent ice-sharpened rays through the window above the kitchen bench, Kichlan pushed aside his plate and stood.

"Lad," he said, in a tight, commanding voice. "You must dress."

His younger brother continued to poke at a swimming yolk with a tarnished fork. He held the implement so hard his knuckles were white, the veins on his hand prominent and purple. Eugeny sat very still, and I followed his example.

"Tired," Lad spat gooey flecks of egg onto his plate with the word.

"I know, Lad. But we have a duty. We need to get up early and work very hard."

"Tired!" Lad roared, and with a great swing of his arm launched his fork across the room.

I ducked, lifted arms to cross over my head. But Kichlan was faster. Kichlan was faster than I'd imagined anyone could be. His suit leapt from his wrists, shot out fine and accurate, and caught the fork in mid-air.

He retracted the thin silver arm slowly, and Lad watched the fork the entire time.

"Why did you do that?"

Lad blanched, and I didn't blame him. Kichlan's voice was low, dark with anger and disappointment. Lad twisted in his chair, peered up at his brother, and the pouting frustration fell from his face as tears crested over onto his cheeks.

"Kich—"

"Why?" Kichlan didn't let up. He placed the fork on Lad's plate with a clang. Lad's palms pressed the table on either side of the plate, and shook. "Don't you want to come with us? Don't you want to be a collector?"

"Kich—"

"After how hard I worked so you could collect with us, don't you want to come now?"

"I do!" Lad jumped up, knocked the table with his knee and sent cutlery clanging across the surface. "I do!"

Kichlan eased his straight shoulders and thunderous face. "Then you'd better get dressed, hadn't you?"

Air returned to the room.

Lad flashed me a quivering smile as he hurried upstairs. Kichlan, however, only spared me a scowl.

"This is your fault—" he started, but Eugeny stood, suddenly, and began collecting plates.

"Now, now, we know that isn't true," he said, voice soft, but his words cut into Kichlan's like glass. "Not at all." The old man glanced at me. "Got your coat, girl?"

I didn't hear the words, but I caught Eugeny and Kichlan murmuring as I left the room and pulled my coat

137

from the line close to the fire. They were both quiet when I returned.

Now inspired, Lad only took a moment to dress and was soon back in the kitchen. Eugeny pressed food into his hands, a few slices of bread and possibly cheese, but offered nothing to Kichlan or me.

"We'd better hurry." Kichlan strode down the hallway, dragging on his patchwork coat as he yanked the door open. Cold Movoc-under-Keeper air reached into Eugeny's warm house, smelling of food and clothes, to slide icy fingers down my collar. I tightened it, and jammed my hat down so it covered my ears.

Kichlan stepped into the street, Lad ran after him, but I hesitated for a moment in the hallway. Eugeny stood in the kitchen door, watching his boys leave.

"Thank you," I said. "For everything."

The old man was inscrutable. "You just remember what I said."

I closed the door and hurried to catch up to Kichlan and Lad, where they waited on the street corner.

"Eugeny," I started to say, and waited until I knew Kichlan was listening to me. His face was stony. "Eugeny, is he one of us?"

One of us. Of *us*.

Kichlan's eyebrows rose a half inch before he remembered he needed to hold them still to keep that stony expression going. "You mean a debris collector?"

I swallowed hard. "Of us" seemed to be echoing in my head, like I'd shouted the words down a tunnel. Just saying them felt like a betrayal of my old life, of the hope I had been holding on to. The hope that this was all a big mistake. "Yes." Or maybe it was time to stop fighting the inevitable?

"No, the old man doesn't see debris."

"But he doesn't use pions either," I continued. Couldn't stop myself now. "He does things the hard way. Dries clothes and heats rooms with fire, or heals wounds with paste made from plants." I hesitated, and realised the stitches hadn't bothered me at all that morning, not even their usual post-sleeping ache. But I couldn't exactly strip in the middle of the street to check how effective Eugeny's gold mush had been.

Kichlan said, "No, he doesn't." Ahead of us, Lad was humming to himself, but not walking with the brisk enthusiasm I had seen the day before. How long could memories of Kichlan's anger keep his morning mood at bay? "Eugeny is an old man, and his sight is failing."

"Oh." That, really, explained nothing. Eyesight had nothing to do with pion sight. Even the blind could navigate a city like Movoc, lit with deeper, bright lights.

"That's how he explained it to me," Kichlan said. "But then, I don't understand that pion-binder talk. Said his sight was fading, his real sight, and his pion sight. He says he knows they're there, but he's happy to leave them there, not interfere. Happy to do things with his hands instead."

To choose to abandon one's binding skill. To choose. It was difficult to imagine.

But 384 Darkwater was so much closer to Kichlan and Lad's house than my own. I hadn't noticed properly, stumbling there the previous evening. A few blocks and slush-wet steps and we arrived. I felt foolish for holding onto my apartment, as Kichlan unlocked the door, collected something from the step, and led us down. My inconvenient, over-expensive home.

Sofia had been waiting in ankle-thick snow at the locked door. "You're late," she snapped when Kichlan turned the key. She walked behind me down the stairs, her arms crossed. "And she's early." I ignored the jibe.

"Never mind," Kichlan said. He headed straight for the table and began piling empty jars into his usual battered leather bag. Quietly, the other team members arrived.

Sofia, arms so firmly crossed they might never unwind again, glowered between Kichlan's hunched shoulders and me. "What have you done?" she hissed at me from the side of her mouth.

"Me? Nothing." That was true enough.

"Here, this has arrived," Kichlan said, and pressed something into my palm. "Your pay." He flashed me a dark grin, devoid of any pleasure. "You're really one of us now."

A scrap of paper. It crinkled as I unfolded it, edges tearing beneath my fingers. Cheap, sewn by pions none too interested in the task. A single figure glared at me from the off-white, fibrous weave. The black letters were blocky, all sharp edges and uneven ink. I blinked, certain there was something wrong with my vision. But no matter how many times I tried blinking, how slowly or how purposefully, nothing changed.

I became aware of silence and glanced up to find the collecting team watching me. All but Lad, who was struggling with his coat and humming softly in his throat.

"It's not a mistake," Uzdal said. Was it that obvious?

Five hundred kopacks.

Five hundred?

"How long is this supposed to last?" I asked of no one in particular.

"We are paid every second sixweek and one," Kichlan answered me anyway. "And it will not change, no matter how long you serve the veche. Or how well."

140

The top of my head was very hot, my skin tingling cold. "Oh."

I couldn't keep my apartment on this, I couldn't afford coaches to travel here, I couldn't eat, and I would have to dismiss the cleaner – if I could catch her before I had to hurry in the morning. Other!

I contracted a fist around the paper and touched it to my forehead. The edges of the paper scraped against my nose and tore.

"That reminds me."

I lowered my hand. Sofia stood before me, holding out a small silver half-disk.

"Meant to give this to you yesterday. Guess it wasn't much use to you until now." She waited until I took the disk, before guiding Lad into the stairwell and helping him with his coat.

Footsteps trooped past me. The disk was a hollow semicircle with a small, dark screen, and made of familiar dull silver.

"It fastens to your rublie," Kichlan said. "That way you'll know how much you have left."

Of course. I pulled my rublie from its pocket.

"Come on." Kichlan slung the full bag over one shoulder and gestured to the stairs. "It's time to begin."

I attached the semicircle to my rublie as I followed him out of the sublevel. The blank screen flickered once, the same green as the lights that flashed when the rublie was transferring kopacks, before shining a clear and steady number.

Six thousand.

I very nearly tripped.

"Watch out." Kichlan grabbed at my arm, but I braced myself on the wall instead. "What's wrong?"

I stared up at him. Six thousand. What had happened over the past day, what payments had come and swiped kopacks without my knowledge? More debts to veche torturers? The cleaner, the apartment? "How do you live this way?" How could I?

For a moment, I showed Kichlan my fear. My absolute panic. Because I didn't belong here, he made that clear every time he so much as looked at me, and my old life would fade away with every kopack I could no longer earn. All choices had been taken from me, left me empty as the rublie in my hand.

He straightened, face firming into a determined expression. "You'll get used to it. We all did, you will too."

What had I expected, sympathy? Words of advice that would, somehow, miraculously solve my financial problems?

I flipped the rublie – now clipped like crutches for a crippled leg – into my pocket. I vowed, as I followed the uneven hem of Kichlan's coat into the sharp sunlight of a pale morning, that I wouldn't think about that depressing number again. Not until I had no choice, and certainly not until I had survived the day.

"What happened to the ceiling?" Sofia waited for Kichlan at the top of the stairs, and glared at me as she asked. Who else could have damaged it, after all?

"Never mind," Kichlan snapped his answer off.

"If she did that you know she'll have to repair it."

If? Sounded to me like she had already made up her mind.

"Do you hear that?" Sofia addressed me over her shoulder. "You need to repair it. If the veche does an inspection and they see that hole, it's coming out of all of our pay. Not just yours! Are you listening?"

"She heard you, Sofia." Kichlan jammed his hands in

his pockets and hunched his shoulders against the cold and, it seemed to me, her tirade. "We all heard you."

"As long as she'll fix it!"

"She will."

"And she understands this is serious. She's not some architect who can get away with–"

"She understands."

Six thousand kopacks? How could I repair that break in the ceiling? Before *Grandeur* I could have done it with nothing but a gentle, soothing whisper. How much would I have charged a collector who came begging at my door?

Six thousand. How was I going to do this?

Lad's temper held out until mid-morning. Until then he smiled at Mizra's jokes, submitted to Sofia's fussing, endured Natasha's waspish apathy. It was the debris that undid him, in the end. He sniffed out – or whatever it was he did to find it – a small cache in a crack in a faulty lamp, but couldn't manage to slim his suit down into tweezers fine enough to retrieve it. When Kichlan offered to do it instead his younger brother turned on him.

I yelped and leapt away as a sword-like appendage sprang from Lad's right hand. It glinted as he leapt at Kichlan, howling like an injured, possibly rabid cat. But Kichlan was ready. He caught his brother's sword on his own suit, which now resembled an iron bar from his right wrist and a large, metallic shield over his left. Kichlan knocked Lad's thrust aside and kneed him cleanly in the gut. As the large man doubled over Sofia was there. She jumped on his back and clamped her own suit over his wrists, ploughing the metal into the cement to pin him to the floor, while Uzdal tipped Lad's head back and Mizra poured half of the contents of a small, dark jar into his mouth. I caught only a small glimpse of the syrupy liquid, but knew the sweet scent well. I had never seen someone take half a jar of it in one go. A few drops in the bottom of a Sweet Night cocktail at *The Bear's Smile* was more than enough to knock you out for the night.

"Thank you, Tanyana, for undoing all my hard work so quickly." Kichlan retracted his suit with a shudder. Lad, meanwhile, lay limp beneath Sofia, Uzdal and Mizra, breathing evenly and looking almost serene. "He hasn't had one of those since last autumn. Happy now?"

I glared right back. "You can stop blaming me for everything Lad does."

"I will when it stops being your fault."

"Going to blame me for whatever happened—" But I bit my lip before I could mention Eugeny's scar, or his warning.

Sofia was staring between us, whipping her head back and forward so quickly I wouldn't have been surprised to hear a bone break. Mizra and Uzdal studied the paving stones intently. Natasha yawned behind her hand and glanced up at the sun with an "oh, won't you move faster, please" expression.

A vein bulged in Kichlan's neck. He opened his mouth, and I braced myself, the image of those sword-appendages vivid. How quickly I could work out how to do one? But Kichlan snapped his mouth shut and shook his head instead. "You're not worth it," he muttered.

I clenched my teeth against argument.

"Mizra, Uzdal, help me get him up." Kichlan set about giving orders, leaving me feeling that something unjust had happened and I wasn't exactly sure what. "Sofia, will you help us take him home?"

Sofia's grateful nodding reminded me uncharitably of a starving dog salivating for scraps.

"Natasha, you and Tanyana finish here." He tossed Natasha his bag of jars. It clinked as she caught it in awkward hands. "Tomorrow is Rest. Do that. See you again Mornday."

"Fine," Natasha answered.

"Thanks to this episode and the fiasco that was yesterday we are significantly behind our quota. Mornday will be long. We have a lot of work to do to make up for this."

I said nothing.

Kichlan glowered at a carefully selected spot on the road as the silence stretched. Then he gestured at Mizra. "Let's go." The three men hoisted Lad's boneless body up between them, and began half dragging, half walking him away. Sofia scurried ahead, talking over her shoulder to Kichlan about keys.

"What did you do to poor Kichlan?" Natasha held the bag out to me in loose, lazy fingers.

"I didn't do anything." I took the bag, uncertain at her growing smirk.

"Of course not—" Natasha broke off as Sofia ran back, clutching the large, dark iron keys to the sublevel.

"Make sure you lock up," she said to Natasha, breathless, before returning to Kichlan and the other collectors.

Grinning, Natasha tossed the keys to me. I fumbled with them, still in the process of slinging the bag over my shoulder. "You must have done something. Bring up a bad memory, perhaps?"

I swallowed hard. "Maybe." I glanced down at the keys. "You're not staying?"

"You don't need my help to finish up, do you?" She flicked a suited wrist at the crack in the lamp.

"Um, I guess not." What was I saying? What was she doing?

"Didn't think so." She rested a hand on her hip. "What did you do to annoy him so much? Ask him what he did before he became a collector? He used to be a binder, you know, but he won't talk about it. Gets cranky if you so much as mention it. No matter how nicely you ask."

I blinked at her. Kichlan was a binder? But he'd said he didn't understand pions, or trust them. "Ah, no. It's his brother. He thinks I upset his brother."

"Oh." She yawned. "Well, you can't expect me to stay here if I don't have to."

"But isn't it our–"

"Our what? Duty?" She laughed. A hard, forced sound. "Don't be ridiculous. The rest of this collecting team don't seem to think much of their duty. Why should we?" Kichlan, Lad, Sofia, Uzdal and Mizra had already disappeared around a corner. "You should understand better than anyone. Collecting isn't duty, it's just bad luck. Nothing else. So thanks again." With a toss of her hair and a smirk, Natasha left me. Alone.

For a moment I stood, holding the bag and wondering how, exactly, this had happened. Other's hell, I still didn't actually know how to use all this silver in my bones. It wasn't like anyone had bothered to teach me. But still, Kichlan had left me here to do this, and I was hardly going to give him another excuse to be furious at me for things I hadn't done.

I fished a jar from the bag, propped myself on my elbows. Deep breaths steadied my hand, and gradually I extended two metallic prongs. I pursed my mouth and managed to narrow them down to two reasonably sized points, and gently, gingerly, reached inside the crack in the base of the lamp.

There was only enough debris to fill half a jar. How many were we supposed to collect in a sixnight? Seventy jars, wasn't it? The single jar looked pitiful in my hand.

But still, I had collected it. Without help, without lecture or instruction. Had to feel a little proud of that.

It was still early afternoon when I found 384 Darkwater. I'd only spent half a bell wandering completely lost, which wasn't bad for someone with no knowledge of the area who hadn't anticipated being abandoned and as such hadn't paid attention to where she was going. I separated the half-full jar as Kichlan had so laboriously instructed, put the rest of the empty ones on the table and hung the bag up on one of the hooks. Then I left the sublevel, fighting with aging iron to lock the door, and realised I had a day and a half all to myself.

No debris. No walls falling on me. No snide remarks, no being pointedly ignored. No volatile Lad to worry about. And no Kichlan.

No Kichlan.

A day and a half suddenly seemed like a whole moon's holiday.

I couldn't take another coach home, not now that I knew how few kopacks I earned. Instead, I started down Darkwater toward the Tear River, and the ferry.

Movoc-under-Keeper's ferries were an historical institution. From the sleek wooden ships of antiquity, rowed by gangs of burly men led and enslaved by a single pionbinder, to the steam-driven boats of the city's relatively recent, pre-revolution past. Or so I had learned, on my frequent trips to stare at the wrecks preserved in the Ferry House, near the city's northern gate. My mother had taken me there often. It was a free way to entertain a child, and always heated, even in the darkest of winters. Inside, ferries of all shapes and ages were suspended behind thick sheets of strong poly, protected from time and the elements by the constant attention of caretaker pions. A veritable history of Movoc, written in its ships. Modern ferries didn't need to rely on manpower, steam power or anything in between. Since Novski's critical circle revolution they were propelled through the water on waves lit by the bright crests of busy pions. This meant they were quiet, smooth, not restricted by the flow of the current or worried by the varieties of the weather. But still, Movoc's ferries were designed with that proud history in mind. Polished wooden decks, sleek hulls painted white, glass windows that rattled in the wind, and even dark, ornamental stacks that would never produce steam.

I planned my evening as I walked. A drawn-out bath in my own home, not constrained by fire-warmed water or meddling old men. Clean bandages and no golden root-gloop to smear on my skin. I wasn't too confident about the contents of my pantry, but knew I would be happy with anything, as long as I was eating it, or drinking it, in my own home.

I almost broke into a run as the Tear came into sight. It shone like glass in the clear day, like a fold in *Grandeur*'s dress. And for the first time the memory of her didn't tug at my heart with cruel, hooked strings, and I wondered, just briefly, if I was starting to let my poor broken statue go.

Then I stepped onto the warm lacquered boards of the ferry. The ferry master smiled as I touched my rublie to his in payment. I smiled right back, turned away and met bright, pleased green eyes.

"Well," Devich said, before I had truly realised it was him. "I know they say all roads lead to the Tear, but this is a surprise."

All my dreams of a day and a half of freedom fell away. "Devich."

His smile changed, became less pleased and more pained. But he didn't drop it completely. "Still not happy to see me, I guess." He rubbed at his shoulder, gaze slipping away. "I wouldn't want to dampen a bright Olday afternoon like this one. So I'll just leave you alone–"

Passengers crowded behind me, pressuring me onto the ferry, pushing me to step forward. "No, please." I summoned a light tone to my voice. "You don't have to go."

A little encouragement, and Devich swooped. He wrapped an arm around my shoulders and guided me cleanly from the gangway, around the steadily filling seats, and into the cabin. Without a word he led me up a tight set of stairs half hidden in a dark corner.

The second level was nearly empty, its lacquered wooden seats less worn by bodily friction and abrasive river spray as those below. The windows were clean of the long-left imprints of curious noses or balancing hands. Only two more people were pressed into one of the corners, and a furtive glance in their direction told me they probably weren't aware of any presence than each other's.

A strange place to take me, and I hoped I wasn't blushing.

"I prefer it up here, don't you?" Devich said, his hand gentle and casual on my shoulder.

I wouldn't know, and couldn't trust my voice to respond.

"Not so fond of the noise and the smell below," Devich continued, oblivious. "You know what I mean, of course."

"Why are you here then? Why not take a landau?" I hoped he wouldn't turn the question back at me.

Devich simply laughed. "A coach to the city on Olday afternoon? I'm a debris technician, Tanyana, not a veche architect. I could throw myself beneath them and they still wouldn't stop, not on the busiest evening in a sixnight and one."

Fair enough.

"Well, my dear lady." Devich leaned against the brass railing beneath the windows and peered through the glass. The ferry was pushing off from the wharf and starting its steady way up the Tear, against the current. Afternoon sunlight glinted on the water. It cast the buildings on the far bank as pale ghosts with shimmering, dark windows for eyes. "Where were you headed when you so carelessly crossed my path?"

"I told you, I'm no one's lady." But I leaned against the railing beside him. He shifted and his bent elbow touched mine. I didn't move. "And I'm going home."

"Ah." He watched a small vessel whip past us as it flew downriver. It looked more like a seedpod than a boat, and I wondered what colour the pions were that kept it afloat and gave it so much speed. "Hard day, then?"

"No words could explain it. No words."

But even now the past few days were fading, becoming grey like a half-remembered and unsavoury dream. Kichlan's house, Eugeny's warning, Lad's sudden and violent temper hardly seemed real when the sunlight hit the Tear just so and Devich smiled like that.

"I'll have to take your word for it then."

I was glad he didn't push the issue. Debris technician or whatever it was Devich called himself, he still didn't need to hear how far I had fallen.

I listened to the low creak of wood and the drum-like slosh of water below. "And you? Where were you going?"

"Oh, out for a night of fun!"

"Olday night and Rest morning," I murmured, and bent forward so my nose came close to the cool glass.

"The very same."

I could recall the end of many sixnights so celebrated. Frosted drinks so potent they kept you warm despite their rim of ice; pale pink pions lighting a room where women in improper outfits of snakeskin and white feathers danced to bells; old-world balls where everyone dressed in voluminous skirts of velvet and lace, and I – no matter how many times I arrived in dress suit and top hat – could still cause a stir. Just another distant dream, far nicer than my nightmares of debris.

"Where will you spend your Olday night?" I asked, before I could stop myself scratching at the old wound.

"This sixnight? *Underbridge* ballroom, I believe. I'm meeting someone..." Devich trailed off, perhaps at my expression. I knew the *Underbridge*. Blue stone, blue lights, blue liquor, the soft blue music of viola and oboe. From the door, on a clear Rest morning when the new sun was touching the Keeper's Edge, you could make out the ice-cream mounds of my art gallery on the opposite bank of the Tear.

A perfect place to meet a nameless someone. I had done so, at least once before. "Sounds lovely." My words frosted the glass.

"A night at home after an indescribable day has its good points."

"I'm counting on them."

Devich hesitated for a silent moment, then said, "You know, you could join me–"

"No." Could I tell him the charge just to enter the *Underbridge* ballroom was more than I earned in two sixnights? Could I tell him I preferred the dream of a past life to remain a dream, for now? A memory softened by pretended sleep. "But thank you."

"It doesn't seem right." Devich gave up any pretence of watching the river. "You, in that apartment of yours, all alone."

"Doesn't it?"

"No." His fingers toyed with a splinter of wood where it had risen close to one of the brass railing's hooks. "No one should be alone after a day they can't even talk about."

I allowed myself to let his easy charm trickle into my stomach, his smile to warm my cheeks. "You really care about that suit of yours, don't you?"

He blinked, confused. "I do?"

"Isn't that what you said? That you wouldn't leave me alone, because you'd put so much work into my suit?" I waved my wrist in front of his face. He tracked the circle of silver that peeked out of my sleeve like a cat with a feather on a string.

"Sounds like something I would say, yes." When his hunting-cat eyes met mine they lost none of that intensity. "And I should probably check its condition."

I longed for my bath, for my bandages. I was quite sure I still smelled faintly of sewage and yellow root mush. But Devich had been going to meet someone, out there in that pion-sighted, kopack-rich real world. And now, it seemed, he didn't want to anymore.

"What about your someone?" I whispered.

"There's plenty of someones in the *Underbridge* ballroom. She'll be fine."

My heart did a small flop, the kind of nervous activity it hadn't done for years, and I answered a messy "Yes" by nodding and waving one hand aimlessly.

Devich and I disembarked a few wharfs down from the bridge, and walked home together.

I hadn't entertained guests in my apartment for a very, very long time. Before *Grandeur* was even a twinkle in the veche's eye, back, perhaps, to a time when my bluestone art gallery was a haphazard sketch in lines of sheer light.

My home had, since then, been my own. My slice of quiet, of stillness, of the soft dark of half-lit lamps and comfortable chairs. I frequented ballrooms like the *Underbridge*, and night-stays with views of the Keeper so exclusive you had to hope you were more important than the next amorous couple just to get in. With commissions from the national veche I hadn't worried about being turned away.

So my home was not fitted to have guests. It was nearly empty of food, particularly at the moment, and never hosted anything to drink stronger than Hon Ji tea.

But Devich was a different kind of guest. The kind who had already worked his way inside my well-but-sparsely appointed sanctuary, and who had done this when I was vulnerable, when I was ill. Like a family member, perhaps. And yet, nothing like family at all.

We walked in silence too comfortable to bear.

"Designed any new suits since I've seen you?" I winced at my own staggering lack of tact.

He took it well enough. "Oh yes, dozens. I'm a hard worker."

I ignored his wink. "Same as mine, or something special?"

"Nothing's as special as yours, my lady."

"I already told you—"

"—you're nobody's lady."

Not without a circle of nine, I wasn't. "Then will you stop calling me that?"

"Not while you are mine."

We turned onto Paleice and I focused on the buildings so I wouldn't have to look at Devich, with his bright eyes and roguish smile.

Gate thirteen was closed and wouldn't open for me anymore – or, rather, I didn't have the skill to open it – so I was forced to crouch and scramble beneath it. Devich chuckled, and vaulted over with an unseemly show of strength and agility. Together, we headed to my ground level apartment. As I slipped my gloves off to touch bare fingers against the crystalline lock, Devich bent and collected a folded sheet of paper from the step. He sidled close to me and tapped the paper lightly against my shoulder. "This would be for you, I assume."

"Of course it is." I struggled to take the paper and unlock the door at the same time. "Anyone else in this building lose their pion sight recently?" The lock rejected me with an angry-wasp buzz. "You're not helping."

Devich leaned in, nose close to my temple, breath warm against my neck.

I concentrated, kept my hand steady, and the lock clicked open, echoing from marble tiles.

"You still are," he breathed into my ear. His lips brushed the very top of my cheek, and the hair along my forearms stood on end.

"Still what?" I asked.

"A lady."

My gloves and the piece of paper tumbled to the tiled, courtyard floor.

Scowling, I bent to collect them. But Devich was faster – easier to move without stitches and bandages and the bruises from falling bricks – and snatched them up.

"Give them back." My fingertips were cold and quivering as I held out my hand.

Grinning, Devich tucked the paper under his arm and wove his fingers through the gloves, as though he and my disembodied hand were clutching each other. It was disconcerting. He said, "You can't pretend. Not to me."

I held out my hand again, cutting the air, trying to be firm.

"And ignoring me won't help either."

"Really?" I swallowed. "Well, what do you know about being a lady?"

"I know." Devich held the gloves high above his head as he stepped closer. In my previous life, I would have been able to take them, a single jump and a quick snatch with a well-directed hand. A previous, pain-free life. "I know that scars can't make you less than you are." And before I could stop him, he touched the bandages on my neck with his free hand.

I jerked back. "Don't!"

"Why?"

"It hurts." You arrogant, rich bastard, I thought. "Maybe this wasn't a good idea." I sighed. "Give me my gloves."

But Devich shook his head. "You were a lady because you were a circle centre, is that it? A skilled pion-binder, a rich one."

A respected one. "That's the way it works. 'My lord' and 'my lady' aren't applicable without a nine point circle of your very own. Unless you happen to be a member of the veche, of course."

He shrugged like none of it mattered. "You might not be a skilled binder any more, Tanyana, but you are a skilled debris collector. And this city need collectors just as much as it needs binders."

But it didn't respect them as much, did it? I said, "Perhaps I should have explained the past few days in greater detail."

"Other!" Devich nearly bit into his own knuckles. "Other's balls, you can be frustrating!"

I grinned, and again held out my hand.

"But you're still my lady."

Devich dropped the gloves, heavy with the warmth of his skin, onto my palm. I tucked them into my jacket pocket and opened the door. The smells of home, and its cool darkness, invited me.

"Well?" Devich, no longer lounging against the door frame confident and cheeky, stood tall, tense, and hesitating.

"The door's right there. You know the way in."

I let Devich into my home and shut the door behind us. In the cool dark his warmth radiated like light. I turned, my back to the door, and he leaned in against me. I pressed my mouth to the hollow of his neck. He breathed into my hair.

"Welcome home, my lady," he whispered.

I tipped my head and sought his lips. They were hotter than the rest of him and his tongue, as it slipped out to touch the inside of my lip like a tentative finger, was cat-rough and quivering. Then his hands slid down my shoulders and pulled me forward, away from the door's supporting solidity. I tasted his teeth and wrapped both arms around his waist. He was thin beneath his coat, not an unhealthy thinness, more something lithe and sensuous.

156

Then he cupped my head with two hands, pressed our lips together so forcefully they ached, and caught the corner of a bandage with his little finger.

"Other!" I gasped, and pulled away.

He resisted for a moment, tried to pull me closer to him, and rocked his hips against mine. The overall effect was nearly enough to overwhelm the simple pain of a stitch tugged out of place.

"Wait." Cold air rushed between us as I stepped away. "The bandage."

He let go immediately, almost took half of my neck with his left hand, and ended up torn between an awkward distance and tempting closeness.

"Your bandage is stuck to my sleeve," he croaked.

"I noticed. Here, shuffle with me." Somehow, we came to the lamp in the entranceway's far corner. I turned a small valve and let the invisible particles rush in to create light enough to see by.

"Can you see it?" I asked, unable to work out how, exactly, my neck connected to his shirt.

"Let me." Devich stuck the tip of his tongue out as he concentrated, and I found myself wanting to nibble it. "Here we go."

I smoothed the bandage down as Devich frowned at the cuff of his pale sleeve.

"It's sticky and... yellow." He sniffed the stain. "Why is your bandage yellow?"

That was far too long a story to tell. "Never mind."

Another two delicate sniffs and Devich seemed to remember what we had been doing. He smiled, ruefully. "It's a shirt." He leaned forward, warming me again. "Just a shirt."

Bandages couldn't be dismissed so easily. I didn't let

him close the gap, but headed down the entranceway and hung up my coat. "Good. Tell me, were you going to eat anything in that ballroom of yours?"

Devich checked himself, but had the good grace not to look too disappointed. "I believe that was part of the plan, yes."

"Pity, because I doubt we'll be able to eat here."

"Oh?"

"Let's look, shall we?"

I brushed past Devich and headed for the kitchen. He hung up his coat beside mine and followed.

The pantry was more deserted than I had feared. Tea leaves rattled in a large glass jar. Crumbs, and a few remaining nuts, occupied another. Very empty and very clean. I had to remember to speak to the cleaner.

"How much time do you spend here, anyway?" Devich asked, an eyebrow raised. I couldn't bring myself to tell him the only proper meal I'd had in a long while was in another man's house.

"Not a lot." I closed the doors. "Would you like to make us tea again?"

Devich laughed. "Tea won't quite fill my stomach, I'm afraid. But I know what will." He held out his arm, crooked at the elbow. "Care to join me for supper, my lady?"

I shook my head. "Not really."

His face and elbow fell. "Oh."

I tried a tender expression. "Listen, Devich, I wanted a night at home and that's what I intend to have. Food or no food."

"You need to eat."

"Not as much as I need to bathe." I could smell worse things than sewage in my clothes, now I had taken off my coat. I could smell Eugeny's homemade

158

soap, clothes-drying smoke, and golden roots of the waxseal plant.

"For you, my lady, I will compromise." The smile returned. "You clean yourself and I will bring you food."

I hesitated. The tea leaves rattling in the bottom of the glass jar was really about all I could afford.

"My treat."

When I was a real lady I wouldn't have agreed. But I was right about that, and Devich, poor boy, simply wrong. I wasn't that kind of lady, not any more. "That sounds like it could work."

"Fantastic." Devich clapped his hands together. "I'll, well, get going then."

Drilled into the wall beside my door was a smaller crystalline screen, a miniature of the pion lock at the front. Reprogramming it without access to pions would have been impossible, but together, Devich and I managed to alter its systems so it would accept his touch as well as mine. He had to tell me what the pions were doing, and move them around while I kept what I hoped was a calming hand on the screen. Pions are not easy to fool, and they rejected him three times before gradually coming to accept that he could be trusted. The whole process left me feeling shaken and exposed. It was like Devich had just helped me walk, or see, or talk: any of those faculties I'd always taken for granted.

When we were done I kissed his warm lips. "Don't be too long." He didn't quite run out of the apartment, but it was close.

Alone in the quiet and dim light I had craved all afternoon, I felt strangely at a loss. Rather than dwell on it, I unfolded the piece of paper that had been left on my doorstep.

I recognised the letterhead before I had read any of the words, scrawled on thick paper in heavy ink. My heart dropped. Walrus tusk and bear claw clashed in vibrant orange and yellow against a pale violet image of the Keeper at daybreak. Proud Sunlight was one of the top universities, accepting only those with the strongest skill.

It is with regret we hear of your misfortune. Please accept our condolences. We trust you will understand our position...

I scrunched the Other-damned thing in my hand. I knew what it would say. Sunlight had a reputation to look after, couldn't have the name of a lowly debris collector sullying its spotless honour roll. For a long and heavy moment I cradled the ball of paper against my stomach like a wound. But there was no point standing like that forever. So I did as I'd told Devich I would. I bathed.

The bandages came off grudgingly; Eugeny's paste had stuck to the fabric and to my skin with equal vigour. But, when they did come off, they left me surprised and pleased. The horrible red puckering from the night before was gone, the wounds were smooth and pink. Nothing itched, nothing ached. My stitches, my scars, they felt normal.

Normal.

A knot, at the arch of my hip, was loose. I gave it a little scratch, and the thread broke, slipping from my skin clean and quickly. A few tugs and the whole thing unwound, leaving only a line of pink skin and the promise of a scar. I stared at my reflection for longer than I should have. The scars from *Grandeur*'s fall were part of me now. They weren't some ghastly second layer of skin that did not belong. Sure, the rest of the stitches would slip away,

160

the raised scarring would retreat, and the whole thing fade to white. But I would never be free of them.

They were my scars.

Shivering, despite the room's steady temperature, I ran my bath. A light pat of the switches above two bear's head taps and water gushed from their roaring brass mouths. And it smelled. Eugeny's water, heated by flame and carted up stairs by a volatile young man, hadn't smelled like this. Like metal, like rust, like something else I couldn't identify. The scent of the sky before a lightning storm, heady, and tickling the back of my throat.

I dropped capsules of aloe and oil into the running water, then a small shovel of earthy Dead Salts, and finally crystalline petals that dissolved and released a smell like roses. Yet, as I eased myself in, wincing as the golden paste washed away and a few of the wounds stung, I could still smell that lightning-sky tang.

Devich returned as I was dragging myself from the still-warm water. I wrapped myself in a towel as he strode down the hallway, a large box in his arms, and called me.

"I have a treat for you, my–" he stopped short as he spotted me "–lady."

I watched his eyes trace over my short hair, darkened by water and slicked out of any shape. As they took in the unbandaged scars on my face, the openings in my neck, the cuts along my shoulder and my arm, and down beneath my towel. I waited for the grimace, for the excuses, the reasons that weren't truly reasons to leave.

He gave me none.

"You're beautiful, Tanyana."

I raised my eyebrows at him.

"And you wear your suit so well."

The suit. I lifted a naked arm. The cleaned bracelet shone bright ciphers against my shoulder, on Devich's face, on the wall and the ceiling around us.

"It's beautiful, on you." Was it me he stared at so hungrily, or the shining metallic creature he had created?

"I have to clean these." I swept a hand over the scars on my shoulder. He spared them barely a glance. "I won't be long."

And his silent adoration vanished with a grin. "Don't be. I told you it's a treat." He hurried to the kitchen like an excited schoolboy.

I washed my scars with fresh water, but couldn't quite remove all of the golden paste. The new bandages were rough. My collector's uniform was so uninviting I almost felt physically ill at the prospect of dragging it on. But I couldn't ignore Kichlan's warning, however much I wanted to forget about both brothers. As I pulled it over my head I noticed that the thick, boned, strangely stretching material that held no bodily smells, no dirt, and no stains, somehow smelled like Eugeny's fireplace and a goosedown bed.

I didn't bother fussing with my hair. Devich had said to hurry.

He didn't seem to notice the uniform as I entered the kitchen, wearing satin bedclothes over the top and hoping their design of dark water and red carp would keep it hidden. He stood, chest wide and thrust forward, arms open over a feast laid out on the clean kitchen bench.

And it was a feast. Good enough reason, I supposed, to feel insufferably proud of himself.

"My lady." He mock-bowed, arms sweeping forward, brushing against a decanter of wine and grabbing it before it could fall.

162

"How did you do this?" I gaped at the food, and my stomach rumbled loud appreciation.

Devich laughed. "Don't question how the food is come by, care only for how it tastes."

"Devich's own words of wisdom?" I arched an eyebrow.

"Hardly. Something my father used to say, when his rublie was particularly empty. Now–" he rubbed his hands together "–can I help you to your table?"

I mused over this small slip as Devich held out a chair and sat me at my small pale lacquered table. Not from a family of debris technicians then? Not the kind of family who had always worked for the veche, always created arcane and complicated suits, and had rublies full enough to prove it. There was more, perhaps, to Devich's easily cultured civility.

"What can I offer you first?"

I found it difficult to keep my attention from his shoulders, as they strained a shirt that simply couldn't be wide enough to fit them, or his narrow, belt-tightened waist. Scrounging through the drawers he found cutlery enough to serve his feast, and rolled his sleeves up to do so. His forearms were muscled, well defined, their hair fair.

I swallowed against a lump in my throat. "Give me a bit of everything." My stomach gurgled at the idea of a measly *bit*.

Devich had brought fish. Fish. Raw salmon in slivers with lime and pepper dressing. Two large tuna steaks, grilled, and topped with thickened sour cream. Trout in a gelatinous sauce with root vegetables so fresh they were still topped with leaves. A salad of crab and green beans. Even prawns, darkened to red by a chilli crust.

More food than the two of us could eat together, even though we focused on the eating in near silence.

Finally, he heaped sugar-sprinkled strawberries on a plate, and we picked at them.

Devich leaned in his chair as he dusted pale sugar onto his knees, smugly. I supposed he wanted compliments for the food he didn't prepare, or perhaps, for the kopacks that bought it.

"Delicious," was all I could get out.

"Wasn't it?" He stood, graceful and smooth, swept plates from the table and piled them on the bench. For the cleaner. I stared at them. There were boxes in a heap on the floor beside the bench. Had he carried them all himself, or simply directed a young chef's apprentice to do it for him? Had he walked, or hailed a landau for the trip?

"Now, my lady, if you're still interested in tea." He held out a hand, and helped me to my feet. My stomach felt strange, not what I would call pleasantly full, just heavy. The result of such rich meat and thick sauces, I supposed.

"Yes. Tea would be lovely." As long as I didn't have to watch him drink it.

"You look tired." Devich traced his finger beneath my left eye. I glanced away. "Sit in your chair, and I will bring you tea. Can't have you too exhausted, can we?"

Despite myself, I grew hot as I left the kitchen and sank into the chair in my study. The lamp was low, its flicker unsteady. Like flames in a fireplace.

Devich brought me tea, and to my unmeasurable relief, hadn't made himself one. He sat on the floor, leaned against my legs, and wrapped an arm around my knees as I sipped. He was very, very warm.

"There's something I want you to do for me," he murmured, voice as soft as the lamplight.

"One meal and you'll think I'll do anything, is that it?" I sipped again.

He didn't laugh. "This is a favour. One friend to another."

"Is that what you are? I thought you were my over-enthusiastic tailor."

"And this is me being serious, Tanyana."

"Then this is me listening, Devich." What right did he have to sit at my feet and be serious?

"Good, then this is what I want you to do. I want you to stop hiding yourself, my lady. I want you to stop believing any of what has happened makes you different."

The porcelain rim of the cup rested against my teeth. Steam moistened my upper lip. "Stop hiding?" I squeezed the handle so strongly my hand began to shake. "How dare you—"

"No, I'm not going to take any of that from you." Devich unwrapped himself and sat back. His green eyes seemed darker, the lines of his face stern. But far from making him unappealing, I found him arresting. More than with his smiles and easy laugh.

I set the cup at my feet. "You don't know what you're talking about."

"Yes, I do." He held up a hand. I surprised myself by shutting my mouth against a building tirade. "I've told you this before. You're not the first debris collector to pass through my door."

"Only the strongest," I murmured, and didn't say what that really meant. That I'd had more to lose, and fallen further.

"I fitted a suit once," Devich said. "To a woman not much younger than you. She was beautiful, and had been talented. An artist, I believe. Something to do with sculpture."

Had she fallen through glass so half her face was unrecognisable?

"She mastered the suit well, although with none of your natural flair, and was allocated to a team in the outer western rim of the city. Far from the Tear."

"You followed her around too, did you?" I asked.

"It was a good suit. I'm interested in the performance of all my suits."

"Helped that she was young and beautiful."

Devich flashed me a frown, and looked for a moment like he might argue, but ultimately did not rise to the bait. Pity. An argument would have been more interesting than any moralising tale. He said, "I watched it happen in fragments, in the flashes of her life I saw each time I stopped to check and tune. I watched her fall apart."

I collected my tea and began sipping again. If Devich was trying to frighten me he had no idea how far I had already fallen.

"She lost her home," he continued. "Her colleagues, her friends. Then, well, I can't quite say what she lost next. Nothing you can touch, nothing you can buy. I suppose you could call it spirit."

"She lost her spirit?" I couldn't hide the cynicism I my voice.

"Whatever made her, her. Her identity, maybe, her reason to be."

Was he really that blind? Did he really think I was still holding onto those things like a cat clinging to a tree? Surreptitiously, I sank into my antique leather chair. I tried to ignore the food I had just eaten, the bath I had just taken, the apartment address so far from my collecting team I could conceivably take a tent and supplies each time I travelled between them.

No, not holding onto any vestiges of an old life. Not at all.

"I saw it happen," Devich said. "Her clothes weathered and her hair grew tattered and her skin dirty and grey. She stopped cleaning, she stopped washing. Finally, she stopped eating. I'm glad I didn't find her. By the time I returned to check on her she had been dead for nearly a moon." He sat back against his heels. "It was a fine suit, some of my best work. A waste."

"Is that why you bought me evenbell supper tonight? Think I'm going to starve myself to death, do you?"

Devich jerked his head up. "You don't do serious very well, do you?" he snapped.

With a sigh, I wrapped my hands around my tea and let its warmth seep into my palms. "I understand what you're saying, Devich. I do. But I don't know what you want me to do about it. This–" I gestured at my face, at my wrists, and nearly unbalanced tea into my lap "–I am different because of this. I'm not even a pion-binder any more, let alone a circle centre. So when I say I'm no one's lady any more, I mean it. That title no longer applies to me. I am less than I was, in many ways. Only you don't see them."

But when I looked up to meet his fervent eyes, his flushed, defiant face, my certainty wavered. He really didn't care about the scars, did he? Or the bands of silver. Or the loss of status, and lack of kopacks. He saw me, only me. Not the difference between me as I once was, and me as I was now. Just me.

I swallowed hard. Only me.

"What do you want me to do?" I whispered, uncertain.

With a triumphant smile he leaned forward, he eased the cup from hands reluctant to give it up and clutched them instead. "Come with me, back into the world. Put on your old dresses–"

I arched an eyebrow.

"–your best suit then," he chuckled. "Come with me and show this world who knew you, who respected you, that you are still the same. That nothing has changed."

I tugged a hand from his and pressed it to the scars on my face.

"You have nothing to be ashamed of," he whispered. "So promise me you will."

Slowly, I slipped from the chair and sank to the floor by his side. I held his face in my hands, kneeled, pressed my chest to his and felt him breathe.

"I will," I whispered onto his lips. "I will." Then I took his mouth with my own, and his knees gave out and we fell sideways, locked together, fighting the chair legs and the pale-fringed edge of a rug.

The floor was cold and hard, and Devich soon stood and pulled me to my feet. We made our way from wall to wall. He pressed me against them, ran his lips over my cheeks, my neck, and made no comment when he came to the thick collector's uniform. I realised he probably knew what it was, and had always known I must have been wearing it.

I no longer cared. My bedclothes fell in the hallway. I yanked his shirt apart, impatient with buttons, and left it hanging from the handle of my bedroom door. His pants were a thick, woollen weave that must have been hot, must have been itchy. I noticed this dimly as I undid more buttons and let him step out of them. They fell smoothly.

"What about this?" Devich hooked his fingers around the collar of my uniform.

I stepped back from him, breathing so quickly and strongly my chest strained against the boning. Devich, wearing only underdrawers but not awkward in the least, watched the rise and fall of my breasts with satisfaction.

"Collector's uniforms are so very interesting. At least, they are on you."

For a moment, I hesitated. Hysteria bubbled up within me as I realised Kichlan hadn't explained the sex etiquette regarding the uniform. Was I supposed to lie with Devich with the damned thing on too?

"Not so interesting as what's underneath." Devich grinned at my hesitation.

Kichlan could be damned to all the Other's hells, as far as I was concerned. I stripped the uniform off. It left lines on my waist and chest, thin pink indents from the boning.

Devich didn't say anything more. He simply wrapped his arms around my shoulders and nearly squeezed the breath from me as he kissed me.

I didn't see him remove his underdrawers, but in a moment he was spreading me on the bed, hot mouth kissing my lips, my forehead, my cheeks and neck. And he was hot and hard against me, rubbing the inside of my thigh, smearing something warm and moist onto my skin. Gasping, I arched, thrust up my hips. But he held back.

One hand stroked my forehead, fingers light and gentle. The other cupped my right breast, squeezed it slowly, tipped my nipple upward so he could dip his mouth down and taste me like cream.

I groaned and clutched his buttocks. I squeezed them and tried to push him into me.

A flash of delighted green and a soft laugh. "But, what about..." His hand left my breast to wave softly over my belly.

"I have the necessary precautions." I didn't want to think about such pragmatic, sensible things. "Don't worry."

"Gladly."

Then Devich slid into me and I arched again. He bent his head, tongue flicking over my erect nipples with each thrust, until I grabbed his head and forced him to suck. To squeeze. To nibble.

I lost all sense of time with Devich upon me. Beside me. Behind me. His touches were warm, his tongue hot, his body muscled but lithe and dexterous. He held me like I was more than a coat rack to hang his precious suit on, like I was indeed a lover. A friend.

Finally, when I was sore and content, when my bandages were lifted and loose with sweat, he spent himself within me and lay quiescent at my side.

For a moment I stared down at his face, young in the lamplight, without his serious or mischievous mask on. Too young and handsome for someone like me. He was an image of life before *Grandeur*, of its pleasures and its beauty. He did not fit with the fallen and scarred.

I placed a soft kiss on his lips. He stirred enough to return it, but I eased him down and told him to sleep.

They were in a small jar at the back of one of the drawers in my dresser. I had bought them years ago, and hoped the pions were still active.

The pills were small and bright red. As I held one up I remembered the way they used to look, filled with buzzing lights, a hive of activity.

I swallowed the pill with a dry throat, and returned to

Devich's side. As I lay flat, hand on my naked belly, I hoped the pions from that pill were already doing their work. I hoped they were destroying the possibility of any child that might have come from Devich and me.

7.

Light snapped on and flooded my dark bedroom, jerking me from a dream that might have involved Kichlan being chased by a giant cat. That, or talking brickwork.

With a cry I lifted my hand to block my eyes, but that only made the radiance brighter. I struggled to sit up, tangled in my own sheets and tipped fighting to the floor.

"Other!" Devich swore from the bed. "Point it at the wall!" He yelled. "The wall!"

"Point what?" I screamed back. Why were we shouting at each other?

"Suit, Tanyana. The suit!"

Kicking against tight blankets I wriggled until I could press my back against the side of the bed. Then I waved my wrists around, no idea how to point the suit at anything without crashing into it and causing yet more unaffordable damage. But I must have done something right, as the band on my right wrist gave a low clicking sound and as quickly as it had sprung to life the light dimmed. I opened my eyes a crack to see the suit's shifting symbol patterns beaming from my right hand and reflected large on the bare wall opposite the bed.

"Oh, Other!" Devich swore again. "You've been called."

"I've been what?" I freed my feet, pushed myself into a sitting position still wearing the sheets like a cocoon. "What are you talking about?"

But Kichlan's warning muttered in my mind before Devich could answer, "It's an emergency. Something's gone wrong."

"With debris?" Feet on the floor, free arm pressing sheets against my chest, I hauled myself up. Where was my uniform? Why hadn't I put it back on? Wasn't this what Kichlan had said could happen?

"What else?" Devich slipped from the mattress with delicacy and enviable decorum. Nude, he crossed to the signs. They ebbed and glowed the same way they did on the suit, only writ large, and revolved in great slow arcs as I gradually turned my wrist.

"How do you know something's gone wrong? How can you be so sure it's debris?" And why hadn't I been told this was going to happen? Symbols on a wall, bright lights in my sleep, and I had no idea what any of it was trying to tell me.

"Because I designed your suit." Devich ran a hand on the wall beside the reflected ciphers. "I tested it for three solid moons, I know a call when I see one."

"Then what does it mean?" The floor was cold; wooden floorboards seeped chills up through my calves. I flexed my toes, shifted weight from the ball of one foot to the heel of another. The symbols moved with me.

"Keep it still!" Devich snapped. He ran a finger over the top of a box-like symbol before it shifted away into nothing. "Your team leader must have explained this to you."

"No." Kichlan had started, hadn't he? Wear your uniform, Tanyana. Because you'll be called, Tanyana. By the suit. The suit. Always the suit. Perhaps I hadn't been all that interested in listening. Yet, as Devich frowned, I found myself explaining, "But really, it's been hectic, accidents, snow storms." Why was I defending Kichlan of all people? "At least I have you here to teach me."

He shook his head. "I don't know how to read it. The men you met in the hospital, remember them? They send the call, they could tell you what this all means. Technicians like me, we just make sure your suit can hear it."

"Oh." My heart did a half-beat. Those men, oh yes, I remembered those men. "Can you try?"

I kept my wrist up as I scrambled on the floor with my left hand for the bottom half of my uniform. I had managed to pull it up to my thighs before Devich answered "The call is a map. Of a kind."

He didn't fill me with confidence.

"Not of the city, though. It's a map to debris."

Was it? I glanced down to the signs beating out their light on my wrist. Did it only respond to a call? Or was this how Lad found his debris so well? Somehow, the idea of Lad reading a complex set of symbols imbedded in his own suit didn't make a lot of sense. Particularly if Kichlan and the others couldn't do it.

"How does it work?" Topless, pants scrunched around my thighs, I shuffled close to the wall. Devich glanced at me and flashed a sudden and very filthy grin, before helping me pull them up the rest of the way. I tried to focus on the map and ignore the occasional slip of his fingers.

"Well, from what I have been able to ascertain, although I've never actually been taught, this one, here–"

he tapped on the box symbol again, although this time it looked like it contained a bolt of lightning and some dots "–this is the one you need to pay attention to. This is the debris you need to find."

It was the darkest of the symbols, the most solid, and hovering around the top of the roughly rectangular band beamed onto the wall. It swam on the crest of so many ciphers all with strokes and dots and jagged lines and was difficult to differentiate. "The debris that set off the call?"

"I think so."

"How am I supposed to know how to get there?" I spotted my uniform top half hidden beneath a cerulean throw that had been kicked from the end of the bed.

"You need to find your symbol first." More searching, face so close to the wall I was surprised the light didn't hurt his eyes. "Ah, here we go. This is the suit owner. I think."

I abandoned the attempt to fish my top out from the throw with my toes alone. Devich pointed at a squiggly image, the brightest of the symbols, but tucked all the way down in the bottom left corner of the rectangle. It looked like a dot under a small hill.

Devich sucked his teeth. "You have a long way to go."

Just what I wanted to hear.

"The debris symbol is far away from your symbol, and it's dark. The closer you get, the brighter it will become, and the closer *you* will move to *it*."

"What about the rest, that mess of symbols?"

Devich shrugged. "Don't know. But as long as you head toward the debris symbol, you should get there."

"Assuming you're right about them."

"Yes."

I had to finish dressing then, map or no map. As soon as I lowered my arm the light disappeared, and for a moment I panicked in darkness. But it wasn't fully black. My suit still glowed, giving me just enough to see by as I fumbled for the lamp valve. I tugged on my uniform top.

"Now what do I do?" I didn't bother with proper clothes. A knit with a warm neck, the thickest pants I could find, boots that wouldn't close around my suit properly, and gloves. I had to leave gaps, a space between the clothes at my waist, a way to expose the bands on my neck, wrists and ankles.

Devich had pulled on underdrawers and his shirt. He shivered. "You should hurry," he said, and wrapped his arms across his chest.

"Why don't you come with me?"

But Devich shook his head. "I would be in the way. A single useless pion-binder, unable to see, unable to help. You don't want me there. This is your chance to help people, to show them what debris collectors can do. I don't want to get in the way of that."

What could debris collectors do? And how, exactly, was I supposed to hurry across Movoc-under-Keeper without a full rublie? I headed for the door anyway. Devich followed, and helped me drag on my jacket.

"Be careful. Hurry, and be careful."

Be careful? How dangerous could it be? I thought he didn't know anything about debris collecting, anyway.

With the map clear in my mind and nothing else to go by, I decided to head right. If I was in the bottom left of all those bright symbols, somewhere, then I should probably head right.

At first, I tried running. But my lungs burned with the cold air, and my stiffened muscles and stitch-sore skin protested painfully. I resorted to a brisk walk, which simply did not feel fast enough.

The snowstorm had passed through and the night was clear. Frigid, and clear. The Keeper Mountain loomed large against the quiet night, its snowcap and sides like dull silver in the moonlight. My calves burned, my boots soaked through, the bottom of my pants grew wet, heavy and dripping. I kept walking. Each time I aimed my uncovered wrist at a wall, the map shone forth and I changed direction slightly, heartened that I seemed to have the right idea, but frustrated by how slowly my sign made its way through the others, the ones I did not understand.

A bell rang, I had no idea which one. The snow seemed to soak up its deep artificial chimes so they didn't even echo. I nearly ran into a small Fist of enforcers, patrolling the streets closer to the river. They were dressed all in black, and a small blue light bobbed close to the ground in front of their feet. Lamplight and moonlight wasn't enough to march by, apparently. I darted into an alleyway and waited for them to pass, not even sure why. I had a legitimate reason to be running around at moonbell, or silentbell, whatever the time was. But still, it felt safer to wait, and continue once they had gone. The streets all looked the same: the snow concealed landmarks, brickwork, anything that would have helped me identify where I was. At one point I passed what had to be a lamplight factory. Working through the night, of course, when their pion-binding skills were needed the most. Loose beams of light danced around the building like smoke: pions that had escaped the systems that should have sent them out across the city, I guessed, and were happily creating their light right here, right now. I slowed at the sight. It was beautiful, in the middle of so much darkness and snow.

Eventually, one of the factory workers stepped outside. He waved his hands and spoke to the errant particles in a weary voice. "Come now, what is this? What do you all think you're doing? Stop playing and get back in line. You have a duty, remember?" Slowly, the light dimmed. I could imagine those pions once dancing across walls and rooftop and out into the street, now subdued and following as their binder headed back inside.

A duty, like I did. I hurried on, feeling just as weary as he sounded, and just as constrained by duty as his pions. But I seemed to be making some progress, as the debris symbol was growing brighter, sharp as a star carried on my wrist. And it was in this brightness that I saw tracks in the snow. Wheels, and unbelievably, hooves.

I could think of no one but debris collectors who would rely on a horse-drawn coach. I ran again, pushing my body beyond its soreness, beyond the cold, and followed the horse tracks around an unlit corner.

And into chaos.

Debris clung to the side of a building like a great, wiggling fungal mass. It was nothing like the little pieces of dark flesh I had seen so far. This debris looked alive. Alive, and threatening. But worse than that, worse than the squid-sentience in its bulging, thrashing appendages, was its shadow. And that, surely, was all it could be. Something dark, flat, wrapped over the wall of the building like a sheet of taut fabric. It stretched further too, away from the debris mass, lancing across streets to the roofs of adjacent buildings. Black sails. Grey sheets of paper. Great, gaping holes with sharp, straight edges and nothing but darkness, impossible, impenetrable darkness worse than the night on the other side.

I shivered, remembered the debris Devich had shown me when we first met. The same thing yet many, many times larger. Behind poly it had been strange. Here, arching over me, it was terrifying.

And there was so much of it.

Lights flickered along the street and in the windows of the surrounding buildings. Lamps desperately trying to cling to life, flaring brightly as their pions overcompensated, then sputtering back into darkness. The debris was doing that, it had to be. Interfering with the systems that carried the pions here, and then weakening their bindings when they arrived. And that wasn't all. Steam gushed from vents in the ground: heat that should have warmed homes all going to waste. I gave the hot, hissing air a wide berth and imagined that spurting into my apartment, scalding anything and anyone it touched. Water had burst from a pipe running the height of the building the debris clung to. How much longer did we have until the rest of the pipes gave way, or the bonds holding the very buildings themselves crumbled?

A semicircle of spectators curved around the building and its parasite, closer than I would have risked to the falling water, the steam and the lights. They watched as Kichlan and his collectors fought in vain to cut the debris down.

I pushed my way through.

Kichlan – arms and suit immersed in a lower section of debris – turned to face me, and his expression grew as dark as the night.

"Where have you been?" he hissed. The veins in his neck, the twitch of his shoulders and jaw told me how much he wanted to roar those words at me. But not with so many people watching.

I didn't bother answering. We could have that argument another time. Instead, I focused on the debris. I could see what Kichlan and the others were trying to do. Jars lay scattered on the ground at each collector's feet, some full to their seal with debris, most open and ready. Piece by squirming piece the collectors were slicing the debris with knives of sharpened suit, cupping it in hastily made spoons, and tipping as much as they could into the open jars.

It was slow work, imprecise, and I could see instantly that it simply would not work.

"What about the sails?" I asked Kichlan.

He was focused hard on a piece of debris, too large to fit through the lip of a jar. He used one hand to cup it and another, suit metal flattened and rounded, to keep it still. But shadows, smaller planes of darkness, were flickering through the gaps between his hands, arching into the air and back to the mass on the building wall. So, for each slice the collectors cut off, they managed less than half into the jars, and the debris was just as big, if not growing larger, than it had been a moment before. This was not a battle they were about to win.

Not a battle *we* were about to win.

"What in Other's hell are you talking about?" Kichlan snapped.

"The flat ones." I fumbled for a word to describe what I was seeing. "The shadow."

"Plane form." Sofia approached, one hand carrying Kichlan's brown leather bag, the other wrapped tight and silver around a squiggling clump. "The normal debris is grain form."

Yet another vital-sounding piece of information Kichlan had not to bothered to tell me. I was gathering quite a list of those.

"Plane form, then. Why aren't you collecting them too?"

Kichlan funnelled most of his debris into the jar and forced the lid closed. I was surprised by how much the container could hold.

"We're going to run out of jars," Sofia said, and placed the bag at Kichlan's feet. It clanged with thick metal.

"The veche will send another team to help." Kichlan jerked his head to the debris cluster. "They have to. We can't handle something this big ourselves."

"What if they don't?" Sofia asked. In the light from our suits her face was worried, grave. "What will we do?"

"What are you doing?" a spectator called from the crowd behind us. "Can't you see what this is doing to my apartment? Can't you work any faster?"

Kichlan gritted his teeth and said nothing.

"What about the plane form?" No one had answered me.

Sofia sighed, loudly. "Just follow our example and help us, Tanyana. We need to work quickly, and will explain things later." She walked around the debris, and selected another protrusion to start slicing.

"But if we don't contain those planes we'll be here forever," I hissed at Kichlan, very aware of the anxious eyes and ears behind me. "Just look at them. They're growing. For every solid bit you all cut off, those planes just stretch out a little further. Ignoring them won't help."

"You can see the plane form?" Mizra came to deposit his full jars in the bag.

I nodded.

"Haven't got any more surprises hidden there, have you?" Mizra grinned. How could he be so relaxed?

"Could we please focus on the debris?" Kichlan asked with a long-suffering groan.

"Exactly!" Another voice from the crowd followed by rumbling, general agreement.

The suit on Kichlan's right wrist expanded, narrowed into tweezers and stretched until he could grip one of the debris's dark protuberances. His left hand curled into a long, fine blade and sliced it free from the mass.

"I am." I grabbed Kichlan's elbow. "We need to focus on all the debris. The planes too."

"Then how would you like to handle this?" Kichlan rounded on me. His grip on the piece of debris slipped. It spilled into the air and floated, wiggling like a maggot, back to its friends. "There're only four of us who can differentiate plane from grain. Me, Sofia, Lad and you. What do you want us to do, try and catch them all ourselves?"

I ignored his scorn. "Can we catch them?"

"If you can hold a beam of light in your hand, then yes, you can catch them."

For a long moment I studied the planes. They stretched across the air, from grain mass to rooftop, lamp, or the ground. They lanced out of any debris the team was trying to collect like rays of sun through cloud, only black, or a very dark grey. But they did not set out on their own, arcing over the city like the sails of some ghostly ship. In fact, all of the debris, even the grains I had watched Kichlan and Sofia collect, had tried to return to the body.

"We need to spread our suits out–" I started thinking out loud "–if we can wrap around the whole thing, I think we could contain it enough to cut it from the wall."

"We don't want to contain it." Kichlan breathed heavily, like was all he could do to keep himself from shouting. "We need to get rid of it."

The team had started to converge. Sofia watched me avidly, like I was a fire about to run out of control. Lad, no longer tired and violent, smiled broadly. Natasha, Uzdal and Mizra appeared cautious.

"But we can't get rid of it if we can't contain it." I poked my toe at the bag of jars. They rattled loudly in the night. I found it curious that debris made no sound. Its planes should have rocked the street with thunder, its shuffling grains like snake scales.

"She's right," Mizra said in my defence, against the gathering shadow on Kichlan's face. "Isn't that what the jars do? Contain the debris, so it can be taken away?"

"Who has the strength to hold all that?" Kichlan shouted as he pointed at the debris. His suit sliced out into a long, thin spike. The spectators behind us gasped, and shuffled back a pace. "You think you do, is that it? You might be able to pick up bits and pieces we find in old lamps but this is something far beyond you!" Spit flew from his mouth. My suit lit it brightly as it fell. Both my wrists were shining fiercely and I was certain, if I rolled down my collar, untied my jacket, or undid my boots, the rest would be too.

"Not on my own, perhaps. But I am not alone, am I?" I turned to the others. Apart from Lad, who had began nodding violently and grinning like a madman, they stood like statues. "I thought we were a team. Why can't we do this together?"

"We were doing this together," Kichlan said between clenched teeth.

"Not properly."

Not the way a critical circle would.

I rolled my collar down and pushed up my sleeves. Bending, I undid the few laces I could tie on my wet leather boots, and hiked up my woollen pants. I shrugged my jacket from my shoulders and let it fall onto the wet street. My ankles, wrists and neck beamed cold blue light into snow and ice and stone, brighter than any of the others, brighter than Kichlan where he stood, gaping at me. It shone from my waist too, when my clothing moved enough to allow it to peek through.

I could forget the gaze of crowd behind me, and the small sense of decency and decorum I had left, to be working as a circle again.

"Are we ready?" I asked the collectors – my collectors – and tried to ignore how silly I must have appeared, with my clothes rolled up and my jacket in the sludge.

"We can't do this without you," Sofia told Kichlan, saying what I had not been able to.

"She doesn't understand any of this," he muttered. "She has no idea what she's doing."

"But we will need you anyway." Sofia placed a hand on his shoulder, and he seemed to shake himself beneath it.

"What would you have us do?" he asked me, voice thick and rasping.

"Make the circle." The words slipped from me before I could check them and my collectors took up the call. They spread out in a crescent around the corner of the building. "Alternate. Sofia, Mizra, Lad, Uzdal, Kichlan, then Natasha." I squeezed myself between Uzdal and Lad, and longed for the days of *Grandeur*, for standing high above the earth and watching as the sky filled with energy. "Right." I rubbed my hands, I loosened my wrists. "Plane first."

I raised my arms and extended my suit, using its silver to reach for sails of plane debris. It responded easily, eagerly, knowing what I wanted, doing what was needed.

Why was that a surprise? It was, after all, a part of me. I flattened it, curved it, linked left and right hand together and arched toward the debris like my hands – my suit – were a domed metal ceiling.

Kichlan, Sofia and Lad followed my example. Their suits spread out, spread up. Edges knocked mine like seams without stitches. Together, we slipped between plane and building, between debris and lamp, street, rooftop. The planes flickered, at first. Unsure. Then they fought back.

One large grey arc buzzed out of existence, then flared back into life a deeper, solid black. It battered against my suit with a sharp, clutching corner, fighting for the building, for the purchase I denied it. I felt each blow. Vibrations echoed through the suit, down into my arm and further, deeper into my skin, bones, head and mind. I steadied myself against it, pushing away memories of crimson pions and what it had felt like to be dragged to the edge of *Grandeur*'s palm. I would not let debris undo me the way the pions had. I would not fall from this statue, eight hundred feet in the air.

Sofia yelped, and her suit withdrew like a frightened cat.

"No!" I shouted over the rattling in my ears. "Keep your suit up."

Expression pained, Sofia extended her suit again.

"That's it! Now–" I glanced over at Mizra, Uzdal and Natasha waiting in anticipation. "We'll contain the planes, you slice the mass from the wall! Hurry!"

The planes flickered faster, as though in desperation, as though they knew what we were about to do. Sofia began to shake, but held her line.

Mizra and Uzdal darted beneath our silver dome. They reached the building wall, aligned their hands with the brick and shot sharp blades up through the clinging debris. The spectators gasped again. Quiet words reached me.

"Other!"

"How can they do that?"

"How horrible."

Natasha hesitated, suit extended to short knives.

"It's starting to give!" Mizra called. Natasha, with a jerking shake of her head, darted in to help.

"That's it, keep it going–" I called. The next smack against my suit knocked me to one knee. "What happened?" Another crash. Sofia faltered, her suit retracted, and Natasha leapt away from the wall with a curse.

I wasn't about to fall. My suit shot out from my ankles and tunnelled thick spikes into the road. The next push didn't budge me, I was buried too deep.

"Tell me what's happening!" I demanded.

"Doesn't want to, Tan!" Lad yelled, his voice high pitched and panicked.

"What doesn't?" I jerked my head around, searching for only the Other knew what. Some kind of interference, someone wielding fierce and fiery power.

"It's the debris," Kichlan answered.

Sofia faltered again. A wide plane flashed out from the debris mass and threw her to the ground. Her limp body jerked as her suit whipped back into her wrists. Kichlan withdrew and ran to her. Uzdal abandoned the attempt to cut debris from the wall and was tugging on his brother's hand, begging him to do the same. And still the stuff was growing, planes lacing the sky, grains bulging and wiggling. It pushed against my suit, but my ankles held firm and I realised that my legs would break before my metallic supports ever gave way.

Still Lad held his position beside me. Our suits were smooth and light-reflecting patches of sanity, of quiet and stillness, among the chaos and the sudden violence only we could see. Tears ran in thick rivers down his cheeks, but he did not falter.

"Doesn't like it," he whispered, over and over. "Doesn't like it."

"That's ridiculous!" I cried. A third spike, five inches thick and sturdy as earth, shot from the back of my waistband to crash through paving stones. I couldn't control it. "This is debris. It is a by-product, a waste. It doesn't care what we do to it, Lad. It doesn't care about anything. It doesn't think, it doesn't feel. It's waste, just waste."

I pushed my suit to spread further. If Kichlan and Sofia couldn't stand in the face of some particularly putrid garbage, then I would do it for them.

I wrapped my suit around Lad's, all the way over the bulging mass until I touched solid brick. Something burned in my arms, a deep and fiery ache, a scraping and a tugging at my bones. I didn't dare look down at them.

"Give up, Tanyana," Kichlan said, wearily, from Sofia's side. "You can't do it all yourself."

But I pushed on. Silver liquid poured out of the band around my neck. It coated my shoulders, my chest, the top of my arms before joining with the bands on my wrists. There, it boosted them, it sent its own strange metallic shape-shifting metal into the large, curved plates I had wrapped around the debris and helped me spread them further. But the burning replied in kind. It raced up my neck, caught in my throat, and it was all I could do to breathe around it.

"Careful," Mizra said, approaching me. "Don't push the limits."

My waist began to do the same thing. I couldn't stop it. I had called upon the suit and it was giving me everything, more than I wanted it to give.

"Kichlan!" Mizra shouted. "Get over here and help!"

Running feet and scuffles at my side.

"Tanyana, you have to stop it. You'll empty yourself. Tanyana, stop it!" Kichlan tried to grab my elbow. But a silver hand whipped out from my waist and smacked him away. I was wrapped in silver, a crawling armour coating me from my wrists to my waist.

"Doesn't like it," Lad kept murmuring beside me, rocking on his feet and crying. "Have to stop."

I nearly had the whole mass wrapped in silver. Just a snip from the wall now, a bend in my suit and a slice. I could do that.

"Lad!" Kichlan's voice cut through his younger brother's mumbling. "Stop her!"

In the corner of my eye I saw Lad flinch. He blinked, he stopped rocking, and he turned to me in horror. "Oh no!" he whispered, lips red and wet with his tears. "No."

He pulled himself from the sphere we had made, and wrapped a metal-coated hand around my forearm. Silver into silver. Suit to suit. He sank into me and distant, hissing voices surrounded me.

Don't like it, they whispered. *Don't like it*, they pleaded.

Shocked, I stared into Lad's concerned face. He was talking to me, red lips moving, but all I heard were the whispers.

Don't like it. Don't like it.

And then, like the clear chime of a bell.

Please stop.

"I'm sorry," I said. But not to Lad. Not to Kichlan hovering in the hazy background. Or Sofia, presumably still

188

lying prone on the damp paving stones. "I'm sorry," I told the whispers, and they were silenced.

"Sorry won't help you," Kichlan was saying. "You need to withdraw. Where do you think the suit comes from? How much metal do you think they've crammed into your bones?"

Lad had gone silent, and tipped his ear toward the debris, expression puzzled.

"If you dig any deeper you'll empty yourself out," Kichlan continued. "Your body will break. Your bones first, then your muscles, then your skin. You'll collapse in and the suit will still hold you up, keep you like this while you die. Do you want to stand here forever?"

Like a statue? I'd had enough of statues. I breathed, grounded myself with the air pressing in my lungs, just as I would have done before calming recalcitrant pions. Another breath, and I brought myself under control.

I eased my armour away. It slipped from my chest and arms like oil. The supports I had sent crashing into the earth withdrew, leaving gaping tunnels beneath the road.

But I continued to hold onto the debris. It had stopped fighting. Nothing pushed against my plates of silver, no planes were clawing into my very bones. Everything was silent, everything was still.

I realised Lad had his bare hand on my arm, his suit also withdrawn. His thick fingers were so warm I could feel them through layers of uniform and clothes.

"That is better," he said, and broke into his usual smile. "Doesn't hurt anymore."

"It is better," I said. Gradually, I retracted the rest of my suit and it felt like gorging on a large, fatty meal. My skin seemed to stretch, to bloat, and my bones were suddenly heavy.

"Oh, Tanyana," Uzdal gasped. "You did it."

I had kept my eyes on Lad's face as I summoned my suit inside. His encouraging, simple joy. But at Uzdal's words I turned to the debris and my hard-won calm fell away.

Gone was the parasitic mess of plane and grain. A single clump wriggled in the air beside the building's corner. I stepped forward. Nothing squirmed, no black sails fluttered. It was debris. The simple kind we found behind aging brick walls and in the cracks of lampposts. Nothing more.

"Here." Mizra handed me a jar.

Numb, I extended the very tips of my suit, pinched the debris out of the air and slipped it into the jar.

Thank you, something whispered.

"Thank you," Lad said.

As soon as I sealed the lid, the lights in the windows and nearby streetlamps steadied. Steam died with a soft hushing, and the broken water pipe stopped gushing. Pions re-established their systems, took back control. Even as we stood there each affected system would be activating emergency protocols, sending signals to the veche's city planning department. In the morning the relevant six point critical circles would arrive, and they would fix the damage.

The crowd, who could not have understood what they just witnessed, gave us a smattering of applause. Face hot, jar in hand, I found I had no idea what to do. It seemed somehow surreal, and the urge to bow or lift the container where they could see it, bizarrely out of place.

The rest of the collectors were equally bemused. Kichlan helped a shaking Sofia to her feet; Uzdal and Mizra grinned and waved; Natasha kept her back turned and Lad joined in the clapping, laughing loudly.

The accolades didn't last long. Soon, the chill of a Movoc night overwhelmed the appreciation of the crowd. The clapping petered out, and the spectators dispersed.

As I met Kichlan's furious eyes, I wished I could dissolve into the night with them.

In the middle of the snow-padded, ice-whitened street, he said nothing. He collected the bag of jars from the stones, took the one I was holding, added it to the clinking pile and tied the bag tightly.

"Natasha," he called her. "Could you bring the transport around, please?"

Puzzled, I watched Natasha head behind the building. We waited in the cold silence, Kichlan staring at the ground, until Natasha reappeared on the coachman's seat of a small, decrepit wagon pulled by a squat, shaggy horse.

A rusty axle squealed in the night. Painted in a peeling drab green, with cracks in what could once have been quite nice stained glass windows, I had no real way of knowing how old this former coach was. The wheels were wooden and bowed precariously, which gave it a bizarre, bobbing kind of movement. Where Natasha sat, all the cushions, the backing and any railings to give her some kind of safety were long gone. And the coach had no doors.

Kichlan caught the expression on my face. "Feel free to walk the way you came." He helped Sofia climb rickety stairs into the coach.

Mizra saved me from admitting I wasn't at all sure which way that was. "Don't be silly." He grabbed my hand and dragged me toward the coach. I was surprised to find Uzdal at my other shoulder, his hand at my lower back a gentle but no less insistent push to his brother's pull. "She's with us."

"She's one of us now," Uzdal chimed in.

I allowed the twins to bundle me into the coach. Sofia sat hunched in the middle of the opposite seat, left arm cradled around her middle, cheeks pale. Lad, Uzdal and Mizra squeezed in beside us. Kichlan told us there wasn't enough room for another body, and sat with Natasha at the dangerous driver's seat.

I had never ridden in a coach drawn by a horse before. The ride was bumpy, cold and slow. There were no cushions inside either, and the no-longer-sealed wooden seat was hard and threatened splinters when I tried to brace myself with my hands. Icy air washed in from the gaping holes that should have held doors. By the time we came to Darkwater, dawn was brushing faint pink against the Keeper, and ice clogged the steps and edges of the coach's empty door frames.

My collecting team disembarked in silence. Kichlan gave Natasha directions that could have led to Eugeny's house, and watched her, the horse and the coach rattle off into pale streets. The silence held as he unlocked the door, as he led us down the narrow stairs, and until he'd emptied the bag of full jars onto the shelves.

And then, the inevitable came.

Kichlan spun, he advanced on me like a hungry dog on a meal, and I fought to hold my ground. "You're dangerous!" He poked the air with a sharp finger. "You don't know what you're doing, you don't listen to instructions, you think you're still a veche architect and act like you're in charge and you nearly get people killed!"

"And you made a hole in the ceiling," Sofia added, her voice soft and words slightly slurred.

Briefly, I wondered how badly she had been hurt.

"Yes!" Kichlan was almost on top of me. I met his fury squarely. Veins purpled his neck, a blotchy red flush darkened his cheeks and forehead. "You've been nothing but trouble, like I knew you would be! We don't need collectors like you, collectors who think they're still too good for this role. You're a burden, and you're trouble."

"That would be two things," Mizra drawled.

I peeked over Kichlan's shoulder. Mizra lay on one of the run-down couches, his feet up, studying a stray thread he was pulling from his gloves.

"What?" Kichlan stopped trying to poke my eye out from a foot away and crunched the hand into a fist.

"You said she was nothing but trouble, and then that she was a burden too. That's two things. She can't be nothing but trouble and also–"

"Mizra, shut your useless, Other-made mouth!"

"Yes, Miz." Uzdal sat in the couch beside his brother, chin resting on the palm of his right hand. "Give Kichlan his due. I'm surprised he waited until now to start shouting."

"True, Uz, true," his brother answered. "We knew it was coming the moment he worked out who she was."

"You two." Sofia, face pale and hand shaking, made wobbly cutting motions in the air. "Stop it."

Kichlan seemed to be having trouble controlling his breathing. I watched a muscle twitching in his neck as he closed his eyes and squeezed his hands. "Where was I–?"

"Trouble," Mizra said.

"And a burden," Uzdal said.

"Brother?" Lad's voice was a small squeak in a room of loud voices. "Brother, please?"

If Kichlan heard Lad, he chose not to acknowledge him. "You–" he resumed his pointing-at-my-face violence "–should have listened to me. You're not too good to do what I tell you to, to come when you are called, to keep your mouth shut when I tell you to. To... to..." He seemed to have run out of words.

I looked straight into that red, panting face, and was calm.

Kichlan knew nothing about losing your temper. He did not understand putting the lives of others in peril. He did not know pressure, expectation, failure or horror. And he could not scare me.

"Have you finished?" I whispered.

The twitch started up again, fresh and violent. He opened his mouth; nothing came out.

"Then you will listen to me." I stepped so close his finger touched my forehead, just above my eyebrow. Right on a bandage. "Do not tell me what I think. Do not put attitudes in my head or words in my mouth."

"You–"

"No!" I cut across him, snapped at the air like I could bite it, like I could take a chunk of it into my mouth and tear at it with my teeth. "No! You have said enough. You will listen."

I was the head of a circle of nine, back in my life before *Grandeur*. I had kept the best under my control. The wealthy, the educated, the elite of the oldest families. This debris collector was a smudge on the bottom of my polished leather boot with the silver bear-head clasps.

"Whatever problem you think you have with me was yours before we met," I continued. "I fell far. I fell from wealth and status and you know that, and it eats you. Well, this is it. No more. Keep your attitude buried somewhere with your decency, somewhere the sun will never touch it. I don't want to hear about it again. The problem is yours, not mine. Not ours."

Sunlight glanced in through the narrow windows. A stray beam caught on the metal of an empty jar and sprayed across my face.

"I have not come here to wrest your petty leadership away. I do not want it, I do not want to be here."

"There, did you hear–?" Kichlan turned from me, imploring our small, silent audience. But I didn't let him. I reached up, grabbed his finger and jammed it against my bandage.

"What would you expect? That I would want to fall? That I would want this pain, this disfigurement? I have lost more than you understand. More than kopacks. More than status. More than the respect I worked so hard for so long to earn! What can you expect? That I should have wanted that all to happen just so I can be here, with you, chasing garbage for the rest of my life?"

He gaped at me, and had stopped trying to pull away.

"What else did you say? That I don't listen? That I don't do what you tell me to do? I have listened to what instructions you gave me, but do not criticize me for failing to follow the ones you didn't give!" I released his hand and waved my wrist in front of his eyes. "If you'd chosen to explain these things to me I might have known what to do when the call came, I might have known what a call was! As it is, you were lucky to have my help at all."

Not even Sofia leapt to Kichlan's defence.

Pale, still breathing quickly, as though he'd been running as I shouted at him, Kichlan lowered his hand.

"Now." I straightened, smoothed my sleeve and

brushed my hair from my forehead. "Was there any-thing else?"

"You still need to fix the ceiling," Sofia ventured.

Stiff, I gave her a curt nod. "And I will. When I can af-ford to do so." The last words tasted dry, sandy.

"You need to learn to control your suit," Kichlan said, when he had stopped panting. He stood tall, hands by his side. All thunder was gone from his face, in its place a kind of understanding. Like a clear sky.

"And I will." I hoped he could see the same in my face. "You know I will."

"Yes, I do. I should have realised earlier, I should have listened to L–"

Together, we looked at his brother, and the argument was instantly banished. Lad was pale, shaking. He had wrapped his arms around his chest and wept silently.

As one, the debris collectors went to his aid. Kichlan spoke softly into his brother's ear. Sofia, one arm still pressed against her waist, patted him with her free hand. Mizra and Uzdal hovered like fretting pigeons. I pried Lad's hands from the nook of his elbows and held them tightly.

"Stop shouting. Can't shout. He says not to shout," Lad murmured, rocking from heel to toe.

It took the rest of the morning to quiet Lad down. Fi-nally, when the noon sun was as yellow as a layer of cloud would allow, Lad was calm enough to be guided home.

I kissed Lad on the cheek and Kichlan graced me with a smile as we parted at the Darkwater street sign.

As it turned out the ferry did run on Rest, but its trips were few, slow and far between. By the time it had taken me to the second Keepersrill and I had walked the long streets home, Devich was gone. He had left a note under the remaining strawberries from the night before, and I ate them hungrily as I read.

Don't work too hard, my lady.
   Devich

8.

The next morning I developed a system. I rose at dawn-bell and pulled on loose clothes over my collector's uniform. Then I walked to the Keeper's Tear River and rode the ferry to Section ten. Each trip cost only twenty kopacks, but it meant a long trek down the eighth Keepersrill to Darkwater.

I knew, somewhere at the back of my weary brain, that I couldn't keep doing this forever. Travelling each morning was hard enough, and I couldn't afford the apartment itself for much longer. But it was my home, and so exclusive I had acquired its lease solely through the veche contacts of a member of my nine point circle.

I would hold onto it as long as I could.

The smell of food coaxed me down to the Darkwater sublevel. When I came to the bottom I realised some of the furniture had been moved. The table that held the empty jars was shoved inelegantly into the middle of the room, up against the end of a couch. The shelves had been pushed over to a corner. All this exposed an ancient, blackened fireplace, around which the entire team was huddling.

"What's this?" I called as I approached them.

"Morning!" Lad bellowed, and left the fireplace long enough to sweep me into a brief, crushing hug.

"Morning," I croaked once he had let me go.

Large, dusky embers glowed inside the fireplace, beneath two heavy iron pots. Something bubbled away under their half-closed lids and that was where the smell was coming from. The smell that set my stomach rumbling.

"Guess what?" Lad, torn between me and the allure of the embers, rocked as he shifted his weight between the two of us.

"What?"

"Guess what Kich did? He said we all did something wonderful last night and he was going to give us something. So, you know what he did? He cooked!"

"Did he?" The pots reminded me pointedly of Eugeny.

Kichlan smiled at me over his shoulder. "When Lad and I first came here the old team leader would complain about the loss of his fireplace. A lot. You know how some people can't stop griping about the same, small, pointless–"

Sofia cleared her throat discreetly.

"Anyway, before we weighed down the shelves with yesterday's jars, I thought I'd give them a bit of a push and see if the fireplace still worked."

Lad made inarticulate spluttering noises.

"Well, I asked Lad to give them a good push. Better?"

His brother nodded wildly.

"Big sixnight ahead of us, and nice to have hot food before we head out, don't you think?"

As the embers warmed my face I wondered how early Kichlan and Lad had arrived here, to get this all organised.

199

It was worth the effort. Lad collected seven wooden bowls into which Kichlan spooned a kasha of buckwheat and raisins, thick with butter, crunchy with pecans, spiced with cinnamon and sweetened with honey. On this he poured apricots stewed in vanilla and a splash of what had to be brandy. I ate it hurriedly. It made me warmer and more comfortable than I had felt for a long time.

Kichlan ate little, and gave most of his bowl to Lad. Before the rest of us had finished eating Kichlan was up, filling his leather bag.

He waited, bag over his shoulder, for us to stack used bowls, lick spoons dry and give him our attention. Then he crossed his arms, lifted his chin and addressed us like a general to his troops. "We have a lot to catch up with. Thankfully, due to yesterday's emergency we have managed to bridge the gap somewhat, but you can be damned sure the veche will take that into account. So we need to work hard. I see long days ahead of us this sixnight. We must stop at every corner, look under every lamp—"

Behind me, Natasha groaned. To my left, Mizra and Uzdal shifted simultaneous feet. Lad was watching his brother with something close to awe, and Sofia wasn't much different. All I could feel was a tired ache in my legs, but resolved not to let it show. This was my fault. I would help Kichlan correct it.

"—we must find every last grain of debris there is to be found!" Kichlan's voice rose, it echoed from the sublevel walls. Did he expect us to start cheering? "And we will rely on you, Lad, to do that." He stepped forward. He placed a hand on Lad's shoulder, looked him in the eye. "Can you do it? Can you help us?"

"Yes!" Lad shouted. Wincing, I pressed a hand to my ear.

"Then it's time to start." Kichlan pointed to the stairs. "Let's move."

Lad bounded out of the sublevel. Kichlan strode behind him with Sofia fluttering in his wake. The rest of us followed grudgingly.

"It's all for Lad's sake," Mizra murmured. "Just so you don't think we've all completely lost our minds." As we emerged into the sunshine he cast a hard look at Sofia's beaming, enthusiastic face. "Well, not all of us."

Lad was already ahead, pushing his way past boxes and down a narrow alley. I immediately understood why an eager Lad was an asset, and why keeping him happy so very important.

It didn't take him long. At the end of the alley he found a broken pipe, and smiled proudly as Sofia scooped a jar's worth of debris from its jagged hole. I didn't think he noticed when she got too close, however, and caught the back of her hand on its rusted edge. "Other," she whispered a curse, dug a kerchief from her pocket and wrapped the wound tightly.

The next cache squirmed with a nest of rats, beneath a large crate overflowing with rubbish. Sofia refused outright to collect from it. Mizra and Uzdal played some kind of complicated game involving hand gestures to decide which of them had to do it. I gathered the task was given to the loser.

By the time Uzdal, looking pale, had collected it all, we had another three full jars. I held back a sigh. Was this my life now? Rummaging in rubbish with vermin?

As we continued, Kichlan walked beside me. "I have done you a disservice." He clasped his hands behind him.

"Are you about to lecture me again?"

Lad pushed ahead, crossing a wider street and down

another alleyway. He looked intent, head down, whispering under his breath.

"I should have done the first one properly." As we followed his brother Kichlan explained about the symbols, about the map, things I should have learnt from the start. I listened, nodded, and didn't mention that I had heard most of this before. Or where I had heard it.

We stopped by a sewerage vent. Even I, with my untrained debris-collecting eye, could tell this would be a good spot: steam lurched haphazardly through the bars. Mizra used his suit to lift the grate without standing too close. Together, he and Natasha lay on the wet stones, shuffled as close to the edge as they could without burning their faces in the steam, and sank long, wide spades from their suits into the sewer. Unable to see what they were collecting they simply dredged up everything that was down there, and Sofia picked grains of debris from the mess. I looked away.

"What about the other ones?" I asked Kichlan, determined to do anything to try and ignore the smell rising with every spoonful Mizra and Natasha scooped up. I peered down at the turning and glowing of the ciphers on my wrist, their rising and sinking.

He was looking pointedly away from the sewer as well. "The other ones?"

"The other symbols. What do they mean?"

"Don't know. The map finds debris, that's what we're all told at the beginning. All we need to know is how to find and follow it in a crisis. The other symbols don't matter."

"Oh." Unsatisfied, I ran a finger along the smooth edging of the suit, brushing both metal and skin. Almost in response, two signs turned over and rose to the top. They shone brighter than any of the rest, but I had no idea what they were saying.

Even Lad was subdued when Natasha and Mizra finished with the sewer, and Uzdal replaced the vent. Four jars that time, but it took a whole bell to get it all.

Mizra stood, patted his wet, fragrant coat down. "Next time you see one of those, Lad my boy, ignore it. Please."

"Sorry." Lad sagged even further.

"Now, now." Kichlan hurried to his side. "That was the best haul we've had all day! It was worth the effort, and no one else could have found it."

Lad managed a small smile. I noticed Kichlan had positioned himself between his brother and Natasha, who looked decidedly unimpressed by his miraculous find and wasn't likely to be diplomatic about her opinions.

"So we'd better keep going," Kichlan continued. "Lots more to collect today."

Lad glanced around and lifted a cupped hand to his ear. "This way!" Again he was leading us, out of the alleyway and into a street lined by roaming food stalls. I was struck, suddenly, by the contrast between the dank lanes where we had spent our morning, and the bright, open, delicious-smelling street.

The food stalls looked very odd without their pions. Essentially a large box of clear poly inlaid in parts with steel, about four feet high and four feet wide, each one was attended by a three point circle. Together, the three pion-binders prepared the food and kept the stalls floating above the street, moving gradually so they could cover as much of the city as possible in a day.

The nearest circle was selling sweet potatoes. Deliciously hot, crunchy-looking, golden sweet potatoes. The vegetables were stored at the bottom of the poly, where they could be easily seen. For ten kopacks customers could choose their own potato. It would rise, tied in bright pion threads, to be roasted behind a metal screen, before finally emerging wrapped in a fresh, white napkin.

Without the entangling, driving lights the whole contraption was disconcerting. Hovering boxes, floating food, heat that seemed to come from nowhere. But despite how strange it all looked to me now, my stomach still urged me to slow. And as I turned to the food and the warmth, a man who had just bought one glanced at me. And dropped it.

I knew him. He knew me. And he left his food in the street, spun, and hurried away. I watched his back, his furtive glances over one shoulder, until he disappeared inside a building on the corner.

Construction for the Furtherment of Varsnia. Just some administrator, always behind a desk, pushing around kopacks and making sure I, and my circle, was paid on time. I couldn't remember speaking more than a few words to him. Certainly no reason for him to drop his food and run.

"Tanyana?" Kichlan called from far down the street. "Hurry up!"

I stared at the building for a moment longer, before shuffling as fast as my tight skin would allow to catch up with my team.

"What was that?" Kichlan asked.

Lad had found debris at a faulty heating valve. Of course, the valve was on the roof of a six-story-high building and surrounded by scraggly pigeons attracted to the warmth. Apparently, it was my turn to collect it.

"Someone I recognised," I answered, as I sent poles into the ground from the bands on my ankles to propel

204

myself upward. Like I had done the other night, only this time on purpose. The birds flew away, I scooped the debris in a deep pot I made with my hands and was down again in a moment. Natasha looked disgusted, Uzdal gave me a nod.

Kichlan held out jars for me to fill. "A pion-binder?"

"Yes."

"Someone you worked with?"

"In a way." I hesitated. Torn. I needed to turn back, I knew it, I needed to find that man and all the veche representatives he worked for. But the quota... and Kichlan had gone to so much effort to make us dawnbell supper in the morning. "I need to talk to him." I swallowed guilt in my throat like a lump. "Now." I had to find that building, that administrator. I needed to pin him down and get answers.

Why had he run like that?

Kichlan held my gaze for what felt like a long and heavy moment. I knew what I was saying. I knew we had to use Lad's help while he was still in a good mood. But debris collecting wasn't my world, at least, it shouldn't have been. If I hadn't been pushed. If I hadn't been silenced. And I couldn't let it just go on. I had to grasp at the straw that had appeared so suddenly, then fled like I was the Other at its heels.

"I will go without you," I whispered.

Strangely enough, Kichlan wasn't angry. His neck didn't bulge in the kind of frustration I seemed to be able to bring out in him without trying. No disappointment either. "We have a long sixnight ahead of us," he said again. "Will this take long?"

"I don't know."

"Then we'd better come with you and make sure it doesn't." He smiled. "You can be useful to have around."

He gestured to the roof I had just cleared. "Can't just let you leave."

Together, Kichlan and I turned back to the street. Looking confused, Uzdal, Mizra and Sofia followed. Lad, easily distracted, bounded after us.

"As long as she gets the next sewer," Natasha muttered, and hung at the back.

I felt strangely strong as I walked down the wide street, flanked by my debris collecting team. Even though pigeon feathers had stuck in my hair, Sofia had a bloody kerchief wrapped around her hand, and Natasha and Mizra smelled like sewage. Even though Lad had started to skip, and attract wide, shocked stares.

The door was locked. I ran fingers over the soft crystalline pad and it buzzed an angry rejection. An old bronze plate was screwed into the brickwork beside the door, green with age and almost unreadable. I could make out "veche" though. Was there a sign below it, in bright pions I could no longer see? What was the administrator doing here? I had never travelled this far from the city centre to meet with anyone from the department, I didn't even know they kept offices outside of the city centre.

"It won't open. Pity." Kichlan leaned close to the panel, lifted his hand to rap against it. But he missed, and his suit knocked it instead. The crystal wobbled like water, sent out a high-toned screech, and the door unlocked with a click. "Oh my." Kichlan straightened. "What do you know?" His eyes were too wide, his face too innocent.

"How did you do that?" Sofia glanced between door and suit.

He shrugged. "It was an accident." He smiled down at me. "Well, didn't you want to get inside?"

It hadn't looked like an accident to me. Either way, he had opened the door. I pushed inside to a narrow and dimly lit hallway. Kichlan and the rest of the team followed.

There was something eerily familiar about the hallway. Its beige walls, the tiled floor, the lighter squares on the walls where pictures must have once hung. The whole place reminded me of the hospital building. Of where I had woken, and been suited.

It made me shudder.

The door at the end of the hallway was open a crack, letting out sharp beams of bright light. I pushed it, and sure enough the administrator was there, sitting behind a desk as he had always been, but looking pale, and flicking fingers and rambling at invisible pions.

He looked up, saw us, and lurched to his feet. "How did you get in here?" He looked around, eyes wide. What was he looking for?

I entered the room. It was far too warm, but I could see no heater. "Do you know who I am?"

He shook his head. "Of course not. Should I?" Sweat dripped from his chin.

I approached the desk, and could feel Kichlan and Lad close behind me. I said, "Don't bother lying." I placed my hands on the wood, flexed my fingers. My suit shone in his eyes and the administrator flinched back. "You recognised me, now you can tell me why you ran like the Other-cursed wind when you did."

The administrator's eyes flickered fast and panicked from my face, to what I could only imagine was Kichlan's thunderclouds, and up to Lad.

Then the large man crashed his fist on the desk beside me, and all of us jumped. "You tell Tan!" he bellowed, and the administrator stumbled back against the wall. "You stop lying to her and tell her!"

"Lad! It's all right, don't shout." Kichlan reached for his brother's arm, but Lad easily shook him off.

When I looked up at him, Lad had tears in his eyes, and his face was red. On him, it was frightening. "Not nice," he hiccupped the words, sniffed loudly. "Doesn't feel nice in here. And don't lie to Tan."

"All right." The administrator ran a finger around the edge of his high-collared yellow jacket. No wonder he was hot, wearing that in a room like this. "No need for threats."

Lad sniffed again, shifted and crossed his arms. Kichlan patted his elbow, looking helpless.

"Yes, I know who you are." The administrator drew a kerchief from a pocket and used it to wipe his face. "But if you're here for the kopacks you should know there's nothing I can do. I allocate payments, or retract those payments, based entirely on the instructions given to me. I can't just produce kopacks, no matter what you threaten me with."

I blinked at him. "Kopacks?"

"Don't tell me this is about kopacks!" Sofia snapped from behind me.

"It isn't." I straightened. "I don't remember your name."

"Pavel," he murmured. "I wouldn't have expected you to."

"Pavel, then." I walked around the desk to stand in front of him. Kichlan, I noticed, remained attached to Lad. "I haven't come to get my payment for *Grandeur* back, if that's what you think."

If anything, Pavel paled further. "Why are you here then? Trying to make things worse for me?"

"Worse?" I frowned, waved a hand at the room. "This isn't where you used to work, this isn't where I met you. So I could ask you the same question. Why are you here?"

Suddenly, he grinned. It was like a crack through his face, jagged, violent, harsh. "You really have no idea, do you?"

"What?"

Lad let out a damaged-animal groan.

Pavel said, "I'm not the only one. Everyone else in my office, all of the other administrators who helped you at some stage in their career, have been relocated to Otherholes like this place. Your circle members survived, they're too well connected to be pushed around so easily. But everyone else." He laughed, a ragged sound. "Even heard some woman on a desk at the tribunal chamber spoke to you and was sent to work in death records in the colonies! Death records! Can you believe it?"

Something hard and cold seemed to have been dropped in my stomach. "No." It set me shivering. "No, I don't."

He laughed again. "What are you here for, then?"

"I—" I swallowed. "I need your help, Pavel. You have contacts, you must have, in the veche. Like the people who send you those instructions! High up. I need... can you tell me who they are? Where they are? I need a tribunal opened, I need to tell the truth!"

"The truth about what?" Natasha muttered at my back. Lad sniffed loudly.

Pavel simply shook his head. "Did you hear me? No one would listen to me now, thanks to you. Whatever contacts I had, whatever career I had been building, they're gone. Gone! Because you touched my life, and you are Other-damned cursed."

Cursed? "Tell me who they are then, where they are, I'll–" I said.

"Listen to me, you debris-collecting bitch!" Pavel lurched off the wall and I realised how tall he was. He lifted a hand, I held a wrist above my face and my suit shone brightly on us both. "It's over! Over. Look what they did to us, we who hardly knew you. And we were lucky. Pale bastards with their wooden walk and those vacant, empty faces. We're lucky all we lost was our livelihoods, our careers, our status and our friends. Got no pity, got no feelings, got no limits to what those men – those things – will do! Truth, is it? Don't you understand? The truth is what the veche say it is, and you better just shut your mouth and do whatever it is they want you to do. Or people will stop disappearing and start dying, until finally, they get rid of you. Do us all a favour and kill–"

With a roar Lad tore himself from Kichlan's hands and barrelled forward. He knocked me to the ground, grabbed Pavel by his upraised hand, lifted him from his feet, and sent him crashing against the wall.

"Lad! No!" Kichlan stumbled after him.

Sofia dropped to my side. "Are you all right?"

I struggled to sit up.

Lad picked Pavel up again, held his shoulders in those huge hands and lifted him high. "No!" he roared into the man's terrified face. "You cannot lie to Tan! You cannot hurt Tan! No more!" And with a great twist and a heave he threw Pavel across the room, to crash over the desk and onto the floor.

Tears streaked Lad's face. He batted Kichlan aside like a fly, reached again for Pavel. Mizra began digging in his jacket for the little bottle that could quell him.

I stood. "Lad?"

Lad dragged Pavel up by the front of his jacket. He sniffed.

"Lad?"

He turned his wet, guilty face to me. "Tan?"

"It's all right, Lad. You can stop." I walked past Kichlan, I touched a hand to Lad's back. He shook beneath me. "He's not hurting me. He's not shouting any more. Thank you for protecting me. Please, Lad, put him down now."

Pavel dropped like a doll. He looked up at us with wide, frightened eyes. His forehead and left cheek were red and already swelling. One arm lay at a strange and painful-looking angle on the floor.

Lad turned into me, wrapped arms around my shoulders and started to cry. As I held him, I stared down at Pavel, who still hadn't moved. "I'm sorry." And I was. Not just for Lad. But for what his life had become, because of me.

Because I was cursed, and the puppet men seemed to be wreaking evil on everything I touched.

"We need to go." Kichlan gripped Lad's elbow, tried to peel him away from me. "Now." In his eyes I read fear and urgency.

I nodded. Together, we eased Lad into walking and left Pavel's office. I didn't look back.

I knew, without needing Kichlan to tell me, that there would be no more collecting today. The bell was late, and the streets full as we made our slow way back to the sub-level. Kichlan kept as close to Lad's shoulder as he could without tripping over his feet, and eyed each person that passed us with suspicion. Lad watched the ground, and sniffed constantly.

I'd ruined the rest of the day, created more work for the next five days, brought out the kind of violence in

Lad that Eugeny had warned me about. Strangely, Kichlan's silence made me feel worse. Spitefulness was, I supposed, easier in its way to deal with.

But I didn't feel as guilty as perhaps I should have. Because anger burned inside me again, even deeper than the suit. Pavel's story had fanned the flames.

None of this was right. I'd known it, felt it that moment on *Grandeur*'s palm, and every time I tried to speak the truth since. While the veche could silence me, while it could keep me busy with this garbage collection, keep me exhausted, aching and out of the way, it couldn't quench that fire. It could alienate the people I had once trusted, it could ruin anyone even remotely connected to me, but that wasn't enough.

Someone had summoned the crimson pions that had thrown me from *Grandeur*. Someone had done this to me. I would not, could not, forget that, not until I exposed them. Not until I proved to everyone that I had not been responsible for my own ruin. I would have my tribunal, I would tell the truth. No matter what I had to do to get it.

The crowded streets parted around our small debris-collecting team like weed-riddled water. I tried to ignore the affronted expressions, the touch of fingers to nose, the wrinkling of foreheads and the turning away. But still, I was glad when we stepped into Darkwater. The sublevel was a haven. Quiet, isolated and dark, with only sputtering lamplight flickering in from the windows near the ceiling.

I breathed in the memory of Kichlan's meal, and tension in my gut eased.

There in our space, we tarried as dusk fell in the world above ground. The thought of the ferry ride home during the night was less daunting than swimming through those crowds again. Instead, we pushed the furniture out of the centre of the room and arranged it so the fireplace was accessible. We discussed the possibility of more dawnbell suppers by ember-light. And each of us watched the windows, glanced at the glass-shadowed image of feet walking by, waiting for them to thin.

Sofia made the first move. She touched Kichlan lightly on the shoulder. "I have to go." Her free hand was on her stomach again, her cheeks still pale. What had happened when the debris had thrown her to the ground? Surely, if she was still hurting, she needed help? "I need my sleep."

I followed her, held her leather-lined coat with the embroidered floral buttons as she wrapped a scarf around her neck. It was so thick, and she so small, that she looked like a child in her parent's clothes. "Are you hurt?" I asked, voice low, glance deliberately shifting from her eyes to her hand.

She blinked away a moment of confusion. "Oh. No, Tanyana. I'm not."

"When you fell, when the debris hit you, it didn't, you know what I mean, hurt anything?" Now that really was my fault.

She must have seen it in my eyes. "Nothing to worry about." Her lips were also pale and they didn't reassure me, despite the rueful smile. "I made certain of that."

"Oh, good." Made certain? How much had that cost her? I itched to offer to pay for the healer, but I didn't even have enough kopacks for myself. "I was worried."

"I can tell." Sofia did the buttons on her jacket and tucked her scarf into its low neckline. The purple wool did compliment the jacket's green, I had to give her

213

that. "I'd feel better if you'd worry about the hole in the ceiling."

I blushed, and muttered something that didn't sound like real words, not even to me, as she left the sublevel. Only Mizra, it seemed, had noticed our conversation and he, thankfully, was watching Sofia instead.

Natasha followed Sofia's example and was above ground a moment later. Mizra and Uzdal told Lad stories for another bell, but left as the large man began to snooze where he was sitting.

Kichlan didn't hurry. He lit two gas lamps on the walls, apparently able to ignore their noxious smell. He cleaned his pots with snow gathered on the doorstep and melted by a small fire. He brushed ash from the floor in front of the fireplace and took it upstairs to dump on the paving stones.

I sat on a couch, watching Lad sleep and his brother fuss.

"He likes you," Kichlan said when most of his chores were done, and the silence had stretched out so long, and so comfortable. "That's why he acted like that today. He is not a violent man, just easily confused. He thought that Pavel man was hurting you. He just wanted to help."

"I know. And I like him too."

Kichlan picked up an empty collecting jar and tapped it against his palm. "I would tell you to be careful, but I think Eugeny must have done so already."

"He has." I stood, carefully, slowly, so I didn't disturb the sleeping man opposite me. Lad had his hands tucked up under his chin and was drooling gently onto his knuckles.

"Eugeny has much to warn others about." Kichlan set empty jars in straight rows on the tables we had repositioned against the wall. They reflected the lamps like fireflies against a steel sky. "And he cares about Lad nearly as much as I do. He wouldn't want to see Lad taken away, he doesn't want him imprisoned."

I stopped, my hand hovering above the tension in Kichlan's shoulders. "Imprisoned?"

Kichlan sighed, and seemed to droop. To grow old. "That's why I have to be here, with him." He turned to face me. "Do you understand? Always with him. And that's why we need to avoid inspections, avoid missing our quotas or doing anything that could draw attention to our team. And to him."

Guilt caught in my throat again. Lad was a beautiful man. But said like that, with age and weakness and a broken voice, he could have been a chain. "What happened?"

Kichlan eyed me for a moment. What did he debate in his head, in that silence? "I wasn't there." He half-sat on the edge of the table. I fought the urge to cross my arms. "I was stupid. I thought I could leave him. He was—" with a frown, he mouthed numbers "—young. I don't remember how many years. But he was already large."

I waited as he paused.

"I still don't know exactly how it happened. Mother never would tell me. I tried once to pry it out of him. Took a sixweek and one before he forgave me. Didn't talk the whole time."

Lad twitched in his sleep and drew his knees up. A giant child on a small couch.

"I knew he liked the girl, I knew he followed her, smiled at her, gave her flowers. Weeds that grew between paving stones. I knew she was kind to him, indulged him, treated him like a large baby to be coddled." Bitterness crept into his voice. "She shouldn't have encouraged him and I shouldn't have let him talk to her. It was my fault. Do you understand, Tanyana? I always have to be there."

"What happened?" I asked again.

He shook his head. "I told you, I don't really know. But I returned that afternoon to find my mother insensible. She had discovered the girl. Lad had tried to hide her, like he hid toys and trinkets and shiny scraps of metal he found, in the space between the house and alley wall." He held up his hands, measured a foot or so. "It was only this wide."

"Other." I pressed my hands to my mouth.

Kichlan just nodded. "She was bruised, bloody, broken. But not dead. He didn't mean to hurt her, I think he–" a swallow "–tried to play with her. Like a doll. That's what I think, but I do not know. And the way he talked, you can't understand it, like someone had told him to do it. Like he had listened to a voice that wasn't there, and obeyed.

"The local veche wanted to incarcerate him. We had to fight for him, and in the end I was the reason they let him go. Because I promised I wouldn't leave him again, go out into that real world, that bright world, and let him loose in the dark. When I fe–" He broke off, looked away from me. I shuddered, from my head to the very end of my toes. "So you understand why Eugeny and I, why we have to be careful."

Together, we watched Lad sleep.

"You are a good brother, Kichlan." My words felt inadequate, but the silence was worse. "You have sacrificed more for him than he will ever know." More than Kichlan had even said. More, perhaps, then I wanted to guess at.

"I try to help him." Kichlan roused himself with a shake. "There are more ways than following him everywhere. Things to calm him, to help him think straight, to keep the v–" a hesitation this time "–the voices at bay. Don't get much time, of course. But I try." He gave a shrug. "Anyway, it's late. Don't you have a long way to travel home?"

Ah, home. "Don't remind me."

"Bit inconvenient, that."

"You noticed? Can't hide anything from you."

Kichlan shook his brother gently. With a wide-mouthed yawn and a stretch that nearly caught Kichlan in the face, Lad sat up. He blinked and grinned broadly at us. "Is it time for supper, bro?"

"Almost. We'd better get home or we might miss it."

Lad jumped to his feet. "Is Tan coming home again? Is she?"

"No, Lad. Not this time. Tan has her own home and she needs to go there."

Lad's face fell, but he still managed to squeeze the air out of me. "Have a nice day at home, Tan."

"Night," Kichlan murmured with a sigh. "It's night, Lad."

As I left Kichlan helping Lad into his jacket, their voices followed me up the stairs. "Bro, is Tan lonely when she's at home?"

"I don't know. Why do you ask?"

"She never wants to go there. It's home, isn't it? Means you should want to go there."

I plunged into Movoc's dark, icy night. He had a point, that large man with a childish, volatile mind. But it was my home. And I shouldn't have to give it up because of kopacks, because of lies and threats.

I would make the veche listen to me. Pavel thought I was alone, he thought the veche could get to everyone who might have listened to me and cared what I had to

217

say. He was wrong. True, my circle had turned their backs on me. True, the few people I knew who worked for the veche had been demoted and sent away. But I still wasn't alone.

I had Devich.

9.

I'd promised Devich.

The next Olday night, I dug clothes I'd assumed I would never wear again from the bottom of my closet. Somehow they needed to look respectable, fit over my uniform and hide as much of my suit and its lights as possible. Tailored pants of black silk and satin; they wouldn't do up around the band at my waist and I was forced to wear them low, so my heels stood on the hems. A fine layered shirt, with a gauzy top layer, of white and icicle blue, and a loose undershirt in silver. It opened wide at the neck and wrists, and I stood in front of the mirror for bells, trying every scarf and necktie I owned. Finally, I settled on a cream silk scarf with bluebell stitching. It was long enough to loop twice around my throat and I tied it tightly. My wrists were harder to hide. I did the buttons on the overshirt, glad the cuffs were solid against the gauze, and hoped any glimpses of silver might be mistaken for jewellery.

Hair, at least, was still simple enough, although it had grown over the past sixnights. I ran a handful of the remnants of my precious cream through the blonde strands so it swept back from my face and curled into wisps behind my ears. There was hardly any of the cream left, a faint clogging at the bottom of the jar. I couldn't remember how many kopacks I had paid for it, and that said enough, really. I wouldn't be able to afford it again.

I lacked the appropriate cosmetics and jewellery. With bandages still stuck to my neck and shoulders, and pink scars wriggling on my face, neither would have helped.

I pulled on flat-heeled boots that were low enough to button up, and examined myself in the standing mirror. A parody of my old self smiled grimly from the glass. The pants no longer hugged my hips and thighs; indeed, they hung baggy and too large over my abdomen and legs. The extra length and the flat shoes made me short. The shirt too had lost its once-feminine look. No longer tight around my breasts, no longer tailored to highlight my waist, it was floppy and loose.

I wavered in front of the mirror. Feeling short, feeling baggy, feeling tired from a sixnight of debris collecting and missing the Darkwater sublevel, with its smells of Kichlan's cooking and its footprints of ash across the cement floor.

Then Devich knocked.

He greeted me with a grin as I opened the door, and swept inside. One arm wrapped around my waist as he pushed me up against the hallway wall and kissed me.

"You are lovely," he said, as he allowed me to catch my breath. His eyes flickered over me, starting with hair, to scarf, to shirt and pants. "Like I imagined."

With a frown, I straightened, and pushed him away. "The trousers certainly look better on you than me."

"Hardly." And he whipped out a pale lily from his jacket.

I took the flower, not entirely sure what I was supposed to do with it. Devich wore pants similar to mine, of a thicker cotton and with a satin stripe down the side. His shirt was the colour of sunset, his jacket black with a crimson satin lining. He looked roguish, charming, and his clothes fit altogether too well.

"I don't think this is a good idea," I murmured, more to myself than Devich. But he heard me.

His face grew serious, not quite stern. "You promised me, Tanyana."

I lifted my eyebrows at him.

"I don't understand the problem." He shoved fists into his jacket pocket and actually pouted. "You look lovely, you will fit right in. You belong with us."

With a controlled breath, I kept my hand from my face. "Too late to back out now, anyway." Oh, I wished there was a way.

"Not that you want to." Devich smiled again. "Trust me."

He helped me into my jacket like a true gentleman and I realised it probably wasn't suitable for a ball, or whatever this event was going to be. It smelled like the streets, like damp snow and road dust. But the other jackets I had owned were veche-marked, or sewn with the pattern of Proud Sunlight. Still, Eugeny's fire-drying room scent was there, somewhere in the weave, as well as traces of Kichlan's cooking. I took the comfort they could give.

Devich tucked the lily stem into an empty buttonhole on my breast, and I hoped it was enough to draw the eye away from the smudges, the dirt and the damp patches.

There was a waiting landau hovering in the silvering twilight. I sat beside Devich, his arm wrapped around my shoulders and pressing my hair against his cheek, and tried to forget the last coach ride I had taken. I tried not to compare the icy night that whipped us through the torn doors of Kichlan's coach to the pion-heated air and down-soft cushions in Devich's. I closed my eyes to the four small lamps lighting the interior, looked down from the gold inlaid handles and ignored the plush, blood-coloured carpet.

We headed into the centre of Movoc-under-Keeper.

The veche chambers took up most of the centre of the city. They spanned the bridge itself, local courts on the east bank, national and province buildings on the west. In the shadow of these buildings, the city changed. It still looked haunted to me, but instead of the apparently un-aided movement of otherwise inanimate objects – from walkways to coaches to food stalls – the older parts of the city were occupied by the ghosts of time. Age wore down on them. Not in a way that dulled the handcrafted beauty of polished marble, or blunted the pointed grace of rows upon rows of tall conifers. Rather, as the apart-ments and the factories fell away behind us, as the streets narrowed and the landau was forced to slow down, it felt like a weight of memory, of bells and moons and years, draped over us. These were the foundations of Movoc-under-Keeper as we knew her, built in the pro-tective shadow of the Keeper Mountain. Our history, our ancestry, our past. And my own face, reflected in the coach window, could have been the spectre of any long-dead debris collector.

Not all the buildings we passed were veche chambers. Indeed, some of the most beautiful were the homes of the oldest families in Varsnia. My reflection paled further as we pulled up at the gates to one such family home.

Devich was from a younger family, I had been certain of it. How could he have been invited to a place like this?

"Just what circles do you swim in?" I asked. To my horror, my voice shook.

Devich simply laughed. "Me? Oh, I'm not much of a circle swimmer. But some veche members are interested in what we do. They consider debris somewhat of an oddity, they're curious. Lord Sporinov is one of them." His face brightened. "Oh, he'll be happy to talk to you!"

"Wonderful." Just what I wanted. Now I was an oddity in baggy, inappropriate clothes.

But as I glanced at Devich from under my eyelashes I realised what this meant. Lord Sporinov? An old family, then, and a member of the national veche. If he was interested in debris then maybe he would be interested in listening to how I came to be able to see it. And just why I needed a tribunal of my own.

"It is a great opportunity," Devich said.

More than he could know.

A small army of servants pulled the large silver gates open. At first I thought that was odd: I'd expected them to be powered by pions. But perhaps a wealthy man with an interest in debris collectors liked the old-fashioned touch.

The landau glided down a long driveway, flanked on either side by dormant fruit trees. They would look beautiful as the weather warmed, sprinkled with pale flowers and the bright green buds of leaves. For now they were all gnarled branches in bare grey.

The house itself was big enough to be a veche chamber, and as intimidating. Marble steps, warmed by the light from many lamps, led up to a set of large wooden doors opened wide. Colour and light spilled from them. Silhouettes meandered at the top. Fainter shapes danced behind.

All too soon we were at the steps. Devich leapt from the landau with unhealthy enthusiasm and held out a hand for me. What would he do if I refused to come out?

"Come with me, Tanyana." He smiled his beautiful smile, and his large hand didn't waver. "You belong with me."

I gripped his hand and let him lead me down the coach's tight steps. Then he hooked his arm in mine and was sweeping me up the carpet of light, to the open doors and certain doom.

There were a few men smoking fragrant cigars at the top of the steps. They spoke in a low and constant whisper that lulled as Devich led me past. I held my head high and tried not to step on my hems.

An aging servant dressed in a shirt and pants of imitation gold thread gazed down his nose at us as we stepped through the open door. Devich flicked his fingers – doing something I couldn't see to invisible pions – and with a nod and a sweep of his arm, the servant invited us inside the Sporinov home. I realised, as I stepped into warmth and light and noise, that the whole exchange had happened without a word being said.

But then I entered Lord Sporinov's home, and it cast all other thoughts from my mind.

I may have been employed by the veche, but I had never been invited to an old family ball. I had worked for those newer to power. Architecture and planning were not high on the veche agenda. Old families, whose pion strength had established them as rulers long before the revolution even happened, they controlled the enforcers, they dealt with foreign powers, they dictated how much of Varsnia's binding knowledge we wanted to share. I had never been important enough, never been vital enough to the future of Varsnia, to warrant an invitation before.

I couldn't imagine why I was now.

Gold-edged carpets ran in smooth lines over a polished marble floor. Different coloured lights shone in flame-shaped glasses that hung from the ceilings on gold chains. Curtains the colour of buttery cream swept over wide windows. And the house was full of beautiful people. Women in dresses that hugged their body shape and were sewn of silk and light-reflecting glass beads. Some women wore a wider skirt, layered with satin and lace. No colour repeated itself in their attire. I saw blue like the sky before dawn, green as the newest sprout from the trunk of a tree, and icy white. Jewels sparkled from ear lobes, necks, wrists and hair.

I realised, with a strangely satisfying kick in the gut, that I wore jewellery far brighter than these women ever would.

Men followed these painting-perfect images of femineity around like shadows. Each was a mirror image of Devich, only older and without the mischievous smile.

Still latched firmly onto my arm, Devich guided me past these, the oldest, the richest, and the most beautiful in Varsnia. I caught sight of a thin young woman, dressed in a skirt that nearly swallowed her. With her large eyes, dark skin and ever-so-charmingly mussed hair, she looked closer to a skittish deer than a woman at a ball. Men hung about her in a circle and vied for the attention of those dark, luscious eyes. I had never seen anything as beautiful, yet Devich's expression darkened when he noticed her, and he looked away. The awkward way she stood, the jerking, fumbling way she tried to walk, started me wondering. What was happening to the pions inside her body? I remembered the rumours, the members of the old families who would snatch pretty women from the streets like gems hidden in mud for their entertainment. What better chains to keep her here than those that already existed beneath her skin?

Devich kept up his pressure on my elbow and she was soon lost in the crowd.

"Here we are," Devich murmured. His cheeks were flushed, his eyes bright and focused with a frightening determination. "Our host."

A tall and greying man stood straight, proudly, on a small step that kept him a few inches above the rest of the ballroom. A much younger but no less proud woman held on to the crook of his elbow. She wore so much silver sewn into the fabric of a long, thin dress that she shone in the light like she was a jewel herself. Together, the couple surveyed the ballroom like shepherds over their flock. They listened politely to the men and women before them, nodding, answering in monosyllables when appropriate, and being altogether gracious and lordly.

I wished I could have taken off my jacket. Surely there was a servant hovering around for that express purpose. But Devich didn't slow, and all too soon we had broken through to the front line of the Lord and Lady Sporinov's audience.

Devich released me long enough to bow, but hurried to grip my elbow again as if I was about to make an attempt to escape.

"My lord Sporinov," Devich said grandly, silencing the constant twitter of the people around us, their bird-like vying for attention. "And my lady Rana. I thank you, again, for your gracious invitation."

The lord and lady turned their faces toward us in a slow and bizarrely coordinated movement. "Devich," the lord said. "You came." His regard was an abrading wind, his wife's cold as ice.

I dipped into the best bow I could manage with Devich still attached.

"I did, my lord."

"And what have you brought?" Rana asked.

I flicked my eyes up, met hers and held them until she looked away. I was no thing.

"Allow me to introduce Tanyana Vladha." Devich didn't seem to realise how uninteresting I was to these people, how low. "The debris collector."

A murmur ran though the crowd around the lord and lady, and gradually spread. I could feel heat beneath my cheeks and knew it would make the scars stand out more.

The lord Sporinov suddenly seemed to animate. One moment he was doing an accurate imitation of a wax statue and the next he was alive. Even had colour in the face and movement in his eyes. He shook off his wife and descended from their single step.

"A collector? Truly?" He held a hand out to me. I shook it, fairly certain I was about to wake up.

"Indeed, my lord." Devich glanced around at the jealous faces, and his smile turned from enjoyment to triumphant. I wished it hadn't. "You spoke to me of your interest in my work, and I thought I could bring a friend who knows far more about it than I do."

"A friend?" A dry voice muttered from the circle.

"Yes." Devich caught my eyes and winked at me. "A very close friend indeed."

"Well, dear lady, this is quite an occasion." Lord Sporinov

maintained a hold on my hand. His palm was cool and dry. "Yes, indeed."

With a toss of her blonde hair, Rana stepped down and stalked to a table laden with drinks. Most of the crowd hesitated, seemed to notice the lord's distraction, and decided to follow the lady instead. Only a few of the older men remained.

"I'll return in a moment." Devich headed off in search of a drink himself.

I was left alone, ringed by the aging heads of old veche families, and feeling like a moth pinned to a board, surrounded by butterflies.

"Let's have a look at you." Lord Sporinov studied me, from hair to toes. "Bit of a strange one, aren't you?"

I coughed. "I wouldn't say so, my lord."

He chuckled. "Got a bit of spirit, then? Always good to have."

"Do they all dress like you?" asked a large man with a bald forehead bright with sweat. "The women, I mean."

"No, my lord." I had no idea who any of these people were, but had decided I couldn't go wrong with the title.

"Just you then?"

"Just me."

"Because of that?" He pointed at the scars on my neck and cheek.

"No, sir."

"Curiouser still." Sporinov patted my hand. "Now, tell me all about it."

"My lord?" I asked.

"Debris, of course. Tell me what you do."

"Well, my lord, to understand that you must understand how I came to it. I used to be a pion-binder. I was a strong one. Then–"

"Start early, do you?" A thin man with yellowing skin interrupted me. He touched a long ivory pipe to his lips, drew a deep breath and released smoke into my face. I blinked, coughed. It smelled nothing like Eugeny's tobacco.

"My lord?" I asked, unsettled.

"When you collect." He waved the pipe in a slow arc. "Early morning?"

"Y-yes."

"Long way to travel?"

"Yes." What was this? What did it matter how far I needed to go in the morning or how early I rose to get there? "But, really, that's not important. If you will listen, sirs, I will tell you about how I fe–"

"And do you do a lot of walking?" This time I was interrupted by a truly ancient man. His eyes were white and he carried a long, ebony cane with a gold handle. Walking? What did it matter?

"Please, my lords–"

Lord Sporinov had been holding my hand the whole time, his eyes trained intently on me. He patted the back of my fingers. "We're just old men, dear girl," he said. "Interested in your world. Please forgive us our curiosity."

"My lord, there is nothing to forgive. But I am trying to tell you something no one else has heard. Something strange and unique." I latched onto my oddity status like it was a lifeline. "I know you are curious about debris, and it is vital to understand how one comes to see it in the first place. I fell, my lords, from a great height. And they said it was an accident but I know–"

"Tell me about this." Sporinov drew back the sleeve of my shirt with a lazy finger. "What is this beautiful thing?"

So I explained the suit, and was obliged to show it shining on my wrists. I explained about jars and teams.

"And now," I tried again. "If you will just listen–"

But all at once the old men turned away, as though they had lost their collective interest in me at the same time. A few smiled at me, a few gave easy nods, then they wandered away and rejoined the ball. Only one hesitated, watching me intently. And I realised that I knew him: the inspector who had visited my construction site the day of *Grandeur's* fall.

I lifted my free hand to him, I tried to take a step forward, but Sporinov held me tighter that I had realised. "Wait," I said. "You were there. You saw them, didn't you? The crimson pions, the ones that destroyed my statue. You're a veche inspector. You must have seen them too."

But the old man just shook his head. "Let it go, girl," he whispered. "It really would be easier if you just let it go." Then Sporinov coughed pointedly, and the inspector disappeared into the crowd.

I stood, still beneath Sporinov's hand, mouth open and unable to understand why I hadn't managed to tell them the truth. To press for my tribunal. The perfect opportunity and all they had let me talk about was the ridiculous and the mundane.

"Thank you, dear girl, for sharing that with us." Sporinov patted me again.

Share what? I hadn't, really, told them anything.

"You're quite a determined young thing, aren't you?" There was an indulgent humour in Sporinov's smile that I didn't understand. I felt strangely like a pet beneath his gaze. "Even when the world aligns itself against you, you keep trying. It pleases me. But I wouldn't try too hard, if

I were you. Not everyone would find it so amusing."
Then he caught sight of his wife, and pushed purposefully through the crowd toward her.

I was left among the guests and their finery, to endure the surreptitious glances and outright stares. I
lifted my chin. What did it matter that I stood out
among the tailored and the diamond-encrusted like a
stone among pearls? What did I care that the host
treated me more like a rare animal on a leash than a
guest? Or that Devich, who had convinced me I belonged here, who had dragged me to the door, had
suddenly disappeared?

Devich. He had left me with these men. Sporinov's
words shuddered through me. They had almost, if I
thought about them hard enough, if I twisted them with
the image of Pavel leaning so angrily above me, sounded
like a threat.

Where was Devich?

Shoulders straight, chin high, I pushed my way
through the guests to a long table heavy with full glasses.
Rich amber brandies, deep red wines and faint blue spir-
its twinkled in the light like a constellation against the
pale tablecloth sky.

I caught edges of conversation.

"Let them try it! Hon Ji thinks they can rival Varsnia,
we'll show them true meaning of power."

"Heard they had spies in Movoc-under-Keeper. Even
Sporinov is hiring enforcers, just in case."

"By the Other, I swear it. The veche is hiding something even from us. A weapon that will put Hon Ji firmly
back in their place."

The usual speculations and proclamations of Varsnian
supremacy. I'd heard them all my life, and paid them

little heed. The critical circle revolution began in Varsnia, but it had spread. Around us, nations grew strong on their borrowed technologies, and occasionally rumours of war would trickle down from the veche. I wasn't sure how much I believed them, because nothing ever came of it. Deals to share pion technologies, promises to stop training soldiers, even the odd skirmish. Part of me had always thought the veche made them all up, just to start conversations like these.

I selected the largest glass of red I could find and headed to a corner where I could sip it in peace, until the guests and the host and the loss of Devich simply wouldn't matter.

"T-Tanyana?"

I turned to a soft, restricted-sounding voice, and found Tsana, resplendent in a gown of rich tree-leaf green sewn with tiny, white beads in the shape of flowers. Her cheeks were flushed with the heat of the room, her eyes – set off so well by the colours in her dress – swam rich and brown. Her thick brunette hair was piled high on her head so her neck seemed longer, the skin paler and more delicate. Another flower, made this time from diamonds, shone on her neck.

For a moment, I considered pretending I was someone else. Because the bright flowers that decked her so beautifully reminded me hauntingly of the critical circle in which she had once stood. And my scars tightened, perhaps remembering the panic and pion skill that had created them.

"It is you." Tsana stepped forward as I stepped back, pressing us both into the corner I had tried to hide in, the unsteady shadows an inefficient cloak. "What are you doing here?"

And that snapped me out of my fear and bad memories. I held the wine easily at my waist and lifted an eyebrow. She had always seemed shorter when I was her critical centre. Somehow easier to look down on.

"I am Lord Sporinov's guest." I bent the truth just a little out of shape. "As, I assume, are you."

Tsana, flustered, waved a flat hand like a fan at her face. "Of course. I... I'm sorry. I hadn't expected to see you."

Ever again, I didn't doubt. I took a larger than usual sip. "You were wrong."

"Yes. I'm sorry." She glanced over her shoulder. "Grandda is a friend of Vladir. We're always invited. To the balls." She fussed with the pleating below her waist. "It's good to see you, my lady."

Now she was someone I wasn't about to correct. But I gave a sigh. "I'm sure that's not true."

If anything, Tsana's flush deepened.

"Come now, I know what happened. Volski told me." I hoped she could see every bandage and scar, hoped they were all plain and unavoidable.

"V– Volski?" Tsana began to tug on the pleats so violently I was surprised the seam didn't tear.

That was strange. "Yes, we met, accidentally. A few sixnights ago now. Didn't he tell you?"

She shook her head before glancing around the room, and I realised how terrified she was, how much she didn't want the elite here, the old families who had always counted her among their kind, to know what she had done to me.

I took pity on her.

And it felt good to have someone to pity.

"Is there a balcony somewhere?" I asked. "I could do with some air."

233

A grateful nod and Tsana gripped me by the hand. She led me across the ballroom, through a throng of revellers gathered to watch as the dances started, and out of one of the large, gold-edged doors that rimmed the ballroom. She ignored the calls from a group of young men gathered to smoke by the carriageway, and found a seat in the shadows between house and night-flooded garden.

With a graceful sweep of her skirts, Tsana sat. With a wince at my uncomfortable and out of place waistband, I joined her. I wondered why Volski had kept our meeting to himself. Was he ashamed of me, of what I had become? Or was he trying to spare us both? Tsana her guilt, and me my humiliation.

"What happened to you?" Tsana breathed the question into the cool night. Beneath my layers, and with my wine to warm me, I barely noticed the bite of the chill.

"Isn't that my question?" I swallowed a large mouthful of the wine. It was spiced with cloves and elderflowers, their combined scent threatening to make me sneeze.

Tsana shuddered. "Oh, my lady. I am so sorry. *Grandeur* broke. I saw you fall. I tried to catch you but glass was falling and I got, I got–" she made a hiccuping noise in her throat "–I got confused."

If I was still the lady she called me I would have drilled her on that. How could a professional pion architect get confused and nearly cost the circle centre her life? But I wasn't, and I didn't know how long it would take Tsana to realise that. The relationship between us was as fine, as fragile, as the thin glass stem in my hand.

"Do they hurt?" she whispered.

"Less than they used to."

A moment of silence.

"What happened?" Tsana did not give up, and it made that glass stem that much finer.

"I was–" Pushed? Did I really want to tell that to another of my old circle who wouldn't believe me? Was there really any point trying that again? I knew the answer. "I don't know. *Grandeur* broke, as you say. I fell, as you say. But *Grandeur* hit me on the way down." I touched the top of my head, the wound for which there was no scar. "She knocked something out, and took the pions from me." I rested the glass on my knees to keep it steady. "When I woke up I couldn't see them any more. I could see something else instead."

And for the first time that exchange didn't seem quite so poor. Not with Kichlan's cooking scenting my clothes.

"There was something strange happening, wasn't there?" Tsana stuttered.

"When?"

"On *Grandeur*. Something, I don't know how to say it, it felt like something was pushing us around. Like every time we tried to help you, something got in our way. I thought you might know what it was. I thought you might be able to explain it. But if you can't..." She gave a shrug with one smooth, graceful shoulder.

I gaped at her. Of course, the one person who would believe me was the one person I had decided to lie to. "Did you tell the tribunal that?" I eased my hand where it gripped the glass too hard. Wine rippled. "Did you tell anyone that?" Maybe this was what I needed? Maybe, with Tsana supporting me, someone would listen!

"But it was nothing. You said you didn't see anything."

"No, but did you–?"

"I was lucky to get out of the tribunal in one piece, my lady. Considering what happened, what I did to you."

She swallowed hard; I could see the moment in her neck. "I could have lost my place in the circle, I could have been charged for negligence and shipped to the colonies to– to–"

She closed her eyes, and my stomach dropped.

"So I held my tongue."

"And now? You know something happened out there, Tsana. You're the daughter of an old family; you're a member of a nine point circle! The veche would listen to you. Have them open another tribunal, I will stand beside you and together we will tell the truth!"

Tsana touched a shaking hand to the diamond at her throat. "A tribunal?"

"Yes!"

"But they already had one."

"So we make them open another. They will listen to you."

But Tsana shook her head. "Oh, I couldn't. I disgraced myself. So did you. And I don't think I really saw anything that day, maybe I'm just feeling guilty. It was my fault you got hurt so badly. That must be it. I'm sorry. Really."

I looked away from her pale face, from the panic and the fear there. Perhaps she was not the best ally to have. Perhaps she wasn't strong enough to help me. Or so inclined.

"So." She cleared her throat. "What are you doing now?"

With a frown, I turned back to her. How could she not know? But then, I hadn't known what it took to make a debris collector before my fall.

"I can see debris, Tsana. I'm a collector."

"Oh." She lifted her head from its conspiratorial tilt, levering her shoulders away from mine. And as cold air rushed into the distance she had put between us I realised this was where residual respect ended, and the realisation that I was different began. I had told Devich. I had always known. I did not belong with these people any more. "That explains why Vladir likes you. He's fascinated by debris." She shifted, barely half an inch, but away from me. "Is it that terrible?"

"Collecting? Not really. Dirty, disgusting sometimes. Not terrible."

Tsana gazed into the garden as I answered, showing the graceful line of her jaw, the fine muscles in her neck.

"There's a lot of walking," I continued.

"Oh."

When would she excuse herself? Had she assumed I was still an architect, was that why she had bothered to talk to me again? A scarred architect with a horrible past, but a binder of some skill?

Something in me refused to let her go, refused to be snubbed by a pretty fool with family connections who had nearly succeeded in killing me.

"Will you do me a favour, Tsana?"

I regained her attention. "A favour?"

"Yes. Repayment, let's say."

Her straight back grew rigid, her jaw set. But she nodded jerkily. "Of course, anything I can give you."

Did she think I was going to ask for kopacks? "I need to borrow your skill to fix something. I can't do it. Not any more."

"What is it?"

"A hole in the ceiling where I work. Foot or so wide, a few inches deep. Cement."

"Is that all?"

I remembered days when that could be considered small. "That's all."

"Payment." She dug into a small pocket in her skirt and drew out a slide. Small, glass and impenetrable. "Have a messenger contact me. We will arrange where and when."

That easy, was it, when I couldn't use the slide and couldn't even afford a coach ride to her door? But I took it anyway, rather than explain. I would walk to Tsana's doorstep one Rest, and arrange a time with her maid. I wasn't above those things, was I? To get Sofia off my back.

I held the slide tight against my palm. Its edges were hard, and bit into my skin. "Thank you, Tsana."

"You are welcome, Tanyana." She stood with the same sweep of her skirts. "I should return. My mother can fret if she does not know where we are. Old families are made and broken by their honour."

I remained sitting. "I'll contact you soon."

Tsana nodded and hesitated for a moment, before gathering her dress and hurrying out of the shadows and back into the mansion.

I held the slide and sat in the darkness.

Above and behind me, music played, people laughed, and the smell of food wafted out to churn my stomach.

How long could I sit hidden in the cold shadows?

"There you are."

I turned to see Devich leaning against the mansion wall, looking down at me like I was a lost kitten, or an errant puppy. Light from the window striped his face with warm, diffused lines.

"You're missing the toast," he chided me, not really angry, rather amused.

I stood. "Where did you go?"

He chuckled. "Missed me? You had Lord Sporinov and his closest cronies eating out of your palms like a bowing,

238

preening flock of pigeons." He grinned at his own wit. "You didn't need me at all!"

"I didn't say I needed you." How had he convinced me to come here? How had I allowed myself to believe nothing had changed? I was too different now; I had moved on. "I think it's time to leave."

Devich, taken aback, tried take my hand. I didn't let him. "They are toasting, Tanyana. You know it's rude to leave before the toasts are finished."

"No one will notice."

He opened his mouth to protest.

I said, "They won't."

For a moment I thought Devich would leave me to fend for myself, as he glanced over his shoulder to the open doors and the carpet of light running down to the carriageway. Was the landau waiting for us? Had Devich paid the driver? Could I walk home before dawn came?

But he sighed, and shook his head. "This is a mistake. But if you really want to leave, we will."

"I do."

Devich held out his hand again and I continued to ignore it. I walked past him, and heard his shuffling feet follow slowly.

Applause echoed from the open doors. I headed for the stairs, but a low, gravel-dry laugh slowed me. A man leaned against stone beside one of the large open doors. His face was hidden in shadow, save for the fiery end of a cigar he was sucking.

"Don't like them either," the man said in a voice as dry as his laughter. "I've tipped my glass at too many toasts, and they never change." He straightened, and stepped from the shadow.

I realised then how very old he was. He stooped beneath a coat that was too big for him, and walked slowly, his shoulders hunched, his knees bent. Faint wisps of pale hair hung like cobwebs over a bald and sun-spotted head. His eyes were sunken, blue lost in watery red, and his hand, where it clutched the ivory head of an ebony walking stick, shook so the point rattled against stone. The long, thin cigar remained in his mouth as he walked and he breathed smoke in and out with every pronounced breath.

A bright pin lanced his silver necktie. On its woven pewter head, a bear roared. An ancient ruby was clutched in its jaws.

Devich sketched a sharp bow. "My lord Sporinov."

The old man chuckled. "You're a sharp one."

It took me a moment to understand. This was Vladir's father, surely.

"Thank you, my lord." Devich glanced at me, and made tipping movements with his head.

I repressed a groan and bowed instead. "My lord." Why was it so difficult to leave this place?

"You're a lady?" The old man leaned forward, putting so much weight on his walking stick it bent, and peered at me. "Don't look much like a lady to me." He laughed again. "But don't let that upset you. Nothing looks much like it used to do."

It hadn't upset me.

"Ah, now I know you." A smattering of empty spaces broke up the teeth as he smiled. "You're the one Vladir's so excited about. You're the Unbound."

From legend, from children's tales and fanciful stories, that word reached out to grab me.

"Unbound?" I whispered.

"Heard that before, haven't you? Didn't you know what you were? Didn't my son tell you?" He made a strange snorting sound. "Acts like he knows everything, doesn't he? I can still teach him a few things, if he'd shut his mouth long enough to listen."

I knew what I was. "I am a debris collector."

"That's a pretty name for this new age. Not always called that, you know. Didn't always collect, did the Unbound."

Didn't they? What other purpose could we have, if not to collect the waste of the world and keep its systems working smoothly, cleanly?

Devich, suddenly, was at my side, gripping my elbow, turning me around. "Your pardon, my lord," he said to the old man. "But our coach is waiting."

"Well, go and catch it. I won't keep you." He shuffled so he could look over his shoulder through the open doors. "Toasts still going? I'd never bore my guests like this." He spat out the nib of his cigar, still glowing. "Yugeve? A cigar, boy! A cigar!" And he shuffled slowly inside, calling to some servant I couldn't see.

I turned. Sure enough, the landau was waiting. The driver had been watching us with interest, but was suddenly absorbed in his own knees.

I allowed Devich to guide me into the coach. We sat in silence as it slid through the streets of Movoc-under-Keeper. When it pulled up at my apartment I opened the door myself, dropped to the paving stones, and had unlocked my front door before Devich had even paid the driver.

I was about to close the door when Devich hurried up the path. He jammed an arm in the gap and winced as I pushed against it. "What are you doing?"

"Good night, Devich."

"Not without an explanation. And please, keep doing that. Let's see who tires first."

I took my weight off the door, and he nudged it open. With a sigh I stepped away and he entered the hallway, rubbing his arm, pouting.

"What's wrong?" He wasn't exactly angry, but he was close to it. Somewhere in between anger and hurt. "Why did we have to leave like that? Why did you jam my arm in there?"

Only then did it occur to me that he could have let himself in, whether I had shut the door or not. I had opened myself to this man. He wasn't going away that easily. "I told you I didn't belong with those people any more. And tonight only proved that."

He shook his head.

I scowled at him, and tore the scarf from my neck. I picked at the shirt buttons near my wrists and pulled the whole thing over my head. It felt better without the bulk of clothes.

"Tanyana." Devich stepped very close. One hand cupped my chin, the other slid over my hair. Gently, he placed a soft kiss on my lips. "Tonight I saw you hold the attention of some of the most powerful men in Movoc-under-Keeper, and the whole of Varsnia itself. I saw you walk into a room filled with the rich and the powerful with your head held high, with your back straight, and a bearing that said 'This is who I am, and I don't really care what you think about that'. Do you know how amazing you looked beside the puffed-up finery and the artificial smiles? You were magnificent, you are magnificent." Both of his hands held my head. "I wish you could see that."

I wanted to ask him if he'd seen the woman who was once my subordinate lose all her respect for me. Or if he knew what it was like to be treated like an oddity, like a specimen under glass. But his smiling lips were so close, and his hands were so warm. And Devich had made a place for himself among those people, he had been given the invitation, and he had melded well into the dancers and the feasters and the drinkers. If he thought I belonged there, if he still respected me and knew me as a woman, not an insect, then perhaps I did.

It was enough. Enough to let go of the angry ache in my belly. Enough to lean against him as he kissed me, and work the buttons in his sleek shirt. As he did the same to my ill-fitting pants I remembered the jar of pills in my drawer and wondered how long they would last.

10.

Dawn, Mornday, with the Tear splitting silent and smooth around the prow of the near-empty ferry. In the raw sunlight on river spray, I thought of the Unbound.

The Unbound were troublemakers, always in the background, always sabotaging the work of good, honest pion-binders. They were the figures in dark cloaks who would not show their face.

My mother had told me few fairy tales when I was a child. "You should learn about real life," she would tell me, "because in real life there are no magic solutions, there are no first sons to sweep you from the arms of dark danger. There is hard work, kopacks, and status. Remember that."

But I knew a few. There was one about a knight and his princess. Rusclan and Ludmilla. On the day they were to marry Ludmilla was carried away by one of Rusclan's rivals. Through many trials Rusclan hunted and found his beloved. But that wasn't the point. The point was his supposedly faithful and Unbound friend, the only man Rusclan would trust with his powerful and pion-strengthened sword. The night after Rusclan had regained his bride his friend broke that trust, and killed the hero with his own weapon.

After which Rusclan was healed by a good binder and went on to save the princess again and probably the day. Something like that. But again, that wasn't the point. It was the Unbound that called to me, skulking from his place in the darkness. What could it have felt like to play shadow to a knight like Rusclan, to care for his pion-powerful sword when all it looked like to you was a hunk of steel? Would you feel used?

The man didn't have a name. He was just Unbound.

So, that's what I was. Untrustworthy, unnamed. Unbound.

I felt dark against the rays of the new sun. But as I disembarked from the Tear and made my way toward Darkwater I realised how wrong the fairy tales were. We did not skulk in the darkness because we belonged there. We stuck to the darkness because that was where we had been pushed. Because of the crowds and the offended looks.

And because that's where the debris was. If debris didn't like the shadows, the crevices, the cracks and the darkness, then we wouldn't have to walk in it.

Debris skulked, we merely followed.

Breakbell had not yet sounded as I reached the door to the sublevel, but it was unlocked – Kichlan had arrived before me. I glanced up before I stepped into the stairwell and caught sight of clouds rushing over the Keeper's Peak, whipped along by a wind as strong as the Tear's current had been. They shaded the promising morning sun.

Sure enough, Kichlan and Lad were alone in the sublevel, and both avidly poking at a young fire.

"Morning," I said, and shrugged off my heavy jacket. It was pleasant in the sublevel, warm and sleep-inducing, far nicer than the outside promised to be. "Clouds are coming." Hands thrust out, I warmed myself by the struggling flames.

"Tan!" Lad leapt to his feet, opened his arms, checked himself visibly and compromised by patting me on the shoulder. "Good morning, Tan."

"Good morning, Lad."

He beamed, and crouched down to the fire.

Kichlan and I shared a raised-eyebrow glance. "He's being good," Kichlan mouthed, before standing up, and passing me something wrapped in linen.

"What's this?" I flipped open the cloth and found a cool pastry, about the size of my hand.

"Eugeny and I have been talking," Kichlan said. "We decided you don't eat enough." He couldn't quite meet my eye.

"Did you now?" I hardened my expression and fixed him with my gaze. I didn't need handouts, least of all from Kichlan, Eugeny or Lad. They who had hardly anything to share.

"Didn't," Lad said, from his position by the fire, leaning so far into the fireplace I expected him to topple at any moment.

"Lad!" Kichlan snapped. "Get your head out of there."

His younger brother sat back, expression puzzled, verging on hurt. "But you didn't, bro. Geny said Tan was hungry and you said she wouldn't want to. You said she's too..." he screwed his face up. "Don't remember."

With a sigh, Kichlan patted his brother. "Ever the diplomat, Lad."

Lad grinned, and returned to his fire.

"Too what?" But I couldn't feel angry, not at the embarrassment colouring Kichlan from neck to forehead. "What am I, exactly?"

"Proud."

I thought of the ball, of sitting alone in the shadows. "Then you don't know me as well as you think you do." I bit into the pastry. Potato, pumpkin, and turnip were soft. I tasted pepper and the faint dripping of lard holding it all altogether. Before leaving I had drunk my usual tea, and scrounged leftovers from a meal Devich had made on Rest: the crusts of bread he hadn't wanted to eat, and browning apple peel.

I just had to hold on. Another night like the ball, more of Devich's important friends, and I would make someone listen. I would make someone understand. Or Tsana would wake up to her cowardly self and together, we would open a tribunal. We would tell the truth and the veche would find whoever was behind those pions burning fierce, and with the compensation – surely, I would be compensated – I would have enough kopacks to eat. To keep my home.

Just a little while longer.

"Thank the old man for me, won't you?" I sucked oil from the tips of my fingers.

"I'll tell him you said that with your fingers in your mouth." Kichlan grinned. "Trust me, that will be thanks enough."

As breakbell sounded above us, the rest of the team filtered in. Uzdal and Mizra were wrapped in extra scarves and knitted hats, their pale features nearly lost amidst the clothes. Sofia was so heavily layered she walked like a child dressed for the snow. A few strands of her dull hair escaped a large knitted hat, to stick against her cheek and nose. Natasha followed, brown hair tucked into a tight dark cap pulled down as far as her eyebrows.

"Lovely day outside," Uzdal muttered. Even in the sublevel warmth he kept his layers on.

"If we're really lucky it might snow on us again," Mizra added. "Wouldn't that be nice?"

Kichlan collected metallic jars and filled his brown leather bag. "Then the sooner we fill quota, the better."

"Other's oath," Uzdal muttered.

We left the Darkwater sublevel and entered an outside world growing rapidly dim and cold. I tucked my hands into the pockets of my jacket, tugged my leather-lined cap down to cover my ears. The wind that had whipped the clouds along started whipping us as soon as we stepped into the street. It was funnelled by the buildings and careened down Darkwater with a scared-dog howl. Above us, clouds settled in like hounds for the night, dark fur raised and shaggy.

It was hard to believe I had ridden the Tear in clear sunlight that morning.

"The snow will start any moment," Mizra said as we turned the first corner in what I was beginning to learn was our usual Mornday route. "And then, if Lad finds another sewerage vent, the day will be complete." He clasped his hands behind his back in a fair imitation of Kichlan. "Because if collecting doesn't make us as miserable, as cold, and as dirty as possible, then we're simply not doing it right."

I grinned at him and glanced at Kichlan. He was entertaining Lad that morning who, as usual, led us from the front. Together they were pointing at lampposts, rooftops, effluent vents. But at each one Lad just shook his head. Not a good sign, as far as the quota was concerned.

"What is it with this place and brothers?" I asked, keeping my voice low.

Mizra shrugged. "Don't know about those two, but twins always end up as collectors."

"Really?"

"Truly."

"Other's oath," Uzdal muttered again.

What had started Uzdal's sudden fascination with the phrase? I thought for a moment. "I haven't met many twins like yourselves." Had I met any at all? No binders that I could think of, not at any circle level.

Both made identical faces of disgust. "Sad truth about the world, Tanyana," Mizra said. "Twins aren't particularly, how shall I put it? Desired."

I did my best to appear perplexed, and assumed that it worked when Uzdal gave his head an exasperated shake.

"Most twins end up like us." Uzdal pointed to himself and his brother. "Debris collectors. Fallen. So, most mothers, if they find out they're expecting twins, well, they do something about it."

"They abort the children," Sofia, walking behind us, interrupted. "That's what these two are trying to say, although they obviously don't want to. Of course, if you'd just thought about it for a moment you might have worked that out for yourself."

I ignored the criticism, and stared horrified at Mizra and Uzdal. I had heard that some healers could see a baby as it grows by the flow of pions between mother and child. What did a baby destined to collect debris – an Unbound baby – what did they look like to pion sight? Would the flow be interrupted, the womb dull compared to the rest of her pion-bright body?

"That's horrible," I whispered.

"We know," Mizra said.

"That's real life." Sofia pushed past us, to walk with Kichlan instead.

"Why do they kill them?" I asked the twins. "Why are twins, most twins, why are they like us?"

Uzdal glanced ahead, where Lad walked between Sofia and his brother, laughing. "Why is Lad one of us? Because he is broken, Tanyana."

"And we are broken, all of us, in some way," Mizra continued. "We're like that crack in the wall that fell on you. Debris likes broken things. It likes us."

Likes? He reminded me of Lad, talking about debris as though it could think, as though it could feel. But I knew what he meant.

Me, with my scars, with the bone *Grandeur* had knocked into my brain. Lad, with his crooked smile and childish laugh. But the twins?

"Being twins doesn't make you broken. A shattered skull—" I swallowed "—that makes you broken. So I don't understand. And Kichlan isn't broken, Sofia isn't broken."

"Nice of you to say so," Mizra said.

"Yes, terribly nice," Uzdal said. "But we know what we are. And not everyone who is broken has the scars to prove it."

"Although we—"

"—are not among them."

I blinked at them. "You're not one of the ones who don't... what?"

The boys chuckled. "When we're somewhere warmer."

"Less windswept."

"We'll show you what we mean."

Lamps spluttered into life as we walked, and as I tried to work out what under the Keeper they were talking about. Broken was a good word for it. Broken was the bones in my head, the skin on my left side. And Lad, yes, I could see how he could be broken. There was something in him that didn't work the way it should have. But what? I knew what had broken me. What had broken Lad?

Could any of us be fixed?

"Guess it's dark enough to turn the lights on." Kichlan had started to hang back as the twins, evidently tired of confusing me, moved forward to engage Lad.

Thunder rolled above our heads, low and near. Lightning flickered against the dark sky.

"We still collect in the rain, do we?" I glanced up at Kichlan, trying for an innocent and hopeful expression.

He nodded. "Today we do. We just scraped above quota last sixnight, and that was with an emergency. But those are rare, we can't rely on another one and I will not risk something that close again."

Lightning flashed, suddenly bright, suddenly plunging the street into darkness. In the heavy silence that followed Kichlan and I looked to each other and turned to the lamp we had just passed. In a moment it flared, so bright I expected the glass to break with the strain, then it cut off suddenly into the cloud-weary darkness.

"That's not lightning," I whispered. As if on cue, my wrist sprang into brilliant light. "Again?"

As soon as our suits lit up, then Lad, Mizra, Uzdal and Sofia hurried to Kichlan's side. Even Natasha, dragging further behind than I had noticed, ran to join us.

"Where is it?" Uzdal asked. Kichlan drew his sleeve up, exposed his wrist and tilted it at the bare wall of a nearby building. It shone steady, sharp and bright, while down the street the lamps blinked on and off.

"It must be near," Natasha murmured. She stood beside me, watching the lights.

But Sofia shook her head. "No, I don't think so." She pointed at Kichlan's projected map. It was larger than the one Devich had helped me to produce, the ciphers clearer. I found Kichlan's *me* sign easily. It was solid, bright and purposeful. I remembered my own, lost in the jumble of images, and twitched the sleeve of my jacket to cover my suit. But as my fingers brushed the band, I felt the symbols move in short bursts of pressure and warmth. With a gasp, I flicked the sleeve up again and I saw it. The symbol, my symbol, throbbed beneath my fingers as if I had called it.

"There." Kichlan pointed to his map, and soon the rest of us saw the debris cipher. It flickered in a far corner. Not bright, not steady, not close.

"Why is it so far away?" Mizra asked.

Something large and wet splashed on the top of my head. Then another on my arm. Even as I realised they were raindrops, I felt the symbols move again. They rolled beneath my touch, tugged and pressed, tilted and guided. I followed them, smoothed my fingers to the left and turned my wrist. When they stilled, and I peered beneath my fore and middle finger, the debris cipher was there, ready like my own. Beating. Living.

I considered the path my fingers had followed. The crests, the dips and the corners. I looked at the symbols sprayed on the building wall.

Didn't make any sense to me.

"Why are they calling us?" Mizra continued. "We're too far away! There has to be another team closer than us."

"That's why." Sofia gestured to the flickering lamps.

Kichlan, who had been studying his map, turned to her. "Factory?"

"Has to be." She looked grim.

Kichlan said, "Then we need to hurry. Time to run."

"Run?" Mizra's voice rose, in both tone and volume. "What, no horse?"

"There's no time, Mizra. Shut your mouth and run."

Kichlan grabbed Lad and pushed him forward. The big man easily outpaced us as we struggled to follow Kichlan. My legs and lungs quickly ached. Rain fell in ever larger, ever more frequent drops. The wet pavement was slippery, and in the darkness of the skies and the uncertain light of struggling lamps, I came close to losing my footing and crashing face first to the stones.

Kichlan grabbed my arm and helped keep me steady.

"It's raining!" Mizra yelled, as he ran ahead of us, breath loud and hoarse in the artificial night. "That's even better than snow."

"What's happening?" I gasped to Kichlan as we skidded around a corner. He stopped long enough to flash his map against a nearby wall. My fingers itched to touch my suit, to follow the symbols like he was doing.

"It's probably a factory." We waited as Sofia screamed at Lad, who had continued to run ahead, and the large man returned. "Hub of pions, large amounts of debris can collect unnoticed. If it's left long enough this is what happens." We both glanced at the dancing lights. "Someone hasn't been doing their collecting properly."

I gasped in breaths, sagged against a wall and clutched at my chest. "What has that got to do with us?"

"Problem like this could shut down the city. Imagine no light on the streets when night comes. No light at home. How do other factories work if the lights go out?"

"Quite well, I imagine." I swallowed against a very unladylike urge to spit on the paving stones. "Don't need light to see pions. But I get the idea." And on a day like this, in the storm and the darkness bearing down on Movoc-under-Keeper. I couldn't think of a worse time.

"They call in more than one team for work like this. For factories, construction sites."

I knew too well what he meant.

"Sorry!" Lad, only barely out of breath, ran to Kichlan's side. "Sorry, bro!"

Kichlan shook his head. "Pay attention from now on. This way!" He pointed, and set off again. With a groan, I pushed off the wall and followed.

This time, I gave in and I kept my fingers to the symbols at my wrist. They hummed with the pace of my running, jostling with the stones that threatened to slip me, with the hidden dips and sudden, uneven steps.

That's when I realised that wasn't all they were doing. My fingers were guiding me. A moment before a loose stone came close to tripping me, a cipher pushed up against my touch. I knew a corner was coming before Kichlan took it because my fingers were guided that way first.

When Kichlan stopped again to check his map I realised I wouldn't have had to. My fingers, my suit, already knew the way.

I peered through heavy rain to the symbols he had splashed across a wall, that mesh of unintelligible figures I had been told had no meaning. Beside Kichlan, on his map, was a long, wiggling line. I walked fingers up from my own position, and sure enough, there it was. I scanned the ground. Beside Kichlan, mere inches from his shoe, a gutter had burst. The symbol buzzed like an insect as I saw it. Nearly invisible in the darkness a torrent of water gushed down the edge of the street, weaving its way like an imitation of the figure on the wall. On my wrist.

Realisation was a breathless kick to the gut. The symbols were the map. All of them. They were the streets, the buildings, the dips and bumps in the road. And all we did was follow two of them. What could we do if we understood everything on the map, if we could read the city on the back of our wrists?

But Kichlan and the collectors didn't know about this map. Devich and the technicians didn't either. So who had put it there, who was keeping us all in the dark about the power of the suit on our wrists?

And why?

"This way." Kichlan called against the beat of the downpour and the rush of hidden water. "We're close now!"

"Bro!" Lad, ahead again, straining to be moving like a dog against a leash. He pointed to an alleyway curtained by rain and spray. "Found it, bro! Found it!"

Kichlan flicked his wrist, and the map disappeared. "I'll trust you before any map, Lad."

Grinning so widely his teeth were clear in the muted light, Lad started off down the alleyway. We followed, and my fingers vibrated, suddenly warm. Below them a symbol was growing strong, vibrant. Another dot under a hill, but not me. I was still there, still clearly marked and separate. The hill was crossed by two vertical lines either side of the dot.

It took me a moment to realise what I was seeing, what the suit and my guided fingers were following. This new figure moved along a thin path, a clear patch between the mess of other signs that made up my wrist band. And I was following.

I glanced between Lad's back, half obscured, and the cipher tugging on my arm.

He had his own symbol.

Kichlan didn't exist on my wristband. Neither did Sofia, Natasha and the twins. Only Lad. What was special about Lad? Why did he have a symbol all of his own?

Then the alleyway ended, and my hand slipped from my wrist unnoticed.

A fat, squat building sat like an ill toad on the other side of a wide street. The lights were dark here, no longer even flickering, and figures ran, frantic and hard to see, in front of the monstrous work of architectural torture.

Debris leaked from its every pore.

"Hurry!" Kichlan drove us forward.

The debris was watery this time, like the rain had diluted it. No sails arched darkly, no growths bulged from the side of the building. It ran instead, oozing from windows, from doors, from the gaps between brickwork and cracks in cement. There was something sickening about its liquidity, its runny porridge texture. It looked fetid, like it should stink.

"Other!" Mizra hissed.

Kichlan rushed forward. The rest of us crossed the street hesitantly. Even Lad eyed the debris with a squeamish expression.

"Who's in charge?" Kichlan called. Fingers pointed, curious faces met ours in the unnatural dark. But even in the cloud cover, even with the rain, I could see their exhaustion, their horror.

Judging by the rough numbers I could see, there were at least two other debris teams here. Possibly more. How long had they been fighting, to look so tired? And yet the muck kept coming, kept rolling out of windows, through the cracks of doors. Was anyone trapped inside, a factory worker who could not know what was happening? Could it hurt, to be covered in debris like this? To breathe it in, unknown? Would it undo the pion systems within a body, unravel blood from muscle, muscle from bone?

We had to stop it. I didn't want to find out.

"Eighth Keepersrill, Section ten," Kichlan was telling a man with greying hair and defeated, sagging shoulders as we reluctantly caught up.

The man nodded. "Don't know how much of a difference you'll make, but it's good to have help." The sound of his voice, the shake and the fatigue, made my bones ache.

"Have the veche sent more jars?" Kichlan asked, his face set in a convincing show of determination.

"On their way."

"Good." Kichlan slipped the bag from his shoulder and tossed it to Uzdal. "We'll do what we can with ours to begin with."

"Can't imagine you'll be much use." The collector gave a weary shrug. "But feel free."

"They're a pleasant lot," Mizra murmured as we moved away.

"They've been here a long time," Kichlan told him. "Can you blame them?"

"And we've had a nice little jog in the rain, have we?"

"Not now, Miz," Kichlan said, voice firm. "Now, we need to do what we can to help these teams. They're exhausted, and could do with some relieving." His eyes flickered to mine. "I think we should follow Tanyana's advice."

"You do?" I asked, before I could stop myself.

"Well, you managed to control the outbreak last time." He nodded. "Yes, we're going to do this your way."

Sofia rubbed her upper arm and shoulder, pointedly, but Kichlan pushed on regardless.

"Everyone spread out. Let's see if we can scoop this up and start pushing it back. I'm willing to lay kopacks down that there's a main body mass inside the factory, somewhere this is all coming from. And I think if we collect that, we'll have this place clean in no time. Tanyana, come with me. The rest of you, see what you can do."

I followed Kichlan as he ran to the front of the building. A large, slatted wooden door was rolled up and debris surged from the entrance in thick waves. Most of the collectors were concentrated before it. Their suits shone like dull silver as they caught the debris in great shovels, then passed it back, where it was dispersed and sealed away in jars. But the debris kept rolling, and the collectors kept shovelling, and I realised they could end up in those spots, collecting, forever.

"This is not working," I murmured to Kichlan.

"My point exactly." He glanced around at the sorry lines, the slushing dark muck, and the ever-growing pile of full jars. "We need to get closer. Right to the front."

I kept close as Kichlan pushed his way through. "So, this happens a lot, doesn't it?"

"What does?" he asked.

"Emergencies." I waved my hand. "Buildings and factories under attack. Like this."

"Actually, no." Kichlan gave me a sorry expression over his shoulder. "You've had an unlucky run."

"So two in a row like this is a bit strange?"

"Very strange, more like it. Usually you'd go more than thirteen moons and a day without a crisis half the size of these two." He grinned. "But then, you haven't been having the best luck, have you?"

Luck. Was that what it was? "You could say that."

We came to the front line of collectors. A middle-aged man, with thick hair plastered to his skull and neck, blinked at us through the rain.

"Here to help?" he asked. He scooped as he spoke, the motion automatic, and twisted at the waist to pass the debris he had collected to the line waiting behind him.

When Kichlan didn't answer, I said, "Yes." Kichlan was staring at the debris, his hands loose by his sides, suit retracted.

"Well, we could use the help. First call came at break-bell and I've been here since. They've been calling other teams all morning. Not that you'd know it was morning... hey!"

Kichlan had stepped past the front line. Debris surged over his feet like mud.

"What's he doing?" The collector paused in his shovelling. "We need to hold the line!"

"Tanyana," Kichlan said, ignoring the collector. "Shall we?"

I nodded, and waded through the debris to stand at his side. It was warm, where it brushed over me. The strangest feeling. Touching but not touching, like wind if it had weight and heat.

"Hey!" More collectors were shouting at us now. "What's going on?"

Behind us, the lines faltered.

"Can you mesh our suits together, the way you did with Lad?" Kichlan asked.

"Don't see why not." Except I had no idea how I'd done that, and less of an idea if I could do it again.

"Let's try, then."

Together, Kichlan and I raised our hands and spread

259

our suits out like a shield. The edges of silver touched at first with a screeching, metal scraping against metal. But then they softened, grew pliable, and sank into each other.

A strange shiver rattled through Kichlan as the same thing passed through me. I remembered Lad's hand on my arm, the connection between us, the whispers I had heard. Kichlan felt entirely different. Where Lad had been open, too open perhaps, Kichlan was closed. His suit became mine, but there were no whispers, no hints of the voices in his head. Did I feel the same, or could he hear my doubts clear as if I was shouting them?

"Lower!"

I glanced down. Debris was oozing from a gap between our suits and the ground. We grew them until only a trickle remained.

"They can collect that." Kichlan clenched his teeth; his eyes were hard and focused. "Let's start moving."

Feeling oddly light compared to the weight Kichlan seemed to be carrying, I walked beside him and helped force the debris back into the factory. It pushed against us as we advanced, but had none of the energy of last time. It did not crash like lightning against us, but merely tried to ease itself past us, like cupping a gentle trickle of water.

"Come on," I thought to it, I whispered in my own head and hoped Kichlan truly couldn't hear. I was wet, already tired, and shaken. All I wanted was for the debris to move easily, to retreat to its source and wait for us to collect it.

Murmurs behind us.

We came to the rolled-up door and were forced to pinch our suits in to fit through. I waited for the explosion, for the debris to roll through the gaps we made, for it to surge to sudden life as it sensed weakness, and carry us along with it.

Nothing happened.

"What's going on?" I whispered to Kichlan.

"Kichlan!" a voice called, echoing.

With a quick glance between us, Kichlan and I lowered the shield so we could see over the top. The factory was almost empty. Debris lay in patches of the floor, puddles after a storm. But of the fountain that had spewed forth from the doors, windows and cracks, there was no sign.

"What did you do?" Uzdal was clambering in through a window. He clung to the steel bones of the building and peered down at us. "Where did it go?"

Kichlan was just as shocked. "I have no idea."

Uzdal surveyed the cement walls and steel structures around him and began gradually climbing down. "I just got up here, was about to try and squeeze the debris and—" he mimed an explosion motion with his free hand. His right arm was wrapped tightly around a thick, load-bearing shaft "—it was gone."

"We walked inside..." Kichlan raised his eyebrows at me.

I replied, "Don't ask me. I've got less idea than you do."

"Kichlan? Tanyana?" Sofia called from the other end of the factory. She was crouched behind another wooden door, only rolled a few feet up. "What happened?" With a wince, she crawled her way through.

"Trying to work that out." Uzdal finally made it to the factory floor. He patted rust and dirt from the front of his jacket. They turned to mud on his wet clothes and hands.

Gradually, the other team members appeared. Lad and Mizra came together, descending from the second floor on metal stairs that rang loudly in the empty, cavernous room. Natasha ambled in through the front door.

"The teams outside are looking spooked," she drawled. "They really want to know what you've done, and why it worked so well."

Kichlan, apparently sick of the same question, rounded on her. "For the last, the final, the absolutely I will not repeat myself ever again time, I do not know!"

Her face set into a sullen cloud, the same colour as the sky outside. "First time you told me, you know."

I approached one of the larger debris puddles. It bubbled as I crouched beside it. How long before it started growing again?

"You might as well tell them to come and collect this mess up," Kichlan said.

"Your messenger now, am I?" Natasha grumbled, but still turned to leave the building.

Gingerly, I extended a thin dirk of my sharpened suit toward a particularly large bubble.

"Still need to find where all the debris came from," Kichlan said.

I popped the bubble.

Are you pleased?

I snatched my suit back so quickly it slammed into my wrist and pushed me to the floor.

"Watch yourself." Mizra chuckled.

But I didn't respond. Instead, I turned my head until I could see Lad. He was smiling, a happy, contented smile that widened when he caught my eye.

"Likes you," he said. "Listens to you."

I gaped at him.

"That's lovely, Lad." Kichlan dismissed his brother's rambling. "Now where do you think we should go?"

His younger brother pointed to the floor. "Down."

I returned to the bubbles. Underground made sense, yes. It was all bubbling up from underneath.

"Right, down we go. Anyone see some stairs on their way here?"

I sat up. Again, I carefully extended my suit, this time as the usual tweezers. My hand shook as I pried a slightly more solid selection of debris from the puddle. I brought it close to my face, frowned at it.

It remained quiet.

A breath I hadn't realised I was holding eased from me in a sigh. The debris rippled.

"Come on, Tanyana!" Kichlan called. He was helping Lad squeeze under the door Sofia had come through by holding it further from the ground. "Sofia's found our way down."

I stood, holding the debris, and hurried to his side. I slipped beneath the door – with far greater ease than Lad – and helped Kichlan do the same. The debris sagged from my suit. It felt warm, wet, and wiggled weakly.

"Where to?" I asked Sofia, once Kichlan was through.

But I didn't hear her reply.

Are you coming to see me?

I nearly dropped the debris. Sofia had already started leading the way and no one seemed to notice me standing there, white by the bloodless feeling in my cheeks, staring at a small, wiggly piece of debris.

No one, apart from Lad.

Still smiling, he nodded. "We should go," he said. "He is waiting."

"He?" I whispered.

I am.

Lad turned, and I caught up to him. "You can hear him, can't you?"

Lad followed the team into a narrow, dark hallway. Without the pion systems in place to keep the lights working, the way downstairs was perilous. I clung to a railing with my free hand and sought each step with a fumbling foot.

"Can you smell that?" Uzdal's voice echoed up from the darkness below.

"Smells like a sewer," Mizra answered. "I knew we'd end up in a sewer today, somehow."

I ran into Lad's back as the stairs ended and the ground levelled out. He steadied me with a large hand in the dark.

"This is no good," Kichlan whispered. "I can't see a thing."

I agreed with him, silently, and the light from my suit strengthened, deepened into a stark, silvery blue. The symbols rolled, pressed together, and became a thickened mess of colour and shape.

"Tanyana?" Kichlan turned, shocked. "What–?" He looked down at his own suit, glowing only the usual soft light. "How are you doing that?"

I shook my head. "I don't know," I whispered. Somehow, it felt right to whisper at the bottom of these dark stairs. "I really don't know."

"We should use it while we have it," Sofia said, ever practical.

"Yes. Tanyana, could you?" Still frowning, Kichlan stepped aside so I could lead the way.

Lad kept close to me as we walked. I couldn't help but glance at the symbols, hard to read in the light and in their bloated closeness. Sure enough, there was Lad, his hill with a dot close to mine. And there was debris, right in front of me, the lightning strike sharply detailed amidst ill-defined lines. But as I lowered my wrist I saw it. A cipher I hadn't noticed before, not while the rest of the figures were spaced out. Made of the map itself, yet brighter, sharper, very much a symbol in its own right. Another debris sign. One that encompassed all of us, one made up of us. It was everywhere, it was everything.

I looked up into the darkness, to the grey shapes of a curved roof and snake-twisted pipes.

"What is that?" I whispered to myself.

I am here.

And sure enough, my suit-light fell on a crack in the floor. A pipe ran beneath it and we could hear the sound of water rushing through iron. But from the gap, the dark corners between pipe and cement, debris grew like a fungus. Bulbous, patchy, and swaying as though in a breeze.

"That's it." Kichlan crouched beside the crevice. "Oh, very well done."

I said nothing. Something was tickling my stomach, something like the first buds of laughter. If I opened my mouth nothing but giggling, inane chuckling, would burst out. Beside me, Lad let out a little laugh, and was ignored.

"Uzdal, the jars." Kichlan held out his hand, and Uzdal slung the bag's strap into his palm. "Let's work, shall we."

I have been waiting. I am glad you came.

As the others set to scooping, prying and pinching the debris from its hold beneath the building, I lifted my hand and stared at the scrap I held between my fingers.

"Why are you talking to me?" I breathed over it, and it jiggled.

They are here, did you see them? Watching you like they watch me. Together we can fight them. Together, we are strong.

Then something touched my shoulder. A hand, light, warm. It brushed my neck with soft fingers and a warm breath.

I am sorry for you, Tanyana. Truly, I am. But I cannot be sorry you are here.

I spun. The room behind me was empty, save for storage crates and shards from broken ceramic loops.

"Tanyana?" Kichlan looked up from his work. "What's the matter?"

"He scared her and now he's gone," Lad answered for me, his words nonsense. "He didn't mean to."

"You didn't scare her, Lad," Kichlan said, full of patience.

I stared between them. The phantom memory of the hand on my skin was warm, and everything jumbled together in that heat. Eugeny's warning, Kichlan's explanation. Lad, with his inexplicable connection to debris and the voices within his head. The voices he had always heard and sometimes, the voices he obeyed.

And I had no idea which one of them was right, if anyone understood anything properly, if I had any idea what was going on.

"Tanyana?" Kichlan stood. Concerned, he approached me, a half-filled jar held in front of him. "It's been a strange morning, hasn't it? Are you all right?"

I nodded. A lie, if ever there was one.

He held out the jar. "Drop that grain in here and take a moment to rest. We've almost got this finished."

I held the debris over the open jar. It felt like a chasm, the lip a gaping mouth.

"Go on." Kichlan smiled.

Goodbye. For the moment.

I dropped the debris and watched Kichlan seal the lid. "Where do the jars go when they are full?" I asked him. I had to concentrate to retract my suit, and my hand shook.

"To the technicians. From there, I don't know."

"Oh." The technicians. Devich.

"Come and give us light. We're nearly done."

Leaning over the rest of the team I watched them collect. Sure enough, the fissure was close to empty. What had caused the debris to rise, to swallow the factory whole?

Lights started to reignite in the factory above us. Voices echoed down from the stairwell.

"It's come up from the old city, hasn't it?" I whispered. The Movoc-under-Keeper built long before Novski's revolution, and the small patches of it that still remained. Like the wall that had fallen on me on my first day as a collector. I squinted hard into the tiny gap between pipe and cement, but try as I might I couldn't see deeper. No ruins, no hand-laid stonework, and not the wellspring I believed had to be there, the untapped oceans of debris.

"No," Sofia answered. "Debris like this is created by the new world, by massive levels of pion manipulation." She hesitated. "But I know what you mean. It likes old places, doesn't it?"

Lights flickered on in the basement, drowning out my suit. In the crevice, no shadow of debris remained. Not even a grain.

When we climbed out of the basement to a world lit again by steady, strong lamplight, I saw them. At the edge of the crowd of surprised but grateful debris collectors, half hidden by the rain and the shadow of a building, stood two of the puppet men. Their faces pale, expressionless, bodies wooden and unmoving, they watched me.

11.

By the time I returned home, it was late Mornday evening and the skies had not brightened once. Rain fell constantly, I was soaked through and so chilled I couldn't keep my finger steady on the lock. It took three tries to convince the pions I was me. And I had just managed to unlock the door and shrug off my jacket when footsteps sounded behind me.

"Vladha?"

I spun. Two large men filled the small, paved court-yard. Both were swathed in coats constructed of dark material, heavily patched, and wore tight knitted hats pulled down to prominent eyebrows.

"Are you Vladha?" the left one asked again. His voice was low as the thunder, his eyes two glinting spots in the shadows of his face.

"Miss Vladha," I answered, already stepping back into my hallway, already reaching to close the heavy wooden door between us.

But large, meaty hands held it open, and wide arms kept it there.

"Landlord sent us," the man on the left said.

"He's not happy," said his fellow.

"Doesn't like tenants who cannot pay."

"Doesn't like losing kopacks."

"Doesn't like it at all."

I stumbled into the hallway, coat dropped to the floor. Suddenly they were inside, filling the small space, invading my home.

"You can't," I whispered.

They gave an identical snicker of contempt. "Oh, we can," the left one chuckled. "We do, in fact, more often than you'd think."

"Places like this." The other was walking down the hall, eyeing the walls, the pictures, the lamps. The little statue of princess Ludmilla that Mother had given me when I graduated, the best she could hope to afford. His eyes were like fingers the way they touched, the way they caressed and pried. "Always in demand. You're not the only one. Buy out of your range, live beyond your kopacks. But there's always someone willing to take what you drop. Always the next arrogant idiot with an overfull rublie in line."

"You wait right here."

The wall I stood against moved. Hands reached from the marble and wallpaper. They gripped my arms, clutched at my waist and thighs. The man chuckled as I strained but had no way to hold back the pions, no way to calm my own wall into submission.

"What have we got, then?" He followed his fellow into my bedroom and left me pinned to the hallway, straining like a fly in a web.

My rublie felt heavy in the pocket of my pants, but I knew with a horrible certainty that they wouldn't go for it. There was nothing left in it, not enough, at least, to cover the debts I had so wilfully ignored. The rent, the water, the pion heat. How many kopacks did I owe and what would these men do to get them?

Unwelcome hands rattled through my bedroom. Voices laughed. Something smashed. I tried to ignore them, as though I could will them out of my home, out of my memory, by staring at the closed wooden door.

"Hey!" A gruff voice spoke and a large hand gripped the side of my head, shaking until I snapped my gaze to his face. "None of that!"

They didn't know that I was a collector and I couldn't have undone the bindings they worked in my wall, no matter how hard I concentrated.

"You should leave," I rasped out of a sore throat. "Don't you know what I can do? I'm an architect, employed by the veche itself. If you don't go, now, I will undo your bonds and turn your pions right back on you! Trap you here, call enforcers, and then who knows what information would get out? I don't think my landlord wants anyone to know the kind of associates he employs, do you?"

The large man smirked between tight knitted cap and unwashed beard. "Yeah, we were told about you. Pity you can't pay your bills, Miss Employed-by-the-veche." He leaned forward. A breath like rancid meat and old onion washed over my face. It set my eyes watering. "We were told to keep you busy, if you went and tried anything. Keep you occupied." He wrapped a hand across my jaw and tipped my face. The back of my head pressed into the wall, my neck strained until I thought the scars would tear. "We could give you prettier cuts than these." He flicked a pink ridge on my cheek. I sucked air through my teeth. "So you keep quiet." He released me, cuffed the top of my head with a casual backhand, like I was a dog that had displeased him, and rejoined his fellow.

They had moved on to my study, I realised as my body sagged against the restraints. To my books, my footstool. The chair I had sat in while Devich drank tea and touched my knees. Devich! I sent out a mental call, a need that welled up from my gut into my head. Come tonight, Devich! Find these bastards and... and what? Walk blindly in through the door and be found dead, clogging one of Tear's more obscure rills tomorrow morning? Did I really want him here, did I want him to fight for me, to suffer for me? Possibly die for me.

Die? I shuddered.

I had to be overreacting. It was just a few kopacks, wasn't it? And this was Varsnia, the civilised world.

I cleared my throat. "Um, excuse me?" No reaction, just more rummaging and plunder. "Hey!"

One of the large men stepped out of the kitchen. "Want us to shut your mouth for you too?"

I refused to be daunted. "What, exactly, is going to happen here?"

A smile broke through the untrimmed beard. "Already happening, bitch."

With a breath I clamped down on sudden anger. But anger was good. Anger was better than cowering attached to the wall, willing for a saviour to come. "Fine. What is happening, then? What–" saying this took a steadying pause of its own, I refused to sound afraid "–are you going to do with me?"

The smile widened as he chuckled. "You're a confident one." He made a sweeping gesture with one thick-as-a-pylon arm. "We take what you owe. Compensation. Apartment for the apartment, goods for the kopacks.

You're lucky there. By the looks of it you'll cover everything you owe."

My throat was suddenly very dry. I didn't ask what would have happened if I hadn't accumulated so many memories, so many treasures with my hard-earned kopacks. How they would have made up the gap.

"So you take my home, you take everything I own. Then you let me go."

He roared with laughter, smacked his own knee and nearly doubled up against the wall. Hardly inspired confidence.

The other man was drawn into the hallway from the study. He carried a small bear statue in one hand and a very old book in the other. The bear was set in solid burnished copper, with an old mechanical clock in its belly. The clock no longer worked. The book was Velchev's *Principles of Architecture*. An original copy, hand written in ink on vellum, complete with diagrams and pencilled-in notes. Both were priceless. Both were gifts, given to me by old family members of the national veche on the completion of the gallery.

I looked away.

"What?" he asked. Biting the word off like a barbarian, barely able to speak the language, let alone appreciate the true value of what he held in his thick hands.

"Reckons we're going to let her go, this one does," the comedian answered.

Barbarian added a chuckle of his own. It sounded hungrier than his companion. He liked his work, liked the consumption of another person's life, particularly someone who thought they were better than him. He enjoyed the process of biting, ripping it to bits and devouring until there was nothing left.

To Comedian it was just all one big, black joke.

"Now why would we do that?" Barbarian asked.

I tried to find his eyes. "Because you'll have got what you came for."

Comedian shook his head. "Apartment goes to the landlord, your stuff gets sold to pay off debts. You, we're supposed to bring in all nice and in one piece. Not the way we usually work it. Most of the time the landlord's happy to let us beat 'em to a right mess. But he's been getting visitors, said they wanted you brought back. You had a lesson to learn–"

"Quiet down!" Barbarian growled.

Comedian shut his mouth, pressed it into a thin smile. "Look at you, got me talking too much."

"You hand me over to the landlord, then?" I tried to remember if I'd ever met the man. Savvin's father had set me up with the apartment in exchange for taking his son into my critical circle, when I had earned my right to head a circle of nine. He had organised everything, and I'd been happily relieved of the chore.

Did Savvin's father know, then, the kind of man who owned these apartments? Was he laughing with Savvin at how low his former centre had fallen, at what would happen to her when she couldn't pay her rent?

"To his visitors, I'd say." Comedian's grin broadened. "And by the look of them, they'll teach you to ask too many questions. Never seen such a strange–"

"Quiet!" Barbarian roared.

"No." I straightened as much as the clutching wall would allow. "No." I would fall no further, and I would not fall away from Kichlan, from Lad. From the twins with their sad humour; Sofia with her serious eyes; even silent, pouting Natasha. I would not leave my team. "I

274

can't go with you. I won't go with you."

Both laughed together.

"Feisty!" Comedian crowed.

"They will break you, bitch," Barbarian said. "I hope I see it. Hope I'm there."

"Break me?" I couldn't control my words anymore, couldn't tell which ones were foolish and likely to get me killed. "You don't know what breaking is! Brains full of the Other's piss, that's all you've got. You useless, little men."

Barbarian strode toward me. "Shut your mouth!" He lifted the solid copper bear, eyes glinting, terrible with purpose and anger.

"One piece, Ngad!" Comedian ran forward, gripped the copper bear and fought to pry it from Barbarian's grip.

"No one breaks a person like *Grandeur* breaks a person!" I laughed at their shocked faces, at their hulking dance around the bear, held frozen in his roar above their heads. "She smacks you and she cuts you and she leaves you all alone."

"What's wrong with her?" Barbarian paused in a bulky pirouette and peered at me, large eyebrows crunched into a caterpillar frown. His hold on the bear loosened enough for Comedian to yank it from his hand.

"What does it matter?" Comedian scowled between us both. "Stupid bitch's mad, not our problem. They can deal with her."

"She breaks you," I continued, only half hearing the two large men supposedly stripping me of my world. Little did they know how much had already peeled away. "But you find your feet again. Falling just means you're someone else when you stand up." I looked up, met each

275

face. "I didn't get up again to let you push me down."

"Other's stinking balls," Barbarian muttered. "She's insane."

"I'm not coming with you."

"You don't understand." Comedian leaned close to my face, the bear still clasped in his hand and safely behind his back. "You don't have a choice. You'll stay where you are until we're ready, then you come with us. And you either come nice and quiet, or we rig your bonds and drag you the whole way. Don't want that, do you?"

I chuckled. "That supposed to be a threat, is it? Do you dream I still fear humiliation?"

"Insane," Barbarian muttered somewhere behind Comedian's head.

"This is ridiculous." Comedian straightened. "I'm not wasting time with you any more." He smacked me with his empty hand. It knocked my head against the wall, stinging the bruise already there, and cut the inside of my bottom lip. My blood tasted warm and rich, tingling. What could I taste there? Was the suit in my very blood? Was that the silver metal that buzzed on my tongue like something living?

"Shut up or I'll rig one of those binds across your mouth." Comedian turned away, his face red with anger, hand wrapped so tightly around the bear his knuckles were white, and the veins along his wrist and the back of his hand stood out.

But it was too late. Laughter bubbled up unchecked from my belly, from the taste of suit on my tongue, from the crude and simple pion-bonds I had no hope of escaping. And from the thought that things could get any worse. That they could break me, these large and simple fools.

Both turned again at the sound of my laughter and both wore identical masks of rage. This only made it worse. Tears ran down my cheeks, blurred their approach. I was laughing so hard my stomach ached. I could barely breathe.

But somehow, I managed a word. "No."

And the suit reacted. It knew what I needed to do, before I had realised. And out of my control, feral and protective like a bitch over her litter, it did what needed to be done.

The bands at my wrists arched out and over me in a wide, metal shield. The band at my neck grew, it flattened over my body in a second silver skin, while my ankles and waist did the same thing until they met, until I was cased in a metal shell.

Wrapped up, enfolded, I gasped in air already growing stale. I could hear voices, hear the shock and something that might have been fear.

"This is no good," I whispered to myself, to the buzz on my tongue. "We need to get out. Hiding won't help."

Gritting my teeth, struggling for control, I summoned my wristbands back and broke the shield. Comedian and Barbarian were arguing, staring at me in shock and shouting at each other. I pushed their words aside and sharpened blades over my hands. "One at a time."

The blades became snakes and slithered in silver over my sleeves, down my arms and toward my chest. At each bond they stopped and cut upward, severing the chains of cement and paint. My suit was sharp, my suit was strong, and nothing made of such coerced and unimpressed pions could hold against it.

Bond by bond, in a trickle of rubble, I cut my arms free.

"–tell us she was a collector!" Barbarian was shouting. "Why wouldn't they–" He had seen me. "Other! She's getting out!"

"That's not possible–"

The argument shut off as both Comedian and Barbarian snapped into concentration. Bodies still, eyes down, hands set in identical clutching claws. I had to give them that. Brutal, senseless they may be, but they had some discipline, some binding skill.

Not that I was going to let them use it. My blades shot out, and it was all I could do to blunt them before they connected with a face each. My left hand smashed into Comedian's nose. He roared and gargled and fell against the front door, clutching his face as blood ran beneath his fingers. My right was not as accurate. It clipped the top of Barbarian's head, just above the temple. He made no sound as he collapsed, crashing to the marble in a boneless heap.

For a moment, all I could do was stare at him. My suit retracted slowly, my left hand red with blood from Comedian's nose, my right strangely clean. It was the cleanness that gripped my gut, more than the blood did. It seemed worse, strangely. A wound without anything to prove it existed.

I hadn't considered the possibility – even after watching Lad launch himself at his brother, and seeing Kichlan respond in kind, their suits like swords and shields – that the suit could be a weapon, that it could do more than scoop debris like so much dog shit on the street. That I could protect myself with it.

Or that it would protect me. Perhaps that was more accurate.

I sharpened my blades again and set them to work on the bonds around my waist and thighs.

The final few shackles crumbled as I stepped from the wall. I was still encased in metal, from my neck to my ankles, with only my arms bare. I kept my blades up, like a sword in each hand, and wished I knew was I was doing with them. Wished I was the son of an old family, and had learned to fence as soon as I learned to walk.

Comedian had sunk to the floor, propped against the wall and clutching at his nose. I hesitated. I had to leave, that was obvious. I had to get out and go very, very far away. But with both men incapacitated, I had time. I could take my memories with me.

Barbarian had dropped the book when he fell. I collected it, trying not to see the trail of blood seeping from his nose or wonder what that could mean.

"Where do you think you're going, bitch?"

I spun. Comedian was on his feet, copper bear in his hand, his face slathered in blood. He launched himself at me before I could raise either of my blades. I turned in the face of his wrath and the copper bear came smashing down on my suit-coated back.

I didn't feel it. Behind me, he cried out again, and I looked over my shoulder to see him gripping his wrist as the copper bear fell from his hand. Its face was dented, squashed into something morbid and horrible. The clock face had smashed, rings loose, bells rattling against cracked glass.

That was it. No more memories were worth searching for. I retracted my blades as I ran past him, book under one arm, and slammed the door behind me. Still coated in suit silver I dashed into the street and ignored the shocked faces of pedestrians and carriage drivers. I just ran.

By the time I made it to the Tear, I could hardly breathe. My chest was afire within me and the book was so heavy all I wanted to do was drop it. I stopped in a narrow, sewage-stinking alleyway. Leaning against cold stone I fought for breath and struggled against the suit. It didn't want to move, to ease the protective shell from my skin. Gradually, as my breathing and my heart slowed, I could convince it everything was okay, that there weren't any strange men to fight and nothing to protect me from.

When the suit had settled, I realised how cold I was. I had left my jacket on the floor in the hallway. I hugged my arms over my chest, hunched forward and plunged into the street. I made for the ferry, and didn't look over my shoulder. Who knew who was following?

I stood outside of 384 Darkwater as twilight fell, and re-alised as keenly as the wind that was slicing through my shirt and to my uniform that I couldn't stay there. I couldn't get through the door. And as darkness and a true Movoc-under-Keeper night fell, complete with clear sky and stars like icicles, it hit me that I didn't have any-where else to go. I didn't know where Devich lived, or even if he would have welcomed me destitute and homeless on his doorstep. Would he ever find me now?

There was only one place I knew would let me in. But I wasn't sure how to find Kichlan's home, the last trip was more of a haze than any real and useful memory.

There wasn't much else to do. I tucked the book more tightly into my armpit, thrust my hands as deep into the pockets of my pants as they would go, and wished that longing for a hat, gloves and jacket kept you as warm as the real things. Then I tried to follow the path to Kich-lan's house.

I lost the trail several times and found myself on unknown street corners. I could feel the chill settling into my chest and neck the way the darkness settled over the city, creeping but inexorable. By the time I found his squat house nestled between two large and faceless apartment buildings I had developed a shiver that ran through me and rattled the metal in my bones.

Kichlan's house was quiet in the night, windows closed up and dark. For a moment I stood shivering on the step, wondering if I could find where the horse lived and sleep next to him. Apart from straw – or whatever it was horses nested in – I probably wouldn't be all that worse for wear. Then I could work it out on my own. I shifted the book. I could make enough kopacks out of this priceless heirloom to find somewhere to live, to buy a new jacket. But that wouldn't do for tomorrow. And horses had a smell, didn't they? How could I explain straw and a horsey smell?

It wasn't that hard. Kichlan had helped me once, I could go to him again. Grovel like a weak chick cast from her nest, snivel because I had nowhere else to stay.

"Stop that," I whispered to the closed door, my teeth rattling in tune with my bones.

I knocked on the door. The knocker was steel and cold. It bit into my bare fingers and kept scraps of my skin as payment.

The house remained still.

I knocked again; my hand shook so much I wasn't sure I could control it. A long breath of darkness, of quiet and cold, and I started to doubt this was the right house. Started to believe I was standing in front of some deserted ruin knocking my way into a cold and endless sleep.

Then voices murmured behind the door, and I heard shuffling. A light peered out of a gap between door and top step. Keys rattled.

The door opened with a groan, exhausting to hear. It split the darkness with a crack of lantern light that hurt my eyes. And Kichlan was there. Only half of his face, the rest of him was hidden. And that half a face was squinting and scowling, concerned and angry all at once.

Perhaps intended to frighten off an intruder.

Or confuse them.

"Who's there?" His voice cracked. He had been asleep, I realised. A sleep he dearly needed and I had pulled him from it.

"I have a problem," I stuttered. My words jumbled over my rattling teeth, and my breath wove a thick haze in front of Kichlan's widening eyes. "I have... a problem."

I wasn't really sure what else to say, there on the doorstep. Without my jacket.

"Tanyana?" Kichlan opened the door wider, saw me properly. "Other! What are you doing?" He grabbed my shoulder and pulled me into the house.

Eugeny and Lad waited behind him. The old man held a fire stoker above his head as though ready to strike. Lad sat on the stairs, chin in his hand, eyes drooping and expression bored.

"Tan!" Lad stood when he saw me, all sleep falling from his wide eyes. "Kich! Tan is here!"

"Yes," Kichlan's gaze took me in with one long, unimpressed sweep. "I can see that. Give me your hands."

I blinked at him. "Hands?" I pried them from my pockets, and still trying to hold the book firmly beneath my left arm, held them out for him. My fingers were blue,

282

the colour broken only by white beneath my nails and red where the door knocker had nipped me.

"Other's eternal darkness, girl." Eugeny joined Kichlan in peering at my frozen, battered skin. "What happened to you?"

I stared at the old man, his scowling tenant, and the younger brother's unconcerned grin. "It's very hot in here." Sweat was running beneath my uniform, itching where it trickled between my breasts.

Eugeny placed a rough hand on my forehead. "Other," he snapped. He turned to Kichlan. "Get her warm, that's a fever I can feel. Lad!" He drew Lad's willing and now firmly wide-awake attention. "Help me, boy. Tan needs medicine or she will be sick."

"Oh!" Lad, shocked, went a strange shade of mottled green and white. "Oh... oh no!" He ran off into the kitchen, overtaking Eugeny.

"Lad locked himself out of the house one Rest a few moons ago, gave himself a fever." Kichlan shook his head. "He hasn't forgotten it. Trust me, he'll hover over you and feel every ache and pain."

"Why is everyone calling me Tan?" I asked him. The idea of a fever was too difficult to understand. It wobbled away in a fog somewhere in my head, ineffectual and quiet.

Kichlan gave me a strange, tilted-eye look and didn't answer. "Why don't you sit down, Tanyana?" He still held my hands and tugged on them gently. I hissed through my teeth. My fingers were numb, but the back of my hands felt fiery beneath his touch. "Come and sit down."

He drew me into the drying room, where I had slept the last time I came here. I suddenly realised how exhausted I was. But Kichlan didn't let me lie down. He found a collapsed couch somewhere behind the forest of hanging clothes and bed sheets. He propped me up in its cushions, drew a blanket from a line close to the dim fireplace and draped it around my shoulders.

I struggled against its weight. "Hot," I murmured.

"No, Tanyana. It isn't. Not really." He wrapped long fingers around the book under my arm. "Give me that. You can sit, then, and have a nice drink."

Was I thirsty? "No." Maybe, it was hard to tell. My mouth felt dry, but the thought of anything in my stomach made me nauseous. "You can't take it."

Kichlan leaned very close. His breath smelled of cinnamon. "It's me, Kichlan. I'm not going to take it away, I'm going to look after it."

Kichlan. That's right, it was Kichlan. Not Barbarian lying on my floor, not Comedian clutching his wrist and howling. Kichlan. Kichlan I could trust. I eased my arm open and he slid the book out. He gave it half a moment's glance and placed it on the floor.

"Be careful," I whispered. "That's all I have left."

Eugeny entered, a tray in his hand and Lad at his heels. Lad carried a mug, steaming faint trails of haze over his face, with a reverential delicacy.

"Drink." Lad bent at the waist to hand me the mug. His eyes were focused on the surface of its dark liquid so intently they nearly crossed.

I tried to take it from him but Kichlan was much faster. He took the cup with a click of his tongue. "Fingers like that, you'll spill it all over your own lap."

"Don't want to do that," Lad told me, solemn. "Need to drink it all."

Kichlan held the mug up to my lips. I scowled at him. "I'm not a child, I can hold my own drink."

"Don't be stubborn." A firm light came into Kichlan's eyes, the kind I had seen when he spoke to Lad in one of his moods. "You came here for help, didn't you? So take it."

Help involved a roof and a space away from the snow. It didn't involve being fed like an invalid or a child. But as I opened my mouth to protest, Kichlan pressed the mug against my lips, and I ended sipping something hot and bitter instead.

I coughed, and Lad gave me a knowing smile. "I know it tastes bad," he lectured me in a fair imitation of Kichlan's voice. "But you need to drink it all."

"What is it?" I made a face at Eugeny, certain he was the cause of this particular problem. "Not another gold plant."

He lifted his eyebrows at me. "Golden roots of the waxseal plant? No, not this time. Hyssop, liquorice root, thyme."

Words in a language I didn't understand. So I glared, puzzled, at him over the rim of my mug as Kichlan – with gentle, but inexorable hands – forced me to drink.

Eugeny shook his head. "You always come here in a state, girl."

I swallowed and leaned my head back long enough to gasp some much-needed air. Kichlan's idea of drinking, it seemed, did not involve enough time to catch one's breath. "Here is a good place to be in a state," I said, before I finished the drink's grass-murky dregs.

"Bro?" Lad, having satisfied himself that I would in fact finish the disgusting but no doubt beneficial brew, collected my book from the floor. "What is this, bro?"

Before I could move, Kichlan smoothly turned, stood, and took the book from his younger brother. "It's Tan's. She brought it with her."

Lad seemed content to peer at the cracking leather cover from over his brother's shoulder. "A book!" Excited, he clamped his fingers over Kichlan's upper arm. Kichlan winced. "What does it say, bro? Do you know what it says?"

Kichlan ran his finger below the embossed lettering on the jacket. It had once been gold, I had been told when given the gift, but years and use had eroded the title to the point where it was almost illegible. "Its title says *Principles of Architecture*, by Eldar Velchev."

I waited for the gasps, the wide eyes, the "How ever did you come by such a remarkable piece?"

Lad leaned back again, and wrinkled the skin at the top of his nose. "Oh." His eyes slid sideways to his brother. "That's not very interesting, is it?"

With a chuckle, Kichlan shook his head. "Not really." He turned the book over in his hands. "But it is very old. Isn't it?" His gaze flicked to mine in a question.

"Yes," I said.

"Old things can be valuable. Can't they?" Again, that quick, but searching and suspicious glance.

"Yes," I said again.

Lad bobbed his head as he searched for something valuable in the old book. "Doesn't look it, bro. Doesn't look it."

"People with too many kopacks have strange ways of seeing things," Kichlan said, grinning.

"Oh." Lad squinted at the book and leaned even closer to it.

I scowled between the both of them. "If this becomes a morality lesson, I'm going outside again."

"No, you won't." Eugeny, who had remained silent and in the background, pushed his way forward. He rested the tray on my knees, and a far more appetising bowl of soup stared up at me. "You're going to sit and eat, and Kichlan will put that somewhere safe. Where hands, unwelcome or simply curious, won't find it."

My gaze followed the book as Kichlan took it from the drying room. My life was in those pages, all that was left of my memories, my ambition and achievements. Something wrenched in my gut as I watched it go, but it was in Kichlan's hands and strangely that was enough. I knew it would be safe, because he carried it.

Eugeny watched me; I caught his pursed lips in the corner of my eye. Then he placed a spoon in my hand, and I was occupied by rich vegetable-and-grain stew.

Without anything new to excite him, Lad drooped. When Kichlan returned he managed to convince Lad to go back to bed. I received a wet kiss on the cheek before Lad was led upstairs, stumbling on the way.

By the time my bowl was empty I was feeling warm – no longer hot while tickled at the extremities by cold – tired and comfortable. I sat among the cushions and closed my eyes to the quiet conversation between Kichlan and Eugeny. Whatever decision they came to, I didn't hear it. For the couch was soft, the room was warm, and for the first time since I had unlocked my front door, I felt secure enough to fall into an easy sleep. I felt like I was home.

12.

We kept the details from Lad. All he needed to know, Kichlan said, was that I had left my old home and needed a new one. He didn't need to know about large and violent men who burst into the one place you're supposed to feel safe, and take your life away. I rather thought I didn't need to know about such things either, but the choice had, unfortunately, been long taken away.

Wetday and Thunderday I spent under Eugeny's herb-obsessed supervision, not allowed to move, not allowed to do much other than drink strong doses of various herbal tea and eat stew until I was tired of the very sight of it. For Frostday and Olday, Eugeny pronounced me well enough to join Kichlan and Lad in the collecting field. The team showed me small sympathy.

"About time you toughened up to the cold," Sofia told me with a superior sneer.

"I've spent half of my life with a fever because of this Other-damned collecting," Natasha muttered. "Get used to it."

I gathered Kichlan hadn't told them the whole story, and rather marvelled that Lad hadn't let my homeless-ness slip. I felt a deep thankfulness to both of them.

By Rest, I was chafing to be free of Eugeny's scrutiny and stew, and wished to be a burden on Kichlan no longer.

Lad woke me early, tangling and stomping through the drying clothes. "Tan! Early morning, Tan! Time to get going."

My bed had once again been made before the fireplace. I levered myself up on my elbow and squinted at him. "Today is called Rest, Lad. Rest. Don't you get the hint?"

He blinked at me, bird-like, studying me separately with each eye. "But it's time to go. Kich said we won't have time if we don't go."

"Go where?" I sat up and stretched. No amount of use could make this temporary bed comfortable.

"To find you a home, of course," Kichlan said, from behind veils of drying sheets. "What did you think we were going to do?"

In all honesty, I hadn't considered it. I scooped my clothes from the floor and struggled into them. After my late-night flight, two days of rest and two days of collecting, these clothes needed a wash the way a drowning woman needs air. Unfortunately, they were the only ones I had.

"Continue to enjoy my company for a little while longer?" I swept past the clothes, Lad in tow, and smiled at Kichlan where he leaned against the door frame.

He flashed a grin that reminded me, for a moment, of Devich. My stomach lurched and I wondered if he was missing me. If he had called at my apartment and found the place ransacked, blood-splattered and empty. If he feared for me.

"A man can only do that for so long." Kichlan chuckled. "Before he starts to lose his mind."

Lad let out an explosive laugh, although I wasn't entirely convinced he understood us.

"No houses on an empty stomach!" Eugeny called from the kitchen. As Lad ran in, the old man peered at us across the hallway. "And if you two keep that up I'm going to lose my appetite."

I felt hot and flushed as I spooned runny, honey-drizzled porridge into my mouth. Judging from Kichlan's red face he felt much the same, but I could guarantee he wasn't as confused about it. That he didn't have Devich, out there, somewhere.

Once we were fed to Eugeny's satisfaction, he tipped us out of the house in a way that made me feel like a child sent to play. "You remember what I told you?" he asked Kichlan. "Here." Eugeny placed a heavy bundle, wrapped in felt, in my hands. "I'm afraid you'll need that." Then he closed the door on my forming question, and left us milling on the step.

"Shall we?" Kichlan gestured to the street, as I pried the edge of the material apart, and recognised my book nestled within.

I covered it, and ran a hand slowly down the spine. It was worth enough kopacks to build a life with, surely. And in a way, it was a fair bargain. An old life for a new one.

"You know you don't have any choice." Pragmatism was somehow better than sympathy, at least coming from Kichlan.

I held the book tightly against my chest, and said, "I know."

We walked in silence below a bright blue sky. Cold fingers of wind played with the flaps of the overlarge jacket Kichlan had lent me. The ice had melted, and the faint colours of small flowers could be seen peeking through cracks in the poorly tended paving stones.

"What is it?" Kichlan asked. He seemed to know where we were going, and I had been following him out of unconscious habit, seeing the city only as a grey haze, unclear and unreal. "The book. Why does it mean so much?"

"A gift," I answered him. "A symbol."

"It's a book," Lad added helpfully. "It's a book, isn't it, bro?"

"Sometimes books are more than books," Kichlan said. He hesitated. "It's rare, Tanyana. Isn't it?"

"You know that already." I sighed, and gave in. "Eldar Velchev was a leader in the critical circle revolution. He composed a set of principles for nine point pion circles that architects still use today. The usual concerns: weight and pressure, distribution of mass. And the broader ones like propriety and symmetry. But more so, he applied the same concerns to the pion circle working the building. He came to realise that a circle must also be balanced, that too much pressure on one point could destabilise–" I broke off. Two blank faces were staring at me, as though I'd started gibbering in another tongue.

"Um... What?" Lad asked.

"My thoughts exactly," Kichlan added.

"Right." I shifted the book into my armpit to free up my hands. "When I was a pion-binder, I was an architect. I designed and made buildings."

"Like these?" Lad pointed to an unnaturally ugly mound of cement that, I supposed, could have passed for apartments if one squinted or covered an eye.

"No." I stuck out my tongue and made him laugh. "No, I made beautiful things. Big things. Important things."

Important things? I shook my head at myself. "This book is written by the man who started the pion revolution in architecture. At the same time as they were working out how to put together factories to generate and distribute light and heat, he worked out how to build cities like the one we live in."

Both brothers nodded.

"Well, this book is all his theories. Written in his own hand, with his own notes. It's very old, like Kichlan said, and very rare. And to an architect, it's probably the most important thing ever written."

Kichlan was silent. Lad, after a moment, said, "Ooh." A long and low exclamation, like he'd eaten something particularly delicious. "Why do you have it then, Tan?"

His acute question surprised Kichlan and myself, and we exchanged a quick, shocked glance. "Well, Lad." I reached up to pat him on the shoulder. "I built something very special. Very beautiful." My throat choked before I could catch it.

"Very important?" Lad continued.

"I suppose you could say that." Rueful, I smiled at my own words in his mouth. "When it was finished the people who had asked me to build it gave me this." I patted the book awkwardly. "To say thank you."

"That was very nice," Lad said, tone approving.

"It was indeed."

After a moment, Kichlan said, very softly, "We would like to see this building, one day."

After a longer moment, I answered, just as softly, "One day, perhaps."

"Where are we going now, bro?" Lad asked. He glanced between the road and the book under my arm, as though gradually putting the two factors together.

"Where are we taking Tan's special book?"

Kichlan's shoulders sagged as he answered. "To a nice man that Eugeny knows who will buy it from Tanyana. So she can have somewhere new to live."

"Oh." The glances grew worried. "But, bro, it's a special book. It's a thank-you book. Tan shouldn't sell it. Should you, Tan?"

I patted Lad again. "A home is better than a book."

"You could stay with us then, and keep the book."

My stomach gave a different lurch, a fluttering as Lad tugged at my heart. "That's a lovely thing to say. But there shouldn't be too many people in Eugeny's house. It wouldn't be fair."

"And Tanyana deserves her own home, don't you think?" Kichlan added.

Glum, Lad nodded. "Guess."

The man Eugeny trusted owned an odd little shop, built of wooden offcuts and sandstone fragments held together by a clay-based mortar. Its windows were made of many small shards of different types of glass, woven together with lead, and they caught the morning sunlight in a mesh of light and colour. Stone steps led up to a wooden door with an old iron handle, and a sign scrawled into the wood that I could not understand. Strange signage for a shop. It sat in small, squat contrast to the rest of the street: from the hulking apartments to a landau crawling its way past us on invisible insect legs.

"Lad, will you wait here?" Kichlan asked.

I expected his younger brother to pout, but Lad, still glum, huddled himself out of the wind beside the stone steps.

I followed Kichlan through the door and into a quiet, dim world.

"We don't need Lad trying to convince you not to sell it the entire time," Kichlan murmured as he threaded his way between dark shelves. "Or knocking over only the Other knows what."

I grunted in agreement.

The shop was a hushed place, where any voices raised above a whisper didn't belong. It smelled of dust, cracking leather and silver polish. Floor to ceiling, wall to wall – at least as far as the short distance I could see – was full of shelves. These were built of wood that looked like it had, at one time, been dark and smooth, but was now so heavily laden with dust it was hard to tell colour or texture beneath the grey. All the shelves were full of pots, leather straps, old porcelain, dolls or spoons and more, and all were covered in their own layers of dust or marked with rust spots and stains. The further we crept into this rubbish graveyard, however, the thinner the dust became, until the shelves opened up to flickering light and an ancient man standing behind a desk. The desk itself was equally laden, but instead of the haphazard growth of accumulated time, the desk was clean, neat and organised. A long curved sword, with a golden tassel on the hilt, glinted beneath a glass case along the front of the desk. A full set of plates painted with dancing bears was arranged for a meal at one end. The other was heavy with leather-bound, gold-embossed books. These caught my eye more than the old man. They were ancient, but the gold more legible than that under my arm, and the leather softer. I caught some words on the spines: *Principles of the Six Pointed Circle, Rural Classes and the Pion Revolution, Old Varsnia: A History*.

The old man had been tinkering with something like a watch. Its face was dark, the glass old and misted, and the inside opened up to reveal dozens of tiny gears and screws. He set it aside as he stood, hands at his back, a smile creasing his weathered and wrinkled face.

"Welcome," he said. "May the bear be ever at your back." He rocked on his feet and chuckled. I gathered Kichlan's expression was as confused as mine. "Old saying, that one. A greeting, or a farewell perhaps, when meeting travellers on the road. Translation isn't the best, so we cannot be sure."

"Um, hello," Kichlan stammered. Perhaps Lad, with his easily infectious enthusiasm, might have done us some good. "Eugeny sent us."

"Ah!" He unclasped his hands and reached over the desk to shake ours with a remarkable display of dexterity for someone so wizened. "Eugeny, you say? How is the old man?"

"He's well," Kichlan answered, and cast me a by-the-Other-say-something expression.

I responded, "He sent us, sir...?"

"Yicor." The old man took my hand a second time and held it for longer than strictly necessary. "To you, my dear, I am Yicor."

I tried to look as flattered and feminine as possible, although I had little in the way of experience. "Eugeny sent us, sir, with something you might be interested in."

"Well, he was right." And Yicor took my hand again.

Beside me, Kichlan let out a sigh.

"I meant this, sir." I shifted the book into my hands. "We have something to sell, something he believed would be to your tastes." Oh, Other I hoped so.

"Well, let us see."

I handed the book across Yicor's desk. Its weight left a lightness in my palm when he took it, a brush of air and a understanding that I would never hold anything as valuable again.

"What have you got here?" Yicor unwrapped the book, lifted it, and turned it to examine the spine. His indulgent smile faded to a thin line as he read, and his breath slowed. Eyes riveted to the worn lettering on the cover, he placed the book on his desk, and tenderly opened the pages. His fingers shook as they caressed the lines of finely written words, stopping to hover above the pencilled-in notes as though they were precious, too fine and beautiful to sully with touch.

Finally, he lifted his eyes to mine. I felt open to them, bare, and I knew Yicor saw right into me, into scars deeper than those on my flesh.

"Are you certain you wish to sell this?" he asked, although he knew the answer. Why else would I have brought it here, why else let anyone else touch it, caress it, covet it?

"I must." It wasn't a real answer, but he accepted it.

"Then my old friend is right." He closed the book carefully, his shivering fingers gliding over the worn leather. "This is something very much to my tastes. And I will buy it from you, although it grieves me to be forced to do so."

The shop was too stuffy, the shelves too full and dust-coated. Suddenly, I wanted nothing more than to be out in Movoc's crisp sunshine and stinging air.

Kichlan, oblivious to the lines of tension strung up between Yicor's eyes and mine, clapped his hands. "Glad to hear it. Now–" he rubbed them together "–how much?"

I turned my head away. I didn't want to hear them haggle over my old life. But Yicor leaned forward, while keeping one hand on the book's cover, and touched my wrist. "How much do you need?"

"To live this life?" I didn't truly know.

Kichlan, however, had begun ticking off his fingers. "You'll need a surety payment, that'll be four hundred and fifty, I'd say. Three sixnights' lease is the usual. Of course, the more you have to spare the better you'll be. What else? Clothes, food, something to sleep on."

Yicor eyed him with pity and I realised how keenly the old man understood me. How much more he had seen, in that single glance, than Kichlan had for all his lecturing. "I cannot offer you kopacks for something so priceless. At least, I cannot offer you kopacks alone."

Like a dog on a leash, Kichlan bristled.

"What will you offer me then?" I lifted a hand to stay Kichlan and focused on the shop owner.

"Somewhere to house you," Yicor said.

"We can do that on our own," Kichlan interrupted. What about this man and his generosity had Kichlan so agitated?

"Somewhere safe, around people I know and can vouch for. Clean, well kept, warm. With furniture and a place to sleep."

I rather liked the sound of it. Kichlan, sulking, crossed his arms and hunched his shoulders.

"For I cannot pay you the worth of this." Yicor's hand had not left the book cover. "I only hope to fill the gap with what help I can."

I nodded. "How much, then?"

"Twenty-five thousand is all I can spare."

Kichlan dropped his arms, and whispered a curse under his breath. But I knew how poor a sum that was for something like the *Principles of Architecture*. Yicor knew it too.

"I accept," I said, and gave the old man a small and

rather shaking smile. "As long as you find it a good home." And, I hoped, not the home of someone I knew, who would realise it was mine and how much further I had fallen.

"Of course," Yicor said, his eyes solemn.

I drew my rublie, sad and clunky in its crutch, from my pants. When I held it out to Yicor and he pressed his own against it, only then did I understand. For his was also sheathed in that sad cover, although it read considerably more than the five kopacks left in mine.

Kichlan, looking away, already muttering about the best way to spend my sudden wealth, didn't notice. Yicor and I shared our understanding alone.

"Where is your team stationed?" Yicor asked casually, as we watched the bright numbers on our rublies flick over.

"Eighth Keepersrill," I answered.

He seemed to think for a moment, and once my rublie was full, he found a scrap of paper in a desk drawer. He scribbled an address using a quill and ink from a crystalline glass jar. The entire odd and antiquated process fit in perfectly with the atmosphere in the shop. "Somewhere close, somewhere safe." His letters were flourished, l's high and g's curled. "Try them."

Kichlan eyed the paper like it was mess at the bottom of his shoe. "I'll tell Eugeny you were helpful." He rested his eyes on me. "We'll wait outside for you to finish." He strode from the shop.

Yicor handed me the piece of paper. "Your friend should know better. You need somewhere you can be protected. He just does not want to admit it."

My fingers stilled, touching the paper lightly. "Protected?"

Yicor clicked his tongue. "Eugeny sent you to me for a

reason, more important than the book. Perhaps you are involved in something you do not understand. Perhaps there are people, strange people, dogging your heels. Perhaps they appear when you do not expect them. Perhaps they are watching, always watching. He sent you to me, so we can watch you too."

I folded and tucked the paper into my shirt, my hand shaking. "Thank you." My voice shook too. "How did you know all that? You're not even a collector, are you?"

Smiling, Yicor lifted his arm so his shirtsleeve fell back to reveal a bare wrist. "Not all of us are."

"How is that possible?" How had he fallen through the cracks while I was caught, shackled, and forced to roam the streets for a pittance of kopacks and less respect? How many of us ran free?

"Just good luck." And he would say no more. So I thanked him again and left him with the last piece of my old life, knowing I would never see it again, and hoping it would rest somewhere safe now, behind glass.

Kichlan was unimpressed by Yicor's help. "What do you think he knows that I don't?" he huffed as we walked away from the shop. Lad stared sadly at the empty space under my arm.

"He's one of us, you realise," I said, keeping my voice low and hoping Lad was too concerned by the book's disappearance to listen carefully. "A coll– no, not a collector. But he can see debris, not pions."

Kichlan puffed up his cheeks and let out an explosive breath. It gave him a froggish air. "Hardly."

"But he is. You didn't see his rublie!"

"Didn't need to."

I was shocked by this. "You knew?"

"Of course." Kichlan scowled down at me. Just like old times. "Not all of us—" he waved his hand and light flickered from the silver on his wrist "—do the right, the responsible thing."

"Oh." Still, how exactly did one avoid doing the right, responsible thing? How did one escape the puppet men? The strange men that were, indeed, forever watching, following, appearing. And to be protected against them, to be watched by more faces I did not know in shadows of their own, it hardly filled me with confidence. If anything, it was worse. "Don't you wish you had that kind of freedom?"

Kichlan looked at Lad as he answered. "Hardly. We have a purpose, Tanyana. Something more worthwhile than selling ancient junk."

"I don't think a book worth twenty-five thousand could be considered junk."

"You know what I mean."

True, I had never seen such a comprehensive collection of dust.

"Still." I flipped the scrap of paper over, reading the address yet another time. "I want to try his suggestion first."

"If you'd rather trust an old man you hardly know more than me, that's your prerogative."

I sighed. "I suppose you already had a plan, did you? Knew exactly where to look?"

Kichlan said, "You could say that."

"You were going to wander around and hope we found something, weren't you?"

"What have you got against spontaneity?"

"Will you help me find this place? Groundlevel, 754 Lightbrick. It's the seventh Effluent, Section ten. Should be close."

"Sounds delightful."

"Will you help?" I asked.

"Of course we will."

"Of course!" Lad broke in with a grin. I could tell by the lightness in his face, the ease, that he hadn't understood a word of our argument. "We're here to help Tan, aren't we, bro?"

"What if she doesn't need our help?" Kichlan asked him, words lightened by the twist in the corner of his mouth. "What if she doesn't want it?"

"Of course I do." I hooked an arm into Lad's elbow. He squeezed my arm against his chest. "I always do."

All roads led to the Tear, and so did all rills and effluents. So we headed to the river to get our bearings. The sharp sun warmed us as the morning aged, tempering the crisp wind and melting what was left of the ice, huddled in windows, and the muddy snow crowding the edge of the road. A large street cleaner ghosted by, prying out dust from the walls and muck from the street with wide-ranging tentacles of now-invisible light. Kichlan and I averted our eyes: there was something disturbing about a floating wedge of clear honeycomb gradually filling itself with dirt. Lad watched it avidly.

"Spring's finally here," I mused, because it was better than arguing about Yicor.

"Wouldn't have known it this morning," Kichlan answered.

I nodded. "And it's taken its time."

"Hasn't it? Didn't think this winter was ever going to leave us."

Some conversations are so much safer. Lad, however, was not so interested in the weather. He yawned widely. Pointedly, I thought.

"Not boring you, are we?" I chuckled, and squeezed his arm.

He blinked in an overexaggerated, tired way. "Where are we going, Tan?"

I showed him the piece of paper. "Here is someone who can help us."

Lad barely glanced at it. "Oh." His hands fidgeted.

"Your turn," Kichlan murmured out of the side of his mouth. "He's getting bored."

"My turn to do what?"

"Entertain him." He grinned, vicious and self-satisfied. "Call it payment."

I remembered all the effort Mizra, Kichlan and Sofia usually went to, to capture Lad's attention. Stories, speeches, and constant praise. It really was a lot of work to keep him in a manageable mood through the day.

Was I up to the challenge? "You know lots of stories, don't you, Lad?"

He brightened instantly, as though I'd opened a shutter and let the sunlight in on his face. "Mizra tells them," he said. "I listen and I remember them. Don't I, bro?"

"You do." Kichlan cupped his hand and said in a loud, exaggerated whisper, "He's very good at it."

Lad's light swelled.

"Well, maybe I can tell you a story you don't know," I said.

"I know a lot of them," Lad replied.

"He does," Kichlan said, supporting his brother and enjoying every minute of this. "That would be difficult."

"Hmm." I pressed a finger to my lips and pretended to be thinking hard. Lad's eyes were wide, his gaze and riveted on my face. "No, I think you won't know this one. I think I'm going to tell it to you, and see if you do."

"Oh, will you?" Lad scrabbled for my hand, nearly crushing it as he squeezed. "Yes, please!"

"Careful," Kichlan warned him.

Lad released my hand instantly and stroked the red skin, his motions awkward, like his hand was too big for his arm to control with any precision.

"Yes," I said. "I will."

I waited a moment to collect my thoughts as Lad patted away. I knew few myths and children's stories, but I had learned things in my time at university neither of them would have heard. The history of the revolution, and the great men who made it happen.

"This happened a long time ago," I began. And didn't get far.

"They all do," Lad interrupted.

"I can't tell the story if you are talking, Lad."

He pressed a hand against his mouth.

"That's better," I said, with an approving nod.

Kichlan turned away to hide a smile.

"Now," I continued. "This happened a long time ago. Before there were cities like Movoc-under-Keeper. When the veche was young, and made up of lots of groups of people who didn't agree with each other. Before lights in the streets, before factories, carriages or debris collectors." I wasn't certain of the last one, but it sounded likely. "Before all this there were men who wanted to create these things. And who worked very hard to make them."

Lad dropped his hand long enough to ask, "Like the book?"

"Yes, very good. Like the man who wrote the book."

He clapped his hand tighter over his face.

"One of these men was Uric. He came from outside of Varsnia, so he was strange. He thought he was as

303

smart as a Varsnian, and as strong, and maybe he was. For a while."

Both brothers were watching me now, intent.

"He was a pion-binder," I continued the story. "And a very good one. But he wanted to be better. And that was when everything went wrong."

"Isn't it always," Kichlan muttered to himself. Lad shushed him, blowing spittle into the air.

"He brought together twelve other binders, all as strong as he. And he said, 'If you make a circle around me, all twelve of you, then we will be able to do great things. Greater than anyone has done before'."

This was the point in the story where pion-binders knew what was going to happen to poor Uric, for his foolishness and pride. Kichlan and Lad continued to listen, expressions blank.

I continued, "But the pion-binders were Varsnian, and they knew no circle could be larger than nine–"

"Why?" Lad interrupted.

"Because that's the limit," I answered. "Any more and the circle will be unstable."

"But why?"

"Do you want to hear the story?"

The hand clamped back on his face.

"So they told Uric that what he wanted was impossible. But Uric laughed; he said, 'Just because it has not been done by a Varsnian does not make it impossible. Work with me, and you will see a miracle.' And the pion-binders agreed only so they could be proven right."

"Oh dear," Kichlan drawled. "He was prideful, wasn't he? And rude. I think I know what this particular myth is trying to teach us."

"This is not a myth," I snapped at him. "It happened. It's in the books, recorded by people who were there at the time."

"Mizra says his stories happened too," Lad said. "The ones with knights and swords and how they rescue people and sometimes they get hurt."

"My point exactly," Kichlan muttered.

I rubbed my forehead with my free hand. Whose idea was this again?

"Then what happened, Tan?" Lad, less able to foresee the morally dictated ending than his brother, squeezed me again, expression intent.

I gave up trying to argue the difference between history and legend. "Uric, unable to be dissuaded, set up his twelve point circle. The pion-binders, for all they didn't believe him, really did try to help. For a moment, the circle was bright, brighter than any ever made. It shone like the sun in the village centre, and all the windows were opened, and people peered out to see the light. It shone with many colours, but the centre, where Uric stood, was as white as a star."

"It sounds beautiful," Lad said.

"It would have been." I didn't tell him he would not have seen it, that none of us would have seen more than thirteen people making a circle with a dot in the centre, standing still, talking to themselves and possibly moving their hands.

"For a moment the circle shone. But the Varsnian binders were right, and Uric should have listened to them, because the circle was too bright, too strong, and after that moment it started to collapse. Uric was at the centre and it all fell on him."

"Oh no," Lad gasped.

"Oh no, indeed." I left it hanging.

"What happened?" Lad squeaked out after a moment of silence and tension.

"If he goes home healthy and well to his family, I'm going to eat that." Kichlan pointed to a particularly filthy heap of grey snow squeezed between the corners of two buildings. The street cleaner must not have taken this path, then.

I ignored him. "No one really knows," I answered Lad. "All the colour and the shine rushed into the centre, piled on top of him, and when it faded away Uric was never the same."

"He was hurt?" Lad's large eyes were frightened.

I squeezed his hand for support. "Not his body, there wasn't a scratch on him. But when the light was gone and the pion-binders tried to talk to him, they discovered he had lost his mind."

Lad blinked. "Lost it? How?"

I had to smile. "He went crazy, Lad. Do you know what that means?"

He shook his head.

"It means he couldn't do the things he used to do, it means he started seeing things, hearing voices that weren't there–" I stopped. Hearing voices? Oh, Other, hearing voices?

Why hadn't I realised it? This wasn't the right story to tell Lad, it wasn't the right story to tell myself. What had happened to Uric in the centre of that twelve pointed circle? I knew now.

He had fallen, and he had fallen hard.

Lad, considering the story for himself, hadn't noticed my concern. "That's not good. It's not good to listen to strange voices you hear, is it, bro?"

"No. We know that already, don't we, Lad?" Kichlan was staring at me, so focused I could feel him like two hot points on my forehead. "We didn't need a story to tell us that."

"No." Lad thought for a moment more. "What did he see?"

I said, "A man." Not debris. No grains or planes or anything he had described as dog turds. A man.

"There's a man over there." Lad pointed to an elderly man wrapped in a large coat the colour of dying grass. He was hunched against the wind, and shielding his eyes from the sun with a flat hand.

"Yes, but he saw a man no one else could see. He heard a man no one else could hear. A man who wasn't there." Saying it out loud like that cooled my sudden panic. Uric had gone mad, it was documented, it was fact. He hadn't become a debris collector; he had started seeing people who didn't exist. He had forced the pions too hard, and they had broken him.

Still. I shivered as the river wind's fingers started up their prying again. All those pions, too many to control: the image was familiar. Were they crimson, those pions? Had he dug too deep inside reality and pried free a furious force that shattered his circle, destroyed his systems, and turned on him? He hadn't fallen eight hundred feet onto a bed of glass, but had they pushed him regardless? Forced him down onto that cobblestone floor until something inside him broke, something vital that no one, it seemed, had ever understood? And the voices, I couldn't ignore the voices.

I glanced at Lad. A frown creased the edges of his eyebrows. I wasn't the only one who had heard them, was I?

307

"I think that's a good story," Lad finally decided, his voice firm. "It's like Mizra's stories."

"It is," Kichlan added softly. "A lot like the myths."

I groaned. We weren't here again, were we? "Except this is real. They locked him up in the ruins of a Movocian castle, three bells' journey from Movoc-under-Keeper. Kept him there until he died, trying to work out what happened to him. They never did."

"Really?" Kichlan kept his voice low. "How fascinating."

It was highbell by the time we came to the seventh Effluent. Beneath us, water rushed into the Tear as we followed the slightly raised path. A vent at every five yards released warm, rank air to steam into the cool wind.

"Not exactly pleasant," Kichlan murmured, pinching the end of his nose between two fingers.

I said, "I won't be living on top of one of those, you do realise that." The buildings lining the seventh Effluent were painted an insipid grey, and none had windows over the raised path.

"It's dull."

"It's not much different from a rill." I had a feeling the houses could be built of marble with gold window-lattices and Kichlan still would have disapproved.

"They're all pale, how are you supposed to find Lightbrick?"

"They have street signs here. That always helps." Apart from the vents and the dead-skin colours, the seventh Effluent was in much better condition than the eighth Keepersrill. No rubbish crowding the streets, signs still intact, buildings standing. I kept that observation to myself.

Lightbrick wasn't too far along the seventh Effluent, and it didn't take long to find 754. The numbers were clear here, and closer together than along the eighth Keepersrill.

"They're small."

I sighed, and didn't bother answering.

Number 754 was wider than the rest of the tall thin buildings, and reminded me of Eugeny's out-of-place home. It had only two stories, with a set of rusty and rather unsteady iron stairs twisting tightly up to the second level.

"Those don't look safe," Kichlan muttered as I knocked on a wooden door with peeling and faded white paint. Had he noticed the heavy iron lock?

The door opened slowly, creaking like an old man, and I had enough time to glance at the paper in my hand. A large woman, with ruddy cheeks and silver-laced blonde hair pinned up beneath a blue scarf, peered around the slightly open door. She didn't speak, but her eyes were sharp and settled on each of us.

"Valya?" I asked.

In silence, she continued to stare at me.

"Um, Yicor gave me your name–"

"Yicor did? Well–" she pulled the door open with a sudden burst of speed and strength. "Then in you get." She shuffled off into a warm, dark hallway.

I hesitated at the doorway.

"Hurry now!" she called. "You look hungry. You will all eat."

That was enough for Lad. He barrelled his way inside and we had to follow.

The house smelled of food, not the constant stew-smell of Eugeny's home, but something vastly more complicated. Charred chicken skin, fresh bread, potatoes baking and hot olive oil all surged around us.

"Got anything to say now?" I muttered to Kichlan as we followed Lad, who was evidently following his nose to the kitchen.

Strangely enough, he was silent.

Lad, it seemed, could follow food with as much accuracy as he could find debris. He wound his way easily through a dim living room, another small and cool room lined with shelves laden with jars of preserves, and into a wide kitchen. A long table took up most of the space, and the cool wind was blowing in from an open window above an old gas stove.

Valya stood at the bench, slicing bread that steamed its freshness with each new cut. "You sit," she commanded us without turning around. Soon she placed the bread, sliced and warm, with a tub of garlic-infused lard on the table. "Begin," she told us, and Lad launched into the food as though he had not eaten for days. This was soon joined by a porridge-like dish of chicken, carrot and buckwheat.

Then she sat at the head of the table and watched us eat. Her sharp eyes took in every bite. "He is a good eater, that one," she said, pointing to Lad, who would have happily eaten everything himself if Kichlan weren't keeping him in check. "I like that. Good eater is a good person."

Lad beamed at her, mouth full. Kichlan ran his hand over his face, and was forced to protect his own bowl from his brother.

"So." Valya turned to me. "You are here for upstairs. Yes, you may stay." Her eyes narrowed. "But you should eat more."

After at least two sixnights and one of living on tea, the occasional stew and Devich's charity, I was finding the rich food difficult. But more than that, Valya's sharp eyes and assumptions were putting me off my appetite.

"You don't even know who we are." I put my fork down and turned in my chair to face her. I did not eat on command.

"I know enough." She straightened. "You are collectors, all three of you. Yicor sent you, so he believes you need help. You are the one who will stay here, your friends already have a home of their own."

Lad stopped eating long enough to show the half-chewed food in his mouth. "How did you know all that?"

"I have eyes, boy."

And she called Lad, who hulked above all of us, a boy. Those eyes were sharp.

"Yicor's recommendation and our collecting suits I can understand," Kichlan said, voice soft. "But how did you know we weren't also asking to stay?"

Valya gave the first smile I had seen on her face. It wasn't joyful, more a triumphant twist of the lips. "She doesn't eat enough. She isn't happy, she isn't content. You two have been looked after. She is the one who needs a home."

Lad, swallowing a large chunk of food, nodded. "Yes, and she didn't like her home when she had one. A home should be somewhere you want to go."

Would I want to go here? Those eyes were sharp, those words were blunt, but really, what did I have to hide from Valya? She already knew me for what I was.

"I am Tanyana," I told her. "And I appreciate you taking me in."

Valya made a scoffing noise. "You don't, not a lot. But that is okay." She stood. "You can come with me."

Lad looked up, despairing of the food he still had in front of him.

"They can stay."

So I followed Valya while Kichlan and Lad continued to eat.

"You eat down here, so I know you have enough," Valya said as she lifted a key from a hook near the door and pressed it into my hand. "Everything else you do yourself." We stepped into the street, and I realised how warm it had been in her kitchen. How pleasant. "Careful of the stairs, stay to the left." The iron stairs rocked as we climbed them, metal creaked beneath our feet and flecks of rust came off against my gloves. "Here." There was a small platform before the upstairs door, barely wide enough for one person. "Open it."

I edged around Valya's ample frame, and turned the key in the iron lock. It undid with a heavy clunk, and the door swung inward at a gentle push.

The upstairs was about half the size of the house below it. It was a living room with a window so close to the building next door there wasn't enough room to push the glass open more than a few inches. A table and a few chairs filled the space; there was an ancient wood stove in one corner. The wall above it had blackened over the years. The floor was cement, but padded with rugs, most made from animal pelts. A bunch of dried lavender mounted on richly stained wood decorated one wall. There was a bedroom behind the main room, large enough for a bed and a small chest of drawers. One of the handles was loose. Beside the bedroom was a bathroom, complete with a narrow, shallow bath. The water worked, although it ran a slightly dirty colour and left tiny grains of sediment in the cracked porcelain. There were wide windows on the back wall of both bathroom and bedroom, draped with lace. They opened out over the rest of the roof and what I realised was a small greenhouse, crowded with plants, at the back of the house.

It was small, not exactly in the best condition, and bare. But, I realised as I peered down into bright glass above newly budding, wavering green, it was home now.

"You cannot bring anything," Valya told me as I returned to the living room. "Only furniture is already here."

"I don't have anything." Absolutely true.

"No, you don't. I can see that." Her eyes bored into me. "Yicor sent you to me, and I will look after you. We won't let them get to you."

"What does that mean? Let who–"

"Tsk!" Valya pinned my shoulder with a hard finger. "You are not so good at lying. You know whom we mean, you know the pet creatures of the veche, they follow you, they use you. Those misbegotten seeds of the Other's lust!"

The puppet men. "How do you know about them? You and Yicor!" And Eugeny, I realised with a sinking certainty. Eugeny had sent me here. Did that mean Kichlan was involved? But no, he hadn't even wanted to listen to Yicor's advice. What was going on? "He said you would be watching, that you would protect me. From what? And how?"

"You are not the first those creatures have set their sightless eyes on. We cannot do much, we are few and old, but we will try. Girl, we will try." Then just like Yicor, she refused to say more, and took me down the stairs, only talking about the room. She lectured me on keeping the door locked, on minding my key. She told me she would ask for one hundred kopacks each sixnight and one, but didn't want to see my rublie until I had stayed there that long. "Don't take kopacks for something not yet given," she said. I would also pay for my food, all of which sounded too reasonable to be true. But I certainly didn't question her.

When we re-entered the kitchen Lad had finished off the chicken dish and was looking very large and sleepy, slumped against the table. We stopped Kichlan in the middle of worried pacing. I shared a nod with him, and he immediately went to Lad's shoulder and started the long process of getting him moving.

"I need to, ah, replenish my wardrobe," I told Valya. She had started collecting the plates from her table, and prodded Lad's arm with a long fingernail to get him out of the way. Had far greater effect than Kichlan's murmured coaxing.

"Come and go as you wish," she said. "Just make certain you eat."

"Fair enough." I helped Kichlan heave Lad to his feet.

"Goodbye," he said to Valya around a yawn as he rubbed his red eyes. "I hope we come and see you again."

Considering the size of the dish he had devoured, I wasn't surprised.

"I think you will," Valya answered.

Kichlan and I supported Lad out the door. Lad started making noises about seeing my new home upstairs, but I feared for the rickety staircase beneath his careless weight.

"And we need to help Tanyana buy some clothes," Kichlan, evidently fearing the same thing, came to my aid. "We need to hurry or the day will be all over."

That was enough to capture Lad's interest. He snapped awake – probably aided by the outside chill – and hurried us along toward the Tear. The shops that lined the water were smaller than the ones I knew in the city, and poorly lit. Their wares were cheaper, secondhand and mended. Kichlan and his brother piled hats, gloves and scarves into my arms. They even found a stiff jacket, tailored for a man but small enough to fit me well, with panels of hard leather sewn onto the thick wool to keep out the wind. As a replacement for the jacket I had left in the apartment it was poor, the leather faded, thin at the elbows, and a large stain sullied the inside left breast. But it felt appropriate, somehow, as Kichlan draped it over my shoulders and tugged it together at my waist, muttering about the need for a belt to hold it together. It was a collector's jacket, to hang in a collector's rented room and brace the cold and the dirt of a collector's life.

I found scissors, small things with wooden handles that wobbled on a loose hinge, but they would do. I had noticed a mirror on the chest of drawers in my new bedroom, and my hair was growing uncommonly long.

The clothes barely scraped the bottom of my newly charged rublie, and we left with arms full of bulging calico bags, the shop owners so flushed with delight they had given us the bags for free. I was sure they would come in useful, somehow. Kichlan certainly seemed pleased with them. I wasn't entirely sure what they were for, but allowed myself to be swept into his enthusiasm regardless.

"For the next time you need to do this, of course," he explained as we trudged beneath a darkening sky to my home at 754 Lightbrick.

"Next time?" I shifted the bag in my arms. "Why would there be a next time?"

Lad, thankfully carrying two of the heavy, awkward things, was walking ahead of us and singing to himself.

"There usually is. They move us, sometimes, break up and rearrange teams. And not all landlords are as accommodating as Eugeny. They don't like having us around for too long."

"Valya seems like the accommodating type."

Kichlan grinned over the bulging bag he carried. My jacket was in there, the heaviest piece of the lot. He didn't seem to mind carrying it. "Don't let her feed you up too much. No use to me if you have to roll around Movoc-under-Keeper."

"Anytime that seems likely just send Lad over for a sixnight," I answered. "Won't be any food left in the house once he's through."

Kichlan nodded, his grin fading. He walked in silence for a long while, expression distant and distracted. "That was an interesting story you told earlier," he finally said.

"Yes." Did he know about the voices too? Had he heard them? Were we all a bit mad?

"Maybe now you understand." He jerked his head toward his brother, singing and walking a yard or so ahead of us. "About him."

"You don't want them to lock him in a castle for the rest of his days. Yes, I understand that."

"It's more than that." Kichlan shifted the bag. His fingers sought purchase in the folds of calico. They squeezed deep indents into the soft clothes. "I think, you see, that some of us fall differently. Like your Ulric fellow."

"Uric," I corrected.

He flashed me a frown. "Yes, whatever his name was. A long time ago I met others who heard things after they fell, who thought they could see faces instead of debris."

I half stumbled on the road's uneven stones. "What? Really? Why didn't you say anything?"

"This isn't something Lad needs to know about. Listen to me, Tanyana, please."

I shut my mouth against more questions.

"I thought I could find out what was wrong with Lad, I thought I could help him. But he didn't give me enough time. He has always been like this. Listening to voices no one else can hear. But they can't find out about it, do you understand? They can't."

"They?" I whispered.

"The veche men. Technicians. Because every one of those people I met, those people who fell hard, were found by the veche, and they were taken away." He drew a deep breath. "I know, because I was there. Because I helped."

I stared at him blankly.

"I wasn't always a collector, I wasn't born like this. Not the way Lad was. And before I fell I thought I could help him, I wanted to use–" he struggled, his hands quivered against the bags he carried "–my skill to help him. My binding skill."

Cold that had nothing to do with the Movoc-under-Keeper weather made me shiver. "I thought you didn't know anything about pion-binding?"

Kichlan couldn't meet my eyes. "I tried to help him. I learned things, but not enough. And when Lad hurt the girl, I knew I had to make a choice. Fall, and protect him. Or watch him being taken away. You know what I chose."

"I don't understand, Kichlan. What was your skill? What did you do–" But I did. The silver hand, that dull metal with its thick cords that had reminded me so much of my suit, on Kichlan's dresser. "You were a technician?" My tongue felt frozen, the words impossible to say.

"In a way. I didn't make suits, not like the ones we wear. The veche had me experimenting, making changes. I was quite skilled."

"You must have been." He wasn't bad at lying, either. "Any reason for the pretence? Or just amusing yourself by lying to the new collector?" The bitterness in my words was too sharp to contain.

"The team don't know this. Lad, I think, doesn't really understand. I gave it all up for him, Tanyana. When he hurt that girl, he took away any chance I had to find out what was wrong with him. To fix him. I fell, so I could protect him. He doesn't need to know. He shouldn't have to carry that." His voice hitched. "It isn't his fault."

I wondered, numbly, why he had told me. Did he think I had the strength to carry his grief around with him? The love in those words, and the resentment, and the failure.

"Where did the veche take them? The collectors you said fell hard?"

Kichlan shook his head. "I didn't find out. I wasn't there long enough. But they never came back." He looked at me, and in his eyes I saw the kind of fear, the kind of desperation and terror I would have associated with his brother's confused mind instead. "I will not let that happen to Lad. They cannot take him away. He's all I have left, Tanyana. He is my everything."

"I know, Kichlan. I know."

I wanted to touch him, to hold him or pat him in a way Lad would have let me easily. But, even if we weren't laden with my new clothes and their calico bags, I wasn't certain Kichlan would let me get that close.

"I'm still going to find a way," Kichlan whispered so softly I almost missed him beneath my own breathing. "I'm going to find out what the voices are, and I'm going to stop them. Then the veche can't take him, they'll have no reason. Then he will be safe."

I watched Lad's back. His head was tipped, with his song reaching a roaring chorus without discernable words.

Did any of this make sense? Did I fall from *Grandeur* and land beside Kichlan and his brother for a reason? Was it anything more than terrible, devastating luck?

Uric's twelve pointed circle burned too brightly in my mind, and I stood beside him, fighting pions of my own. I had known from the beginning, hadn't I, that this was more than Yicor's *luck*. Kichlan had thrown himself from his *Grandeur*, I had been pushed.

What, exactly, was I going to do about that? I felt backed into a corner. Devich and the powerful people he knew weren't accessible to me any more. Pavel and the thugs who had thrown me from my apartment felt like warnings, as though someone was telling me in brutal terms to cast aside all thoughts of *Grandeur*, of pions, of justice and a veche tribunal. To let that life fall forgotten into the past, and get used to being a debris collector.

And most of all, to stop asking questions.

But what frightened me most was how comfortable this corner could be. Lad's friendship, Kichlan's loyalty, Eugeny's care, I wanted these things. I liked them. It would be too easy to embrace this new life, to stop fighting for the truth, to leave the past alone. It even sounded like the most sensible thing to do.

After all, nothing was holding me to my old life anymore. My circle was gone, my apartment was taken, and I had just sold the last piece, the last memory.

Maybe it was time to let go?

13.

Lad leaned into the river spray, one hand wrapped around the railing, the other tangled in mine. I was keenly aware that I had nowhere near enough weight to keep him on the ferry if he fell, and would be sucked into the Tear's icy current behind him.

"Feet on the floor, Lad, not the railing." I tugged at the large man, a lot like trying to shift a steady wall of brick and mortar with my little finger.

"The water is nice, Tan." He leaned over further.

"Not if you fall in it, it won't be."

With a sheepish glance, Lad slipped his feet from the first rung and back to the deck, landing loudly. The few ferries that ran on Rest were filled, but not in a crowded way. There were tired young men making their way down from the city. Middle-aged chaperones supervised younger women who fluttered their eyelashes and were rewarded with leering, sleep-deprived smiles. An elderly couple huddled on seats by the doorway, watching the Keeper Mountain grow slowly smaller, blinking against sunlight on the river. A gaggle of children were doing a fair imitation of Lad's unsafe climbing. I felt sorry for the two governesses trying to pry them all down.

Kichlan stood beside me, also watching the Keeper Mountain. "They weren't like him, you know," he said, soft against the rush of the wind, not loud enough for Lad to hear. "Neither. Both were good binders, respectable people working hard for Varsnia and their children. It's not in the blood. My parents weren't collectors."

"Pion skill has got nothing to do with blood, although the old families won't want to hear that." My mother was proof of that.

"Don't you wonder, then, what it is?" Kichlan's hands gripped the railing, knuckles white, skin blue in the chill. "What made us?"

"I know what made me." I touched the side of my face. "And you made yourself." Kichlan had not been forthcoming with any more details of his fall, but I refused to be dissuaded and continued to pry. "Fling yourself eight hundred feet into the air, did you?"

He said, "Doesn't take eight hundred feet to break a person, and not all of us have to be quite so dramatic." Kichlan looked over my head. "Him then." In the corner of my eye I noticed one of Lad's feet had crept back to the bottom railing. I poked him in the side, and he lowered it with a chuckle. "What made him?"

Over the last sixnight and one, Kichlan, Lad and I had explored the backstreets and alleys between the seventh Effluent and the eighth Keepersrill. Narrow, dark capillaries between wide veins, shaped without reason, blocking often in dead ends or gates. It was this constant companionship, I told myself, that had stopped me searching for Devich. How could I head into the city, or try and find the building where he had suited me, with

Kichlan and Lad like dogs, constantly at my heels. And Olday evening, as the brothers had said their farewells at the bottom of Valya's rickety stairs, Kichlan had asked me to come with them the next morning, to visit his parents' graves. If I hadn't been so surprised, I might have thought up a way to decline.

Devich had to be worried. He must have visited my apartment by now. I owed him the truth; he deserved to have his fears rested. Instead, I was heading for the cemetery.

Graves were not my speciality. Between Movoc's pre-revolutionary walls and the newer townlets that were springing up around the Weeping Lake, the cemetery was a sprawling necropolis, an architect's nightmare dedicated to the dead. I never visited.

We disembarked at an aging limestone quay, just on the other side of the old Tear gates. Once large defences, securing the break in Movoc's wall necessitated by the Tear River, the gates were rendered useless by the revolution and were now entirely ornamental. The iron had been restored to a better condition than it had probably ever been. The bars were shaped like little rivers, starting with a viciously sharp-summited Keeper, and ending with a skull. Lad stared at the skulls as we passed beneath the shadow of the wall, and even I couldn't help but shiver. Their eyes had been replaced with original kopacks, ancient coins of brass, and they glinted cruelly in the glare from the water.

From the quay we filed along a narrow road, just as ancient, cut into a rocky landscape of desolate knolls. Little more than thistles grew. Shadows seemed to lie there without anything to cast them, hugging the cold earth. We weren't the only ones travelling to the necropolis to visit the loved dead that rest. The old couple followed, at an increasing distance, slow over the treacherous, uneven ground.

"Is this something you do often?" I asked Kichlan, feeling breathless but desperate for something to fill the shadowed quiet.

Lad followed a few yards behind us. He hummed a slow, sad tune.

"I want Lad to remember them," Kichlan answered. "So I suppose, yes, we do this more often than most people."

Certainly more often than me. I wasn't even sure I could remember the plaque behind which my mother's ashes slept. I had not known my father when he was alive, and certainly didn't know where he rested now.

Kichlan led the way along thin paths of cracking stone. I felt surrounded. Gravestones with small roofs made hushed, disordered suburbs. Memorial statues and tombs hulked beside older, unmarked barrows. Rosemary grew in thick-scented clumps between stones. And images of the Other loomed from every corner. Featureless faces etched into gravestones; flat, humanoid shadows built of dark rock stretching from the side of a tomb wall. And older, more frightening things. A skull, half buried, its face crushed. The chaos of a skeleton statue, bones put together the wrong way. The Other was death, and disorder, and fear. Surely he belonged here, then, far from the protective shadow of the mountain named after his opposite: the Keeper.

The stonework was coarse, the paving poor. I tried to tell myself that was why I preferred to stare at the skyline, or a square of green cloth that had been used to repair Kichlan's jacket, near the shoulder.

He halted in a newer patch of graves. Each had a headstone, engraved with names, no worn-away faces or shadows. The roofs were well tended, no tiles cracked. Shin-high fences marked them all apart. Lad tugged rosemary from where it grew in a gap in the path. He settled onto his heels before two graves with no fence to divide them, and placed the rosemary gently on the earth. He picked at weeds that had began poking around the iron fence. He brushed dirt and dried leaves from the roof.

"They loved him, despite what he did. Despite what I chose to do." Kichlan remained by my side, hands deep in his pockets, shoulders hunched.

"I'm sure they did." Was this why I was here? To be told how much Lad's mother loved him? "Why have you brought me here, Kichlan?"

Lad, satisfied with the cleanliness of the graves, had started pulling small leaves from the stalks of rosemary. The scent surged up around him like a rising tide, and he muttered to himself, a constant flow of words I couldn't hear.

"After I– when Lad forced my hand, I didn't give up. I tried healers first." Kichlan was as quiet as Lad, nearly as difficult to hear. "They kept telling me the same thing. That no one knows what is wrong with him, no one knows why pions choose to abandon some people. They said it like that. As though he'd been tested, and rejected." The venom in his soft words was a chilling and terrible thing.

I touched the top of my head. "I wish I could tell you I can't imagine how horrible that feels."

Kichlan shuffled closer, so our arms touched through layers of woollen and leather coats. "Too much of that and someone in the veche must have heard. They sent technicians to check on Lad every second day. Even

324

some of those Other-cursed veche men. I stopped asking after that."

I shuddered, and Kichlan leaned against me.

"Eugeny had some ideas of his own. You know what he's like."

Golden root wax plant, whatever it was. "I do."

"Nearly impossible to get Lad to drink his concoctions, I have to say. For all the good it did." He let out a sigh so long it sounded like it had started somewhere close to his feet. "And now, all I can do is watch him, protect him. Make sure he remembers the parents that loved him, and try to make him happy."

"Did you read the veche records?"

He snorted. "Those little glass pion-written things? I did, when I could. They were not terribly helpful."

I could imagine that. "What about researchers? You must have attended a university to become a technician. The texts there, the lecturers, they could have helped you."

Yes, what about them? I knew some strong binders who'd dedicated their lives to the study and the teaching of those little spots of bright light. If I asked them, they might know what made a person lose their pion sight, and they might know how to fix it. What's more, they might know how to summon a horde of furious, crimson pions from deep inside reality. They might even know who could do it.

Why hadn't I thought of this earlier? Jernea, if he was still alive, would not turn me away. I was sure of it.

"Ah." Kichlan looked down at me, mouth set, but unable to quench a sudden hope I saw in his eyes. "Technicians train each other, I'm afraid. If you display the correct skills and make the right inquiries the veche comes calling, and offers you a position. So I did not attend any university that could help us."

I remembered the letter from Proud Sunlight that I had cradled so close to me. *It is with regret we hear of your misfortune.* But if Jernea was still there, he would listen to me. He would help.

"I did," I whispered. "And I will try."

"Done now, bro." Lad was standing, watching us, and neither of us had noticed. "Is that enough?"

For a collector like him. And a collector like me.

"Yes, Lad," Kichlan answered with a smile. "We can go home now."

Together, we rode the ferry on its journey upriver. Together, we took Lad home and gave him over to Eugeny's food and care. Together, we returned to my new home. I felt close to Kichlan, close to Lad. A part of the team, even something like family.

Then Mornday, when I descended to the sublevel and stepped beneath the filtered morning light and the cracked ceiling, Devich was there.

He glanced at me, and his expression didn't change. He had been rotating half a dozen or so small glass slides in the air in front of his face. He stilled them with a whisper, then plucked one and held it close to his eye. I wondered what was written in it.

"Vladha?" he asked.

I realised I was gaping at him. I shut my jaw with a click, and forced my feet across the floor. Kichlan, Lad, Mizra and Uzdal were already sitting in the couches, none of them pleased. A second technician was counting jars.

Guilt knocked the air from me, guilt at Devich's expressionless face. "Yes," I answered with a gasping breath. "Tanyana Vladha."

326

"And are you still housed at the second Keepersrill? Paleice, I believe it is."

Kichlan glanced up at this, surprised. I gathered this was not an ordinary question.

I drew a breath. It was like treading on pale ice itself. "No."

Devich's eyebrows rose. There was something sharp in the motion, something hurt.

"No, I was forced to leave there. Forced. No way to contact anyone I knew and tell them where I had gone, no time to take anything with me." But time to watch Lad lay rosemary at his mother's grave. "Believe me, I did not move out of choice."

The hurt became alarm. His fingers tightened around the slide and it cracked. He didn't seem to notice. "Forced?" he said. "Are you all right then, Vladha?"

"Yes. Only due to the other members of my team." I inclined my head to Kichlan.

Devich did not even glance at him. "And where are you living now?" He repaired the cracked slide with a whisper, and poised his finger above it.

"I rent a room not far from here. In someone else's house."

"Ah." Irritated, he glanced my way. "Address?"

I told him, but I hoped he had understood I could not entertain him any longer, not with Valya cooking below. If he wanted a bed to share with me, it would have to be his own.

"Thank you. Please, take a seat, we will begin when the rest of the team have arrived."

I squeezed in beside Kichlan. "Inspection?"

He made a low, grunting noise. "Yes, but I don't know why. We haven't been up to our usual standard but we've definitely been above quota the past few sixnights." He frowned. "Yes, I'm sure of it. So I don't know why they're here."

I glanced up at Devich. His face was down, apparently focused on the slide, but his eyes had followed me. His expression was cold, and confused, and even a little jealous. But I did not move from Kichlan's side. Devich had no reason to look like that.

Sofia and Natasha arrived as breakbell sounded, dim and distant through glass and cement. They were both surprised by Devich and his fellow technician, but answered their questions easily. Finally, when we had all gathered, both technicians stood together before the table covered in jars.

"Firstly," started the technician I didn't know. "The damage to the ceiling."

I groaned, inwardly. Sofia shot me a venomous expression.

"This has not been reported to the veche, which is irregular to say the least."

"However," Devich interrupted. "You will be given time to have it repaired. Inspectors will be sent in two sixnights and one, ensure it is filled in by then."

His fellow technician appeared surprised by this, but made a note of it and didn't argue. I couldn't remember if I'd told Devich about the damage I'd caused to the ceiling, but I must have. A rush of gratitude flushed my cheeks.

"Now, we will proceed." The technicians employed Kichlan and Mizra to help them set up a large screen they had drawn from a long canvas bag. It was built of hollow tubes and green material. They arranged it across one corner of the room, and dragged two chairs to sit behind it.

"One at a time," Uzdal whispered in my ear. My confusion must have been evident. "They take us behind there one at a time and have a good poke around."

I flashed him an alarmed expression, and he chuckled. "The suit, Tanyana. They poke around at the suit. Make sure everything's working."

"Oh." My face flamed, which set him laughing again.

"And believe me," Uzdal continued once he had calmed down enough to speak. "You want everything to be all right."

"Why?"

"Because if it's not then you need to go back on the table, with the lights and the machines and they do a tune-up. They tighten, they push deeper." He shuddered. "It's not pleasant."

"Did it happen to you?"

He nodded. "The suit never took to Mizra and me very well. Had to endure a few of those to get it right. One time's bad enough, don't you think?"

I remembered the voices, the pressure, and the knowledge of pain numbed by drugs. "Oh yes."

Devich took Sofia first. Far from nervous, she seemed relieved to be getting it over and done with.

"You shouldn't worry, though," Uzdal commented as the technicians led Sofia away. "You're like her. Suit always worked, didn't it? Never had any problems. Can't imagine you'd have them now."

The suit worked too well at times. Maybe working too well would also warrant a tune-up. I hoped not.

Sofia stayed behind the curtain for half a bell. When she emerged, she was relaxed, her suit glowing particularly bright. Devich took Natasha next, and he and his fellow kept her for a bell at least. When she returned to us she was happier than Sofia had been. Even volunteered to find us something to eat.

Uzdal and Mizra were called together, and I sat fidgeting beside Kichlan, wondering if Devich was forcing me to wait on purpose. If this was some kind of vindictive punishment.

"It's fine." Kichlan patted my knee. I jumped under his hand, and he gave me a sympathetic smile. "You've had no problems, so you'll be fine. I know the first time is hard, a bit frightening. Brings back the nasty memories." He tapped his forehead. "But it's not that bad. Trust me."

I nodded, unable to find my voice. None of them understood the torment, the turmoil, that had nothing to do with my suit.

"Vladha?" Devich stepped out from behind the screen. I jerked again, and stood up so quickly I knocked my knee against the corner of the low table near the couch.

Wincing, bending slightly to rub what had to be a developing bruise, I answered, "Yes?"

"My colleague can examine the twins, and we will run out of bells if we don't make this faster." He glanced at a silver watch drawn from the lapel of his jacket. Unlike the one Jernea had given me – and which had not survived my first day as a collector – Devich's watch was powered by pions. Tiny replicas of silver bells rose from its otherwise smooth surface and danced, chiming out the time as they did so. Expensive. "Would you come here?"

"With Mizra and Uzdal?" Why did I feel embarrassed? The twins had already watched me undress once, what more could they possibly see? Surely Devich wasn't about to strip me to my skin and have his poke around?

"There's nothing to worry about." Devich tried for patience, but I thought he looked annoyed. "Believe me."

I glanced at Kichlan, desperately seeking some kind of escape. He just nodded, and made *get going* motions with his hands. I stepped around the couches and approached the screen. Devich's lips were tight. He wasn't impressed.

Movoc's crisp sunlight was diluted faint and green by the material. Mizra and Uzdal stood before the second technician, naked to the waist, their uniform tops lying like second, darker skins at their feet. Neither met my eyes as Devich led me past them. In the green shadows it was difficult to make out expressions, to see anything other than the silver that shone and spun at their wrists, necks, waists and ankles. The technician was leaning close to Mizra, a long, thin instrument of the same shining silver in his hand. It had a hooked end and this was inserted between the symbols on the suit at Mizra's neck.

I shuddered as the instrument slipped inside, as the assistant turned it, as Mizra jerked his head to the side and clenched his hands. Was Devich going to do that to me?

"Watch where you're going," Devich snapped.

I had walked into a chair, placed away from Mizra and Uzdal and angled to face the wall. Scant privacy that would provide.

I gripped the back of the chair as Devich walked around me, my hands shaking against the poly-coated wood. A final glance at Uzdal, a hope for some kind of support, and while his face was darkened by shadow, a beam of light glancing off the steel tubes shone directly on a long scar down his right side. It ran, thin, precise, from his underarm all the way down to his stomach. It was broken only by the band of suit, and disappeared into his pants.

Did Mizra have the same scar on his other side?

Had they been broken together?

"Are you finished staring?" Devich waited for me, his arms crossed.

I blushed and approached the wall. Close to my back, the cement radiated cold though my clothes and uniform. If I was forced to strip like Mizra and Uzdal had, I would freeze. Would Devich show me pity if I started to turn blue?

"Take quite an interest in your fellow collectors, don't you?" Devich muttered. He didn't sit, but remained standing in front of his chair, arms crossed, lips thin. Sharp shadows gave his face planes of anger and an appropriate green hue.

I held back a retort, a spider-bite. "Is it really a concern of yours?"

"They're my team," I answered instead. I fought against anger, against the need to scream in his face, tell him everything that had happened and how desperately I had needed him when he wasn't there. But that wasn't his fault. I could have searched, couldn't I? Found a building I hardly remembered, or a home I had no address to. "Of course I take an interest in them. But I have—" I drew the words out, dropped my voice, hoped he understood and didn't think my association with collectors was making me dull and unhinged "—other interests."

Devich had been sorting through his slides again. He paused, summoned them back into his palm. "Do you?"

"Oh yes, interests outside of collecting. Consuming ones."

Devich looked up. His thin lips struggled against a rising smile. "Consuming? Have trouble controlling these interests?"

332

"Oh yes. But they give me exactly what I want."

"Well, aren't you lucky?"

"I've come to think so." The tension shifted, and I found it easier to breathe. Taking my clothes off was growing rapidly less frightening. "If only I could show you," I whispered the final words, hoping they wouldn't carry further than Devich, past his body to Mizra and Uzdal or over the screen to Kichlan.

Devich cleared his throat loudly. Finally, he sat, looking uncomfortable, his hands in his lap. "So." He cleared his throat again. "Shall we proceed?"

I grinned. "Oh, absolutely." I pulled my blouse over my head as Devich dragged a stiff leather case out from beneath his chair.

He left me in my camisole and the small drawers I had worn beneath my uniform. Both were simple things, secondhand clothes Valya had soaked in lime powder and left in the sun for days before allowing me to wear.

If Devich noticed anything different in the underwear, he didn't remark. But then, apart from the softness that came from factory-spun cotton and inner linings of silk, they weren't all that different from my usual, ever-practical fare.

"Now." Devich stood. "Let me see."

Goosebumps rose along my arm as he lifted it. It wasn't the cold anymore. He turned my hand gently; light from the suit surged and shone in patterns over his face. But he wasn't watching the suit. Instead, his eyes held mine. They swam with strange letters, symbols I could not read and had not seen before.

"What happened?" he whispered. He was so close to me, touching me, and it was difficult to remember that there were other people in this room. That we were not alone.

I breathed in his smell. Tension in my shoulders, tension I hadn't known existed, eased out.

"I was thrown out," I mouthed the words, voice as silent as I could make it. "The landlord sent two men to take me away."

Devich's hand tightened on mine. For a moment we were joined, hand to hand, eye to eye. Closer than sex, it felt, simple and truthful. I squeezed him back. Gently, he placed my hand against my hip and moved to pick up my left. He hadn't checked my suit once.

"You got away?" He pretended to bend over my wrist. Even nodded before releasing my hand and leaning into my neck.

I could feel the heat from his breath, the warmth of his body as it arched over mine. Made it very hard to concentrate. Very hard to keep up the pretence of a reluctant debris collector and her technician.

"Yes. I got away." I didn't extrapolate. I didn't even like to think about that evening in any detail. But he deserved a better explanation than that. "I didn't know where you live. I still don't. I wanted to go to you, but I didn't know where. So I came here instead, found a new place to stay, new clothes."

Not entirely honest, not exactly accurate. But close enough.

Devich touched my waist. He ran fingers around the edge of my suit. They set me shivering. "I'm sorry," he murmured in my ear.

Over his shoulder I could see Mizra and Uzdal's backs. Their technician was fiddling with Uzdal's waist. I took the moment to lean against Devich. He slipped his hands beneath my camisole, stroked upward over smooth skin and scar alike, to cup my breasts gently. His palms were warm, and left a cool breeze when he released me and returned to the suit.

"I should have told you where I live. I should have given you an option. Somewhere safe to run to. I guess–" he touched my chin with one finger and turned my face to his "–I never imagined you would need one."

He kissed me. Something hurried, something desperate, the press of his lips so hard my teeth nearly cut my own mouth. Then he stepped away and drew a sharp instrument from his bag. "I wouldn't concern yourself," he said, suddenly very loud. The bubble we had created around us, the small, warm world popped with the sound. "It doesn't hurt."

A quick glance up told me the technician was watching us. How much had he seen?

"If you say so," I answered. "I hope not."

"Trust us, Miss Vladha. We know what we're doing." Devich crouched at my feet. "Give me your wrists again." I held out a hand. He gripped it softly, and inserted the thin edge of the instrument between my skin and suit.

There wasn't much space to insert it in. He pushed gently, and I winced as it cut into my skin.

"Careful!" I hissed. Blood trickled down from beneath the silver band. He pulled a kerchief from his pale coat and dabbed it away.

"Wonderful," he said.

"Wonderful? That hurt." I frowned down at him.

He balanced himself, one hand high on my bare thigh. My frown vanished.

"Apologies. But it is wonderful. No distinction between suit and skin, even after time, even after use. This is very, very good. And look." He lifted my hand up; I peered at the suit.

Something was moving in the cut he had made. Tiny wiggling things like insect legs, but a pale, silvery blue. They struggled, kicking out into the air he had opened me to, dancing a bizarre and violent dance.

I felt faint, but Devich's grip on hand and thigh kept me upright. "What is that?" I choked out.

"The suit." How could he possibly sound so calm? "It's the best bond I've seen. Look, it doesn't want to be separated from you. It won't allow it."

The legs were sewing me up. Using threads of that same, pale metal, like thinner versions of themselves. Their stitches were tight, and together formed a tiny plate, an extension of the band itself, tugging skin together, covering the cut. Stopping the bleeding.

I didn't know what to feel. Sick, for the thing inside me, the thing Devich had put there. Or a desperate sense of how unfair this was. If I had fallen with the suit on, if Tsana had cut me up with the suit on, would it have sewn me together? Would it have allowed me to be maimed?

"I told you, didn't I?" Devich let go of my hand and started on the other. He didn't prod this time, didn't cut. Merely pulled at the skin and looked for a gap. I already knew there wouldn't be one. "You will be stronger, you will be better." He leaned forward, so close to my pelvis his lips were nearly touching my drawers where they stretched over bone. "Than any other collector."

Did that include my team? I was hardly better than any of them. But he didn't know, how could he understand? Gaps between suit and skin didn't mean anything, not in the tiring, dirty everyday.

"Devich?" A new voice in our close dialogue. The other technician.

Devich, not the least bit fazed, simply leaned away from me and looked over his shoulder. "Yes?" He still held the sharp, hooked instrument in one hand and was touching the skin below my waist with the other.

I realised I had lost track of his hands. With his lips so close.

"I've finished with these two."

"Any progress?" Devich asked.

Mizra and Uzdal were dim shapes pulling on clothes, keeping their faces averted. I caught a glimpse of Mizra's side, and sure enough saw the mirror of his brother's scar.

"The same." The technician was staring at me. I wanted to cross my arms, but couldn't decide if he was looking at the nipples standing hard beneath white material, the scars running pink and stitched, or the suit spinning at my neck. Neither could I be sure which would be more disconcerting.

"At least they haven't regressed again." Devich turned to me and bent to lift my right foot. I gripped the wall with my free hand to keep my balance.

"True."

"Who will you do now?" Devich's breath tickled.

"The big guy. Team leader last. Sound good to you?"

"Whatever you like."

The technician walked around the screen and suddenly my foot was back on the floor, Devich had his hands on my hips and was pressing his mouth against me. He was warm through the fabric, his lips slightly open, promising pressure and moisture.

I let out a gasp. He stole a hand around, wiggled fingers beneath cloth and slipped inside me with a groan.

I fought the need to arch, to lean against the cold wall.

Instead, I gripped his head, held him there as his mouth moved, as he sucked the white cloth clear and his fingers, his fingers roamed.

"I've missed you," he murmured, voice muffled. "I need you."

I said nothing. Dimly, as though a wall of concrete, stone and steel stood between me and the rest of the room, I could hear Kichlan.

"You can't take him in without me." His voice was raised. Every one of these inspections was a strain on him.

I rocked against Devich's hands, wrapped my fingers through strands of hair and bit the bottom of my lip to stop myself crying out. While Kichlan fought for a brother who couldn't thank him. I churned inside, aching with pleasure, drowning in self-disgust. I was the reason they were here, I was putting this strain on Kichlan, on Lad.

"Don't you people keep notes?" Kichlan continued. "I'm his guardian, and you're not doing anything to him without me there."

I clenched around Devich's fingers, quivered beneath his mouth. And Kichlan said, "Finally. Thank you for seeing reason–" As I heard footsteps coming closer, closer, I eased Devich from me, out of me, and panting, whispered, "Why did you do that?"

His eyes were so green in the light from the screen, sharp like a blade of grass. "I told you. I missed you." Then he handed me my uniform pants and wiped his mouth and fingers with the kerchief he had used to soak up my blood.

I was tugging myself into the uniform as Kichlan and Lad appeared around the screen. Lad grinned at me, waved. Kichlan blushed a red that darkened in the green light, and looked away.

Devich, pretending to put away his tools, rifled through the bag he had brought. The sound of steel against glass was jarring, slicing into a dull tension making its way up my neck to nest in my head.

"That's good," he was saying. "But not as good as it could be." He clipped the bag closed and stood. In my uniform pants and camisole, I felt shaky and altogether too exposed. "Here." He had found a scrap of paper and a pencil in that bag, and started scribbling. "Cleanliness, Vladha. Cleanliness is the key." I wished he would keep his voice down. For show or not, I didn't need the rest of my team hearing about my apparent lack of sanitation. "Follow these instructions, particularly the next time something falls on you." He smirked as he handed me the paper, particularly pleased with himself.

An address was scrawled in graphite on the rough weave, and some vague directions. I glanced up, realising Devich was telling me where to find him.

"Follow them carefully." He winked at me, and deliberately ran the back of his hand over his mouth.

"Of course," I answered, and bent to retrieve my clothes. I jammed the paper into the deepest pocket I could find, so it pressed against my uniform, my second skin. It would remain hidden, close to me, even at home. "Good." Devich sat, drew out his slides, selected one, and began directing its pions to take notes. "You can go now."

With my clothes piled hastily over my uniform, I snuck past Kichlan and Lad. Lad was hypnotised by a mirror the other technician was using to flash reflected light in his eyes, and Kichlan watched his brother's expression intently.

Once out from behind the screen the air seemed to grow lighter, grow cooler and fresher. Natasha, with a smirk and a wrinkle of her nose, pressed a warm bun into my hands. The smells of melted cheese and cooked mushrooms wafted up, and sent my stomach growling.

I flopped into the couch and ate through my food, refusing to meet the eyes of the others.

Finally, Kichlan and his brother re-emerged. I was feeling sleepy by then, my stomach and hips warm, slightly fuzzy.

"That's all of you, then?" Devich stood before the screen as the second technician dismantled it. He scanned the slides, fingers sketching rows and columns in the air.

"Yes," Kichlan snapped off the word, his arms crossed, his face dark. "You know it is."

"Mmm."

Devich tucked the slides away again. His fellow technician finished cramming the screen into its bag and looked hot in the face, flustered compared to Devich's distant cool.

"Thank you for your participation," Devich rattled off what sounded like a liturgy, one he must have said uncountable times and the collectors had surely heard nearly as often. "For your service to the veche, and Varsnia itself."

A moment of silence. Were we expected to say anything in return?

Devich and the second technician collected their bags, balancing the large one that contained the screen between them. No one offered help.

In silence, the technicians left the sublevel. The paper Devich had given me felt heavy in a pocket close to my chest. My drawers were wet, starting to cool. My head ached.

"Well, that was a waste of a day." Kichlan took his coat from its hook, tossed one to Lad and handed me my own. "We need to make up for it tomorrow. Breakbell, earlier if we can." He shook his head. "Still have a quota to fill. Inspections are never taken into account."

One by one we filed out. Mizra and Uzdal, so close together, heads down in some silent and shared concern. Sofia, drawn and tired. Natasha, whistling a soft tune. Lad took the stairs quickly, still full of energy after a day spent sitting inside. Kichlan kept close.

I didn't know what to feel. Devich brought opportunities back into my life. He brought his invitations to high-ranking parties, his friends in old families. But he also brought instability to that comfortable corner where Kichlan, Lad and I had existed so peacefully. He brought stress for Kichlan, pressure and fear, and he had brought them because of me, because he had been worried about me. I couldn't tell Kichlan it was my fault, that I had effectively put Lad in such danger.

I would never tell him, but I would try to make up for it regardless. I had to find Jernea, and I hoped the old man still held all the answers. So I could help Lad, and maybe myself.

14.

I heard it before my suit woke me. And there was a moment of ringing and darkness, between the sound that shattered the night and the light that broke it open, when I knew, I just knew, that this would not be anything like the previous debris emergencies. That this was something worse.

The sound was like *Grandeur* collapsing. Metal and concrete and life crumbling in one great roar. The floor shook and a fine crack traced its way into the window beside the bed. As I levered myself upright my suit lit up brilliantly, catching gleams in the splintered glass like a spider's web.

"Other!"

Someone was screaming below me. Valya? I scrambled into shoes and dragged on pants and a woollen shirt as I leapt down the tightly wound, unsteady stairs. The front door had been shaken from its lock and I pushed it open, plunging into the food-fragrant hallway.

Valya was in her bedroom. Her screams led me to her, and in the radiance from my suit she was pale, mouth wide and eyes darkly terrified. She snapped into silence as soon as my light touched her.

"Are you hurt?" I shouted over the ringing in my ears and the oppressive echoes of her screams.

"Did you feel it?" she breathed out a whisper, forcing me closer, forcing me to lower my ear to her mouth. "Did you feel it hurt?"

"Where?" I tried not to shout. "Where are you hurt?"

But she shook her head. "Not me." She stared into the suit's brightness, unblinking. "This is what they are doing, do you see now? Splitting us open. He can't stop them, not any more." Her shaking hand reached for my wrist. "Can't you feel his pain? He needs you, girl. So we have to protect you. He needs you."

I couldn't feel pain, but I could feel a need. An urgency, sharper than the light on my wrists, ankles and neck. I could feel it somewhere in my bones, in the insect legs scratching away below my muscles, the silver kicking in my blood.

"I'm not going until I know you're not hurt." What an effort it took to say that.

"We are all doomed if you don't go, girl. If you can't help him." Valya held a patchwork quilt to her chin like a small, frightened child. "Hurry."

I left the house, plunged into streets that should have been dark and empty. Ruddiness lit cobblestones with a fireside light, dull and red, hanging on the bottom of clouds like a pooling stain. It lit terrified faces as the people of Movoc-under-Keeper spilled from buildings like blood escaping skin. I pushed through a growing crowd – ignored the screams of children, the barking commands of men, the imploring hands of women – and felt vivid against their dull fear. Felt purposeful. Necessary.

I didn't bother casting the map, not this time. Instead,

I followed the symbols on my wrist, wound around streets and buildings and potholes without watching my feet, trusting in the suit, the guiding movement beneath my fingers.

Then Lad's cipher rose vivid and insistent, pushing against my forefinger. I skidded to a halt. Lad and Kichlan stood at a corner, on the other side of a sea of milling people. Kichlan had cast his wavering map on a building wall. Lad, bag full of metallic jars hanging from one shoulder, gestured to me.

I waded across the street. An old woman clutched at my elbow, her hand too much like Valya's. It made me shiver. "What's happening?" she screeched at me, two rotting teeth pale stumps in a dark and gaping mouth. I shook her off and pushed forward.

"Tan!" The suit and the firelight combined to give Lad's cheeks a youthful pink. It jarred with the tension within me, with the light on the heavy clouds. I had no idea where in Movoc we were, only how close the debris was, only that we needed to be there. Now.

"We need to hurry." I grabbed Lad's hand and drew him into the mass of people. "It's this way."

Kichlan flicked off his map and followed. "How do you know?" he shouted. Were his ears ringing too? Had Eugeny woken screaming in the night? Somehow, I couldn't imagine it.

"It's here." I lifted my wrist. "The map, it's all here."

A moment's hesitation I put down to running, to his being out of breath. "You can read the suit? On your wrist?" Even against the ringing I could hear his surprise.

"Yes." Surely he expected no explanations now.

"How? Who taught you?" Kichlan demanded.

"No one taught me." The suit had shown me. Those

wiggling worms I had seen kick out from my skin. They had taught me.

Lad squeezed my hand as we ran. I squeezed back.

I said, "I worked it out myself."

"Ever considered sharing?"

"Now is not the time" hovered on my lips. But then the world was rocked again and flames leapt above the tops of buildings, throwing huge chunks of stone into the air as though they were no more than balls tossed in play.

"Shelter!" Kichlan roared, barely perceptible as chaos erupted around us.

Together we dragged Lad to the nearest building and pressed him into the wall. Bodies pushed us, forced my shoulder onto the cement so hard I was glad for the sturdy uniform. And in the screaming, the press of bodies, the roar and light of flame, Lad watched, captivated, as parts of Movoc-under-Keeper fell from the sky. A wall smacked down into the throng that filled the street. Somehow, over everything, I heard the crack of each bone, the squelch of flesh, and had to fight very hard not to be sick. A column, a great cylindrical pillar, slammed into the roof of a building, shattering tiles, crushing stone. It slid to the street in an over-slow avalanche of brick, cement and – my stomach lurched again – bodies. Dead like dolls, limbs loose. Scorched. Broken. Thrown.

I started to sink against the wall, one arm wrapped around my middle. But Kichlan yanked me upright. "Don't! If you get under all this, you'll never get up again!"

The bodies against us were fierce now. Running, screaming, wailing. Forcing like the current of a rapid, angry river.

I swallowed bile. "We have to get to the debris." The words came unbidden. What I really wanted to do was join the senseless, panicked screaming. It seemed a lot easier that way. "We need to stop it." Was that really me, so calm, so sensible?

Kichlan's mouth firmed, his face grew determined. "You're right."

That made me feel better. I wasn't the only one.

He said, "That means going toward the fire, though."

I touched the suit, nodded. "It does." The dead didn't show up as symbols. The crowd was nothing but a low, indistinct rippling. I swallowed hard. Didn't seem fair.

We ran into the street, both gripping Lad's hands, pulling him forward. His head tipped back and he stared with wonder at the red sky. The crowd thinned as we ran. Some of them tried to stop us.

"Not that way!" a young man screamed. Blood soaked the front of his pale nightshirt. A gash in his forehead painted half of his face red. "They're all dead, and it's getting bigger, and they can't stop it! Don't go that way!"

We pressed on. But his voice echoed in my head, and I feared what *it* was, though somewhere in my gut I already knew. Could debris really do all this? Debris that wriggled, bug-like, through the air on a course of its own?

"Kichlan!" Sofia called from an intersecting street and hurried toward us. Her face was pale beneath dirt, smudges and a fine layer of sand. The collar of her jacket at been torn, bloody handprints smearing the fabric.

"Are you all right?" Kichlan asked, fear in his voice. "Have you seen the others?"

Sofia shook her head.

"Sofia?" I glanced at her hand. It shook and reflected our suit lights with something wet. Something red. "You're hurt!" I reached for her, but she turned away. Her expression hardened.

"Something hit me. Stone, I think." She gestured to her shoulder. "It's not serious."

I bit back an argument.

"We need to get closer." She turned to Kichlan, all business. "The others can find us. We need to work out what's going on."

"Can you keep him close to you?" Kichlan asked Sofia, placed Lad's hand in hers. "Stay here with him. For now. Tanyana and I will see what's happening."

"Tanyana and you?" Sofia asked. And despite the chaos and the blood and the fear the look she gave me was one of betrayal, of hurt. It lasted only for a moment, disappearing so quickly I began to doubt that I had seen it at all.

"Don't worry, Tan," Lad said, as we gave him over to her care. "It will be all right. In the end."

I knew he believed every word.

Kichlan and I left Lad with Sofia, where they huddled under a wide awning that seemed to have maintained some of its structural integrity. Lamps shuddered beside us as we ran, flickering high, then dying, only to burst into painful brilliance.

"Another factory?" I shouted.

Kichlan tapped the solid metal stand of a lamp as he passed it, wrapping a hand briefly around the carved lines and the bear heads peering eyelessly out of dark steel. "I doubt it." His voice hesitated, his feet pushed on. "Things go wrong when factories don't keep themselves clean. Lights fail, heat dies. I've never heard of one disgorging fire before."

The ground rocked again and Kichlan ploughed into me, pressing me up against a wall as stones hailed onto the open street. I felt them hit his back, heard the dull thuds and his low gasps of breath. "Kichlan!" I hissed, struggled to peer around his shoulder, but he leaned more of his weight on me and I couldn't move.

"They're not big. The uniform is taking most of it." Something very large crashed a yard from where he shielded me, spraying the cobblestones with dry rain.

"Liar," I whispered. It was hot, wrapped in Kichlan's body. I had forgotten how tall he was, how large. It was easy to do, with Lad to compare him to.

"See you prove it." He chuckled, breathlessly.

As the stones petered out a voice shouted from across the street, "Hey!"

Kichlan turned; I took the opportunity and slipped around him. "Kichlan! Tanyana!" Mizra from a high window. "Door." He pointed out from the shattered glass, arm strangely angled to avoid the edges. "Get up here. Hurry!"

We crossed the street, pushed in a door hanging loose from its hinges, pion lock buzzing sickly. Two flights of dark stairs and Uzdal was waiting. Firelight lit his hair and the side of his face, as though the room behind him was burning.

"You have to see this." He coughed, spat onto the floor. "Ash," he explained, by way of an apology.

The firelit room had once been a home, though now it was mostly rubble. A decrepit couch remained, and a low table.

"Don't know where the owners have gone." Mizra was staring out a gash in the wall on the opposite side of the room. "Got out as fast as they could, I'm guessing." He faced us, skin dirty, eyes darker than the cinders. "Don't blame them."

I approached him like it was a dream. Those weren't my feet stepping ash into someone else's carpet. Those weren't my eyes watering against grit, my face flushing with sweat as heat washed through the hole in the wall that had, I realised with an architect's detachment, been a supporting structure. The building could fall any moment. But it didn't matter, because it was a dream, all of it. None of it could be real.

"Other," Kichlan whispered the word. It summed everything up rather neatly.

"We can't stay here," I said. "It isn't safe."

The scene outside belonged in nightmares, not reality. A crater in the street, a hole where buildings had once been, so deep the bottom was all shadow and spitting flame. The building beside it – a squat, ugly thing – was torn apart like a limb, spurting water into the flames, hissing steam. Things dangled from the cracks in its walls and floors, soft things. They wavered in the steam, they cooked in the heat. Some moved, and those were the worst, some were still living, torn like the building, fiery like the sky. Bodies.

"What happened here?" Kichlan asked. No answer could satisfy that desperate question. "Why are we here?"

"Can't you see it?" I answered him, because neither Uzdal or Mizra could. Something darker leapt with the flames. Unreflective and dull. Planes of debris. Sails of it, roaring with the steam, surging with the light. It traced itself in a dim web around the building, it arched out of the hole like the wings of a giant, terrible dragonfly, and it leapt into the air, displacing stones, body parts.

Not displacing them. Throwing them.

"Oh, Other," Kichlan whispered beside me.

A glass window winked up at me from the crater. Planes of debris were playing with it. Cruelly. Like a cat. They flicked underneath it, lifted it, tossed it, cracked it.

Silver wire held the glass together in a mangled pattern. Sharp shards dangled like cold flesh.

"Did you see that?" Kichlan asked, struggling with a mouth that must have felt as dumb, as cotton-filled as mine.

I said, "Yes."

Mizra and Uzdal glanced between us, faces pale beneath ash, their fear all too obvious.

"We have to get away," Kichlan said. "We have to get out of here now."

"Yes." I swallowed solid grains of ash in my throat. "This building isn't struct—"

I stopped. Peering from the gash made in the earth, glinting from many levels below the ground, the edge of a metallic table caught my eye. And an arm. A great, silver arm. I remembered a needle attached to the tip of that arm. I remembered Devich's voice from the darkness beyond the halos of hot lamps.

"This is familiar." I gripped loose bricks; I leaned forward. "I was suited in a place like this."

My words seemed to hang in the air as the debris stilled. The planes dropped the window they had been torturing and rose out of the crater like great dark fingers. They swept slowly over the rubble, touching, testing, then with a flash they lashed the side of the building. I cried out as debris, very hot, very black, slashed at the gap in the wall. Slashed at me. I stumbled back. The dragonfly twitched its enormous wings and the next plane that attacked was sharper, more precise. It slammed straight into my chest.

Breath rushed out of me as I was flung back. I crashed into the couch and came to a sprawling halt up against the far wall.

Running, shouting, and everything drowned out by fire in my chest and buzzing in my head. I blinked against a blurred haze, a fog hanging over my vision. Kichlan leaned very close. I watched his mouth, but couldn't hear anything he was saying.

Another voice took his place. *You should run.*

But I couldn't move. Dimly, I realised my arms were silver, my suit activating without guidance and coating me from wrists to elbows, ankles to knees, neck to waist. I closed my eyes, focused on my chest, and pushed against the pressure. Air rushed into my mouth as my suit retracted. I swallowed it greedily.

To be safe. You should run.

"What was that?" Mizra screamed.

I could hear again.

"Debris," I gasped out the word, and something flared in my side. Fire, sharp, hot. Something broken?

"I saw it." Kichlan was still close. His hand under my head, his face beside mine. But he was straining to look at the ceiling. "The building. It's attacking the building."

"It?" Mizra screeched. "What in all Other's hell?"

"Get... out." I fought for each word. "Unstable." The pain was easing, being replaced by a numbness spreading down from my side to my hips. Better, or worse?

Kichlan didn't waste breath. He scooped me up, grunting as he pushed himself to his feet. "Damn, Tan. You're too heavy for someone so small."

I didn't smile. I thought of the numbness, of insect feet and silver sleeves. I was too heavy. How much of what Kichlan was carrying was me, and how much was the suit?

He lurched for the stairs and nearly tumbled down them with Mizra and Uzdal pressing so close behind us.

Another plane crashed into the building as we burst onto the street. Rubble shook from the walls. Tiles slid to shatter on the paving stones.

"Put me down." I pushed against Kichlan's shoulder and he did not argue.

"Are you all right?" His look was searching.

I nodded. "Yes. Knocked the wind out of me."

"What did?" Uzdal at my shoulder, breathless.

"Planes of debris." I flicked a hand toward the building. "They're everywhere in that mess down there. They're–"

"Attacking the building," Uzdal finished my sentence. "It doesn't do that. Kichlan?" He begged like a child for reassurance. "It doesn't do that, it's never done that. Has it?"

"I've never seen anything like that. Holes and fire and bodies." Kichlan frowned at me. "This isn't normal."

And I realised why this felt so familiar, the shock and the violence and the breath pulled from my lungs. I could have been eight hundred feet high.

"We should get away then, shouldn't we?" Uzdal said, through a fog, from a distance. From the ground so far below. "Shouldn't we run?"

Run.

"We're here to do our duty." Kichlan lifted his wrist. "We've been called to collect it."

"Collect that?" Mizra shouted. "We can't collect that. It threw Tanyana across the room."

I looked down as they argued – at my feet, at a distant construction site so vivid in my memory – and knew we were about to be swept away. Knew there was nothing we could do.

"Bro!" Lad ran down the street, Sofia gasping in his wake, clutching her shoulder and dripping blood from her arm. "Angry, bro. So angry."

"I couldn't stop him," Sofia choked on the words. Uzdal rushed to her side, slipped his shoulder beneath her arm to hold her steady, and stared in horror at the bright blood coating her hand.

Kichlan nodded his understanding. "I'm sorry, Lad. I didn't mean to forget about you."

But was Lad really talking about himself? I thought of the debris dancing with destruction like a cruel cat. The whack like a fist against my chest. Lad wasn't angry, was he? But the debris was.

"Who would summon furious pions from too deep inside reality?" I whispered, but there was no critical circle below me to respond. And this was debris, not pions.

Why was it all so angry?

They talked, while the debris consumed. I thought of the bodies in the rubble of what could easily be Devich's building. His work, not his home. He wouldn't have been there in the middle of the night, surely. But someone was there, enough people to plaster blood across bricks and cracked cement. I couldn't stand here talking about Lad, when all I wanted was to know was if Devich was in that pile of rubble.

Pions, debris, the lot, they could take their anger and be Other-damned! I would not be swept away again.

"We have to," I said, firm over the flame and hum. "We're debris collectors. We have to go into that building, and we have to stop the violence." I lifted my arm. My suit, still coating me from wrist to elbow, shone so brightly I squinted against it. "We have been called."

And I had to find out if Devich was safe. I had to know, for certain.

"She's right." Kichlan squared his shoulders, stood tall. "Sofia, you and–"

"Not staying!" Lad cried.

"I'm not an invalid, Kichlan," Sofia said, her tone leaving no room for argument.

"Fine," Kichlan said with a resigned sigh. "What about Natasha, have we seen any sign of her?"

No one answered. Mizra glared at me, Uzdal at least seemed resigned to his fate. Kichlan and Sofia maintained varied degrees of forced determination. Lad looked like he was about to cry.

"We can't wait any longer." Kichlan took the bag of containers from Lad. "We have to do what we are here for. We have to stop this."

"Hurry." I set off without waiting, crossed the street and kept as far from the building as I could. Something licked my foot, and I glanced down to see a dark plane flicker from a scattering of shattered tiles – to glance off the suit that had wrapped me from my knee to my toes.

I shook it off, but Kichlan had seen. Kichlan was staring at me, frowning, thinking, wondering. I began to run. I couldn't start that wondering. Could the debris have heard me, or seen me leaning from the window? What had made it drop the glass? What had made it launch itself at me, and destroy the entire building around me? The same thing that had made the pions throw me from *Grandeur's* palm? What, exactly, could do that? Or who? A pion-binder who could not only see debris, but control it as well?

Nonsense.

The hole where the technicians' building had once been was a scar in the earth, smoking and raw. Heat radiated from its darkness, from its burns. Binders had set up a perimeter around it, urged tall stone fences to spring from the street to try and confine the destruction. They wouldn't hold long. They crumbled as planes and rubble crashed against then, falling faster than the pion-binders could replace them. But the debris was interfering in a far more insidious way. Upsetting the circle systems, destabilising the bindings, wreaking a far more common chaos, but a chaos just as terrible. As we hurried toward them, one whole side of a large stone fence sluiced into mud, and the six point centre who had been working on it roared curses into the flame-lit sky. Planes flickered out of the gap this made, testing freedom with wide black sails.

"We're collectors!" Kichlan shouted as we ran to a huddle of people near the fence. "Debris collectors! Let us in!"

A crowd of brave or stupid spectators had gathered to watch. Nine point enforcers held them back, though why you'd need a powerful binder to convince you not to run into the head of chaos and death I couldn't understand. Between them and the fence, healers worked on bodies and I was thankful that the ruddy light cast everything red. It made blood that much harder to distinguish.

One of the enforcers broke away from the crowd. A circle centre, with bears roaring from his shoulders and lapel. Representative of the veche. He cast us a disdainful glance and pointed to one of the healers. I couldn't make out the mess of flesh the latter was working over, fingers weaving pions I could no longer see in a wild fight for life. "That's all that's left of the other team," the enforcer said, voice rasping. "What do you think you can do?"

"Other's hells," Mizra groaned.

Kichlan paled, but shifted the bag on his shoulder. "The only thing we can do." He held the enforcer's gaze. After a moment the man's salt-and-pepper stubbled mouth eased into a dry grin.

"Do it then. Any chance you can stop this is better than none." He lifted a hand, hesitated. "Good luck." Then turned to the binders on the fence and bellowed, "Let them through!"

We slipped through the gap in the stone. I kept my head down, unable to meet solemn, exhausted faces. The other side of the fence was strangely quiet. As the pion-binders sealed us in, a kind of stillness and dread settled on my shoulders.

"Any great ideas?" Mizra snapped.

I ignored him and scanned the ruins, the rubble. "There!" A body, a lump of pale cloth stained pink, of mushed meat and pooling blood.

Kichlan pushed past me, came to the body first. "Other." He pressed his hand to his nose and mouth. "It's the technician. From yesterday. Other."

Lad took a step forward, peering and curious. Kichlan spun, grabbed his shoulders, pushed him away.

Something had dropped out of me at his words. I slumped to my knees. They clinked against the cement, suit silver on stone. It couldn't be, not like this, not so suddenly and violently. I swallowed an urge to vomit and looked down.

Into the face of the second technician, the one who had assisted Devich, the one I didn't know.

"Tanyana?" Sofia from a distance, her voice like reflection on water, faint as rising steam. "What are you doing? We need to – Other!"

The world swam. I fell forward, too close to the red mush, to the collapse of body and bone, but I couldn't hold myself up. It wasn't him. It wasn't Devich, dead and torn. There was still a chance, wasn't there, that Devich was alive? But if his assistant was here–

"Tanyana!" Kichlan roared.

I lifted my head to see my team retreating to the fence, to see panic and confusion.

"Move!"

Then I was caught again. Something hooked around my leg, high, up along my thigh. Above my suit. It lifted me, dangled me like a doll, and tossed me.

I opened my hands to catch the ground but my suit caught it instead. Two wide, solid poles charged from my wrists into the cement. They crunched deep, held me suspended a moment still struggling with shock, before retreating, easing me down. Bare hands pressed to the earth, I struggled for breath, struggled to understand what had just happened. It had to be debris planes, tossing me around like the broken glass.

I stood, legs shaking. My thigh ached where the debris had touched me, like a bruise throbbing deep.

"Tanyana?" called voices from the other side of the hissing steam.

Where was I?

I turned, prickling dread. A tangle of bricks, of cement and steel frames surrounded me like corpses. Caustic smoke oozed from gashes in the ground. Water rushed in a putrid waterfall from the end of a shattered pipe. I was in the hole. The debris had not pushed me away this time. It had trapped me.

"Tanyana!" Kichlan called, his voice so far away.

I ran to the wall of rubble. I hooked fingers around stone and found it sharp and jagged. But I knew with some hunted-animal panic that I had to get out. That this had been no accident.

"Tanyana?"

"I'm coming," I whispered an answer. "Fast as I can."

357

"Tanyana?" But the voice, though it came from above, was closer. Not screaming, not panicking. I looked up.

Devich watched me from a small gap in rubble. My stomach clenched.

"Other, why are you here? Get away, Tanyana. Run. Please."

But I couldn't run. I could barely climb. "Devich?" I ignored the cuts, the pain in my fingers and palms, and pulled myself up. Suit-enclosed feet fought for purchase, slipped on smooth rock. Hand by hand, foot by painfully slow foot I dragged myself toward Devich.

Where was the debris? It was there, I could feel it like a threat at the back of my neck.

"What are you doing?" Devich gasped. He coughed wetly, and my stomach flipped again.

"Wait," I said to the stones against my face. "Wait for me."

"I'm so sorry, Tanyana. I can't believe it was you. It shouldn't have been you." His voice trailed into exhaustion. Into silence.

Something told me to keep him talking. "What happened here? Devich? Tell me what happened."

Darkness skittered over the rubble close to my left foot. It sent small stones trickling down. I watched them fall, and realised I hadn't climbed very far at all.

"The storage." He coughed again. "Below us, there was storage. For the debris."

"Yes? Keep going." Rubble fell against my face and I blinked sand out of my eyes.

"There was a blast from below. An explosion. Then fire, and smoke, and everything collapsed."

I didn't understand it. Of all the debris I'd seen none of it had managed to move rocks, let alone blow a hole in the ground. It floated in the air, passed through cement and stone. Only certain kinds of poly, and our suits, could touch it, could hold it.

Why had it changed?

"Are you all right, Devich?" My shoulder screamed as I hauled myself up the final stretch, overextending my arm and taking all my weight on one hand. But none of it mattered, because I was close to him. Close enough to fit my fingers through the crack and touch his face. He was very hot.

Devich said, "Something fell on me." He held my eyes with a fearful expression, and something deeper I could only describe as courage. The will to stay awake, to keep talking. "I can't move." He even smiled, small and wry. "But I'd like to get out, if I could."

"I'll get you out." How did I expect to do that? "We're here to clean up. We'll fix it, and we'll get you out."

"I knew they would send a team. But I didn't want it to be you." Devich grunted, shifted slightly.

"Don't move!"

He wiggled enough to drag a hand out from beneath him. I could reach in, far enough, to wrap the tips of my fingers against his.

Devich said, "This isn't right. This is dangerous. Other, I didn't want it to be you."

A scream, and the mountain of rubble rocked. Stones and shattered bricks cascaded down on Devich and me. I hunched forward, let my suit extend two metallic semi-circles, great hybrids of mirrors and wings. Rubble crashed against them, I bore each hit with a grunt, and held on to Devich's fingers. When silence returned I folded my suit inside and whispered, "I'll get you out." And the planes attacked me again.

I gripped Devich's fingers hard as debris wrapped hot

and painful around my legs, but couldn't hold on. I heard him scream as I was lifted into the air.

I reacted this time, determined to be more than some passive body inhabited by a proactive suit. Spikes arched from my hands to catch in the sides of the rubble. No longer flying, I withdrew them enough to skid down to the ground, sending clouds of dust to join the smoke and setting off avalanches of my own.

"I know you're there," I spoke to the clouds, to the grit clogging my throat.

Movement behind me. I spun and lifted an arm as a plane lanced out of obscurity. It smacked against my forearm, slid around the metal and unable to get purchase, glanced off into the air beside my right ear.

The suit. Of course. It had tried to tell me already, if I had only known to listen. The debris couldn't hold my suit. Couldn't hook it, couldn't scratch or pound it. "All right, then. If I must."

Kichlan had warned me against this. But Kichlan believed debris didn't think for itself, that it wasn't vicious, wasn't vindictive. And look where that philosophy had got us.

Something dark glanced against my head, knocking me forward. As I fell I let down the guards on my suit, loosened muscles from the bonds of thought. Silver slicked over my fingers, my palms. It was cool as it shot up to my shoulder, as it spread over my chest and down to cover pelvis and thighs.

I stood to meet the next plane that launched at me, coated neck to toes in silver. I reached for it with my own hands, not extending, not scooping it or collecting it with tweezers' precision. I grabbed debris, wrapped silver fingers around it. And when I held it in a hand encased in the suit, it was no longer the light reflected on stone as Kichlan had described it. This debris was not the unearthly sails I had seen, the shadows with nothing to cast them. It was solid, it was catchable. It was real.

I understood how that kind of solidity could wreak the damage it had done. How it could knock me, break me, bruise me. But I couldn't understand why I had never felt it before, why none of the team had done this most simple thing and gripped debris with suit, with hand, with everything.

I knew you were strong.

I stared at the debris in my grip. Planes still hit at me, smacked against my calves, my back, my shoulders. But these were insects flying, soft, barely felt through the silver.

Something glanced across my ear, cutting a line of blood that splattered wide against the ground. I swiped with my free hand and knocked the plane back. I would not be battered around any longer. Not by pions, not by debris.

"Did you?" I spoke to the debris in my hand.

Yes, and that is why I am glad you are here.

"So I can help you, is that it?" Like Valya had said?

Yes. But for now, will you just end it? Will you give me peace?

"You want to be collected?" To be controlled, crammed in small jars and sent into storage to rot. What was all this about, if not escape?

Peace.

Peace? This thing that attacked me, this unknown voice. How could it hurl me across a room, throw me like a doll, and then demand I give it peace?

I can't stop it doing those things. And the longer I am here, the more danger I am in.

The dragonfly wings quivered, fast and flickering as though prepared for flight.

"Danger? From whom?"

Look up. They are always here.

The puppet men. Pale figures at a broken window, watching from a building beside the ruin.

If I stay, they will attack me too. But if I go, that which you hold will run wild, and wreak more destruction than you can imagine. So bring it peace.

I tried to imagine it. The wings receding, the shadows drawing back, until all that remained was a small, wiggling lump.

They will try to stop you.

The puppet men disappeared. A moment later they were at another window, closer to the ground. They pressed hands to the glass and cracked it, the lines of fracture caught bright in the ruddy firelight.

Above me, the great wings swept across the sky, hissing steam into the air and sending rubble flying. I wavered. Peace? These planes didn't deserve peace. They deserved to be cut, to be sliced into pieces and forced into jars and stored in the darkness for the rest of eternity. They had killed the technician, hurt Devich.

But that's how this all began. Can't we just finish it? Can you give me peace?

"Who are you?"

The voice was quiet. The planes battled on.

I am not like those men. I will not hurt you, I will not deceive you, I will not use you. I can only ask for your help.

"Why are you asking me, what do you think I can do? I can't control debris, no one can control it! Peace?" I imagined that small, wiggling lump again. So simple, so innocuous compared to the chaos around me. Certainly a debris I preferred. "How do you expect me–"

The wings flickered. They stretched, they arched, then they dissolved into the ruddy night, became gloom on the rubble that edged closer, softly, like tired steps over the dirt. Fanned out around my feet they cast for me a hundred thin shadows, strangely expectant.

Carefully, ready for attack, I crouched. The planes kept still. I lowered the debris in my hand, touched it to the ground, held it there as it absorbed each shadow until I held something more akin to a wide, wet towel. It wasn't quite plane form anymore, more like softened, limp grains, stretched thinly.

Thank you.

It was relieved. Absorbed, lessened, and relieved. When I glanced up the puppet men were gone too.

I draped the debris over my suited shoulder and trudged to the mountain wall. Devich was looking down at me, paler, like a ghost face in the rubble.

"Is it over, now?" he called, querulous.

"Yes." I was stronger in my suit. With the debris balanced I found handholds and footing. I climbed smoothly, then lifted cement and exposed Devich to the air. He gasped, groaned. He looked crushed, out of shape around the middle, and delicate. A paper doll.

But he was still able to smile. "You're all shiny. So pretty."

"We have to get you to a healer." I hoped he could afford one, hoped he wasn't broken beyond repair. Like me.

He didn't move. He watched me, eyes open, empty. I bent, wrapped arms beneath him and lifted him against my chest. I knew I should feel fear, feel panic. Be terrified by those empty eyes, be angry at the thing over my shoulder. But all I felt was strong.

You are strong.

I climbed, Devich in my arms, debris over my shoulder.

"–vanished." Sofia sounded exhausted. And closer than I expected.

"She's here, must be here," Kichlan said, too fast, too loud. "We need to search."

"What about the debris?" Mizra snapped. "It's too dangerous."

"It's gone, I told you," Sofia answered him.

"How could it just disappear? How?"

"Tan," Lad spoke above them all, blue sky above their cloud. "She's here."

I stepped out of the rubble to silence. Kichlan gaped at me, a few feet from the edge of the hole. Sofia, slumped on the ground, had been glaring at Mizra. They both turned shocked faces to greet me. Uzdal, restraining Lad as best he could, watched me without readable expression.

"Tan!" Lad waved. "Thank you!"

Kichlan looked down to Devich in my arms. "The other technician." He spoke slowly, as though he couldn't believe the words.

I said, "He needs help."

Healers were already rushing through gaps in the fence. I allowed them to take Devich, ignored their shock before they closed ranks around him and started to work.

"Is he going to live?" I asked them.

The healers did not reply.

"Tanyana?" Sofia struggled upright. "What is going on?"

"Good question," Mizra muttered.

"Here." I pulled the strange debris from my shoulder. As a group, my team recoiled. Only Lad remained still, and looked sad rather than revolted.

"Other's arse, what is it?" Mizra hissed.

I said, "The debris." Wasn't that obvious? "I contained it."

"How?" Kichlan asked.

I couldn't answer, because I didn't really know. I just pointed at the jars. Moving stiffly, he collected one and opened the lid. I tipped the debris inside, pouring it like water.

Goodbye. Again.

Kichlan sealed the lid. I wondered, numbly, that so much had squeezed into a jar so small.

As I retracted my suit and my body flared into stiff, painful life, I wondered how much could fit into me. Before I shattered like glass.

15.

Movoc was silent as I returned to my flat above Valya's house in the smoky mid-afternoon, her streets empty of anyone but the enforcers, architects and healers scrambling to clean up the damage. I kept as far from all of them as I could manage, head down. But my body had not come through the night unscathed and I wasn't as agile as I would have liked to be, nor as hidden.

"Tanyana?"

I stilled with the voice, so out of place in these back-effluents and rills.

"It is!" A second voice, closer.

I looked up to see Volski running toward me, arms open, face smeared with ash and dirt, but glowing with fierce joy. "Tanyana!" Those arms wrapped around me and lifted my feet from the stones. I dangled in his embrace, watching the rest of my former circle from over his shoulder. Tsana, hands lifted to her mouth, was stumbling toward me like a drunk woman, legs wobbly. Zecholas broke away from them too, mouthing "My lady?" over and over.

Then Volski let me go. He beamed down on me and I felt dull – empty compared to their light. Debris to their pions. "They said collectors had been killed!" His hands flexed again, moved for my shoulders before he could pull them back. Did he need to touch me to be certain I was there? "It was an accident, with debris, and six collectors had been killed before they could control it. I thought... we thought... oh, I'm so glad it wasn't you!"

We thought? Worried about me, were they? Their fallen centre.

I couldn't share in my circle's joy. "Many more were killed than that." My voice was raw, it sounded like sand scraped down my throat, uncomfortable to my ears. "Technicians, binders. People in the street. So many people in the street." Was that the suit, scraping words with its legs?

"They were?" Volski's sunlight faltered. "Tanyana, are you all right?"

Devich had been taken from me, but taken to be healed. I had saved him.

I had to believe that.

Zecholas hovered by Volski's shoulder. "My lady?" he asked. His gaze swept from my ash-flecked hair, to the torn clothes, the weight I couldn't put on one leg, the hollowness in my eyes I knew had to be there. A hollowness I could feel tunnelling deeper.

"Not any more," I told him. Then, to Volski, "Let me go, I need to get home." I needed to tell Valya I was well, tell her it was over. Needed to spend a very, very long time lying down.

Across the street, behind the rest of my huddled circle and their probably terribly embarrassed new centre, a spot of darkness drifted by. Not ash, this one. Something solid, flesh-like, wiggling. My suit spun that little bit faster, and tension travelled in spasms from my wrists to shoulder.

It was over. Wasn't it?

"Oh." Volski stepped back. Something in me pulled tight like the suit, something that told me pushing him away like this was foolish. But I had tried to tell Volski the truth, and he hadn't listened. Volski, who had known me so long and so well. Volski, who I had always believed I could trust. If he wouldn't listen, if he refused to believe me, then what chance did I have to get the others to hear me? To help me.

"I'm glad you're well." Such sadness in that face, the same look he had given me on the bench in front of the gallery. It felt so long ago. "We all are."

Were we? Llada's face was so red she shone from the building they were repairing across the street. Was that Savvin's back? I hoped it was, I hoped he couldn't bear to show his face. But Volski was here, and Zecholas, and even Tsana, holding back, still pressing her lips like she was trying not to be sick. That meant something, I supposed.

"Thank you," I managed. Another glob of debris floated by, closer this time. I clenched my hands to try and control the spasms. "Be careful. There was a lot of debris." More than I could hope to explain. "The effects could linger."

Volski nodded, grave. "You be careful too," he told me, and didn't move as I started walking again, just watched me with that same, sombre expression.

A few steps, and I halted. Tsana was here. Tsana, the only person who had believed me. "Tsana, do you remember what I asked you?"

She hurried forward, removed her hands long enough to reach for mine, realised I wouldn't take them, and pressed them back on her face. "Yes," she said behind fingers, muffled.

"While you are all here, in this area of the city, do you think you could?"

"Oh, yes, of course." Her cheeks were growing flushed against her fingertips. Didn't she want the others to know who she met at parties?

"Can you remember an address? Can you be there, tomorrow, laxbell? It isn't far from here."

"Ah–" She glanced over at Llada's red face.

I shifted the weight away from my aching leg again.

"Of course."

"Great." I gave her the sublevel address. "Tomorrow."

And I left the circle, wondering if they would find bodies in that rubble, or if the enforcers had already swept through, diggers in tow, removing every last one. If the healers had saved any of them.

The bruises on my upper thigh flared into painful life as I crawled into the space between a rickety fence and the back wall of a tall building. Mud clung to my knees, it hung heavy from the front of my jacket. I pinched a blob of debris, the last of a cluster we had found clinging to the unstable and rotting fence.

The lights of the whole street, only two blocks away from the sublevel, flickered in poorly kept time. The rest of the team were working on them. It wasn't even third-bell, and we had already filled almost twenty jars.

Groaning, I edged my way out of the gap and straightened. If this kept up we would have no problem meeting quota. And I knew that should have been a good thing, but there was so much of it, I could only imagine the debris was residue, parts of the planes that had escaped. So each glob, either floating in the air or stuck to buildings or oozing from sewerage vents, reminded me of Devich, half-dead and in a healer's care. Or the voice that had pleaded with me. Or dragonfly wings. So I wished things were normal, I wished we had to rely on Lad just to come close to what the veche demanded of us. Because none of this was right.

"At least this is easier." Mizra, hand laden with full jars, stretched his back out, wincing.

I couldn't stop the "Hmmm" under my breath.

"Not risky enough for you, is it?" Mizra must have heard me, and snapped, "No fun if you can't put your life and the life of others in–"

"Mizra!" Kichlan shouted from his lamp at the end of the street. "Enough."

The twins, muttering together, moved on to a lamp as far from me as possible. With a sigh, I nodded to Kichlan, and he just looked away.

I couldn't shake the feeling we'd all moved back a few sixnights and one.

When we could carry no more we returned to the sub-level. I missed the scent of porridge cooked on Kichlan's fireplace. I missed Lad's unerring and probably danger-ous focus on the flames. I missed everything that had, for a moment at least, made this cold room a new home.

As Kichlan arranged the jars on the shelves, Lad and Uzdal sank into couches. I glanced at the sun creeping in through the half-size windows. Lax was bells away. Nothing to be concerned about.

"Tanyana has a point," Kichlan said, suddenly. He turned from the shelves, a jar still in his hand. "This isn't normal."

I gaped at him. "Er–"

"No, Kichlan." Mizra leapt to the fray, eager anger in his face. "No! Walking out of that Other-hole wrapped in her suit, that isn't normal! Saving that cursed arrogant

370

technician, of all the people who died, that isn't normal! What we found out there was debris on lamps. That happens all the time."

"A whole street of them?" I murmured.

Kichlan sighed. "You're not helping."

"A whole city of them for all I care!" Mizra spat the words. "Anything is better than yesterday."

I pictured the dead technician. I could still hear screams as buildings fell from the sky. "Yes," I said. "It is."

"Then stop complaining about it. Stop wanting it to happen again!"

I spluttered, made inarticulate by fury, by a bitter sense of how Other-damned unfair this was.

"Mizra!" Kichlan snapped. "Tanyana doesn't want–"

Sofia, looking pale, drawn, had been leaning on the wall. She pushed herself upright. "Think of everything that has happened, since she stepped foot in here. Three emergencies, Kichlan. We don't get that many in thirteen moons and a day. Something is going on." She pinned me with a vicious, animal-protecting-her-young eye. "And it's got to do with her."

"Yes, Tanyana," Natasha said with her all-knowing, uncaring smile. "You do rather seem stuck in the middle of it."

Shivers traced fingers along my spine. The anger of pions, the rage of debris, all rushed around me like waves.

"She can do things with that suit no one should be able to do," Sofia continued. "She steps into the middle of the Other's own hell and suddenly the whole thing stops? We don't know her, Kichlan, not really. For all we know she's making this happen–"

"I'm not!" Wrapped in their anger, surrounded by memories I did not understand, I struggled for something

371

to make sense. "I didn't do any of this. The pions, *Grandeur*, the planes. I don't know why they are so angry."

Uzdal, face dark from where he lay on the couch, glared at me. "What are you talking about?"

I took a deep breath. After everything we had been through, my collecting team would surely believe me. "*Grandeur* was the name of the statue I was building when I fell."

Reluctant nods. Lad's head was hanging so low I couldn't see his face.

"That wasn't an accident. I tried to tell the binders in my circle, the pupp– the veche men, no one believed me. But someone pushed me off. Someone who dug too deep into reality and summoned angry, violent pions. I'd never seen any like that before." I swallowed, saliva sticking in my throat. "Like the debris was yesterday."

The room hung heavy with silence, broken only by Natasha's unsympathetic snigger.

"So, what?" Sofia pressed on. "What does that mean? Pions are out to get you? Debris is too? Don't be ridiculous."

"Doesn't sound very likely, does it?" Natasha smirked.

"I know," I said. "But it's true. You saw what happened yesterday–"

"You're saying that was your fault?" Uzdal pushed himself off the couch. "All those deaths, they were all your fault?"

Other. Was I saying that?

"Just like the statue?" Uzdal asked. "All the damage that caused, all the debris teams brought in to collect the mess? That was your fault too?"

"No," my voice cracked as I spoke. "Someone else was–"

"They were targeting you!" Mizra shouted. "You just said it. They pushed you off, no one else! If they were targeting you then it was your fault."

"I–"

Then a pit-a-pat like a bird against glass cut me off, and there was Tsana, fist against the door to the sublevel, expression uncertain.

I swore beneath my breath, "Other."

Tsana's large eyes fell on the shocked faces of my team one at a time. "Tanyana." She stepped into the room, one hand held out.

I crossed the floor quickly. Why was she early, of all things? "Tsana." I took her hand. "Thank you for coming."

"Of course." She smiled prettily, and let none of the distance between us show. "Of course."

I would have to introduce her. Another thing I had hoped to avoid.

"Everyone," I said. "This is Tsana. She's here to fix the ceiling, she's an architect." *Like I used to be* stalled on my lips. "Tsana, this is my debris collecting team."

Sofia coughed. She stood, head high and neck uncomfortably straight. "Not that she needs our help. Sometimes it seems she can just do it all herself."

Tsana extended her smile. "She was a very skilled binder too."

She probably meant that as a compliment.

Sofia lifted an eyebrow. "I wouldn't know about that." She fixed me with a sharp expression devoid of any trust. "Lots we don't know about her." She left the sublevel with ice in her wake.

Mizra and Uzdal didn't speak. They followed Sofia closely, heads down.

"Don't be long." Kichlan helped Lad out of the chair, and pressed a coat into the man's hands. "Make sure the door locks behind you." I noticed he didn't offer me the large iron key in his pocket. "Try to make the ceiling as smooth as possible. Don't give the technicians a reason to notice it again."

Tsana, affronted, sniffed loudly. "I only do the best work."

Kichlan raised his eyebrows at her. "Come on, Lad."

Lad continued to stare at Tsana like she was an exotic bird.

"Is he quite all right?" Tsana murmured to me from the side of her mouth.

"He's Lad," I answered the only way I could. "It's just the way he is."

"Come on." Kichlan tugged Lad's hand. "Let's leave them to their work."

"What's the lady going to do, bro?" Lad asked as he followed Kichlan.

"Fix the ceiling, Lad."

"All by herself?"

"Yes."

"Oh." Footsteps receded up the stairs.

"Hello." Natasha, who had waited smiling under sunlight from the windows, approached Tsana. She held out a hand, and the two women shook.

"Hello," Tsana replied.

If their situations were not so vastly different, I realised, the two women would have been a lot alike.

"I'll leave you to it." Natasha flickered her smile on and off like a broken lamp as she glanced between us. "Better make sure there's not a scar left, or you won't hear the end of it."

I groaned and rolled my eyes to say I knew she was right.

Chuckling, Natasha left Tsana and me alone in the sublevel.

"So, that's your new circle." Tsana wasn't impressed. I could see it in her stiff shoulders, hear it in her clipped words.

"Team," I corrected her. "We don't use circles. Debris collecting is done in teams." Except, of course, for the circle we had made when we all worked together.

"Ah." She frowned. "So how do you–?" She made a gripping gesture in the air.

I held up a hand and pulled back my sleeve. Rather than balking at the slowly spinning, shining suit, however, Tsana leaned in and peered at it. That surprised me.

She said, "I still don't understand."

"Stand back." I spread my suit out over my hand, at first in a glove of silver, and then beyond my fingers and into the traditional pincer shape. It didn't want to go that far. The suit fit so well over my hand, so snugly. Like a dog with a new trick, a child with a new word. It had learned to coat me from toes to neck and it seemed now it didn't want to do anything else.

"Amazing." Tsana frowned for a moment. "I can't see it at all. With pions, I mean."

Couldn't she? I withdrew the suit, watching it glint silver in the sunlight. That was strange. Something without pions. Or, I reconsidered, maybe they were too deep, too dense for her to see them. Like the ones that had thrown me from *Grandeur*.

"Shall we?" I pushed those thoughts aside and gestured to the ceiling.

"Of course." She found the crack and stood beneath it.

I figured I should thank her. While we were exchanging white lies. "I appreciate you coming to do this."

"You asked."

Given the circumstances she could hardly have said no.

It didn't take her much, but I'd known that would be the case. I could have done it with a glance, and certainly with more grace, in the days of my old life. Tsana's frown returned, she flexed her hands at her sides and muttered to herself, then the hole began to fill. The cement was fluffy, like foam. I resisted the urge to criticise, to tell her to keep her pions under tighter control. There was too much air. A moment and she realised this, corrected it, and the cement grew darker, harder and solid. Soon, nothing was left, not a scar to prove the crack had ever existed.

Jealousy surged somewhere in my stomach. I had not been patched as elegantly as she did the ceiling.

Tsana shook her hands out, adjusted the colour slightly, frowned deeper and adjusted it again. "There." She turned to me. "Done."

I forced a smile, still tackling acidic envy. "Thank you."

"Are you sure that's it?"

Such a small thing to repay such a large debt. "Yes, that's perfect."

"Good. Great."

It must have been a massive weight from her conscience. At least, I hoped it was massive.

We stood in the sublevel beneath the healed ceiling, staring at each other with nothing to say.

"Well, that's it." I clapped my hands together.

"Yes."

"Shall we–?"

"Of course."

I was careful to lock the door as we left. Last thing I needed was another reason for Kichlan to dislike me.

A landau was hovering in the street, resplendent in polished mahogany and silver. How many kopacks was Tsana paying to have it wait? Or maybe it was her own, the driver's family employed by hers through the generations.

Tsana hesitated at the coach door. "Can I offer you a ride up to the Tear?"

"Ah." I swallowed. "No. I was forced to move. I live near here now."

"Oh." The door swung open with a creak loud in the darkening street. "I am still happy to take you home."

I shook my head. "The walk is not far. I enjoy it." Why did my tongue feel like a strip of torn cloth in my mouth? Thick and unresponsive.

"I see."

I watched Tsana climb in. She was being assisted by pions, I realised with a start, probably looping around her waist in ribbons of colourful light and gathering beneath her feet. It added a graceful, floating quality to her movements. "It was lovely to see you again, Tsana."

She gripped the silver handle, nodded. "It was." She started to pull the door closed, and hesitated. "Goodbye, Tanyana."

The coach glided away the moment the door snapped shut. I stood in the street and watched it disappear in a flicker like moonlight on dark water.

I reached inside my jacket, past my blouse, and into one of the folds of my uniform tight against my chest. I pulled out Devich's scrap of paper, thick between my fingers, scanned the address and turned into the evening. To follow it.

Devich lived further away from the city centre than I would have believed. I could have told myself it was to keep close to his work, to the building that no longer was. But it might have had more to do with a childhood unaccustomed to luxury or city living.

Still, it wasn't the top floor of an old house, above a food-obsessed crazy woman. It had that in its favour.

Devich's home was surrounded by thin triple-story buildings squashed in together along a street that ran close to the Tear. It looked the same as all the others, wind-stripped paint on weather-pocked stone patched with off-colour cement. His, I noticed, had a small garden between the gate and the two sagging steps to the front door. Flowers I couldn't identify, petals anaemic, stems yellowing, wavered against a chill lifting from the Tear. Three small worms of debris wiggled their way through his garden.

Everything was washed out, starkly colourless in the light from street lamps. I pushed open a well-maintained gate, skirted plants, and pressed a pion lock beside the door. It wouldn't unlock for me, but it would send streams of colour and light to let him know someone was at the door.

Devich answered. He was pale. His hand, wrapped around the door frame, shook. His nails were bloodless.

"I can go, if you like," I said as he stared at me in shock. "If you need to heal."

He pulled the door all the way open, stepped out onto the first step and wrapped me in an embrace. One arm held my shoulders; the other, I noticed, was bound to his side. "Tanyana."

Awkwardly, Devich drew me inside.

His home was lit warmly, by pions generating light behind rose-coloured glass. I rather liked the effect, and realised it reminded me of flame. Proper, real, not-a-pion-in-sight flame. An interesting choice for a debris technician.

"Thank you," Devich said. He stood close, face mostly shadow, and ran a finger over my cheek.

"What else would I do?" At least he appreciated what I had done. That made for a nice change. "Couldn't leave you there, could I?"

He laughed, still rich, full, despite his near death, despite his bound arm. "I meant, thank you for coming here. I've been waiting for you. I thought you might have lost the address."

Waiting for me? "You were hurt. Badly hurt. I didn't know where they would send you. I thought you might not be here." Did he remember dangling in my arms as limp and as alive as a cloth doll? "Don't you need time to heal?" I had needed time.

But Devich leaned in and kissed me, deeply. "There were skilled healers on site."

There were skilled healers beneath *Grandeur* too. "What about your arm?"

"This?" He lifted his bound arm slightly and winced. "Dislocated. Apparently the healers can't fix the swelling. Of all the things they can do, they can't fix that."

"What did the healers do, then?"

He looked down. "You don't really want to hear about that, do you?"

I placed a finger on his chin and tipped his face toward me. "I do." I hoped he could see how serious I was. I needed to know what had happened to him. If he was one of us now.

"Fine." But his eyes slid from mine. "They stopped bleeding in my chest and abdomen and patched something that had ruptured, and I'm not talking about that any more. They put my shoulder back where it belonged and patched up a fracture. They fixed three broken ribs and a shattered ankle. That's what they did."

So, that's what a healer should be like. To put all that back together without stitching, without scarring. It left me throbbing between jealousy and relief. With the unfairness of it all.

"And this?" I ran fingers over his forehead. He closed his eyes.

"My head?"

"Yes. Is it okay?" Could Devich still see pions?

"Wasn't hit. You saw me, you saved me. My head wasn't hit."

Did it take a head injury then? I didn't think so. Mizra and Uzdal had not been connected by their skulls.

How could I ask? "So, you are all right then? Nothing that can't be fixed?"

Devich looked at me with confusion for a moment, then eased into a sad smile. "Are you worried that I have to become a collector too?"

A perfectly reasonable concern, I thought. "Well, are you?"

His free hand took one of mine. He stroked the scars. "No, my dear. I am still my same old self."

I wrapped both of my arms around him and kissed him as hard as I could without bruising. His tongue slicked mine. His teeth were cool, sharp.

"Good," I whispered against his lips.

I saw little else of Devich's house that night. We ascended a staircase in darkness, two flights. The carpet was thick and absorbed all sound. His bedroom was sparse, but held books. We were similar in more ways than I had realised.

I peeled away my uniform, helped him with his shirt and pants. Our roles felt strangely reversed, as I eased

380

myself onto him. He was the injured one, the one who needed to be cared for. While, in the long run, I was far more broken than he could ever be, I was stronger for the moment, and I would give him the love and the acceptance he had shown me when I most needed it.

Devich moaned, lifted his hips to meet me. I smoothed him down.

"Just lie there. My turn to look after you." I licked the edges of his smile.

"I will miss this." His chin tipped up, head angling back.

I stilled. "You will?"

"Ah." He gave a soft, rueful laugh. "I would have missed this, I mean. If you hadn't come to save me, if I wasn't here now. I'm glad I am still alive, to be here with you."

"Oh." I was glad too. Even if the team had turned against me, even if Kichlan offered nothing but silence and suspicion, it didn't matter. At least I had Devich.

I put his strange and probably pain-rattled words aside, and I kissed his exposed neck.

16.

I hadn't returned to Proud Sunlight since I had graduated: Three Point Circle, First Class, Architect with Distinction. I would have been welcome before, particularly as my binding skill improved, my circle increased and the number of kopacks I could have donated rose with both. It was strangely satisfying to think that the first time I would return was when I was no longer welcome, when I had no pion-binding skill left, no circle and a pittance for an income. Maybe the fall had twisted something in my sense of humour.

On Thriveday we filled our quota early, with a large cache barely a few yards from the Darkwater door. We scooped it out of a pothole in the street, had not been forced to lie face-down in muck, wade through sewage or scale the side of buildings. However unnatural that enormous heap of debris lying easily accessible in the middle of the street was, I couldn't help but be thankful. Just this time. With our jars filled the remains of the day were left empty. I was not invited to shop, to travel to graveyards or enjoy Eugeny's cooking. I took the ferry into the city and tried not to see the patches

382

of darkness hugging walls, lampposts, even the deck of the boat.

And I returned to Proud Sunlight.

The university was an imposing building of sandstone and marble close to the banks of the Tear River, a few rills north of the bridge. It hulked above the old city buildings, ancient as they yet larger, its pale walls broken by dark stained-glass windows. The Keeper had been sculptured into the stone at every corner, above every doorway. Both the mountain and the myth it was named after, he who defended us from the Other. That kind yet stern face, strong and everlasting.

A tall iron fence enclosed the building and the mani-cured gardens that stretched to the river. An old jetty reached out into the Tear, but I had never known it to be used. Before Proud Sunlight had opened its gates and heavily reinforced doors to anyone with sufficient bind-ing skill, that fence would have been guarded, old family children alone invited to study in its halls. Now the main gates were left open, and enforcers no longer patrolled the corridors or garden paths, but to me it felt no more inviting. As I passed through the gate I felt like an in-truder. So I hunched my shoulders and jammed hands in my pockets and hoped I could remain unnoticed. Just in case enforcers from the distant past did, somehow, re-main. In case they could see through my secondhand clothes to the suit on my wrists and the honour I had lost, and throw me from the rooms I had once studied in so proudly.

But no one did. I attracted few second glances as I made my hopefully unobtrusive way past the main hall-way. Pion-binders were practicing, bathed in colour from the tall windows. They huddled in groups of three and seemed to be altering the temperature of the room. I wondered at that. If Proud Sunlight had stooped so low that it was teaching binders to work in heating factories, then it shouldn't have been so quick to strike me from the honour roll. The university I remembered specialised in disciplines that required precision and skill, disciplines that if not done correctly could put lives at risk. Architecture, healing, military technologies and the more arcane investigation into circle formation and pion skill.

I continued beyond the main hallway, beyond offices and classrooms on the lower floor. A voice droned from somewhere, lecturing in a dull monotone that even Kichlan would have struggled to match. The thought made me smile and realise I missed his lecturing, at least compared to his silence and his distrustful glances.

The building was roughly divided between the disciplines; the kind of unofficial rule new students spent their whole first year trying to work out. Ground-floor rooms were allocated to the military; architects preferred the upper hallways. I knew the ways well, even after all these years. How many was it? Ten years? Yes, it must have been.

I found the half-hidden stairs behind an out-of-place bookcase in an old, empty office. The stairs themselves were an architectural wonder, and I could understand why the first architects who had come to learn and teach here had been attracted to them. They wove their tight way through the building, bypassing the rest of the levels to reach the top. Proud Sunlight had a strange roof. Designed with odd angles, some areas made of great sheets of glass that let the sun or the moonlight in, most built from the stone itself. What might have once been an attic had been divided into rooms, and these the architect lecturers had claimed as their offices. It was here I would find Jernea. If he was still alive.

I made my way down a thin hallway. Deep afternoon sunlight glanced in through patches of glass above me. It lit some of the offices, while others were left in dark shadow. A few faces I did not recognise watched me from desks as I passed them. A small group of ridiculously young students passed me in the hall. They whispered circle theories and hardly noticed me. I remembered what that was like, to have such passion, to be so skilled, and ready to create your future with both.

I had almost given up when one of the faces I didn't know did more than just watch me pass. Young for a teacher, his black gown too big for him, his silver bearclaw too bright, he was twitching through the invisible contents of a slide when I walked past his office. He looked up, surprised, placed the slide on the desk and strode into the hallway.

"You!" He pointed to me, and I stalled as a streak of warm light touched my face. "Who are you?" He approached me, hands hidden in folds of black cloth. The crimson satin edging on his gown surprised me. He must have graduated young and with high honours to have made second-senior lecturer by his age. "You're not a student."

I wondered what tipped him off? The scars? The clothes, or just because I looked colossally older than everyone in the Other-damned place? Which was exactly the way I felt.

"What are you doing here?"

I repressed a sigh. "Just looking for someone."

"Just looking?" He stepped into the sunlight and I noticed sporadic pale hairs dotting his chin and upper lip.

Didn't help my mood. "You can't *just look*. This is an exclusive university, only the best–"

"What's going on here?"

I turned as a woman stepped out of the office at the end of the hallway. She strode toward us, step sure and brisk, and the young teacher took an involuntary step back.

"Who are you, what is–" Then she saw me, bathed in the light from the roof, and she stopped. "Ah. So, you did come." She was still in shadow so I could not see her face, but I could hear the rueful smile in her voice alone. "I suppose they were right." Another step, and the light touched her as well. I realised I knew her. Her sun-browned face carried more lines than I remembered, her dark hair was pulled back where it had always floated free. Dina. Only now, she wore a gold edge upon her black gown. Architect dean. It was rare for a woman to lead any university faculty, but she had always been skilled. Jernea's assistant when he had mentored me, a sub-senior lecturer those ten years ago. Quite a rise.

"Petr, thank you, but you can go now."

The young lecturer made to argue, but Dina cut him off.

"Please. Leave us."

With a final scowl in my direction, Petr returned to his office. Dina watched him go before casting her hard eye on me. "They did better work on your face than I expected, when I was told you were scarred."

Of all the students Jernea taught, why would she remember me? "It will never be the way it was."

"No, it won't." She seemed to hesitate, to be debating something silently within. "I suppose you have come to see him."

"It was my last resort." I had already steeled myself to hear of Jernea's death.

"I'm sure it was." Instead, she gave me a sad smile. "I will let you see him, but you should be prepared. He can't help you, he can't help anyone anymore."

"He is still alive then?"

Dina laughed, full and throaty. "That old bear will outlive us all. He refuses to hear the call of the Other, and you know what he is like when he sets his mind on something. The Other can shout as loudly as he wants, the old man won't listen."

I couldn't help but grin. "That's true." Jernea was one of the most tenacious people I had ever known. A powerful binder, a highly skilled architect and a determined teacher.

Dina gestured to me, and I followed her back to her office. "I must warn you, he is not the man he once was."

Her office was large, but narrow, almost a corridor of itself. Full bookshelves lined the walls, floor to part-stone, part-glass ceiling. Only section of the university's ancient and priceless library. A desk, a few chairs and a rug alone broke up the uniform tones of wood and sandstone and leather-bound paper. Jernea was sitting at the far end of the office, beneath a large glass section. Late afternoon gold seemed to make him glow.

"He is no longer employed by the university," Dina said, softly. "He has not worked here for years. However, he feels safe in this room, he feels more at home here than in an old and empty house." She rubbed the back of her neck and looked at the floor. "Truth be told, I feel better when he is here with me. I don't remember a time at Proud Sunlight without him. He has carers, of course, and they came to me. Explained his situation. His distress. I was glad to have him back, to care for him. He doesn't need much. They feed him every day..." She trailed off as I slowly approached my old mentor.

Jernea sat in a strange chair, wrought of some kind of thick poly. It couldn't have been comfortable: too straight-backed, legs out, arms on hard rests. Not a cushion or any kind of padding in sight. He wore a gown of faded blue that was done up loosely down the front. His bare skin was thin and withered across stark ribs, and there were count-less tiny holes in his chest.

"Other's hell," I hissed. "What have they done to you?"

"Oh, I'm sorry," Dina said, behind me. "I should have thought of this. You can't see them."

"See what?" I glanced at her, angry. There were more holes on his forehead, down his neck, even his arms.

"The pions, of course. It's a complicated system, tied in to the chair itself. It keeps him alive. They're pumping blood down to his extremities, monitoring and compen-sating for oxygen loss, as well as maintaining the workings of his left kidney–"

"Stop." I held up a hand, closed my eyes. "I– I don't want to know." I could imagine pions looping around him, *in* him, binding him to the chair, to this life, like colourful chains. And I wished I couldn't, because I didn't want to remember Jernea like that.

He looked like he had been spun from glass. Nearly transparent skin stretched across the bones of his face and hung in wrinkles around his neck. I could make out the veins at his temples, every sunspot that had ever dotted his cheeks. His eyes were white with cataracts, his hair thin. A blanket was tucked in around his legs and his once powerful and expressive hands were curled and skeletal, shaking on his lap.

"Jernea." I crouched beside him.

His head turned, ever so slightly, but his sightless eyes passed me by. He mouthed words, but they came out only as wet sounds.

"Today is not a good day." Dina stood close to my back. "He cannot talk today. He cannot stop the shaking. Some days he will ask after people I have never heard of. He will talk to the pions in the walls as though they were his friends. Today is not one of those days."

I stood and realised my own hands were shaking, almost as much.

"You picked a bad day."

"I did." I clasped my hands, squeezed them as I fought tears. I would not weep for my stubborn old mentor. It was good, in a way, that he did not know that I had fallen. That he would not understand it, or hear it, even if he was told. In that mind, locked behind age and blindness, I was always the centre of a critical circle.

"Why did you come here?" she asked.

When I turned, Dina's expression was hard. She crossed her arms, bunching the loose fabric of her gown. "You're not really here to try and persuade an old man to open a tribunal for you, are you?"

I gaped at her.

"Because he would be hurt, Tanyana, to think that was all you wanted from him."

"How did you know I wanted a tribunal?" And why did she remember me? Of all the students, why me?

"Tell me why you are here."

I looked back to Jernea, to his shaking and crippled fingers. "No, that is not why I came. Although I might have, if I had thought of it earlier." I shook my head. "I came to ask the greatest pion-binder I have ever known for his expertise, his knowledge, his mind. I came here for nothing."

Dina's shoulders sagged. "I should have known. No one he had touched could use him so thoughtlessly."

"So tell me," I said. "How did you know that?"

The edges of Dina's mouth twisted into a grim smile. "Come now, you must know."

"The veche?" I whispered. "Did they come here, did they threaten you?"

She was looking at Jernea again. "I should not be talking to you. I believed them, when they said even talking to you would be dangerous, that helping you could be fatal. Even for an old man." But when she looked back up at me her face was set, eyes dark and furious. "But I will not be threatened, and as ancient and distinguished an institution as Proud Sunlight will not be bowed into submission. They can take away our funding, divert kopacks into weapons research and warmongering, but we will not compromise our integrity. We will not be beholden to the veche any more than we already are. No matter how many more pale and strange-looking thugs they send!"

Ice shuddered over my skin. "Pale? Did they have no expression, nothing in their voice that sounded human? And did they walk like they were unreal, like they were built of wood?"

"That's an accurate description, if I've ever heard one." Her expression grew disbelieving. "Don't tell me you didn't know it was them. They're watching you, Tanyana. They made a point of coming here, of telling me you were looking for help to open a tribunal, and if I dared to help you both Jernea and I could be in some peril." She chuckled. "They can't understand the calibre of binder Sunlight produces if they think they can threaten us."

I stared down at the old man for what felt like a long time. "I'm sorry to bring them to your doorway."

"I know you are." Suddenly Dina placed a hand on my shoulder. "But I am more fearful for you. The veche must be very, very interested in you. Watch yourself."

I nodded. "I will go, and hope I take all my trouble with me."

She lifted her eyebrows. "What did you want to ask? I might not be the old man, but I have stood beside him for a long time." Dina softened as she spoke of him. "I learned a few things here and there."

"It doesn't matter now. And I won't give them any reason to come for you."

I crouched again, took one of Jernea's hands and then held him. He felt thin and fragile, like so much of my life now. And as I thanked him silently, I realised those questions I had thought so important really didn't matter. Why broken people like me could see debris, whether we could be fixed. What mattered, what really mattered, was why the puppet men had taken such an interest in me. And what, if anything, I could do about it.

A final pat on skin that didn't seem to feel me, and I stood. "Thank you," I said to Dina.

She nodded, seemed to hesitate. "Listen, I don't know if I should tell you this, but I think I will." She looked down to Jernea. "For him. When they came, the strange veche men, I heard a rumour. Kopacks are being withdrawn from us, here and at other universities, and thrown into something very secret. I overheard members of the military discipline talking about war with the Hon Ji, and those veche men seem to be involved. So be careful, Tanyana. Those are very powerful men."

When I left the university the bell was late, the sky streaked with long, drawn-out clouds shining crimson in the sunset. As I travelled the ferry I wondered if I was being watched.

Trudging back to my room above Valya's home, I realised I had no appetite. Of course, that wouldn't make a difference to her.

"You're late!" she called as I entered the house. "Busy, busy day."

I shrugged out of my jacket and draped it over a chair before sitting at her table. It was constantly hot in Valya's kitchen. There was always a fire burning and something cooking. "Not really." I rested my elbows on the table and sank my face into my hands. "I was looking for something and I didn't find it."

"Eh?" She placed an earthenware bowl in front of me and spooned it full of thick soup. She and Eugeny would have agreed on the apparent universality and infinitely appropriate virtues of soup. "Debris?"

"No, we found that." I stirred chunks of potato, parsnip, carrot and onion. Valya ate little meat. "Found that easily."

"It is everywhere now."

I blinked, slowed my stirring. "You've noticed that too?"

"Impossible not to." She shook her head. "Dangerous times. Explosion in the night. Debris left lying on the street. Too much to pick up. Not a good sign."

A sign of what?

"So then, what were you looking for?" Valya asked.

"Answers, explanations. Hope." I caught myself. "Don't let it bother you."

"Answers, eh? Eat." Valya sat at the other end of the table with her own bowl. She watched my spoon like a hawk watches a mouse. I forced myself to eat, if only to appease her keen gaze. "You need someone who knows

392

many things. You know who knows many things?" She sipped delicately. Always gave me most of the chunks. Apparently Valya still believed I needed fattening.

"Who?"

"Yicor. He sees much, he hears much, and he has many books."

I swallowed a large slice of onion without bothering to chew. I had seen books, hadn't I? Hidden in those shelves.

"Lots of books. Books other people don't have. Books other people aren't interested in having. Books only certain people care about."

Slowly, I looked up from the table. It was like surfacing from a fog. Valya's eyes were bright and sharp, stars in a clear sky.

"Only certain people?" I released the spoon and it slid into the soup, leaving only the very end of its wooden handle dry.

"Only some." Valya gestured to the soup. "You eat and you go. He'll be happy to see you, he will want to help. Likes girls."

I pried the spoon up and wiped sticky fingers on a napkin. "I owe you thanks, Valya."

"Eat. Those are my thanks."

I finished the bowl so quickly I burned the top of my mouth. Valya, taking the time to taste her food, waved me away as soon as the bowl was empty. I took it to the tub of cleaning water, grabbed my coat and headed out into twilight.

I hadn't returned to Yicor's shop since he gave me Valya's address, but I could remember the way. He wasn't far. Street lamps sprang into light as I arrived. His windows were dark, the door closed, but as I stood on the step and listened, I could hear noises inside. Footsteps and a solitary voice.

I knocked, rapping cold knuckles so hard on the wood they stung, and the noises ceased. Then a lock turned, the door opened a crack, and an eye looked out at me, lit by the lamps at my back, the only bright thing against the darkness of the shop.

"My dear!" The door opened wide and all of Yicor's face was washed in lamplight. "Now this is the kind of surprise I wish I had more of."

"Thank you, Yicor. I hope I'm not intruding."

"You, my dear, could never." He stepped from the door. "Please, come in from the dark."

I didn't mention that it was, in fact, darker inside his shop.

He shut the door and I waited a moment for him to light an old portable gas lamp.

"Come through, come through." He led me down the shelves, his lamp bobbing like a firefly. "Is everything all right, my dear?"

I hesitated a moment, and blurted out, "Did you find a home for it? The book I sold you."

He placed the lamp on his desk. The face he turned to me was piteous and full of compassion. "I did, if it helps you to know. Somewhere it will be treasured."

I nodded, more than a little surprised by how relieved that made me feel.

He added, "But I'm certain that is not the reason you are here."

No, it wasn't. "Valya suggested I speak to you."

"Good woman, that one."

"Yes, she is."

"Obsessed with food, though."

That made me grin. "So it's not only me then."

With a chuckle, Yicor patted his generous stomach. "Not in the least."

"She thought you could help me. You see, I'm looking for answers."

"Answers?" Yicor's eyes left my face, travelled too casually over the shelves we had passed to rest on the ceiling.

"And Valya told me to ask for your help."

"Did she?" he asked.

"She said you'd be happy to give it."

Yicor stood rigid a moment longer. Then he released a great sigh; his shoulders sagged. "Valya is a good woman. She knows who to trust. If she sent you here, then she had her reasons. I won't argue with her."

Who to trust? Why did I feel like there was a conversation going on that I couldn't hear? Hidden meanings behind innocuous words?

"Come with me." Yicor collected his lamp from the desk again, and headed into the forest of shelves, junk and dust.

He did not take me to the door. The shelves turned around on themselves, became a maze that spread deep into the shop. More deeply than I had realised it had space to go. When we got to a point where I was thoroughly lost, and quite convinced that I could wander here until I starved to death, Yicor stopped. He put the lantern on the floor beside a rug. He flipped the mat up by its corners to reveal a trapdoor in the floor.

He gripped a large iron ring and hauled the door open. The room below was small, walls cut from earth, ceiling low and supported by wooden beams.

"Down you get."

I stared at him in sudden panic. What was he about to do? Lock me in this hidden cell?

But he shook his head. "I'm not about to hurt you, my dear. If I wanted to, which I don't, it wouldn't be worth crossing Valya. She's a good woman, like I said, but Other's little curlies, she can be frightening. I'll hand you the light."

I gripped the edge of the trapdoor and climbed down. It wasn't much of a descent. Standing in the room, my head peeked out of the trapdoor and was about level with Yicor's shins.

Yicor said, "Here."

I accepted the lamp.

"You call when you've found what you were after, and I'll come get you. Coffee drinker?"

I nodded, still not sure what to say.

"I'll boil us a pot." Then Yicor left me, wandering into the darkness. It seemed he did not need the light to find his way.

Crouching, one hand braced on the floor and the other holding up the lamp, I turned into the room. It was longer than it had looked, although narrow and low. And it was full of books. They were stored on metal shelves, behind glass that reflected the lamp if I brought it too close. There was nowhere to sit, no room for a desk or a chair. Only books.

I shuffled further into the room, placed the lamp in an indent on the floor of packed earth so it would stay upright, and approached one of the cabinets. With a little effort the doors slid open. The books inside were clean, free of dust, earth, or damp. They felt new, leather soft, paper crinkly. How old were they, how precious, considering Yicor's rather extreme methods of keeping them?

And what could they tell me?

None of the spines were labelled. I drew one out, and the cover too was blank. I sat, conscious that the dirt would mark my jacket. I shivered. The earth was cold.

When I opened the cover I did not find words. Symbols rose at me from the page. Not imprinted in ink and applied with pressure on the vellum, they floated from the paper, hooked somehow into the weave but struggling always to escape. Like bubbles in black.

I shut the book with a snap that echoed through the room.

A breath and I opened it again. The symbols were still there, flattened by the board and leather, but rising gradually as though filling with air.

One symbol caught my attention. Smaller than the others, down at the very bottom of the right-hand corner. But I had seen it before. I had, I realised with a chill that had nothing to do with the cold, followed it. An eye stuck in a gate.

Lad's symbol.

What was Lad's symbol doing written in a strange bubbly–

I lost all feeling in my fingers and watched the book as it fell. It dropped gradually, like a feather, spreading over the packed earth in a smooth motion.

"Worked it out, have you?" Yicor was peering from the trapdoor, one hand holding onto the floor, the other gripping a steaming mug. I hadn't heard him approach, hadn't noticed footfalls on the wood above me.

"How?" I swallowed a multitude of questions that struggled in my throat; they fought each other to be voiced and choked me. "It's written in debris, isn't it?"

"Yes. Here–" he wiggled the mug "–you'll need it."

I crawled to the door and took the drink. "But how?"

"I don't know." His face was a mask. Impossible to tell if he was lying, if he was sincere. If he cared, or had any opinion at all. "That art is lost. Long gone. And so much else with it."

A viciously strong coffee smell smacked into my nose. It cleared my head. "What about the symbols?" I lifted my wrist. I had followed them, read them like a map. But if books were written using the things, then perhaps they meant more.

"No." Yicor, however, did not look at my suit. "I cannot read them. Another art lost with the revolution. Taken with our history, our dignity."

Then why was I inscribed with them? If none of us could read them, if even the technicians didn't know what they were for, then who had decided to use these symbols? And why?

"Our history?"

Yicor gave me a sad smile. "We did not always collect debris. And we had a language in those symbols, a language just for us. Traditions and ceremonies and more, gone from memory, lost from history. Before the revolution came. Before it brought the technicians, the national veche, and their twisted men."

"What good are the books, then?"

"Not all of them are written in cipher, my dear. Persevere." Yicor left. This time, his feet were heavy above me. They sent trickles of dust through the wooden ceiling.

Coffee in one hand, I crawled back awkwardly to the book. I dusted dirt from the cover. I flicked through more pages and found nothing but more bulging symbols. So I replaced the book and began my hunt.

The first book I found that I could read sent quivers into my stomach so fierce I had to swallow deep mouthfuls of coffee. The liquid was thick, so strong my head buzzed with each sip. The book was a long description of a ritual that, while I could understand the words themselves, made no sense to me. It ranted about invisible body parts – hands that were not, mouths that were not – and a way to connect with them that seemed to involve a barbaric level of violence. It sickened me to see something so brutal written about debris. I felt culpable, somehow. Because only collectors could have read those words, so only collectors had wanted to do the things they described. Collectors just like me, although I could never imagine myself driving a metal skewer into the head of a friend.

I was halfway through the shelves by the time I found it. The coffee was long gone, although its scent remained, keeping with it that tingling buzz. Yicor had not returned and I couldn't begin to guess how late the bell was. I had no thoughts of giving up, however. The symbols alone, that impenetrability alone, was enough to keep me looking. Even if I ran out of books.

I knew the text was different the moment I drew it from the shelf. Where the others had been plain, covers unadorned, this had a single symbol in embossed silver pressed into the bottom right corner.

The gate and the eye.

Lad's symbol.

My hands shook as I opened the book. I had wished for few things with the fervour I now wished that the book contained words – legible, readable words.

The first thing that must be made clear is the childishness. The Bright world will see this as a defect. This is a lie brought on by misunderstanding and fear.

What may look like childishness at first is but an eye divided. In experiencing both worlds one cannot truly live in either. Distraction is not distraction: it is looking at things we cannot see. Talking to oneself is not talking to oneself: it is conversing with those who we cannot hear. Idiocy is not idiocy: it is understanding a world beyond ours.

I sat so hard it was almost falling. This was it, it had to be it. Distraction, hearing voices, a degree of idiocy. There was Lad, spelled out in rising black. And there was his symbol, cool against my fingers as I held the book open.

Shuffling, I sat up straight to ease a crook in my upper back. The desire to read quickly, to turn chunks of pages and hope I landed on the right one was so tempting I ached to deny it. But I kept reading, moving through the text slowly.

Halves are born into this world already cut in two.

Halves? Uzdal and Mizra immediately came to mind.

Half in this place, half in the world beyond. No ritual can create them, no blade or blow. The Keeper calls them for his purposes. Who are we to second-guess him?

I glanced up, though I could not see the Keeper Mountain though floor, shelves, wall and buildings. I scanned the words again to make sure I had read them properly. *The Keeper.* Our Keeper, weeping over Movoc? Or the mountain's namesake. A guardian against the Other and his darkness. In myths he was a kind guide, an unseen presence who heard pleas for help and protected us from nothingness and death.

But he was a myth, an ancient deity no longer needed in this pion-bright world. Now, he was just a mountain.

So look for them within the first years of life. Halves will not learn speech easily. They will not take to play as other children do. They are slow to understand, slower to obey. Walking may be difficult, games even harder.

I did not know about Lad's childhood. This wasn't helping.

I gave in and flicked through further. How would this help Lad? How could it help Kichlan? What did he want, what had he always wanted for Lad? An end to it all. A normal life that did not involve hiding and random acts of violence he could not control.

...because without them, we are surely lost.

I stopped, frowned at the end of a sentence and scanned to find its beginning.

A Half within the family is a blessing. Do not send them away. Do not lock them behind walls. Do not wish they had been born other than they are. Each Half is more precious than gold, because without them we are surely lost.

Halves will hear the words of the Keeper.

When the Keeper comes to close the Gate, who will hear him if the Halves are gone? And fear for the worlds, both Dark and Bright, if the Gate is opened and he is not there to close it.

Fear for everything.

Fear for everything?

I continued to skim, and the book gave up more of the

same. Tales of a Half who had heard the words of the Keeper and not understood him. He had thought the Gate would open in the heart of a girl he loved, and had opened her body instead. But mostly it was full of warnings against the very thing Kichlan was trying to do. To rid Lad of his affliction. To make him – to use a term too close to the book to make me comfortable – whole.

But how could I tell Kichlan any of that? To let Lad hear his voices, to pay attention to them, to try to make sense of what they were–

I closed the book with a loud, echoing snap. I had heard his voices. What was more, I had spoken to them, communicated with them. With an unseen presence. Was that the Keeper, talking to me from the debris? The Keeper warning me about the puppet men, about debris he could not control?

Fear for everything? What did that mean? And why could I talk to the Keeper? I was not a Half like Lad.

Fear for everything. I thought of the puppet men, and shuddered.

I replaced the book, closed the cases, collected the lamp and the mug. At the trapdoor I stood, placed both on the floor and called Yicor before climbing out. He meandered out of his maze as though he had been waiting only a few shelves away. I wondered how late it was as I rubbed redness from my eyes and suppressed a yawn. The old man didn't look tired.

"Did you find your answers?" Yicor asked. He retrieved the lamp. I carried the empty mug and followed close.

"Only more questions," I replied.

"The books are like that." The light bobbed as he watched me over his shoulder, feet finding their way with surprising surety and steadiness. "No matter how many times you bring them out, they fill only the gaps they want to fill, and leave too many spaces."

I tapped earthenware against my fingernails. "There's lots of knowledge that has been lost, isn't there? About us, I mean. And the debris."

"Yes," Yicor said. "Lost, and taken away. I don't like it. It frightens me."

"I know what you mean." *Fear for everything.* Yes, I understood him well.

Yicor took me to his front door. He opened it to an icy, black night, pierced with lamplight like icicles. "It is not a nice night for walking," he said. "I can offer you a bed."

I shook my head. "I don't think Valya would approve." And that was not an excuse. That was the Other's own truth.

He grinned. "Yes, you're right about that. Will you be safe?"

The streets were empty. I didn't think anyone would brave that cold to wait for me to wander by, unaccompanied. "I will." And I had my suit, didn't I? If such a person did exist, now I knew how to use it. If I was given no option.

"I'll trust you then, to know your own mind."

I stepped into iciness, and hugged my arms to my chest. "Thank you, Yicor."

"I doubt I was much help," he said.

"Some pieces are better than none," I replied.

"If you insist, my dear. But the whole is our right. When I read the pieces, when I realise how broken they are, it angers me. And it frightens me. Oh yes, it frightens me."

I plunged into the night as the door closed with a soft, well-carried click. I hurried, walking as fast as I could, to get the blood flowing and because the allure of a warm bed pulled me like a rope tied around my waist. A large growth of debris hung springy and well hidden between a set of flickering lampposts near Yicor's shop.

I considered what I'd read as I strode along and every twist of thought, like the turns of the street, led to the same place. The same realisation. One I could never tell Kichlan, even if it was the truth.

I didn't wake Valya, but went straight to my upstairs room. The door caught in the cold and I was forced to shove it open. "Other," I hissed under my breath as I stepped inside, hoping I had not woken Valya. I had started tugging my boots off before I realised a gas lamp was lit in the sitting room, and Kichlan sat at my table, light and shadow draping him in layers.

Gaping, I stared at him, hand still on the doorknob, one foot in the air with the boot half tugged off, the other wobbling as I struggled not to fall. Then Kichlan snored.

He was slumped in the chair, cheek pressed into his hand, elbow propped up on the table. And, it seemed, sound asleep.

I slipped the rest of the way out of my boots, hung my jacket on its hook by the door and tried to tiptoe through to my bedroom.

Kichlan gave another half-snore, coughed, and opened a single eye. "Other, Tanyana, do you know what bell it is?"

With a sigh, I gave up my inept attempt at stealth. "I have no idea." I hadn't heard the chimes. "And why are you here?"

"Came to talk to you. Old woman told me you'd be back so I waited." He stretched his mouth in a giant yawn, and spread his arms wide. He rolled his wrists in the air, wincing slightly. "Didn't realise I'd have to wait this long." One hand dropped to his lower back. "This did me no favours."

"Maybe you should have gone home then," I muttered. My room was warm from Valya's downstairs fires, and the comfort had eased me enough to realise how exhausted I was. I didn't want to deal with whatever Kichlan was here for. All I wanted was sleep.

"I probably should have." Kichlan stood, rolled his shoulders, stretched his arms some more. "But I'm still here. And now you're here."

I had no idea what he was talking about. "If this is going to become a talk that starts 'You're a woman and I'm a man' – could you warn me? I'd like to throw up in advance."

He glared at me. With the gas lamp below him and the night at his back, I was reminded again how tall Kichlan was. He said, "We've spoken about being serious before."

"So you know not to expect it to come easily," I replied.

"At all would be nice."

I held my tongue.

Kichlan let out a huge sigh like a giant bellows emptying. "What is going on, Tanyana?"

I blinked. "What do you mean?"

"I'm not an idiot, none of us are. We might not have your education–"

"–don't start that again–"

"Stop acting like you think we're all simple debris collectors without a brain between us, then."

I scowled at him before rubbing at my eyes. "Kichlan, I'm exhausted. Get to your point or I'm going to start sleeping on my feet."

"Fine," he snapped, and crossed his arms. "What's going on? These emergencies, events, whatever you want to call them, you were right. They're not normal. This is so far from normal I don't have a category bizarre enough."

"I thought so," I said.

"I saw it, don't try and deny it. That debris, those planes, they were attacking you. Not us, Tanyana, you. It shouldn't attack anyone, why you?"

Why me?

I stared at him, and realised I had no answer. So instead, I said, "I told you about *Grandeur*–"

"About what?" he interrupted.

"The statue, when I fell. The pions that attacked me."

"And now you think debris is doing the same thing?" He lifted a sceptical eyebrow.

"I don't know, I just don't know. It isn't possible, it shouldn't be possible. But–"

"It's an awful lot of coincidences, isn't it?"

I smiled at him, hope like a tenuous fluttery bird in my heart. Kichlan, of everyone, might just believe me.

"So, what does this mean?" Kichlan asked. "Either everything is out to get you, from the bindings of the world to the waste it creates, or someone is directing them." He rubbed his face again. "Do you remember making anyone really, really angry?" He flashed a cheeky grin at me from beneath his hand. "Because that I would believe."

"Not anyone in particular."

"I'd imagine you have lots of people to choose from." His grin fell away. "The team is confused about this. Some of us are frightened."

I thought of Lad and my heart gave a little jump.

He said, "They're not trying to be malicious."

I nodded. I understood. I believed him. I really did.

We stood in my rented room, the silence heavy and

straining. It was some kind of understanding, I supposed. The awkwardness and the hopelessness of it all.

"Is that where you went?" Kichlan asked, his voice softer, easier. "Tonight. To look for answers?"

"I'm not even sure anymore." I released a pent-up laugh. "I found something. Not an answer for me though."

"Oh?"

I hesitated. "In other times, Kichlan, you might not want to change someone like Lad. He might have been accepted the way he is."

"Another place too, perhaps." His expression hardened. "But this is not either. And in this place, and at this time, we have to protect him, we have to keep him hidden. Because the veche love debris collectors with skill. They love to test suits on them. Yes, like the suits I used to make. I was a part of it, I've seen it, and I will not allow it to happen to Lad."

Was I part of the *we* again?

"The only way I can think of," Kichlan continued. "The surest way, is to cure him."

I nodded, unsure whether I still agreed.

Then Kichlan pulled his jacket from where it had draped over a chair. "I should go, Tanyana."

"It's late," I said. "Maybe you should stay and we'll collect Lad together? I have a rug and some blankets. And if that doesn't tempt you, Valya makes a mighty dawnbell supper."

Kichlan chuckled. "Nothing is quite as tempting as the idea of sleeping on a rug on the floor. But no, I sadly must decline. I should be there for Lad, when he wakes up."

"I know."

"Thank you though," he said.

"No need."

A smile each, and Kichlan left my room. I didn't envy him the walk.

17.

Devich said to me, "It will be nothing like the last one."

"I don't see why I have to go anywhere. Whether or not it's like the last one." At least Devich wasn't insisting on dressing up again. I supposed I should be grateful for small blessings.

Devich, at my shoulder and reflected in the mirror, kissed the curve of my jaw. "Because you are my saviour. And news of the debris incident is running over Movoc like fire through dry grass. You are at the centre of that, although you don't seem to be able to understand that without outside prompting. These people want to meet you, these people want to thank you."

"You want to show me around to them, you mean. Your saviour." I didn't fancy another night pinned under glass.

"Can I help it that I happen to have a beautiful saviour on my arm?"

"Don't call me that, Devich."

"But it's the truth."

I frowned at him through the glass, but already knew I would give in. The smug smile on his face told me he knew it too.

I owed Devich. I felt it in my core. Never mind his saviour rambling – that was my duty. When Barbarian and Comedian had thrown me from my home, I should have searched for him. I should have told him I was not hurt. And memories of his limp body in my arms evoked so much guilt. Because if he hadn't come to find me, and if I hadn't saved him just in time, he could have died in that attack like his assistant had, and never known what had happened to me. That I had only abandoned him because I had no choice. Going along with another of his social gatherings would have to do for now.

"Fine," I acquiesced with a scowl. "We're not staying long, though. And I'm not changing clothes."

"Of course!" Devich squeezed my shoulders and turned from the mirror. "This night is about you."

I really wished it wasn't.

"Let's hurry, then." Devich was already in his coat, scarf and gloves. He held out my jacket and waved it at me.

"Why the rush?" It was strange, that Devich who planned and cultivated me last time was happy for me to leave as I was. I still wore the clothes from an Olday of collecting. While the morning had quickly given us more than enough debris to fill our quota, so the clothes weren't dirty or sweat stained, they were functional, not fashionable. Worn for searching the streets of Movoc-under-Keeper, for hours of walking.

"Earlier we get there, earlier we can leave. Isn't that what you want?"

I shrugged, and allowed him to fit the jacket over my shoulders. What did I care how I looked for these mysterious friends? That was Devich's concern.

We found a landau so quickly I suspected it had been waiting. Maybe Devich had known I would give into him. I was making a habit of it. Again, we rolled into the centre of the city. But this time we passed the grand manors and continued deeper, to the tightness of buildings at the edge of the bridge.

"Where is this gathering?" I asked, voice frosting the coach window.

"We'll be there soon."

I scowled at Devich lounging in the seat opposite. His shoulder was out of its bandage, although still stiff. "Not an answer."

He laughed. "You wouldn't know the place, Tanyana. So it's not going to make any difference."

Finally, the coach drew to a halt in a dark alley. I stepped out onto cold and slippery stones, but refused Devich's hand. Buildings towered over us like a forest of dull windows and gargoyle heads. I shivered. These buildings were not constructed of cement and bricks. Sandstone and slate, old handprints and chiselled initials. Older than the revolution, these were. Like Proud Sunlight yet darker, somehow. Where my university had the Keeper inscribed into its every corner, this place seemed to prefer the Other. The grotesque instead of the beautiful.

"What is this place?" I whispered to the dark night. Lamps shone at the end of the alley, but no light disturbed the ancient stone.

Devich swung himself up to the driver and said something I couldn't hear into the man's ear. The driver nodded, and directed the coach to the end of the alleyway. There, he lowered the coach to the street, and relocated to the cabin itself. Waiting again.

"Excited?" Devich hooked his elbow gingerly into my arm. Fearing for his shoulder, I didn't pull away.

"Should I be?"

With a grin, Devich led me to the shadow of a wide awning. He knocked with a large, oval metallic knocker. I looked up as the sound echoed. More gargoyles hunched over the door, stone eyes watching me. The door opened, light burst from the room beyond like a prisoner desperate to run.

I recognised the servant in the doorway, though he was not wearing gold this time. He nodded to Devich and me, and stepped back to let us through.

"Devich?" I hissed as we marched down a long corridor. "What's going on?"

We entered a warm room, redolent of smoke . Even though the lights brightening the walls were obviously pion-generated, a fire had been lit in an ornate fireplace of dark stone, mounted by more gargoyles. Candlelight danced above wooden tabletops, with iron embellishments on the corners and long benches. The room was full of faces I knew. Old men, all of them. The veche inspector. The debris enthusiasts. Not dressed this time in their finest suits, but in strange, dark cloaks tied at the waists. The whole setting made me shiver. There was something so wrong about the mixture of pion-generated light and flame, about these ancient, wealthy men dressed so strangely.

And I didn't want to be left in the middle of it.

"My dear." Vladir Sporinov extricated himself from the small throng and approached me, hands outstretched. "You made it here. We are so glad."

I forced myself to smile at their soft, general murmur of approval.

"See." Devich slipped his arm from mine with a level of dexterity he had not been able to show until now, and nudged me a few steps forward.

"And I heard you saved our young Devich here."

A round of applause broke out. The circle was tightening, the faces menacing in their closeness.

"Yes," I answered, suddenly hot beneath clothing and uniform.

"Good choice. A wonderful young man to, ah, save."

I blushed in the wake of indulgent laughter.

Then it started up again. The questioning. Was it tiring, such constant collecting? How did I coat myself in silver like that? Where did I find the strength to lift a man from the rubble and carry him to safety?

I deflected as best I could, answered the easy ones, and wondered why they were all here again, questioning me. How did they know so many details? Had Devich told them everything he could remember, or had they been there too, watching, like the Other-blasted puppet men had done? Where had Devich gone? He'd evaporated into the sea of dim light and weathered faces.

One old man wrapped a hand around my upper arm. "Did it hurt?" he whispered, voice grating. "When the debris picked you up. When it knocked you back. Did it hurt?" He leaned forward, mouth slightly open, as though he would suck in my answer like air.

"Y-yes," I floundered. Had I told Devich about that? Had he seen it, in his half-sighted pion-binder way? I couldn't remember, I just didn't know.

"But your suit helped you, did it?"

My suit? It had, yes, and it had done so almost on its own. How could he know that, this old binder?

"Came to the rescue? Worked well?"

Vladir unwrapped the old man from my arm, one strong, resisting finger at a time. "Come now, Kadjat, not too hard. Let's be nice to the dear collector while we can."

Kadjat hesitated for a moment, before breaking into a grin. "Oh, yes."

I found myself shivering as Vladir led him away, flushing hot and cold in the close room. More eyes, so close, more hands. Someone stroked the suit around my neck. I flinched away, and the chuckling rose again.

"Did you feel strong?"

"Did it feel good?"

"What did it feel like, that suit all over you? Warm? Nice? Or did it hurt?"

"Did it hurt?"

"Did it hurt?"

"Why do you care?" Finally, I shouted at them, hearing terror in my voice I couldn't control. These ancient faces, this taste for pain, was far more frightening than planes of debris that could throw a building from its foundations. This was twisted; this was cruel.

It reminded me of the puppet men.

"We're just interested in your progress, dear girl." One of the old men, tall and thin, most of his body hidden in his strange clothes, stepped out of their circle. "We have a lot invested in you."

"A lot?" I sharpened my gaze on him. "You're all part of this, aren't you? You and the puppet men." They laughed at that. My pulse quickened, I could feel its pressure in my head. "Worked well? Other damn you! You don't need me to tell you about the suit, you know about the suit. Why are you doing this? What is going on?"

"Now, now." The veche inspector, again. His face

creased like worn leather as he smiled an impish smile. The same look he had given me at *Grandeur*'s construction site, on the day of her fall. "You should be proud, little girl. It was an honour to be chosen. To secure Varsnia's future."

I could feel the suit in my veins, feel it surge hot like my anger. As I tightened my hands into fists I was certain the symbols would be spinning faster, glowing stronger, ready to work with me, ready to show these men how powerful I was, how wrong they were, how little I cared for their honour. Varsnia could go to all the Other's own hells.

"Was it you?" I asked between gritted teeth. "You had no other reason to be there. Did you knock me from *Grandeur*? Did you set this up from the beginning?"

Then Devich reappeared. He stepped out of shadow, face blank, closed, guarded.

"Time?" He reached for my hand and I snatched it away.

"Answer me!" I shouted at the old men, turning to face them all, and found Vladir right behind my shoulder.

"Going already?" His smile was reasonable, a terrible mask surrounded by hunger.

"No! Answer me, I deserve answers."

Devich reached for me again, this time clamping his hand around my elbow and holding harder than I could have believed. "The debris collector is tired." His voice was as empty as his face. "She has had another long day."

"I'm sure."

Silence settled over the gathering. It set my skin prickling.

"Well, you've been entertaining," Vladir told me. "I think we'll miss you when you go."

We'll miss you. *I'll miss you.*

If the old men were behind this, if they were pulling puppet strings or even watching just for the fun of it that meant Devich... Devich who had convinced me to meet with them both times. Devich who always just happened to appear at the worst possible moment. Devich who seemed to know details I couldn't remember telling him. Who suited me, who listened to me, who had supported me... was a lie. Everything he was, everything he had said.

If these old men were behind everything, then so was Devich.

I let Devich help me into the waiting coach in a daze. We sat in silence as it glided into the night. But not for long. "You're one of them, aren't you?" I turned to him, still too shaken to shout, to rail, like I knew I should. Like I wanted to. "What are you doing to me? Did you know the truth all along?" I swallowed bile. The thought that everything – that the love he had shown me, that the love I had shared with him – was all a lie made me sick to my stomach. "Was this all a game? Did you plan it?"

His blank expression did nothing to ease the tension clutching at my voice. "Don't be angry with me."

"How dare you! Did you get yourself hurt just so I would rescue you? I cared about you. You knew I did."

"I don't want you to be angry with me. Not now."

"Why, Devich? What happens now?"

The coach jolted to a sudden stop and I was thrown against the seat opposite. Devich, less agile, let out a weak-dog cry as he slammed into the door and slid to the coach floor. Face bloodless, he gripped his injured shoulder, gasping for air.

"Are you–?" I stopped myself. Did it matter if he was hurt? Instead, I pushed myself from the seat, focusing at the same time on the suit that had sprung to cover my legs and arms. Gradually, it retreated.

"What happened?" Wincing, Devich hauled himself from the floor. He leaned back in the seat, hand gripping his shoulder so hard his knuckles were white.

I glared at him. "That's what I want to know." I forced open the door on my side, gripped the rails, and swung myself up beside the driver. "What's going–" But I saw it. The driver's hands wove pointless patterns in the air, tugging at pions that wouldn't respond. Because the street was flooded with debris. It rolled down the stones in waves, like the Tear had burst its long-held banks and was flushing darkness into the city.

"Other," I whispered.

"It won't work!" The driver, panicked, clutched at the sky. "They won't listen."

I glanced at my suit, cool, slow, dim. No emergency. So what was this? "It won't. There's too much debris."

The driver flinched. He too, it seemed, knew of the accident at Devich's building.

Accident? I shook my head. Was this just another test? Another trial set up by Devich and the veche and their puppet men? But how did they set the debris off? Debris wasn't pions, it couldn't be controlled. At least, not that I knew. And maybe there had been a way, in that history Yicor so lamented. Perhaps it had survived, as twisted and undermined as the language of the symbols.

"Don't worry, it's not going to kill us." I wanted to reassure him, but what could I do to explain the difference? No planes were attacking, no chunks of Movoc-under-Keeper dropping out of the sky to kill us.

417

This was sludge, passive, horrible. But where had it come from? And why now?

"Can you do something?" the driver asked.

I considered standing in the middle of all that, sweeping it back with suit spread wide. I didn't want it touching me. Not again. "There's too much, I don't think I can."

I swung back down into the cabin. Devich, still holding his shoulder, was hitched up against the opposite door, breathing long, controlled breaths. "Debris," I told him. "Too much of it. Interfering with the driver. But then, I don't need to tell you that."

He just stared at me, face blank.

Then the landau lurched forward and I was flung outside again, my hold on the rails the only thing keeping me from falling into a sea of debris. I clambered back to the driver's seat.

"It's moving!" Sweat shone on his face from flickering lamplight as he fought for control of his pions. "Slowly, but it's coming back."

Sure enough, the tide was receding. But something in that disturbed me more than the debris had in the first place. "Get us going as soon as you can, as fast as you can."

"I will." The driver sucked at his bottom lip in his concentration.

Debris brought us to a halt three times before the coach could take me home. Once, when it had wrapped itself tightly around a lamp and throbbed, like a terrible insect sucking the light away. Then debris dripped from the window of a high apartment, onto the heads of a crowd that had gathered in the street, oblivious of what they were showering in, knowing only that the lights

418

wouldn't stay on, the sewage had backed up, and the heating had died.

Each time the landau sagged to a halt and the driver struggled to get it moving again I looked to my suit, but it remained calm, quiet. No maps, no warning lights. No emergency.

I watched Devich as we finally made it home; still he showed no emotion.

"Goodbye," I said, trying to set my voice as hard as I felt. "I won't see you again."

Devich shook his head, he opened his mouth as though to speak, and for a moment I thought I saw something spark in his eyes, some terrible desolation. Then his face clouded over. "No, you won't."

"Why did you do this?" The words rushed from me, unbidden and foolish. "What are you trying to do to me?"

He shook his head. "You know I won't answer you."

"Bastard. Other take you."

He released a great breath and looked away. "I'm sure he will."

I yanked the handle down and pushed the door open with my foot. As I teetered between paving stones and coach floor, I looked back at him. "Then at least tell me this." I waited for him to look up again. "Why me?"

A shudder ran through him. He winced, touched a hand to his shoulder, but held my gaze. "Just bad luck, Tanyana. Bad luck."

I leapt from the coach and slammed the door on his Other-forsaken face. As I watched it lurch away, with debris tugging beneath it, my suit remained still. Quiet.

I did not sleep that night. Debris raged through the streets in a wild stampede, sending Movoc into chaos, and I watched from the top of the stairs. Half-repaired buildings fell. Lights stuttered on and off in a violent dance across the city. The enforcers were out, carrying gas lanterns, emptying buildings one by one. They wouldn't wait for a repeat of the last disaster.

Where were they taking everyone? Where could be safe, with waves of debris rolling through the streets? I couldn't wait to find out. Valya wouldn't listen to my entreaties as I tried to convince her to join the evacuation.

"Nowhere to run," she told me, her expression haunted.

Nowhere but the sublevel, and my collecting team. So that was where I went. Kichlan and Lad were already there, though I had no idea how early the bell was. Their anxious faces greeted me. I lifted a hand and said, "Good morning." What else could I say?

"Not a good day," Lad said with perfect seriousness. "Not a good day."

Watching his sweat-slicked face, I wondered what the voices were telling him. And how could I ask him without Kichlan knowing?

"Have you seen it out there?" Mizra burst into the room, cradling debris in great scoops on his hands.

"That's a good idea." I stood, extended my suit and offered to take some from him. "I should have thought to do that."

Mizra hesitated, his energy and my words battling with the cold distance he was trying so hard to maintain between us. Eventually, he allowed me to pinch a large chunk that had started to float from his pile.

Kichlan retrieved empty jars. As we contained Mizra's collection, Uzdal arrived with more debris. Lad, arms wrapped around his chest, sat on the couch and stared darkly into an empty corner.

"Something's going on." Sofia and Natasha arrived together, balancing debris between them. "Did you see all the debris?" Sofia started decanting.

"Walked through it." I kept an eye on Lad as I answered her. He had started to rock, slowly back and forth.

"You need to look again."

Lad could not be convinced to climb the stairs so we left him huddling into himself. I felt it before we even reached street level. A tightness in the air, a constriction. And heat. Waves of it like a summer day funnelled down the stairs, whooshing with noise and pressure.

Outside was dark. Clouds hovered over Movoc in a swirling mass that had nothing to do with rain. Lights flashed on and off around us. Something rattled against a door down the street and water gushed in a torrent from beneath it. Someone screamed in the distance, over and over like an ineffectual dog's bark.

"What is this?" Uzdal murmured.

I lifted my wrist, stared at the suit. It was dull, spinning slowly. No lights, no map, no call.

"Can't be right."

"Maybe it's the technicians' laboratory?" Natasha ventured. "Maybe they can't call us because it collapsed and that's where they normally do it from?"

Did we really need to be called? I glanced between the faces of my team members and understood their fear. But why were we standing here waiting to be told what should have been so obvious, what should have been so natural?

I had thought about that a lot, as I sat at the top of my stairs and kept my dormant wrist heavy on my knees. Why did we need to be called, to be told what debris to follow, what emergencies to attend? Because that was all we ever knew, and our tools to do otherwise, the things that could have made us powerful, had been taken away. Our language, our rituals, our history. On our wrists we had – at the very least – a map, a way to know where we needed to go, what we needed to do. If we could read it on our own, read it properly, who knew what we might discover? So we had been told we were useless in this bright new world, useless and dirty and not particularly smart. How often did you need to be told something to believe it?

But they were wrong, the veche and the technicians who seemed happy to hold us down. We could be so much more.

At a juncture between two buildings, debris was growing. Like a fungus, a body, it bulged out of bricks and cement. One tendril snaked over the cracked footpath to wrap around the base of a nearby lamp. Light flickered fitfully against the glass like a terrified insect.

An explosion rocked the street. As one, we crouched, hands over heads. Fire leapt from the window of an apartment three blocks away. The same screaming continued.

"We shouldn't be here. Everyone was leaving, as I walked here," Sofia rattled off words as she crouched. "Enforcers were leading them all away. To the Tear. Boats on the Tear. Other, we need to get away."

Lad, panting, crashed into Uzdal's back as he ran from the stairwell. "Bro!" he screamed into the preternatural silence. "What happened, bro?" Clapping eyes on Kichlan he launched himself onto his brother and wrapped his arms around Kichlan's waist. Great tears ran over his cheeks. He gasped in hitching, sobbing breaths.

Kichlan, bent over backwards and struggling for breaths of his own, patted Lad's shoulder awkwardly. "Calm... fine..." he laboured to be heard.

"We go now, bro. Bro, go downstairs. Stay there, shut the door. Wait. Can we do that? Can we do that?"

Fear for everything.

A terrible premonition settled over me, pricking my scalp with a breath of ice. I wasn't going to wait to be told what to do, no matter how low I had supposedly fallen. Even in this bright world debris collectors could be strong. Especially in this bright world, that could create so much, but understood so little.

"Lad." I stepped toward him, shook off Sofia as she scrabbled to hold me back. Mizra and Uzdal watched me like a snake, or an untrustworthy dog. "Lad." I touched his shoulder, drew his gaze and loosened his grip on his brother. "What is it, Lad? What have you heard?"

For a moment he stared at me, blank. Then Lad said, "You know, Tan. I know you do."

"Know what?" Mizra asked, voice high and cracked.

Footsteps. We turned and watched as a man bolted down the empty street. He ran in silence, the only sound his rasping breath and the beating of his feet. They were bare, I realised with horrible curiosity, skin smacking the stones.

"Other's balls," Uzdal breathed.

"Know what?" his brother croaked again.

"Why don't you tell us?" I tried to soothe Lad. The muscles in his forearm shook beneath my hand. "For the others."

Lad released his brother and straightened. "Bad things," he whispered. "He said there would be bad things."

"Lad–" Kichlan started. But his brother pointed at me, and if anything grew paler.

"They are real!" he screamed into the empty street. "Tan hears them too!"

I could truly lose the team, in this moment, if I wasn't careful. I could become another Lad to them, one they weren't too interested in protecting.

"I can hear the voices too," I said, softly. "Because they are real."

Lad nodded, his face a mixture painful to watch. Desperate fear and desperate hope, added to a childish excitement.

"This is what I tried to tell you, Kichlan." I turned to him, not letting the mouths around me speak, battering against arguments and hoping I could wear them all down. "What I meant. Lad's voices are real, he's not the first to hear them and he will not be the last. And I have heard them too."

"Are they speaking to you now?" Sofia asked, tone condescending.

I turned on her. "No. I cannot hear them all the time, only–" when I was wearing my suit. It hit home with a force that made my head ring.

"Only when?" She blinked, face falsely patient and lips pursed.

"Lad can hear them all the time." I ignored her. "That's what makes him so special, so good at what he does. He follows the voices when we use only our eyes. And that's why he knows something is going wrong."

"Follows the voices?" Mizra was leaning forward, his expression animated by morbid curiosity. "How does that help him collect?"

"The voices are the debris." I looked at Kichlan as I

424

said this. "And that is why some things should not be changed."

His face was blank, a badly painted mask.

"That's ridiculous," Sofia snapped.

In the distance, another explosion sent flames into the sky. Heating units overloading? Or cooking benches, perhaps. This was the greatest fear of a nine point circle society. This was debris overrunning the city, turning all its complicated systems into chaos, its life into death. What would happen if it was left unchecked?

Kichlan's mask didn't matter. Sofia's acid or Mizra's panic, both were irrelevant.

"Lad." I held his hands in mine, drew his focus. "Do you know what's happening?"

Lad shook his head. "He says this is the end. He says we can't go backwards."

The Keeper. The debris. I didn't understand it, but I had heard it with my own ears, seen it limp in my own hands. The Keeper, the debris. They were the same thing and they were talking to Lad.

Fear for everything.

I shivered. "Where is he, Lad? Do you know?"

Lad nodded.

"Take me there."

"Stop this!" Sofia lunged for Lad's hands. "Where are you going? We haven't been called anywhere!"

But Lad jerked away from her, and still holding my hands nearly lifted me from the ground. "No!" he screamed at Sofia and she stumbled away in shock. "No! Tan believes me, Tan is my friend. It's true. Never lied!"

Sofia fell hard against the stones and this, at least, dragged Kichlan from his distraction.

"Lad." He didn't shout, but his tone cut through the building tears and anger blotching his brother's face. "Don't shout at Sofia and put Tanyana down."

I found the flagstones again gratefully.

"Say sorry to Sofia."

"Bro, I didn't lie! Not ever."

"Say sorry to Sofia."

A hiccup, and a squeeze of my hands so painful I was certain I heard something snap. Lad turned his head to Sofia but tucked his chin in low, and couldn't meet her eyes. "Sorry, Sofia. That I hurt you."

Sofia said, "That– that's okay, Lad." Uzdal helped Sofia stand. She ran a hand over a large wet patch that went down the back of her dress. I realised the stones were damp. It was on everything, buildings, road, skin. Condensation? So much heat from so much debris.

"That's better. Now–" Kichlan worked his fingers around Lad's and gradually pried up his grip "–will you take us there, Lad? Will you take us to him?"

"But Kichlan, we–" Sofia tried again.

"Don't need to be called." Kichlan straightened, firmed his mouth into a thin line. "It is all around us, obvious that this is an emergency. And we have a duty."

My stomach quivered in triumph. Lad was less optimistic. "Believe me, bro? I didn't lie. Not ever."

"I know, Lad." Kichlan glanced at me. His eyes seemed so open, so full of regret, of gratitude and suspicion, it was overwhelming. "Can you show us the way?"

Lad nodded, grinned wide.

"Then we'd better hurry. Before this gets any worse."

Lad set off at his great pace. I hurried to stay close, with Kichlan at my side. I didn't see the hesitation, nor the fearful looks the rest must have exchanged, but at least the rest of the team followed. Although hunched in a group and well behind.

We headed for the Tear.

18.

As children growing up in Varsnia, we all knew about
the Other. He featured in cautionary tales, in myths, in
threats about going to bed and staying there. But as I
walked through Movoc-under-Keeper, I finally understood him.

This city was his city. Steam billowed stinking and
thick from sewerage systems in chaos beneath our feet.
Rancid water bubbled up through cracks and backed out
of houses. Fires lit themselves and burned untended,
leaped building to building, casting a heavy glow on the
base of the low clouds. The streets were empty, hollow
and ghostly like dried bones.

This was not Movoc-under-Keeper, this was the
Other's city. And if I was right, if only half of what I had
understood and interpreted beneath Yicor's shop was
right, then this could only be the beginning.

We passed quickly through the city, faster than I would
have thought possible. There were no ferries, the Tear was
dark and flat as a slate. The screaming faded behind us as
we ran, to be replaced by wind through empty windows,
by the echo of footsteps and the lonely cry of a crow.

"Where are you taking us?" Natasha called from behind.

Neither Kichlan or I could answer, and Lad did not. I wasn't sure he knew he was being spoken to. His head was tipped, one ear facing the street, eyes at an angle. The Keeper called him.

"Where are you?" I whispered.

But only wind answered.

Slowly, the route Lad was following grew clear. As we entered familiar parts of the city, as I knew the empty shops, the swinging signs and houses, my skin prickled.

"Can't be."

Kichlan sent me a questioning glance. But before I could answer Mizra was running forward. "Look!" he cried as he ran, and we saw it. A body, lying in the street, prone.

Before we reached it I knew what the man was. Not who. What. I saw his suit, silver against all the grey. It spun, though his face was as pasty as the grey tiles, and the back of his skull crushed in.

"Other," Sofia hissed.

"He's a collector." Mizra, who had kneeled by the man's head, reared backwards. He stumbled, and only Uzdal's grip kept him from falling. "He's an Other-buggered collector!"

Sofia eyed the body, pointed up at the roof of a tall building close by. "There are more."

I didn't want to see, but could not keep my head from turning. More bodies hung, wrapped around tiles, impaled on the iron railings of a balcony fence. Blood seeped down polished stones and I wondered if it would stain. What was the building made of, was that marble I could see, decorating the stonework? Yes, marble would stain.

"What's happening? Are they all collectors?"

But Lad, having stopped to glance at the body, kept walking. I touched Kichlan's hand, and he jumped beside me. Silent, I tipped my head at Lad.

"We can't leave him here," Natasha murmured, voice like a groan. "Not like this."

"He fell," Sofia said with certainty. "Or was pushed."

"Stay with him if you want," Kichlan told Natasha. She nodded, face pale, lips grey as the death at her feet, and crouched to begin rearranging the man's splayed limbs. I caught a glimpse of his face where it had pressed into the stones. He had not just hit the street, he had been crushed into it. His cheek was ground into wet red mush, flecks of stone like mineral deposits in his flesh.

I glanced over my shoulder as we ran. Natasha watched us go, her gaze focused firmly on me. She spoke, and though I could not hear the words, by the Other it looked like, "It's here for you."

"Where are the planes?" Kichlan murmured as I caught up to his side.

"Planes?"

"Like last time. Something killed that man, so where are they?"

I shook my head. Where was the debris at all? The muck that had clogged streets, the deeper into the city we ran, the thinner it became.

"Not again," Mizra was muttering to himself, a mote at the back of my hearing. "Not again."

"Tan," Lad said as he turned where I knew he was going to turn, against all reason, against all fairness. "He says he's sorry. He can't stop it."

"So am I." And we turned the corner, crossed the

430

street, and entered an empty patch of scarred earth that had once been *Grandeur*'s home.

They had removed her body and shattered bones. Nothing remained but gashes in the ground, but the great indents where her fingers had hit the earth. Thin grass had grown into them. Nothing new had been built.

And yet, the lot wasn't empty.

"Oh, Other." Sofia faltered.

"We have to get out of here!" Mizra squealed behind me. "Now!"

Grandeur's body was gone, but others took her place. They were small compared to the statue in my mind, to the memory of a woman greater than her name. Small, human and broken, they were scattered about the lot. Two dozen, perhaps, maybe a few more. And all, I knew instantly, debris collectors. Like we were now, they had followed the debris to *Grandeur*'s birthing place and her grave.

To the place where I had fallen.

But where was the debris?

"Don't move!" Kichlan snapped as Mizra tried to stumble from the yard. He dragged Mizra close, wrapped a large hand over his mouth. "Can you see it, Tanyana?" he whispered. "By the beam."

I had been wrong. *Grandeur* was not completely gone. A single steel bone arched up from where it had fallen and impaled the earth. I had missed it, in the shadow. The shadow that fell from nowhere in the middle of an open space.

"Says we should get away," Lad whimpered. "Says this is the bad stuff, right here."

"Don't need any voices to tell us that," Sofia whispered.

I didn't know what it was, plane or grains, it didn't

431

even look like debris. It was darkness flittering like shadows on water, and it was, I realised with increasing horror, steadily stripping a body that lay propped against the steel beam.

"It's flaying her," I choked on the words. "Why is it doing that?" Let alone how, or how we could stop it. How we could collect, control, where the dead around us had failed.

"Get away," Lad groaned.

"If we move, it will see us." Kichlan caught my eye with his steady gaze.

I clamped down on my panic. "It will notice us soon, whether we move or not."

"So what do we do?" Mizra asked, muffled behind Kichlan's hand. Gradually, Kichlan released his grip.

"We contain it," I replied. This was like the other times, wasn't it? The mass of grains and planes clinging like a parasite to the building's wall. The surging muck that had shut down a factory. The mad planes that had destroyed the technicians' offices and nearly killed Devich. This was another form, another surprise, just another test.

"Any ideas on how we would do that?" Sofia asked and edged closer, Uzdal at her side.

We stood in a line, a team, missing one.

"Can't," Lad jittered. "Should run."

I looked at him. The Keeper was being less than helpful. "Can you tell him something for me, Lad?"

Lad looked at me, surprised, and his shaking arms stilled. "He can hear you, Tan. Told me to say he can hear you."

"Right." Where do you look to talk to the invisible? "Well, then." I drew a breath and focused on a spot beside Lad's ear. "If you're going to stay here and talk you

432

might as well help. Dire warnings aren't going to make us run. So stop it."

"Speak for yourself," Mizra muttered as wind blew and Lad listened.

I realised, with a low sickness in my gut, that I could hear the collector's skin being torn away.

Lad said, "Says you should have run, but if it's too late, he will try."

"Right," I murmured. What exactly was I supposed to be asking?

"How do we collect it?" Kichlan asked for me.

"Says you can't," Lad said. "Says it's not normal, won't go into the jars like normal."

"Other's balls," Uzdal growled.

I said, "Why is it different? Why have we been able to—"

A terrible scream sliced through my words. Lad added a scream of his own, wrapped his hands around his head and sank to his knees. Kichlan dropped to his side. Mizra and Uzdal stood to the spot like the steel beam rammed into the earth.

"It's seen us!" Sofia yelled. She grabbed at Kichlan's elbow. But Lad was sinking lower, and I knew Kichlan wouldn't move unless he did. We had to hold it off.

"Come on!" I yelled at Mizra and his brother. "A shield!"

The debris shifted. It didn't float like grains or lance through the sky like planes. It compressed, became thin, transparent, and disappeared. The body against the beam sagged into a shapeless mess of blood and skin.

"It's gone," Mizra whispered. But he knew, I knew, we all could feel it like taint in the air. The debris was here, somewhere.

"Shield them!" I screamed at him. "Quickly!" I spread my suit out over Kichlan, Lad and Sofia like a ceiling of silver. Uzdal joined me a moment later. Mizra stared at the body, lips moving silently.

"Mizra!" Uzdal yelled at his brother.

Then the debris attacked. It slammed itself against the shield and Uzdal fell, a gurgled cry on his lips. I gritted my teeth as shock travelled through the suit and into my bones, but held steady.

"Uz!" Mizra snapped from his distraction and wrapped his own suit over Uzdal's as the debris attacked again.

"Not Lad." I ground my teeth, spat blood and saliva at a flitter of shadow. "You can't have him."

...you soon. Careful...

As suddenly as I heard him the Keeper was gone.

"Hold it up!" I told Uzdal and Mizra. "Can you?"

Pale faces nodded. They could, yes, but not for long.

I withdrew my suit from the shield and began stalking, ringing a wide circle around them. "Where are you? Come on, you dirty Other-skinned bastard! I'm here, try it."

Darkness on my left. I spun, suit up and still oval, and the debris glanced against me. A sword on a shield.

I chuckled. "This is old. I've been here before!"

Something crashed into my lower back. I waited for skin to peel, for bones to crush like all the bodies I had seen. But my suit was too fast. It shot out from neck and waist, and wrapped my torso in silver that knocked the debris aside. Still, I was thrown into the air. Even as I realised I was alive, and whole, I shot stilts into the ground and held myself up.

You are the biggest threat. It hasn't realised that yet. It is still going for the Half.

I replied, "You could tell me something I can't see for myself and that would be more useful."

It is coming for you.

434

Heat around my thigh. I withdrew one arm, lowered the other and swiped at the apparently thin air with a sharp suit. Something screamed, then crashed against my supporting arm. I folded with a cry, fell to the earth. Stone cut into my cheeks.

Roll.

I coughed out dust, saw tiny splotches of red wet the grass.

Left.

I rolled.

Wait. Right. Again. Faster.

Not fast enough. Slices in my arms, over my neck and down to my back.

Suit! Quickly!

I didn't know what that meant. My suit did. It wrapped me again in silver, fingertips to toes to jaw. Where it touched my open skin metal seeped into my wounds, into muscle and nerve. I screamed my throat raw, kicked against the ground, but could not shake the invasion of my body.

Head!

I saw the flicker this time, rolled of my own volition. But something heavy and solid smacked into my temple. A different darkness spotted against the ruddy, dull sky, lit by pinpricks of stars.

The suit moved. It crawled over my jaw, up over the back of my head like creeping hands. Dazed, I couldn't stop it. I was hit again, this time something sharp. It cut my ear, tore hair and grazed scalp. Then my suit was there. It soaked into my ear, into the spaces between my skin and skull. I clamped my lips closed, it sealed them. I squeezed my eyes shut and it was a heavy blindfold. Over my nose, it grew, into my nostrils.

I couldn't breathe. Something was hitting me, clashing with my suit in a sound like a battle of silverware and crockery. But I couldn't breathe. Nothing else mattered, I fought my body, struggled with my addled mind for control.

Just to breathe.

I only wanted to breathe!

Be still.

Sounds in my ears, clamouring and rushing, a cacophony. A smell like burning flesh. Great exhaustion pressed down until I couldn't move anything any more, even if I'd wanted to. My chest burned fit to burst, I was seeing colours on the back of my eyes.

It has gone for the Half. You can breathe now.

Breathe? With silver shoved up my nose?

Listen to me, Tanyana, and breathe. I have waited this long to meet you. If you die now, you will make me mad.

I laughed despite myself and in that involuntary explosion of air discovered I could suck it in as well. Suit or none.

I breathed so deeply it rushed to my head like wine. I wanted to laugh long, loud and hard.

Lie still, catch your breath. Don't let it think you're alive.

The air smelled stale, like body odour and humidity.

And when you're ready, open your eyes.

No point arguing. I could breathe, why not see. Why not talk.

I opened my eyes to a very different world. Gone was *Grandeur*'s graveyard. Gone were the bodies, the chaos. It was a dark world of empty planes and doors. Nothing but doors.

Well, nothing but doors and a man.

He was bent over me, concerned face close to mine.

Pale as limestone, skin translucent, eyes dark and seeming to float in his face. There was nothing inside him one would normally associate with a man, no bones or pumping blood. Just thin veins of darkness like patterns in marble.

He had no hair, I realised, and was naked. Naked and anatomically accurate.

"Are you the Keeper?" I whispered, half expecting my mouth to fill with silver. It did not.

He smiled. The inside of his mouth was black. "I have more than one name. But yes, that is one of them."

I tried to sit up, but he placed a hand on my chest and kept me down.

"Do not move until you are ready to fight it."

That made sense, I supposed. I looked around. Doors for a sky, for the ground, doors instead of buildings and mountain. "What is this place?"

"Again, it has had many names. The Dark World, perhaps, you might have heard. The place that is not."

I peered at his head. The veins were moving, pumping their own blackness as ours would pump scarlet blood. "The hands that are not." What was that? I frowned, looking closer.

"Yes. This, all you see, this is—"

"—debris." I was sure of it. Grains in his body, planes surging them along.

His smile broadened, his eyes shone like beetle wings. "Yes. Oh, Tanyana, I was so glad to welcome you."

Welcome? "That was you, in the beginning? When I fell from *Grandeur*?"

He nodded.

Was I supposed to understand any of this? "So this world is made of debris? Like you?"

"It is debris. Like me. We are one and the same. Your world is made of layers, and particles, of different pieces running in hectic chaos. I am only one. All this–" he swept his arms wide "–is me. It is also debris. I am the door, the guardian, the sign."

"Right." No sense at all. "What are the doors?"

His face settled into seriousness, into sadness in transparency and black. "Joins between our worlds."

"Lots of them."

"Yes, too many. It is all I can do to guard them and keep them closed."

"Closed." I frowned, brain still sluggish. I blamed the blows, the silver and the whole bizarre situation. "If they opened, that wouldn't be good, would it?"

He shook his head. "Should they open, the Dark World and the Light World, my world and your world, they will blend. The Dark World will destroy you. The Light World will destroy me. Everything is changing. Soon, I am not sure I will be able to hold the doors closed."

"Fear for everything," I murmured, and thought of Lad who had done his role as a Half so well, and warned us. Lad.

Lad!

I jerked upright. The Keeper didn't hold me down. "The debris! Is it... is Lad...?"

"Can you see? We are connected, all worlds. If you know how, you can see both."

Like pions, just with an added helping of scary and a little too weird. A frown, a moment of concentration, and shapes emerged from the doors. My collecting team cast thin and insubstantial in wood and shadow. Mizra and Uzdal had fallen, their shield cast down, suits weak. They lay on either side of the empty site, limp and unconscious.

438

"Not dead," Keeper told me. How did he know?

Sofia was wrapped around Lad who still rocked, hands to head, crying. She shielded him completely, exposing her back, and watched as Kichlan stood against the debris-thing. She knew, I could see it in her face, that if Kichlan fell – then she would die before she surrendered Lad. Sofia knew it, accepted it, and thought it rather likely.

"You said it is going for Lad. Why?"

"It knows the most powerful of you, those who threaten it." He shook his pale head. "Do not let it kill the Half. There are so few like him left in this world, and they are so precious. I need them. You need them. To help me keep these doors closed."

I could see all this, but no more of the real world. Kichlan stood – one arm hanging by his side, the other raised with a jagged blade of suit guarding his face – his image mottled with wood grain, in a world of darkness and doors.

The debris-thing was something else entirely. The Keeper's terrible twin. A pale body with dark grains running through it, but twisted. Scarred. Dark ridges ran from fingers to shoulder, torso to leg. Its head sagged to the side. Its legs shuffled. Its skin rippled, new ridges forming, old ones dying, scarring over and over again.

It looked to me, for all I did not want to see it, like it had fallen. And landed on glass.

"What is it?" I whispered.

"Debris. Like me."

"Make it stop." I stood, no longer feeling the dizziness in my head or the cuts to my body. I felt whole, strong. I flexed a silver-coated hand. Very strong. "If you are it and it is you, make it stop."

"I can't." The Keeper stood beside me. He was tall, but thin as a willow branch and as delicate. "They are changing us. Changing me. I am losing control."

"They?"

The Keeper lifted a fine hand and pointed with pale fingers. "Can you see them? They hide in your world, scurry like rats behind walls. But they are always there, behind you. Following."

Where the remnants of a wall from *Grandeur*'s old site would have hidden them in the real world, in the Keeper's home of doors and shadows the puppet men were starkly clear. Three of them stood in a line, watching Kichlan and the debris-thing.

"They see too much," Keeper whispered. "They touch both worlds. I fear them. Their touch burns, and each part of me they scar unlocks another door."

As one, their pale faces and mouldy eyes turned toward me.

Kichlan roared. I spun to see him slash at the debris-thing and miss widely. It flickered around him, dancing like a cruel partner. A warped hand flashed out, struck his shoulder, and sent him spinning.

"Bro!" Lad leapt to his feet, throwing Sofia off like she was a doll. "No!"

"Not the Half!" Keeper shouted, but I was already moving. I ran over to the doors. They were hard, like concrete. Kichlan landed on his injured side. The debris-thing scuttled forward. Lad extended his suit into clubs and lunged.

But I got there first. I held Lad back with a hand, catching his club in its downward swing, lifting him from his feet and pushing him at Sofia.

"Hold him!" I shouted at her.

She and Lad stared at me like I was the debris-thing, like I was a ghost or a creature worse than any imagination could make me. But I didn't care. It was Kichlan I had come to save. I would not let the scarred thing hurt him any more.

The Keeper appeared behind Kichlan as the debris-thing hesitated. It flickered itself around, head twisting like a doll. I realised it had no face; at least, it had none left. There had been a nose, eyes, a mouth. Only ridges, shifting and solidifying, remained. The scars on my own cheeks seemed to tighten in response.

Kichlan looked up, pale and strained. "Tanyana?" he whispered.

The debris-thing lashed at me. I caught it as I had the planes, locking my suit to its arm like weapons crossed.

"Tame it!" Keeper cried.

"Miss Vladha."

As one we stopped. Kichlan, Sofia, Lad, even the debris-thing, the Keeper and I, as the puppet men entered the abandoned construction site.

"What are they doing?" Keeper hissed.

"You?" Kichlan spat the word at them. "What is going on?"

But the puppet men held their attention firmly on me. "We suggest you do not listen to the advice of weaklings not long for either world. We suggest you listen to us, Miss Vladha, and do exactly as we say."

The Keeper placed himself between Lad and the puppet men. He wavered, like a wind was battering the branches of his limbs and the thin trunk of his body. But still, that stance, legs wide and shoulders broad, was defensive and strong. "You know I am here, don't you?" His dark eyes danced between the three identical faces. "You can see me. Hear me."

How was that possible? Even Lad, a Half, only heard the Keeper.

The puppet men turned simultaneous heads, lifted the corners of their mouths, and sneered together. "You should flee. Your time is limited. Run, if you want to make the most of it."

Kichlan rolled to unsteady feet. "Leave him alone!" He didn't know Keeper was there. All he could see was the sight he dreaded most, the puppet men threatening his brother.

But they paid Kichlan no heed. Sneers fell away as they looked back at me. "Destroy it, Miss Vladha. Quickly."

"No," Keeper whispered.

The debris-thing folded, and vanished from my hand.

"Behind the Half." The Keeper vanished with it.

I plunged my suit into the ground. It threw me up and over Lad and Sofia's heads. The debris-thing re-emerged and I crashed right into it.

"It's going to keep doing that." The Keeper reappeared. "You have to calm it."

"I don't know what you mean!" I shouted back.

"That debris is more powerful than anything you have fought before." The puppet men started again. "It will kill your team."

"It will ravage every pion system in the city."

"Will you let that happen?"

"Destroy it, Miss Vladha."

"Destroy it."

"No!" the Keeper cried. "All these doors, Tanyana, they are pieces of me. Like this one below you – broken,

442

twisted, and scarred – is a piece of me. They have all been torn from my body. If you destroy it, you will create another door. Didn't you hear me? If you don't return it to me, I won't be able to keep the doors closed!"

The debris-thing fought, lurched and tipped beneath me. Its faceless visage strained, not to the Keeper, not to attack me, but toward the puppet men. Whimpering, snuffling, a desperate and beaten dog.

"You created this?" I asked them, gasping as I fought to hold on.

"This is the final test."

My hands slipped. The debris-thing skittered toward the puppet men. As one they opened their jackets, together they drew out something bright, sharp, and terrifying. I flinched, and the scuttling debris-thing did the same. Smaller, but still arms – like the ones that had fitted me with my suit. Needled, thick with wires, slightly curved and altogether cruel. The puppet men lifted the devices, pointed them, flipped buttons to start the cords moving and fluids churning. And the debris-thing screamed, flickered in and out of existence, before twisting back toward Lad. It pushed the Keeper aside and I leapt to my feet, but not before catching the triumphant grins on the puppet men's faces.

The only emotion I had ever seen them express and it was horrifying. Lines rose all over their pale skin. Seams of darkness, jagged, covering foreheads, cheeks, and necks. Their mouths opened widely, too widely, their eyes darkened over and they weren't human. No expressionless faces and stilted movements, not any more, just ridges and vast grins and dark, bottomless eyes.

In an instant, it was gone, and the puppet men were pale and wooden again.

I jumped at the debris-thing, plunging my suit into its pale shoulders, pushing the creature down against the doors. The Keeper gasped, faded further, and staggered. They were one and the same. Joined. The Keeper and this manic thing beneath me. Knowing that, could I fight it, cut it into pieces and force it into jars?

"How is this a door?" I panted.

"We told you not to listen to it," the puppet men sneered.

"The doors connect us, Tanyana. They connect the Dark World and the Light World. I am that connection. Debris is that connection. When they rip a part of me away, when they twist it to their own ends, they are tearing the doors from my control!" Keeper straightened, though he still shook. "If the doors open, the worlds merge. If I can't close them, we will lose them both. Both worlds."

"It lies," the puppet men leered, mechanical and unemotional.

"That is why my Halves exist. They alone will hear me should a door open, they alone can help me close it. That is why they are precious. And that is why you cannot do what these men are telling you to do!"

"Superstitious nonsense."

"You must choose. What do you believe?" Keeper asked.

"There is but one choice, Miss Vladha," the puppet men said. "If you do not destroy the debris now, it will kill your team. One by one."

"No," the Keeper whispered. "I cannot take much more. If you do not tame it, the doors will open, and this world will be lost."

"That is ridiculous. Use the weapon we have created in you, and finish this test."

My head reeled. Weapon? I looked down to my silver-wrapped wrists and thought about everything I had done and all that had been done to me. The suit had protected me so many times, caught me when I had been thrown, shielded me from the planes of debris that had killed so many and from threats so mundane as a rotten and falling wall. I remembered Comedian and Barbarian, and what I had done to them. Was that what I was, what the veche had made me? A weapon that could withstand any debris storm, that could break any pion-made bond, that could maim or kill without thought?

"Is that what this is all about?" I asked. Suddenly, it all made sense. "This is why you have used me, all this time." What greater weapon could there be? What pion-powered weapon could fight against an army with suits like mine?

I added, "I'm doing this for our future. My life, for a stronger Varsnia." Dina's funding complaints, rumours of weapons and war, and the obsessive attention of the old veche men.

"You understand." As one, the three puppet men pretended a smile.

This was why I had been thrown from *Grandeur*'s palm.

"I have one problem with it, though." I shook my head. "I am not a weapon." I was an architect. I had worked hard to make my life what it was. And suit or no suit, *Grandeur* or no *Grandeur*, tests or Keepers or doors or debris, it didn't matter. Even Devich. None of them could make me anything other than who I was.

And I was no one's weapon.

"Then you will die, like the others who have been suited, tested and failed before you."

"Others?" Kichlan whispered, his voice cracking.

"Do as we tell you and you will live. Fail, and you will die. You and your team."

The debris-thing struggled, and the Keeper winced. "Please," he groaned. "Calm us. Rejoin us. It hurts, Tanyana. It hurts."

"Destroy it, Miss Vladha. Destroy it before you are destroyed."

The debris-thing thrashed again, kicking my gut, whacking fists against my head and neck. I felt each blow through the silver. How long could I withstand that? How many more times would it have to vanish and reappear before I was too tired to follow? Would Lad be the first to go, when that happened? The first to be flayed alive, to be stripped of skin and life. Then who? Kichlan?

I couldn't let it happen. Not Lad. Not Kichlan. Not another debris collector, not while I had the strength to stop it.

I would have to destroy it. I withdrew a hand from the debris-thing's shoulder. It shivered beneath me and the Keeper cried out, weakly. I lifted the hand above my head, sharpened and curled my suit into a great, shining arc.

"Hurry," said the puppet men.

"No, please," the Keeper whispered.

I was not a weapon. "But I don't know what else to do!" I looked into the Keeper's dark eyes, to the debris that surged through transparent veins and skin across his face, and realised how much the puppet men had looked like him. Just for that instant.

"You do know," Lad said, his quiet voice nearly lost behind them all. "You did it before. Remember, Tan? When you told the debris to go backward, and it did. When you asked it to stop turning all the lights off, and it did. When you told it to stop hurting people, so you could save that man. Can't keep hurting it. That's what he means. Stop the hurting."

How do you stop a scarred mirror-image from hurting? How do you give peace to untouchable sails, to bubbling grains? To waste?

The same way you convince pions to build a building for you.

I eased my cruel suit back, and relaxed my shoulders. I closed my eyes. As the debris-thing bucked under me, thrashed and flickered in and out of solidity, I slowed my breathing.

"Shh," I whispered to it. "It doesn't hurt any more, you know that? Feel it, it doesn't hurt." And I sank deeper. I gave the debris-thing everything I had. No enthusiasm, no wild desire to weave lights and patterns into the world. I gave it peace. I gave it calm.

"Miss Vladha? What are you doing?"

I gave it standing in the cemetery with Kichlan, as Lad placed rosemary at his mother's grave.

I gave it Mizra's wild stories.

I gave it Lad's smile.

And the bucking stopped, the tension eased, the screaming dwindled into a soft sobbing and the body dissolved away.

"Ah," the Keeper whispered. "It hurts."

I couldn't move. I felt empty, brittle. All my strength exhausted, all my knowledge jumbled. The Keeper was on his knees. The debris-thing, as it dissolved, rushed into him like a current of dust mites in the sun. Tears ran down his pale cheeks, great lashings of black liquid.

"They hurt us, Tanyana." He implored me to understand, to correct it. To help him. "They tortured me, to create that thing. I can still feel it! I can still see it. Horrible light, cruel faces, all around me. All playing with me, hurting me, twisting me and changing me, all for this."

The doors around me wavered. My suit was retreating. Perhaps I no longer had the strength to sustain it.

"They made you, Tanyana. And they tried to break you. Don't let them. For me, for everyone. Don't let them."

A cool breeze on my face.

Through the slits of my eyes I saw Lad on the ground, Sofia collapsed beside him.

I couldn't see Kichlan.

Then I heard footsteps over the earth, and the voices of the puppet men above me, "This is unexpected."

"Unexpected."

The footsteps were so close. Shadows blocked the sun. The puppet men. I had to get up, I had to stop them doing whatever it was they wanted to do to me next. Because the Keeper was right. I would not let them break me and I would not let them turn me into a weapon. No matter what they injected beneath my skin and between my bones. I was me, not the suit. Me.

"Disobedience is as bad as failure. The subject should die here."

But my empty, brittle body would not respond. I couldn't move.

"And yet, the survival of the subject can create a new test."

"Further experiments are needed."

448

"Agreed."

The footsteps faded. I allowed my eyes to close, and fell into darkness.

19.

Devich stood on the hastily erected stage accepting thanks he in no way deserved. Not only because he was just a technician, and it was the collectors who had saved Movoc-under-Keeper, but because he was one of the scheming veche bastards who had put her in peril in the first place.

Not that Kichlan and I had mentioned that to anyone.

Still, it made me furious to see Devich up there. To listen to the veche representatives give speeches thanking all of us who were involved in such a rescue, from technicians to collectors. An old man, with a large bear-face hanging from a chain about his neck, droned on about the sacrifice we had made. I knew what he really meant. The veche had sacrificed us. I didn't know the number of collectors who had been killed by the Keeper's debris-twin. But the injured surrounded us. Teams missing members. So many with bandages, splints, even though the veche had commissioned healers to help us.

We were no exception. Mizra and Uzdal had suffered fractures where the Keeper's dark twin had thrown down their shield. Sofia had a broken rib, Kichlan an arm. Only Lad and Natasha had escaped unscathed. I wore my new scars in silver.

"Just be glad Lad isn't up there," Kichlan whispered in my ear and touched a finger to the fists I hadn't realised I was making. "He doesn't need to draw any more attention to himself."

He had a point. Lad stood beside his brother, humming and rocking and generally paying no attention to anything that was going on. I wondered if Keeper was here, somewhere. If this was some strange form of communication.

Puppet men shared the stage with the veche and the technicians. They stood, so still against the wind even their jackets didn't seem to move. Vacant eyes stared out over the small crowd. Since we had been found at *Grandeur*'s grave the puppet men had left us alone, but they certainly hadn't disappeared. They were always there. I caught sight of them on the edges of crowds, listening to healers give reports, following the more important members of the national veche who had come to survey the damage. Always there, always watching.

The speeches droned on. Technicians applauded. The debris collectors around me watched the proceedings with apathy.

Finally, thin ranks of pathetic trumpeters sounded an ending to the torment, and the puppets and veche representatives filed into waiting coaches. The technicians milled around, aimless without ceremony.

Devich looked at me, and approached the end of the stage. "Tanyana?"

Kichlan stepped between us, drawing Lad's concerned attention. "You need to get out of here," Kichlan said in a low, dog-growl voice I had never heard him use. "Now."

"Bro?" Lad whimpered.

I placed a hand on Kichlan's shoulder and drew him back. He flashed me a surprised look. "Look after your brother," I murmured. And as he turned to Lad, who had began wringing his large, fretful hands, I met Devich's eyes.

He looked haunted. A man who had seen things he never wanted to see. "Tanyana?"

Or done them, perhaps?

At my back I could feel the presence of my team. Even injured and scarred they were a strength to me. This was that new life, I realised, the one the puppet men and their debris-creature had threatened to take away. But they had failed, and so would Devich.

"What do you want?" I asked him, trying to keep my tone civil.

"I–" He stretched his hands out to touch me, I kept out of his reach. He dropped his arms and his head, and I quelled a lurch in my heart, a pull of pity. "I'm sorry."

"Is that all you have to say?"

"I didn't have a choice! You must believe me. You know what they are like now, you know I didn't have a choice."

"Pathetic." Kichlan hooked an arm through mine. "You're pathetic."

Devich nodded. "I know."

"And we will not waste our time on you." Kichlan smiled down at me, like sunshine against Devich's low clouds. "Shall we go?"

That was the best thing I'd heard all day. I smiled back. "Yes, let's." Without another glance at Devich's lowered head, I allowed Kichlan and his brother to bundle me away from the stage. Sofia, Uzdal and Mizra said their farewells to us at the Tear. Natasha had wandered away without a word. Kichlan, Lad and I boarded one of the few ferries still running, and headed for the city centre.

The wind that rose up from the Tear was fresh; it was clean. And Other, did Movoc-under-Keeper need it. No amount of scrubbing could clean away all the dirt that had spilled into the city. No amount of spring rain could wash all the blood.

I gripped the railing, tipped my head into the wind, and breathed deeply.

The silver notches in my ear and at the back of my head buzzed pleasantly in the cold. The silver-filled scars in my arms were too rugged up to join in.

"Careful," Lad said, by my side. "Don't fall."

I grinned at him and leaned back, hands firmly on the rail. "I won't."

Movoc was taking a long time to heal. Gradually, its population returned. But they returned to devastated houses and infrastructure so ravaged it would take moons to rebuild. And there was worse. Those few too young, old, poor or sick to escape had suffered terrible fates when the pion world went mad. The stories that ran through the survivors were horrifying. A child, huddled and hiding in her bathroom, drowned when uncontrollable pions filled the room with water. An injured man pulled apart by the roaming threads of a tattered factory system. An old woman on Darkwater found burned alive by the pions of her own heater. I often wondered if that was her we had heard screaming. Mostly I tried not to think about it.

We left the ferry on a quiet, almost empty dock. "Come on." Kichlan, good hand in the pocket of his coat, hunched against the wind.

"Any rush?" I asked, but peeled myself away from the river anyway. I held Lad's hand and together we walked away from the Tear.

Kichlan shifted his shoulder. His arm was hurting again, I suspected. The bone had been healed, the veche had seen to that, but it ached regardless. It would take time, the healer had said. We had waited more than a day at *Grandeur*'s grave before anyone had found us. It was a long time for a wound to fester.

A small group of men stared at us as we walked. They recognised the suits on our necks, and wrists, and bowed. Thanks, I realised, could make up for a lot of things when you got them.

And we were getting a lot at the moment.

"It won't last," Kichlan said. "They'll forget, eventually, and go back to ignoring us."

"All the more reason to enjoy it while it lasts." I nodded to the men, and was graced with a hesitant smile.

Lad ran ahead, gaping at the grand veche buildings, sitting on every bench, picking pale spring flowers. I was glad the city remained so empty. There were few eyes to be drawn to him, few attentions to grab.

"What do we do now?" Kichlan asked as we both watched Lad play.

He had asked this question more times in the past sixweek and one than I could count. I still didn't have an answer.

"Our duty. What else would we do?" I asked.

"You know what I mean."

I did. I had no doubt the puppet men would set up another test. I was their weapon, wasn't I? The veche's precious investment. And the Keeper's warnings would not leave me, his talk of doors and worlds and

454

the kind of destruction I could only sum up with *fear for everything*. Whatever the puppet men and the veche tried next, we had to resist it. Because I would not be used. And because the Keeper's fear and pain was real, too real.

But I couldn't do any of that right now. I said, "Our duty. I mean it. Do what we do, what you have always done. Save the city from its waste. Give the people a reason to thank us." My voice dropped. "Keep Lad away from them." *Them* had weight on it. From now on *them* could only mean the veche's men, the puppet men. Or whatever Other-cursed creatures they were.

"They will come again."

"Then we will be ready, and we will survive."

I was not a weapon, and I would not let the veche turn me into one. The Keeper had put his faith in me. Kichlan believed in me now, and Lad always had. This time, we knew the puppet men would be coming for us. This time, we would be ready.

I would not fall again.

We crossed beneath the bluestone arch and into gardens. I smiled as I watched the haggard expression fall from Kichlan's face.

"Tanyana," he whispered.

My gallery rose out from behind the foliage in ice-cream scoops and cream. It was closed, of course, but seemed to have come through the whole event unscathed. There was little in the way of infrastructure here, I supposed. Most of the old city, after all, had not been built with pions.

"Oh, it's beautiful," Kichlan said, his fingers reaching, apparently without thought, to tangle in mine.

"It looks nice enough to eat," Lad said.

I laughed. "We'll have to return when it's open. You should see what they put inside."

Streaks of deep blue gave the gallery an early-morning-sky hue. It was beautiful, and delectable, and permanent. And a memory. A pleasant one, yes, but gone.

And I didn't much mind.

ACKNOWLEDGMENTS

Tanyana and I know we would never have come this far if not for the help of some truly amazing people.

We can't say thank you enough to the wonderful Rabia Gale and Miquela Faure beta-readers extraordinaire. You two have stuck with us from the very beginning. Your keen insight, sharpened red pen, patience and friendship mean more to Tanyana and I than we can ever say. Plus you've read this book like how many times now?

Extra special thanks to Marianne de Pierres, for so generously sharing your knowledge and time, for believing in us, and guiding us. You are inspiring. Oh, and thanks for giving Jo a right kick up the bum when needed!

To my agent, Anni Haig-Smith, thank you not only for your faith in us, but your sheer determination!

Marc Gascoigne and Lee Harris from Angry Robot Books have been absolutely wonderful to work with, and we are so grateful to have you in our corner. Thank you for bringing Tanyana and I into your robot family. March on, Robot Army! March on!

We also want to shout out to Dominic Harman for the stunning cover image. Tanyana is flattered, and I'm just thrilled. This is always how I imagined the book would look like, and I know how lucky I am.

Even more thanks to Tansy Rayner Roberts, Trudi Canavan, Ian Tregillis, Trent Jamieson, Kaaron Warren and Edwina Harvey, for giving up your time to read *Debris* and then actually saying nice things about it.

And finally, to my husband. Tanyana wants to apologise for demanding so much of my time. I just want to say thank you. For everything.

ABOUT THE AUTHOR

Jo Anderton lives in Sydney, Australia, with her patient husband, faithful dog, one megalomaniac cat and one dumb-as-a-post cat. She'd rather be living on a big block of land in the country, so she can adopt more pets.

By day she is a mild-mannered marketing coordinator for an Australian book distributor. By night, weekends and lunchtimes she writes dark fantasy and horror.

Her short fiction has appeared in *Aurealis*, *Midnight Echo*, *Kaleidotrope*, *Andromeda Spaceways Inflight Magazine*, and been reprinted in *Australian Dark Fantasy and Horror Vol 3* She was shortlisted for the 2009 Aurealis Award for best young adult short story. She is now hard at work on this book's sequel, *Suited*.

joanneanderton.com

ANGRY
ROBOT

We are Angry Robot.

Web angryrobotbooks.com

ANGRY ROBOT

COLLECTING IS CONSIDERED COOL
Snare the whole Angry Robot catalog

DAN ABNETT
- [ ] Embedded
- [ ] Triumff: Her Majesty's Hero

GUY ADAMS
- [ ] The World House
- [ ] Restoration

LAUREN BEUKES
- [ ] Moxyland
- [ ] Zoo City

**THOMAS BLACKTHORNE
(aka John Meaney)**
- [ ] Edge
- [ ] Point

MAURICE BROADDUS
- [ ] King Maker
- [ ] King's Justice

ALIETTE DE BODARD
- [ ] Servant of the Underworld
- [ ] Harbinger of the Storm

MATT FORBECK
- [ ] Amortals
- [ ] Vegas Knights

JUSTIN GUSTAINIS
- [ ] Hard Spell

GUY HALEY
- [ ] Reality 36

COLIN HARVEY
- [ ] Damage Time
- [ ] Winter Song

MATTHEW HUGHES
- [ ] The Damned Busters

TRENT JAMIESON
- [ ] Roil

K W JETER
- [ ] Infernal Devices
- [ ] Morlock Night

J ROBERT KING
- [ ] Angel of Death
- [ ] Death's Disciples

GARY McMAHON
- [ ] Pretty Little Dead Things
- [ ] Dead Bad Things

ANDY REMIC
- [ ] Kell's Legend
- [ ] Soul Stealers
- [ ] Vampire Warlords

CHRIS ROBERSON
- [ ] Book of Secrets

MIKE SHEVDON
- [ ] Sixty-One Nails
- [ ] The Road to Bedlam

GAV THORPE
- [ ] The Crown of the Blood
- [ ] The Crown of the Conqueror

LAVIE TIDHAR
- [ ] The Bookman
- [ ] Camera Obscura

TIM WAGGONER
- [ ] Nekropolis
- [ ] Dead Streets
- [ ] Dark War

KAARON WARREN
- [ ] Mistification
- [ ] Slights
- [ ] Walking the Tree

IAN WHATES
- [ ] City of Dreams & Nightmare
- [ ] City of Hope & Despair